KATHY LETTE first achieved *succès de sca.......* as a teenager with the novel *Puberty Blues*, now a major motion picture. After several years as a newspaper columnist in Sydney and New York (collected in the book *Hit and Ms*) and as a television sitcom writer for Columbia Pictures in Los Angeles, her novels *Girls' Night Out* (1988), *The Llama Parlour* (1991), *Foetal Attraction* (1993) and *Mad Cows* (1996), became international bestsellers. Kathy Lette's plays include *Grommitts*, *Wet Dreams*, *Perfect Mismatch* and *I'm So Happy For You I Really Am*; recently she has presented *Behind the Headlines* and *01* on British television and *Devil's Advocate* for BBC Radio 4. She lives in London with her husband and two children.

THE

LLAMA

PARLOUR

Kathy Lette

PICADOR

First published 1992 by Bloomsbury Publishing Limited

This edition published 1993 by Picador
an imprint of Macmillan Publishers Ltd
25 Eccleston Place, London SW1W 9NF
and Basingstoke

Associated companies throughout the world

ISBN 0 330 32685 6

14 16 18 19 17 15 13

A CIP catalogue record for this book is available
from the British Library.

Printed and bound in Great Britain by
Mackays of Chatham PLC, Chatham, Kent

CONTENTS

FOR GEOFFREY

PART
ONE

THE DICKHEAD CLAUSE

'Strip,' Tash ordered the old bloke.

I watched him peel off his shirt and trousers and stand there in his long socks and those daggy, baggy underpants that American men wear. My best friend Natasha was about to handcuff the president of a powerful movie studio to a brass bed and spank him.

'Who's been a bad boy, then?' Tash said in her Chicago drawl. She had a voice you could grate cheese on, no kidding. A nervous giggle escaped my lips. Tash, too, was on the edge of laughter. She bit her lip hard and shushed me sternly. 'Shoelaces!' She put out her hand like a doctor waiting for a scalpel. I separated five or six strands from the wad of leather laces on the dressing-table.

The old codger stretched out face down on the bed. Tash tethered his wrists above his head. 'Feet,' she instructed me, her voice full of forced severity. His skin was grey, the colour of cafeteria gravy, and his purple socks smelt. I knew absolutely *nothing* about bondage. I'd always presumed that it was just an inventive way of keeping your partner from going home. As I was securing his ankles to the bed base, the old guy swivelled his head to one side. His eyes weren't just glassy, they were double-glazed, and he had this thin, hopeful kind of smile on his chops. I'd seen better heads on a beer, let me tell you.

Tash yanked down his underchunders. The dressing-table was crammed with awesome photos of him armoured in business suits. The navy pinstripe hid the reality of his trembling thighs and flabby buttocks, which were like cream cakes, soft and crinkled. 'Now,' she ordered, 'I wantcha to count.' He clenched his cream cakes. Tash raised the leather belt and brought it down across his bum.

'One . . .' he said feebly. She gave him a second stroke. 'Two . . .'

'Not too hard . . . I mean, doesn't it hurt?' I heard myself squawk in alarm, realising as I spoke that, of course, *that* was the whole point. *What was I doing here?* I was the sort of girl who dental-flossed at night and pushed my cuticles back. I did cryptic crossword puzzles, for God's sake.

'Don't move, scumbag,' Tash instructed him in a low, head-mistressy voice, before leading me, her leather boots creaking, into the bathroom.

'Tash,' I said, as soon as the bathroom door closed behind us, 'this is too weird for me.'

'Where do ya live?' she asked sarcastically. 'In a box? *All* men are into bondage, 'specially if they're real assholes at work all day.' She frowned at the black nail varnish flaking off her index finger.

Tash was tiny and totally held together by nerves. She had a delicate mouth, copper-coloured hair cut short, a silver ring through her right nostril, and massive breasts. (She'd told me once how much she hated having big tits. Men were always drooling and slobbering all over them. 'They forget I'm there! It's like . . . Hey! Excuse me,' she'd demonstrated, addressing her chest as though a man were there, suckling and slurping and carrying on. 'When the three of you are through . . . lemme know, okay?')

I watched Tash relacquer her nail. 'What happens next?' I asked, trying to sound like a woman-of-the-world.

'Well, I'll give 'im a few whacks on the ass then a quick poke or a blow job,' she said with resolute indifference. 'And that's it.'

'Errgh. Yuk.' I cringed. 'You'll let him put it in your mouth? He's probably a grandfather! He's practically a fossil! He's . . .'

'I like givin' head,' Tash retorted with cheerful aggression. 'It gives me a little break, ya know, time to do some thinkin' about other stuff.'

Other stuff? Other stuff? Like *what?*

'But he ain't allowed to come in my mouth.'

'Oh right!' I said with mock relief. I concentrated on the bath-room walls. They were plastered with gold-framed posters of movies I'd never seen and was five or ten years too late for.

'There's only one cure for a cowboy who does that . . . Pretend to kiss him and empty it all back into *his* mouth. Ask him how *he*

4

likes swallowin' half a pint of warm salty porridge.' Tash placed her gloved hand on the door handle. 'And Kat,' – her Moroccan-Beige lidded eyes looked me up and down – 'this is a Power-fuck. Smarten up huh?'

I glanced at my reflection in the bathroom mirror. I looked ridiculous. The empty bra cups in the corset sagged and my suspenders were askew. When I'd asked Tash to get me a job, I'd been thinking more along the lines of a bookshop assistant or a deli delivery girl or something.

By the time I got back to the bedroom, Tash had flipped old Schulman sunny-side up, straddled his huge belly, and was tying a silk rope around his neck.

'I'm gonna count to a hundred,' she said solemnly. 'If you haven't come by a hundred, I'm gonna pull this rope tight round ya tonsils. Got it, cowboy? My assistant is here to help me.'

'Yes,' the mogul meekly said, stranded on the bed like a walrus on a beach.

Assistant? Assistant? The only thing I'd ever whipped was cream. The truth is, my experience in matters sexual is limited. For me, a new position in bed means sleeping on my other side.

Tash slid up and down, pogo-stick-style, counting each thrust. 'One, two, three, four . . .' The old bloke's eyes bulged with pure joy. '. . . thirteen, fourteen, fifteen . . .' It was hard to imagine him sitting behind a big desk, making appointments for power breakfasts. '. . . thirty-one, thirty-two, thirty-three . . .' I had often seen Joel Schulman's picture in *Variety* magazine, with a cluster of stars, chuckling and smoking a cigar; all camaraderie for the cameras.

'Fifty-five, fifty-six . . .' Tash tightened the silk rope round his neck. His skin looked as though he'd been in the bath for a week. I wanted to play 'join the dots' with his goose pimples. 'Sixty-nine, seventy . . .' Her voice took on a sterner tone. 'Seventy-nine, eighty . . .' He became more urgent, flailing about, straining at his leather tethers. 'Eighty-two, eighty-three . . .' His double chin quivered. His big belly wobbled. 'Ninety-six, ninety-seven, ninety-eight, ninety-nine . . .'

He shuddered explosively. His whole body arched up off the bed. He groaned a groan of ecstasy and relief and sheer, perfect pleasure from every pore in his antediluvian body.

Tash dismounted, gave his pale leg a perfunctory pat and

5

motioned for me to follow her out to the kitchen.

She made us both a cup of tea – mine Earl Grey and hers Lemon Herbal. 'There,' she said, 'half an hour and two hundred bucks. Straight into the hot little hand of C.J.'

Tash wasn't a roolio troolio hooker. Well, only part-time, in order to pay off her debts. And it wasn't that she hadn't tried other jobs. In the last year, Tash had been a kiss-o-gram, a road sweeper, a bogus tarot card reader, a fantasy-sex-phone-in-girl and a disc jockey in a hospital reading out the sports and mortuary news. She'd dressed as Santa Claus, eaten fire in public parks and been a human street sign. She'd siphoned petrol and spent all night coughing up her guts in some deserted parking lot downtown. She'd stolen her own car to get the insurance. Once she wrote to three hundred LA restaurants claiming that clam chowder had been spilt on her white Rodeo Drive designer-suit. She'd demanded, and received, a $5 cleaning bill from each of them – but she was still broke.

Most of her money went to C.J., the private detective she'd hired to help her solve some stuff from her past. Tash's past was the classic, Bible Belt, small town catastrophe. Incest, alcoholism and a mum who was into animal husbandry. (She'd had seven husbands, all of them animals.) Any money left over from C.J., Tash used for her singing classes and demo tapes. She wrote her own songs, the best were 'Everywhere I Go, Everywhere I Go, Everywhere I Go, I'm There,' and 'Fuck Me Now'.

As it was only Tash's second night on the game, after a few sips of tea she put in a call to her 'Madam', Candida. The number was disconnected. I wasn't surprised, to tell you the truth. I mean, what could you expect from a woman who was named after a vaginal complaint?

It wasn't till we went in to untie the old codger that I noticed that the phone line wasn't the only thing that was dead. I felt the heat of pure fear flush across my face and down my neck.

'He's carked it!' I bleated.

Tash looked at me uncomprehendingly.

'Kaput. Finito.'

'Huh?'

'He's fallen off his perch.' I dragged my finger across my throat and gurgled. 'He's handed in his dinner plate.' Still she didn't get it. 'He's DEAD, damn it!'

6

'Fuck,' she said, devastated. 'That wasn't supposed to happen!' Then she braced herself. 'But he ain't paid me yet.'

'Well, do something!' I started running from one side of the bed to the other and back again.

'What?'

'I dunno. What about mouth-to-mouth resuscitation or something . . . ?'

'Erggh. Don't make me puke.'

This just about killed me. 'Tash, you just had sex with the guy and you won't *kiss* him? What are you worried about? *Germs?*'

Tash prodded him tentatively with her foot. 'It's too late, anyways. This dude is deadybones.'

I stared at the corpse. The silk rope was still entwined around his throat. 'Don't panic,' I panicked. The blood in my veins congealed. My brain palpitated. I began to think of ways of disposing of his body. We could put him in a bath full of acid . . . No. There was only one sort of acid Tash knew how to get hold of – and that came in tabs. We could chop him up and feed him down the food disposal unit. But all I had on me was a pair of nail scissors. 'We could call it suicide.'

'Oh sure,' Tash said, reviving the cigar Joel Schulman had extinguished in the ashtray earlier. 'He fucked himself to death? Who's gonna believe that?' But then her face lit up. 'Come on! Help me get 'im over to the window,' she panted, tugging loose the shoelaces around his ankles.

'What for?'

'This is a thirtieth floor apartment.'

'So?'

She looked at me as though I were a remedial reader. 'Does the word "splat" mean anythin' to ya?'

The old cove was incredibly heavy. Straining and heaving and swearing like troopers, we dragged him across the carpet. We'd winched him all the way up to the sill, and composed aloud a totally convincing and terribly moving suicide note, before discovering the window was deadlocked.

'Shit!' Tash said profoundly. And we dropped his body back on to the floor.

'God. *Now* what will we do?'

She shrugged, studied his famous face for a moment and gave a small and tender smile. 'Oh well. At least he had a great orgasm.'

'Orgasm!' I screeched. 'Orgasm! That was no orgasm! That was his death throes, you dickhead . . . God!'

Honestly, Americans are the most sentimental breed on earth. They have a sort of psychological sweet tooth.

Tash drew a belch of cigar smoke up her pierced nostril. 'Let's just split. No one will know it was us,' she said. 'I mean, he's a studio executive. There'll be zillions of suspects.'

'Tash!' I was practically hyperventilating. 'You told me he was a Ten-K-a-day-guy, really fit.'

'Well, he is . . . was . . . Check the rosy cheeks.'

'They're not rosy cheeks. They're rosy *veins!*' I snapped, before pointing out that it was too late to run away. We'd bumped and wrenched the old bloke about so much, that now it really did look like murder. Bruises were developing with polaroid speed along his arms and legs and the back of his head. His skin was starting to look kind of corrugated. 'Maybe we should just call the cops?' I suggested.

'What . . . ya really in the mood to fuck the entire Beverly Hills Homicide Squad?' Tash stubbed out the huge firecracker she was smoking. 'The guy we *should* call is Arnie Grossman.'

'Who?'

'He's the Vice President. He'll be desperate to keep it quiet. Ya know, savin' the honour of the studio an' all that shit.'

'Really?' Relief oozed through my body. 'And he has heaps of influence and stuff?'

Tash gave me one those 'are you kidding?' looks. 'This is the guy that got Israel to pull out of Lebanon.' She picked up the phone. 'Is that influence enough for you?' Then, just as fast, she put it down again. 'Shit. But then the studio will cancel the recordin' contract Joel lined up for me.'

'Tash,' I explained icily, 'if we don't do something, the only record you're going to have will be criminal.'

I thought of jail. Of *Miami Vice. LA Law.* The electric chair. There was nothing else for it. *We* would have to commit suicide.

'Okay, okay. Calm down. Whaddabout ya producer, Epstein? Yeah. Give old Abe a call.' She put the phone in my hand.

'Tash, how can I call, when I'm not talking to him?' I shoved the phone back at her. 'I walked out on his show in the middle of taping, remember? The complete dingo-act. There's no way I'm gonna call that son-of-a . . .'

'He's got mob contacts, hasn't he?'

'*Has* he?'

Tash wrapped my fingers around the receiver. 'Call.'

I should never, ever have come to Hollywood. Everything had gone bung since the day I first got here a year ago. I'd fallen for a guy who had love bites all over his mirror. I'd been recruited into a club called 'Ugly Unlimited'. I was sharing a house with a girl who dyed her hair green on St Patrick's Day and slept with older men part-time to pay for taping songs with stupid titles – and had just murdered the head of one of the biggest movie studios in Hollywood. Apart from that, everything was fine, beaut, no wuckin' furries, as we say back home. I dialled Abe's number. 'Answering machine.'

Tash was staring at the body with that forlorn affection usually reserved for a dead pet. 'Okay,' she said, nibbling at the nail she'd just revarnished, 'we'll just wait and call back later.'

Oh why hadn't I listened to my mates? Grub, Chook, Fang, Debbie, Macka, Cara – none of them were wrapped in me going Stateside. Not, as you'd expect, because of the muggings or car crashes or mob murders. What worried them was that I'd turn into a dickhead. At the airport they'd made me sign a 'Dickhead Clause'. It simply said, 'It is time to come home. You have now turned into a dickhead.' It was agreed that this would be posted to me if I was ever caught wearing sunglasses indoors, or using the terms 'power breakfast' or 'run it past me'. Not that I thought I ever *could* turn into a dickhead. Living with a father like mine meant that I'd developed a very finely tuned crap-antenna. Oh, but I'll get to him in a minute.

The reason I was even in a place where people wore sunglasses indoors was because I'd won a trip to Hollywood for a walk-on role in this famous American situation comedy called *DINKS* (Double Income, No Kids). The competition was one of those tacky promotional things. The show had just been released down-under, and the producers thought it'd be kind of cute to have a little Aussie gal make a guest appearance. All you had to do was send along a videotape of yourself, plus the coupons from ten margarine wrappers, and write on the entry form in ten words or less what you thought about America.

That was easy. I loved America. The reason I loved America

was because my father hated America. And I hated my father. I don't know why everybody gets so het up over kids who muck up. What I wanted was a home for delinquent dads. Once, when I was about ten, and he was going on a trip, he made me write all his postcards before he left, in case he was too drunk when he got there to do it himself. 'Hi. Having a great time. Wish you were here . . .' etc. I even had to write one to myself. 'Dear Katrina . . .'

The only birthday present he ever gave me was the offer of either a 'hit' or a 'lean' on any of my teachers at school. A 'hit' meant bumping them off altogether. A 'lean' would just do away with a kneecap or two. This went over really well at Parent/Teacher night, let me tell you.

I also remember going to visit him in jail. The long bleak journeys on the train out to Parramatta prison, through the factories and the housing commission flats. The prison-issue soap that smelt like fly repellent. The pale, seasick-green prison uniforms. The greasy smell of prison stew – chew n'spew, they called it. And how his voice, straining to be bright and casual, was distorted by the voice-box in the visitors' room. And then there were the 'contact visits' – the cruel, condescending look of the prison wardens as they searched my mother's handbag. One day they shredded her sanitary pad. Looking for drugs, they said. Bastards. We'd sit, cross-legged on the bindi-eyed lawn, waiting for his beaming face to loom out of the puke-green sea of men. He'd sit with us for a while, doing card tricks and asking me about a hundred times how tall I was. But, as the sun scorched the top of my head, talk would turn to money and morals. He'd flare up at my mother, calling her a snob and a rich bitch who 'thought her shit didn't stink' – he had a way with words, my father – and then he'd wander off to flirt with the wives of the other blokes.

That's how I remember him.

My mother married 'beneath herself'. A 'scallywag', a 'larrikin', a 'ladies man', my posh aunties from the North Shore suburbs said. Mum found out after I was born that dad had married three times before. She reckoned he got married so much because he was an uneducated yobbo. She said that 'I' and 'do' constituted his total vocabulary.

They reckoned it was cancer that killed her. But what she died of was a Terminal Case of My Father. He was a malignant growth in the shape of a six-foot-two, blue-eyed Irishman with a gleaming smile and a tanned face marked by laughter lines.

The weird thing was, I didn't really miss her. To tell you the truth, there was not that much to miss. Although she died only last summer, she'd actually shut herself down years ago. Her presence was like shopping mall Muzak; there, but not there, merging into the surroundings; in the background, indistinct. In my mind's picture of her, the fabric of her face was pinched, her lips pursed, as though she were sewing, and had a mouthful of pins. I guess she was frightened that if she ever smiled, she might just completely unravel.

But don't worry. I'm not going to wallow in a whole lot of poor-little-me crap. Life for me has always been simple really, much simpler than it was for my mates. I've got a set of built-in beliefs. I just believe in all things my father doesn't. He hates the police, classical music, mushy romantic stuff, television (he calls it the 'haunted gold-fish bowl') and more than all the others put together – America. He reckons that Australia has become the fifty-third state. He's always ranting and raving that if we'd grown up eating Russian tucker, watching Russian telly, wearing Russian clobber, that the rest of the world would reckon we'd been conquered and brainwashed. But just because it is *American* telly and tucker and entertainment, nobody seems to notice. As he chucked out our McDonald's and hurled his thongs at the American movies on TV, my mother would try to argue with him. But to tell you the truth, the only thing my father could really grasp in an argument was a beer can.

Consequently I grew up a classical-music-listening, Mills-and-Boon-reading, law-abiding, telly-watching, closet American. If you could change your name by deed poll, why couldn't you change your genealogy? You know, by gene poll. I wanted to become an American. Desperately.

America made me feel as though I'd longed all my life for things I'd never even heard of before: bathroom scales that talked, folding toboggans, His and Her helicopters, indoor ski machines, a sonic rodent repellent . . . And the thing I longed for the most was to fall in love. I wanted an American Romeo; hot off the press, home-delivered. Nothing special: as long as he had pectorals, a PhD, a nice bum, a non-sexist attitude, a top tan, a well-read penis, pale blue eyes, could cook soufflés, arm-wrestle crocodiles and wanted a loving relationship with bonemarrow-melting sex. Now, was that too much to ask of a billionaire?

That was the other reason for becoming an American. You see, Australians aren't that good at mushy, romantic stuff. Passion's not the Fashion where I come from. Aussie blokes, those without Brewer's Droop and verandas over their toyshops may be bronzed and blond, with laughing eyes and a wit as dry as the Sahara – but they are also *emotional bonsai*. Not only that, you only get affection when there's an erection. The boys I knew anyway.

Tash reckons that I'm 'cock-shy', but it's not that. I've had seven lovers, okay going, I reckon, for a twenty-year-old. Colin Pickles, Chook, Fang, Fido, Scunge, Terry the Tooth and Garry Hudson. Garry was my last lover. He was considered by my girlfriends to be a top spunk rat. Though it kind of annoyed me the way he was always setting fire to his farts, you know, as a party trick. Anyway, one night, I stopped Gaz, mid-bonk, to pledge, in my best movie starlet style, my adoration. You know, to vow lifelong love and devotion. 'I mean,' I pleaded, in my mushiest, mascara-running voice, 'You do love me, don't you?'

Gazza looked down at me, bewildered, and shrugged. 'Jeez, I'm rootin' you, aren't I?'

It was after that I sent in the margarine coupons.

Tash reckons that love is not 'objectively verifiable'. She reckons that believing in 'love' is about as plausible as believing in UFOs. She's right, in a way. I mean, Close Encounters of the Romantic Kind were definitely alien to my house. One day my dad went out to buy a packet of cigarettes and didn't come back for two years. When he walked back in the door, broke, my mum just looked at him and said, 'Didn't they have your brand?'

See, the reason my old man's a delinquent is because he's a gambler. My father would bet on the length of a bee's dick. So now you know the real reason I believe in love. Betting against the odds runs in my blood. And even though my poor old mum had such a bad trot (and I mean that literally: Dad lost his whole pay packet on the horses – the few times he was in work, that is) she still told me that she truly believed there was a bloke out there for every girl. And that one day I'd meet my Mr Right.

Mind you, she also told me not to swim when I had my period.

Anyway, when I won the competition (I told them how I wanted a nationality-transplant) I weighed up my options: a cockroach-ridden squat; a boyfriend who set fire to his farts, who fucked anything that was warm and counted the legs afterwards; and a father who bet against himself in solitaire. It was them – or America. I applied for a visa. I guess that's just the kind of girl I am – impetuous.

'Are ya sure he's dead?' Once more Tash tentatively poked the old codger in the ribs with her stiletto.

'Dead? Of course he's dead. What do you think he is? *Shy?*' I was on the brink of hysteria.

'Try Abe again.'

Dialling the number, I listened to the whelp of sirens on the street below. The moon was like a giant headlight in the sky, focused accusingly on us. 'Machine.' I hung up, squirmed out of the sticky black leather and pulled on my jeans and T-shirt. It was then I realised that I was a dickhead – officially. It was time to fill in the form: I'd put on my sunglasses – *indoors*.

FLOATING TURDS

On my first day in Los Angeles, the Fourth of July, there were three freeway shootings, a mugging inside the Paradise Studios car park, gang warfare outside between the bikies and the Latinos, a report on the radio announcing that the air pollution in Los Angeles exceeded national health standards on 232 days of each year, twenty-six murders, ten rapes, eight suicides and a jogger was mauled to death by a dog. I came from Sydney. The most dangerous thing I'd ever done was to park in a clearway zone.

The stretch limo moved through the streets, as silent and sinister as a submarine. Below decks, we were fully equipped. Telly, bar, video, stereo, probably a bath, gymnasium and tennis court if I'd bothered to look underneath the back seat. We slid, as if coated in Vaseline, past the pampered lawns of the Pacific Palisades. I'd been collected from the airport by the television producer himself. A great honour, he kept assuring me, seeing as he was one of the richest television producers in Hollywood. Not only was he the richest, but also the best, the meanest, the biggest, and the most respected . . . Abe Epstein was a Human Superlative.

I yawned. My body ached and my mouth tasted like the bottom of a canary cage. I'd had about one minute's sleep on the whole flight, during which I woke up four times. I couldn't wait to get horizontal.

Abe then broke the good news that instead of going to the hotel, I was to meet the entire show's company at his Malibu home – hair stylists, stage-managers, couriers, costume designers, warm-up comedians, publicists, production co-ordinators and a whole summit of Presidents. Presidents of Public Affairs and Business Affairs, Presidents of Casting, Presidents of Comedy Development, plus the Presidents of those Presidents . . . and most important of all, the number one star of the show, Rondah Rivers.

Although bald and pudgy, Abe wore the paraphernalia of a World Champion Gold medallist: thermal Gucci tracksuit pants, deep-sea diving watch, high-tech aerobic running shoes. I watched him pop open a bottle of Dom Perignon; it was the most athletic thing he'd done all day. A sip or two later, he flossed his teeth, sucking and slurping, then scrutinised the gunk on the green string before flicking it out the electronically operated window. So, old Abe *was* world-class in one field, after all. Down-under, Epstein was the type we'd call Olympic Games Ugly.

'I haf bin celibate for two yiss, Katrina. Hard to believe no?' What was hard was trying to untangle the thick vowels of his accent. I just nodded a lot. 'Yes, A great vaste for voman kind. It happened ven I got divorced, and my daughters were old enuff to start experimenting sexually, I lost my zex drive.' We were now winding along the Pacific Coast highway towards Malibu. 'Vimmin haff tried to convert me . . . but, eats impossible.'

The car cruised into a driveway flanked on both sides by fluttering American flags. But it was kind of hard to believe that I was in the Land of the Free. The entrance to Abe's house was an electronic portcullis. He pushed the button on his bleeper. The surveillance camera swivelled into action. We were spotlit, like roos on a shoot. The locks unlatched. The giant wrought-iron gate rasped open. And an armed security guard, complete with killer canine, cheerily waved us through. I sunk down low in my seat. This sort of hospitality could hospitalise you.

Abe's house was huge. He had a triple garage, a near Olympic-sized pool and Jacuzzi you could swim laps in. The grounds seemed to me just a little smaller than metropolitan Sydney. The tennis courts were huge. The paintings were huge. The television screens were huge. The Dobermans were huge. But Abe himself was very short. Not to worry. His ego expanded to fill the space. I was soon to find out that this is a law of nature in LA.

'I am zee best television zituation comedy produzer in zee country. Zee best. I make zee funniest shows that run for zee longest time and make zee most money. Because I know vot makes people laugh. You know vye?' He leant into my face, close enough for me to count the blackheads on his nose – there were zillions of them – and pronounced with sombre sincerity, 'Because I am a deeply funny person.'

About as funny as period cramp. 'Oh that's nice,' I said helplessly.

Wading through the shagpiled hallway of his house, he told me yet again how popular Australia was now. If my guest appearance in *DINKS* rated well, they would sign me up. For ever. Abe told me that I was a 'High Concept'. 'Auzzie-girl-in-American-zitcom,' he headlined. (As far as I can figure out, a 'High Concept' is kind of haiku gone Hollywood.) 'Got it cupcake? And here she ease,' he boomed, swinging open the gi-normous doors out on to the lawns. 'All zee way from down-under. Crocodile Dundette!'

I looked at Abe in alarm. Remember that crap-antenna I told you about? Well, it wobbled. The closest I have ever got to a crocodile-skin was a handbag I'd once 'borrowed' from the David Jones Department Store on Mother's Day. (We didn't use the term 'stealing' in my house. Anything shoplifted was simply called a 'five-finger-discount'.) Wincing at the neon sunshine, I stepped out on to the pool terrace.

In stark contrast to the balloons and streamers and glittering 'G'day' signs – spelt 'Gooday' – there were only a measly handful of people at my welcome party. And, judging by their long faces, they looked as though they'd been enlisted by the Good Time Gestapo. Abe gestured across the pool to a group of mostly middle-aged men wearing jeans and jaded expressions. 'Zee viters. Brilliant! Vitten every-sing from zee Beverly Hill Billies to zee Brady Bunch.' The writers looked as though they'd been left standing out in the wind for a decade or two. 'You know vot ve call a group of viters? A *hack*.' He fired a volley of laughter in their direction.

On the other side of the turquoise rectangle were the actors and their human handbags. Two of the show's 'regulars' were frog-marched over to meet me, their high heels clacking on the poolside pebblecrete. They were well-padded girls in their early twenties called Phoebe Mercedez and Ping. (Apparently, Ping's mum thought 'Ping' was Chinese for 'peace'. It wasn't till years later that she found out it meant 'lump'. And boy, did she live up to her name.) 'G'day,' I smiled. Ping looked at me lumpenly.

I tried my luck with Phoebe Mercedez. She responded to my greeting as though she'd trodden in a dog turd. Which was quite possible. It must have been a BYO Dog party. Each actress had a little mohair poodle tucked under her arm. 'Howzit going?' I persisted. But they just kept up with the old Trappist Monk treatment. Embarrassed by their silence, I stripped off to my Speedos and smeared pink zinc sunscreen across my snoz. It took me a minute or two to sus that the other guests were giving me the old hairy eyeball. Disconcerted, I looked down at my black one-piece cossie. I noticed how pale and weedy my legs looked after a Sydney winter, and there was a shrivelled, week-old Bandaid on one knee. I followed their communal gaze to my armpit. A tiny maverick patch of trainer stubble had sprouted there during the fourteen-hour flight.

Ping, turning to the other actors, broke the interrogative silence. 'Well,' she said sarcastically, 'it's a *look*. It's a *choice*.' My crap-antenna started wobbling again.

It was a pool party, but nobody got wet. The only thing they dived into were their paper-parasoled cocktails.

'Whadda ya want?' one of the 'hack' asked me by the bar. What I wanted was to crawl into a nice quiet bed and try to remember what my name was. 'To drink,' she explained tersely. The silver pendant around her neck read 'Amy'. 'A Shark Attack or a Total Wipe-out?'

Amy was dark-haired, about thirty, with a permanently furrowed brow. She reminded me instantly of my mum. A natural worrier. You know, the kind of person who feels bad when she feels good, because she knows she'll only feel worse when she stops feeling better. She poured a beaker of bright blue liquid, added a surreptitious slurp of vodka, then closed my fingers around it.

'Thanks,' I said.

'You're welcome.' She retrieved her own doctored glasses of punch and began to list in the direction of the other writers.

'Hey . . . um . . . Amy, wanna find a place to sit for a sec?' I grabbed her sleeve.

'Listen,' Amy explained, shrugging off my hand. 'It's not that the writers have got anything against you personally. It's just that, as far as we're concerned, being an "actor" is the lowest job possible for a multi-celled animal.'

'Oh.'

As she turned her back on me, Abe burst through the patio doors with all the natural grace of a Mack truck. Apparently, my welcome bash was over and a flood of Fourth of July Party People had arrived. It looked like he'd rung Rent-a-Guest. 'Mix,' he ordered me. And so, for the next two hours, I became a swizzle stick, swirling from one conversational cocktail to another.

'I've left my husband,' a gaunt lady with leather jodhpurs and riding crop said to the crowd. 'I'm currently individuating.'

'At midnight, yes,' a woman in a transparent plastic dress and Calvin Klein designer underwear confided. 'I had to ring the Cat Psychiatrist Emergency Line. My cat . . .' – her voice throbbed with restrained sobs – '. . . my cat was *growling* at his *bowl*.' Someone recommended Cat Holistic Healing as the best treatment. Another guest thought the little feline needed a holiday in Palm Springs at 'Aristocat', the relaxation clinic for cats and dogs.

Dwights and Dwaynes and Wandas and Waynes dropped the names of people I'd never heard of. A glamorous woman who looked like Joan Collins sashayed past me. It *was* Joan Collins. Girls in T-shirts that read 'Nicaragua is Spanish for Vietnam' compared tans and hair tints.

A blow-waved bloke was holding court from a hammock strung between palm trees. I'd heard of padded socks for extra height, well this guy had padded *underwear*. 'Get real. I'd rather *die* than vote for a black man!' he declared.

'Me too,' boomed Abe. He was surrounded by a bevy of blonde girls. These were the models-stroke-actresses that Abe was currently incubating. They smiled interminably, with no idea that they were about as transient as their leg waxes. Abe took a drag on his cigar then added thoughtfully, 'but I'd vather vote for a black man, zan for a *voman*. Imagine it. Every twenty-eight daze,' he elaborated, 'she'd haff to be relieved of duty.' The Dwights and the Dwaynes snickered. The models-stroke-actresses just sipped their drinks and looked bored. I glanced up at the grey duvet of smog above the city. Did they pump valium into the air in Los Angeles or what? Back home if a bloke had said that to a woman, she'd punch him so hard he'd be brushing his teeth out his bum.

'Just made a two-picture deal with *Mel*,' the man beside me bragged.

'*Jack* just signed on. We go in November,' his companion counter-boasted.

'My project's in turnaround at the Sundance Institute,' gushed a girl in leather shorts and an ankle chain. 'Redford is apparently off his face over it! He's zonked. Like totally.'

'Is he a nice sort of a bloke, Robert Redford,' I ventured, 'or a bit of a dickhead?' They all turned their cold, coloured contact lenses on me. I felt like Alice in Wonderland, post-biscuit. I shrank, visibly. It was hard to believe that these people had Oldies who worried whether they were eating their greens or not.

As Abe and his friends nattered on about foreplay classes and dog diets, I looked longingly at the couch in the sunroom, aware how effortlessly these sort of sofas convert into night-and-day-beds. But Abe was still on the side of insomnia. 'You must vait till Vondah gets here. She vants to meet you.'

I screwed up my face against the afternoon sun. The pool looked like one of those paintings by that David Hockney bloke. I launched myself into the frame. Back-stroking up and down, I peered up at the suntanned features of my fellow guests. There was something not quite right about them all. But I couldn't put my finger on what it was. It was like one of those 'What's missing from this picture?' games, you know. And it's always the teapot handle or the dog's tail.

I submerged and the chlorinated whorls distorted their famous faces. Actually, by this stage I was having trouble focusing on anything except the need to find a horizontal surface. A floral Li-lo floated on top of the pool. I surfaced and climbed gratefully aboard.

But no sooner had I curled up in the sun than Abe was prodding the giant plastic blister with his sneaker.

'Vake up! Eets not jet lag, eets *shag*-lag,' he diagnosed. 'Vot you need is a boyfriend. Ve vill get you laid.' Abe ordered me to get out of the pool and come and talk to some 'boize'. I could take my pick of the 'talent'. There were rock stars, movie stars, fashion studs, sports jocks . . . I tried to explain that I couldn't even talk, let alone touch anyone. *Quiet* was about the only sound I could bear to hear right now. I fled inside. Guests gawped at me as I dripped water round and round the house looking for a place to crash. For a 'High Concept', things had sunk pretty low. One of the kitchen microwave clocks read five p.m. *Great*. So far I'd been in America for four hours and was hated by absolutely everyone.

The kitchen was empty except for a middle-aged woman straddling a stool. A book was propped up on the counter in front of her. Her eyes were eclipsed by the wild hair that shot out from her head at all angles. It looked as though she'd swallowed a grenade. Although well on in years, she wore leather shorts and a leopard-skin bikini top. Her skin was stretched taut. This woman was vacuum-packed. As she crossed her legs, I expected to hear that *pzzzt* sound, like when you open a packet of coffee. Her wild eyes glanced up from the coloured pictures in her book.

'You are what you eat,' she announced with hazy enthusiasm. 'Did you know that?'

'Pardon?'

The woman slid off the stool and approached me. She thrust the open pages into my face. I peered more closely. The photos were of human turds. I'm not kidding.

'Your faeces tell you what's wrong with your diet. Heavy and dark – too much carbohydrate. Little pebbly ones, well, that means you need more roughage. If you're real healthy and get lots of fibre, then your turds should float.' She offered me the book. 'Go on. Pick yours,' she said magnanimously, 'Go on, *pick*.'

I backed off down the hall and through the first door I came to. I locked it behind me and turned. And this is where and how I first laid eyes on Pierce Reece-Scanlen Jnr (the Third).

He was straining into the bathroom mirror, nostrils flared, tweezers poised, tweaking the hairs from inside his nose. I was looking at a green-eyed, blond-haired, olive-skinned, red-lipped, living, breathing tribute to the American gene pool. But in this case, the melting pot had boiled over. Light and supple, with a gravity-defying hair cut, gelled to within a follicle of its life and the kind of eyes that had slain a million, trillion women, this guy was a daredevil. You know, the sort of bloke who has no past and no plans. Pierce Scanlen wasn't born – he fell off the back of a truck.

'G'day,' I said guardedly.

He put down his tiny tongs and turned to look at me. Even his most casual movement was deliberate. There was a dangerous luxuriance about him that took my breath away.

'What's your name? What's your IQ? You can't be that goddamned Australian girl. You look too intelligent to work in goddamned television.' He slowly tilted back his head and continued tweezing. 'G'day. G'day,' he mocked. 'What is "G" Day for Chrissake? The day Australians look for their G-spots?' The bathroom acoustics amplified his voice and the mirrors magnified his image. 'I gave up on all that crap. I mean, just when I found the clitoris, they went and moved it.'

I felt my face redden. This was the other reason I wanted to be an American. They were totally and absolutely one hundred percentedly devoid of self-consciousness. The opposite of yours truly.

'I'm sorry to um . . . barge in on you like this, but I just had to get away from this mad woman in the kitchen. She's reading a book about, well, about *crap*.'

Pierce's voice dropped to a sinister, TV announcer's vibrato. 'Welcome to the American Zone,' he said.

'She wanted to have a discussion on shape and colour and – I mean, who would know? Who wants to look? Once it's over, I'm out of there!'

'Really,' he said, not as a question, but in agreement. His voice was low, subtly contemptuous. It had a creamy quality – as though it had just come out of a blender. 'I mean, I wanna get to know you but not *that* well.'

'You'll be the first.'

'What?'

'Person who wants to know me.'

'I *have* to get to know you,' he pronounced, studying his reflection devoutly. 'We'll be working on the same goddamned show. I play the irresistible, upwardly mobile, herpes-free stud,' he said matter-of-factly. 'Mimi, that maniac you met in the kitchen, plays the millionairess-divorcee-mother of Rondah. Rondah's my bitchy de facto on the show. Ping is the token Hispanic. Phoebe Mercedez is the token black. And you're the token, gauche, naïve little Aussie.'

I thought about disappearing there and then, but I'd only get stuck talking to some *other* dickhead. This party was wall-to-wall dickheads, and, well, this guy didn't seem as dickheady as the other dickheads, if you know what I mean. At least he hadn't asked me what sort of car I drove.

'So kiddo, what kinda car you drive?' Mr Nostril-Plucker asked. Shrugging at my silence, he leant on the sink in a nonchalant manner. '*I* drive a black 911 Carrera convertible,' he volunteered. 'A black 928S Porsche – I had the alloy wheels chromed. Bewdiful. A black Ford Bronco 4 × 4, and a Ferrari Testarossa.' The last one sounded the most honest of the bunch. I mean, at least it admitted it was a motorised male hormone. 'I suppose, kiddo, you wanna know my name?'

One thing I hate is being called 'kid', especially by some jerk who's just a few years older than me. 'No. Not partic . . .'

'Pierce,' he said, 'Pierce Scanlen. And, like everyone in this goddamned industry, I earn enormous amounts of money for doin' absolutely fuck-all. Whaddid you do before you won this illustrious part?' Entranced by the miniature one-inch pigtail I'd just discovered at the nape of his downy neck, I didn't answer straight away. 'Hello?' He snapped his fingers. 'Earth to Aussie. Come in. Read my lips. What-did-you-do-before-', he over enun-ciated, 'you-got-sucked-into-this-Croc-Dundette-shit?'

I told Pierce about the squat I'd called home in Darlinghurst and the bookshop where I'd worked part-time. And about how it was ten margarine wrappers that had greased my way into Ameri-can television.

'A bookshop?' he addressed the mirror, almost wistfully. 'You left that to work as an actor in LA? Babe, this is fuckin' Siberia. Except warm. This is hell. You've taken a step so far down, your goddamned ears must have popped. Ouch! Shit! Mutha-fuck-ah! Chrrrrist!' He clamped a wad of tissues to his nose. The lethal little forceps had wrenched off a layer of nostril lining. As he stemmed the flow of blood, he unlidded his impudent green eyes and studied me. 'Lemme fill you in on the ol' score,' he offered nasally. 'Okay, they fly you here first class, chauffeur you round in limos, put you up in the Beverly Hills Hotel – but in less than one god-damned week, you'll be nothin' more than a gag-bag. A joke-nigger. Got it?'

'Abe told me that I was a High Concept,' I said defensively.

Pierce scoffed. 'Whaddaya get when you cross anal warts and a Hollywood television producer? Nothing. Anal warts won't stoop that low. So why not just crawl off back to Lizard-land? You won't survive LA, I betcha.'

If Pierce had known about my old man, he wouldn't have bet me anything. In the family resemblance department, I'd only inherited three of my father's genes. I had ingrown toenails just like his; I could touch the tip of my nose with my tongue; and I couldn't resist a bet. I was born with a pack of cards in my crib.

I learnt to count in the bookie's. I could say 'odds on, two against' before I could say the alphabet. At birthday parties, we didn't play 'spin the bottle' or 'hide-and-seek', but blackjack, pontoon, two-up. My father's only aim in life, besides blowing up the Pentagon, was to die playing cards, just like Al Jolson, Buster Keaton and Wild Bill Hickock. 'You're on,' I said. 'One hundred bucks,' and pushed past him into the inner sanctum of the toilet cubicle.

It was the weirdest dunny I'd ever been in. Oh, not just because of the gi-normous size, but there was a phone right by the toilet seat. The seat itself was covered in a thin layer of Gladwrap. I decided, dropping my togs, that Pierce was up himself. Like all good-looking blokes he had tickets. He was a blow-wave on legs, with bionic teeth. He most likely went out with girls called 'Bambi'. His middle name was probably 'Thumper'. As I flushed, the plastic sheet moved beneath me. More plastic was suddenly ejaculated from behind the cistern and propelled around the toilet lip. Experienced patrons no doubt learnt to leap to their feet like lightning before being embalmed in Gladwrap. My bum, however, had just been turned into the latest Christo creation. Hacking free, I squirmed back into my cossie and bolted into the bathroom. What an inglorious end. Eaten by a dunny seat. 'Even the toilet's trying to kill me,' I gushed.

'AIDS,' Pierce said airily. He was tweaking nostril hairs again. 'They put those goddamned condoms on the seats so that you won't pick up anythin'.'

I sat on the rim of the sunken bath and let my eyes rove around the marble bathroom. Having been awake for forty-eight hours, a hemisphere away from home and insulted by everyone I'd met, I was feeling kind of unrefreshed. Everywhere I looked, there was a mirror hosting a reflection of Pierce peering up his perfectly sculpted nostrils. Even on the ceiling.

'Ummm. What exactly are you doing?' I supposed it was just another strange American custom – like shooting drivers on the freeway for going too slowly, having pool parties where nobody swam, or looking at coloured pictures of crap. I was un-shockable.

'Huh? Oh . . . this. Well nuthin' disarms a woman like a man crying. May have to pull out a few nostril hairs to do it, but it works every time. Even on the Ruthless Rondah Rivers.' He exploded into a volley of sneezes. When they subsided, he checked his wrist and made for the door. He moved, I noticed, like a cat burglar. 'Synchronise watches. Water works,' he predicted commanding-officer-style, 'in six to seven minutes.' Then beamed bionically and left.

I followed him, shocked.

Exactly four and a half minutes later, Rondah Rivers made her entrance. I was standing on the far side of the pool near the writers when she swept on to the terrace in a voluminous green tank dress.

'Oh look,' Max, the head writer, whispered to his pen pals huddled under the sun umbrella. 'It's Sherwood Forest.'

Amy tossed her head back to laugh, but, seeing me, shushed her colleagues with a dramatic roll of the eyes. 'Actor Alert,' she warned, 'ten o'clock high.' The writers, their humour evaporating, glanced suspiciously in my direction.

I was getting the impression that on the job-desirability scale, it went – garbage collector, amoeba, can-opener, actor. I moved away to perch, cross-legged on the barbecue. Rondah was being greeted like royalty. People were practically curtsying, no kidding. Her Raybanned eyes darted like a bird of prey and finally came to rest on Pierce. He was lying supine in a deckchair in front of me, all golden brown, light-haired and luminous. She swooped.

'So, sugar, what happened to you last night?' I heard her snap. Brushing his legs aside, Rondah lowered her amplitudinous body, causing the chair to sag to the left.

'Um . . .' Pierce stalled '. . . would you believe I fell asleep?'

'I rang you.' Rondah had a Gone-with-the-Wind accent with the cleavage to match. 'I dialled my finger to the bone!'

'Yeah, but you see . . .' Pierce sat up, moving with underwater languor, giving himself more time to dredge up an excuse. 'I dreamt that I was . . . John Denver. I was so goddamned bored as John Denver that I even fell asleep in my dream. There was no waking up *then*, now was there?'

Rondah's mouth was painted a ferocious slash of fashionable puce. She used it now to attack Pierce. I strained forward so as not to miss one hiss. He was selfish, irresponsible, insensitive. And how did she feel going to a charity function by herself? Humiliated, that's how. Utterly hugh-mill-ee-aded.

Pierce said he was sorry. Really sorry. Rondah scoffed. But before she could lay into him again with her verbal truncheon, he removed his sunglasses. Pierce's eyes were glistening. His lips quivered. A fat tear welled up and spilt down his cheek. 'I'm just not as good in public as you are, Rond . . .' His voice was swollen with remorse. 'You know, basically, it's just that, well, beneath all the macho bravado and shit – I'm shy.'

Rondah inspected his face suspiciously for a moment, before her rage turned into a maternal rush of mush. She took his head between her manicured hands and kissed him on the nose. 'There, there boojums. It's all right. I believe y'all. Don't cry, sugar.' She cradled Pierce's head on her shoulder. 'There were plenty of other men there to look after me. Oh boojums, boojums.'

Pierce's performance was mesmerising. I searched his face for traces of insincerity. There were none. But just as a clot of sympathy was rising in my own throat, Pierce peered over Rondah's shoulder-pad and winked at me, his treasonous lips parting into a wide and wicked grin.

I began to smile back, then bit my lip and looked away.

Rondah was summoned to have some publicity shots taken for a television magazine.

'Boojums?' I quizzed him, when Sherwood Forest had uprooted.

'It's Persian.'

'What are you?' I asked, 'A *rug*?'

'This morning, no. This afternoon, yes. Rondah walks over everyone. She's top dog on the show, see. Dog, being the operative word. Wanna know her nickname?' He put his sunglasses back on. 'Castrina. That chick has men's balls mounted on her walls.'

'Including yours, obviously.'

He lounged back triumphantly in the deckchair, arms casually knotted behind his head. 'Oh, I see. It's laying-cards-on-the-old-table-time. Okay, number one, I'm a disloyal sonovabitch. Two, I don't love anyone. And three, I'm gutless. Get this – I once faked an orgasm with a prostitute 'cause I didn't want to hurt her feelings. And four, I'm a survivor. After the holocaust, you know who'll be left? Just me and a couple of cockroaches. Anyway,' Pierce continued, 'there *are* aspects of Rondah that are really nice.'

For a horrible moment I thought he was going to try and redeem himself. I looked at him as though he were fake as vinyl. 'Like what?'

'Like when she's asleep.'

Unlike the other guests, Rondah was positively Caribbean in her welcome. Back from the photographic session, she laced her arm through mine. She gave me a sip of Diet Coke. She called me 'Dah-ling'.

'It's ironic, dah-ling, I know,' she lectured me by the poolside bar, 'but bein' in a high ratin' situation *comedy* is no *joke*.' It was the sort of purred preamble she'd obviously polished on many talk shows. '*DINKS* is in syndication. We're watched by thirty-one million people a week across America. We have a very devoted audience. You see, dah-ling,' her voice was saturated with sincerity, 'we fulfil a need.'

'Yeah, you know,' Pierce smirked, 'just like Methadone.' He took a drag from his cigarette, which he was holding between thumb and forefinger, poolshark-style.

'And the reason we're needed, hon,' she continued with resolute affability, shooting her co-star an icy smile, 'is 'cause we radiate a Christian message of lurve.'

'Rondah's a Born-Again Christian,' Pierce informed me with subdued mockery.

'Yeah?'

'Whut's yuh rer-ligious persuasion?' she purred.

'Well, um . . .' I looked at Pierce for a clue, but he was busy playing marbles with martini olives, rolling them up and down the laminex bar top. 'I'm more your basic Born-Again Atheist.' Rondah's mouth contracted as though she'd swallowed a bad oyster. 'Um, I was kinda being ironic,' I added dismally.

Rondah just looked at me coldly. Her sunglasses, perched on top of her head, were like the antennae of an alien. There's an irony-deficiency in LA, no kidding. To tell you the truth, I'm not that cracked on people like Rondah Rivers. She's the sort of person who could smile this great big warm kind of smile at you – while her eyes had the look of a kid about to squash an insect.

'It's goin' to be jest so refreshin' to have y'all round, Katrina, ain't that right, Pierce?' I swear to God her accent was becoming more and more N'Awlins as she went along. 'It's so re-fresh-in' to meet a woman in Hollywood who's not inhibited by small breasts. I mean, a lotta chickadees wouldn't even go into the actin' profession with breasts your size. And if they did, they'd feel the need to cover up. It's so darn silly and, well, so *dishonest*, don't you feel sugar?' I peered forlornly at my undernourished mammaries. 'And ain't you downright *brave* to wear a one-piece. Still, you can't see yourself from the *back*, so what does it matter anyway? Of course I'm not pryin',' she wheedled, flicking her hair over her shoulder, 'but what exactly *is* yer actin' experience?'

'Well um, none really. I've done a little singing and stuff.'

'*Moi aussi*,' she enthused sweetly. 'Do you sing Lieder?'

'What?'

'Lieder.'

'You mean like "Leader of the Pack"?'

Rondah clapped her hands. Eyes glistening, she repeated this for the benefit of the other actors. 'Sweet Lord! Attention every- bodee. We've got a hillbilly on our hands!' she thrilled.

People stopped eating. They swivelled around in their chairs or leant up against each other and leered. Salads wilted. Cream cakes curdled. Plates of oysters congealed in the sun. Okay, so I wasn't exactly a high-brow (until recently I'd thought 'cacciatore' was an opera) but I wasn't a card-carrying yobbo either. Besides, it was Rondah's mates who were acting like barbarians. Some of them sort of started to circle me, giving the odd primordial sniff. I felt myself redden under their gaze. Rondah's contempt was contagious.

'The blushing virgin,' Ping snickered, stroking the fuzzy ball of poodle in her lap.

'Yeah, tell us, Down-Under,' Phoebe Mercedez interrogated, retrieving a piece of chewing gum from her escort's mouth and inserting it into her own, 'do you have a lover?'

Smirking, her muscle-bound boyfriend then shoved his hand down his jeans, poked his index finger through his fly and wriggled it. 'Yo, white pussy, wrap your wet squeegie round this mutha- suck-ah.'

Everyone seemed to think this was pants-wettingly witty. As they chortled, I looked at their tasselled moccasins and designer- ripped jeans, at their too-tanned faces and tailored teeth. (LA is the overbite capital of the world. Everyone has Donny Osmond dentistry.) 'Excuse me, mate,' I said at last, 'I hate to tell you this, but your dick needs a manicure.'

Phoebe Mercedez's boyfriend retrieved his hand, cracked his knuckles and glowered at me.

The laughter died on their lips. The actors looked at me in scandalised silence. I guess they were all a little lost without

Autocues. Phoebe Mercedez's bloke growled, long and low and loud. It struck me then how much he resembled a baddie from a Schwarzenegger movie. You know, the sort of guy who picks his teeth with a switchblade. Pierce must have noticed this too. He suddenly started moon-walking backwards out of the scene. And then the baddie from the Schwarzenegger movie lunged. Two other blokes grabbed him by the shoulders, leaving his forearms to flail about in an indecipherable semaphore.

The photographer oozed towards the front of the gawping 'extras'. At the sound of his finger clicking into position on his nine calibre Nikon trigger, Rondah stepped between us. Oh, not to prevent me from eating a knuckle sandwich or anything nice like that. No, it was just that these were not the sort of photos she wanted to see on the front of *TV Guide*. Especially with 'Sweeps Week' looming – the week they gauged the show's ratings.

'I saw a doc-u-ment-tree on down-under once,' she said with indefatigable sweetness. 'Sweet Lordie. It's not what you'd call an *advanced* cunt-tree. They practically eat their young, *live!*' She brushed her hair back again, in that provocative way she had. 'Our little Oss-sea just ain't bin tamed yet.' She lifted up my arm to reveal the stubbly pit. 'Or groomed. See what I mean? We're talkin' *primitive*.'

Relieved, everyone started laughing immoderately. The photographer uncocked and lowered his camera. Linking arms with my assailant, Rondah led him inside to the dance floor, where an invisible disc jockey was playing a Motley Crue song, 'Hollywood, There's No Escape'.

Pierce stopped doing his Neil Armstrong impersonation and centred me in his green gaze. I reckon he was worried about his hundred bucks.

The Independence Day party flowed into the night. More and more people arrived. By now I was finding it almost impossible to remain perpendicular. The only bed I could find with no one in it was a heart-shaped ensemble in the guests' wing. But as soon as I lay down it went into tachycardia, *cha-cha*-ing back and forth across the carpet. A vibrator-bed is not such a wonderful sensation after seven airline meals, six vodkas and a brush with a modern-day mastodon. Unable to find the 'off' switch, I abandoned the twitching mattress and settled instead for a big comfy chair in Abe's study. The room was wittily decorated with his collection of Polynesian war masks and shrunken heads. I had just sunk into the soft leather marshmallow and was dropping off, when Abe ambushed me. 'Zere you are, Crocodile Dundette!'

His arm clamped round my shoulder, he led me through the rest of his air-conditioned, antiseptic, disinfected, rust and dust-proof, intruder-resistant, mite and termite-free, capital 'T' Taste-ful, Hollywood home. The walls were lined with Monets and Manets. Abe toured me from one masterpiece to the next, expounding on the price of each one. Every painting was hooded by a little light, illuminating the signature. It was beyond me why Abe bothered buying paintings. He should have just framed the cheques. When I shared this insight Abe's eyebrows hovered angrily at nose level, then shot back up on to his forehead.

'I vant you to azzimilate.' He clenched his jaw and moved it from right to left, revealing a little piece of pastrami wedged in the crease of his frown. 'Azz-im-ilate. Savvy?'

In the master bedroom was a marble Jacuzzi. It bubbled and frothed like a giant cappuccino, except it was chock-a-block with naked bodies sharing joints and laughing too loudly at each other's jokes. Abe stripped off and plunged into the tub. Assimilate, I said to myself and followed him in. It was like getting into a pool of piranhas.

'Oh, there's no need to leave your panties on, babe,' a woman with a tattoo on her shaved head said to me.

'No worries. I'm right thanks.' No undies, in *this* crowd? Was she crazy?

'Let *me* wear them.' The voice belonged to Denzil, one of the token black, or rather beige, actors on the show. 'Cross-dressin' is one of the most er-ot-ic experiences in the world.'

Another bloke confessed to wearing his wife's underwear to work. 'Watermelon is my favourite colour.'

A disembodied voice started to cry. How could she cross-dress when she couldn't even find a Close Personal Relationship?

I'd say, being starkers in a Jacuzzi, it was impossible *not* to find a Close Personal Relationship.

The only creature I recognised in this decadent aquarium was Mimi Zarbo. She was instructing a small group in yoga knots. Her half-submerged limbs looked smooth, almost plastic. Come to think of it, all the bodies around me looked just as taut and tanned. They were like Barbie and Ken dolls, on acid. What *was* wrong with this picture? Suddenly it dawned on me. Wrinkles. Los Angeles is a wrinkle-free zone. I had come to a country where there was no law of gravity. Here, skin sagged *upwards*. Mimi was sixty-five, with the skin of a cheerleader. She must have had so many facelifts that her ankles would now be her knees. Her knees would now be her navel. That would put her clitoris at about chin level. Her hand was resting there, below her lips. I strained to see if she was rubbing that particular spot a little too vigorously.

Abe grinned at me and sank into the murky depths of the Jacuzzi. I looked around for him through the bubbles. Just when I was contemplating a full-scale Bondi-Beach-surf-life-saver rescue and resuscitation, I felt something sucking my toes. One by one. When Abe came up for air, I enthusiastically reminded him how chic it was to be a radical celibate. I was getting the impression that his sex drought was about to break.

'You don't want to ruin your record, do you?' I said, edging away from him. Abe, nude, was not such a beautiful sight. He looked like a fur ball that something had vomited up.

'Let's go into zee bedroom, cupcake, and I'll fuck your brains out,' my new producer said suavely. I declined, pointing out that I had a very high IQ. He'd be there for absolutely ages. Years. Decades. Eons.

I practically walked on water to get out of there. I realised that Mimi Zarbo was the only sane person I'd met all day. Turds *did* float. Here they were, at the very top, earning ten million dollars a year, producing American television.

THE CRAZY AMERICAN SALAD

It took exactly fifteen hours for the bumper stickers to appear.
'Don't shoot me,' read a Corvette on the Hollywood Freeway,
'I'm driving as fast as I can.' The stretch limo taking me to the
studio changed lanes incessantly. All the other cars were just as
twitchy. It was like being in a school of four-wheeled fish. According to the miniature television embedded on the back seat, so far
today there'd been a bomb scare at the LA DA's office, only two
freeway shootings, a Rottweiler had devoured a small child, three
people had been shot dead in a drugs bust, as well as the usual
corpse count from gang warfare downtown. And all before breakfast. By the time I got off the freeway, I had severe faceache from
smiling at every passing driver.

Paradise Studios was located in one of the seediest parts of the
city – which in LA is really saying something. The shops catered
for fast food and fast sex. It was a chaos of rubber underwear and
rissoles, hot dogs and inflatable dolls, burgers and bondage gear.
The limo manoeuvred into a congested backstreet. We crawled
past men lounging on street corners, their flies at half-mast. 'Hey,
yo mutha-fuck-uh!' These guys really knew how to greet a girl.
'Show us ya puss-ee!' This entire tangle of crack dealers, copulating dogs, and decomposing car bodies was framed by the massive
letters of the 'Hollywood' sign straddling the barren hill above.

Getting on to the lot was dead easy. I gave them everything
except a urine sample and drove straight through. Stencilled
nameplates in the multi-tiered car park labelled the stalls of each
500 horsepower Mustang, Maserati or Mercedes. I read the
names as we spiralled upwards: Abe Epstein, Ping Sufuentes,
Phoebe Mercedez, Pierce Scanlen, Rondah Rivers. Rondah's stall

was painted pink, the cement floor patterned in a silver star of hubcaps.

I wandered down on to the lot. It was not yet lunchtime, but the air crackled with heat. The lot was like a concentration-camp: chockers with windowless buildings and graffiti-free walls. Almost all the current major situation comedies and soap operas were filmed here every week. I was standing in the nerve centre of America's imagination, the heart of the world's dream machine. And it was a nightmare. During my first wardrobe call on my first day, as I was being hauled in and out of jodhpurs and jumpers, leotards and leisure lounge suits, automatic gunfire rat-a-tatted outside. Hobbled by the lycra jumpsuit I'd let fall at the sound of shooting, I blundered towards the window. Beyond the barbed wire fence, a police helicopter swooped, vulture-like, down over the street, its human prey scurrying. Sirens yelped. People scattered. Bullets thudded. The wardrobe mistress, Betty, nonchalantly informed me that it was a drug bust. Betty levered open the window and called down to the gateman. 'Hey bud, what's the score?'

He cupped his hand over his mouth and called casually back up to her. 'Three dead. Two maimed.'

Pierce, his head bracketed by a Walkman, was being fitted with the latest fad in faded denims. I peeled back one earphone. 'Excuse me, but, um, well, while we're inside making comedy, people are outside being killed.' Pierce shrugged with his lips. 'Well, doesn't that strike you as being just a little bit weird?'

Pierce readjusted his Walkman and tweaked my earlobe. 'I said you wouldn't last long, kiddo.'

The only thing that shocked an Angeleno was someone being shocked. You'd have to have all your limbs sawn off with a nail file and your brain sucked out through your ears by a straw, before you'd get the slightest bit of sympathy. A bump in the fender of a hundred thousand dollar Maserati, however, was enough to send all and sundry into apoplectic spasms. 'You're about as sensitive as a, as a . . .' Pierce took a leisurely tug on his roll-your-own as I squirmed for the right word, 'as a, I dunno, a *corpse*. Didja know that?'

Pierce looked at me lazily, then made for the door. Watching the retreat of his denimed buttocks filled me with a sudden feeling of despair. It was Friday. An empty weekend yawned before me.

At the party, Abe had tried to coerce someone into looking after me. But Phoebe Mercedez had a crystal therapy workshop. And Ping was tied up with her dog psychiatrist, and then she was hanging out with her mates, Cindy and George. (It was clear by the tone in her voice that she meant Lauper and Michael.) 'Um, hey, Pierce, what are you doing, you know, over the weekend?'

He didn't even bother to turn. 'Decomposing.'

After the wardrobe call, I was shepherded into Make-up. The President of Make-up, a middle-aged bloke named Cosmo Vinyl, eyed me clinically, then twirled me towards the mirror to deliver his verdict. For the next ten minutes, I listened while he prescribed a dizzying array of day creams, bust creams, eye and thigh creams, fade and freckle creams. Glossy four-foot photos of his famous clients beamed down smugly from their walnut frames, as Cosmo bombarded me with bio babble about collagen and elastin and liposomes and microsomes – which all just sounded like an insanely expensive array of multi-coloured globs and blobs. I'd always thought the only way to prevent wrinkles was to stay out of the sun. But, hey, what would I know?

'So,' he concluded, 'for today, we'll go for the leg wax, lip depilation, tanning salon, hair cut and streaked, cuticles softened, eyelashes curled, nails . . .' He splayed my fingers and studied them. 'Malibu Sunset, eyebrows reshaped, nourishing emulsion and Brumisateur hydration. Apart from that, we'll go for the *natural* look.' He then gave me a dirty big wink. I kind of liked Cosmo. The poor bloke was halfway through a hair transplant. Up close, his scalp looked like a little plantation of palm trees. And he didn't laugh when I said I wanted to wear my Speedos in the tanning salon.

Rondah was laid out on a slab, rotating every twenty minutes, like a chook on a rotisserie. She was already the colour of my mother's mahogany sideboard.

'Oh, hi,' I greeted her. She stretched a lazy arm towards a bottle of oil and dripped translucent globules on to her big belly. 'Great party,' I lied. Still no response. Cosmo pulled a face behind her back, then handed me a pair of goggles. Cosmo's salon was equipped with two regular full-tanning machines and four high-speed. The ultraviolet rays were 'safe enough', he assured me, 'for a new tanner'. Through the windows I could see the sun shimmering mercilessly off hot car metal.

I stripped and tentatively stretched out on the toasting pad. It was like getting into a Breville sandwich-maker. The mauve beams beat down on me. All that was missing was the marjoram and rosemary. 'Um, so, what are you doing over the weekend?'

Rondah looked at me as though I was radioactive and turned over.

After I'd been basted and browned, I went back to the make-up room so that Cosmo could attack my hair. As my head was dunked like a teabag, in and out of the basin, I caught snippets of the conversation. It was all about Abe's party. Two of the 'extras' related the Jacuzzi confessions on underpants swapping.

'You bunch of deviants,' Cosmo whined with mock indignation. (If his voice had legs, it would have minced.) 'Am I the only like *normal* one on this entire lot?'

I was about to ask Cosmo what he had planned for the weekend, when I felt a hot whisper in my earhole. 'The guy gets cocks shoved up his bum for Chrrrissake. You can't get more normal than that.' Squinting open one eye, I glimpsed a blinding flash of teeth as Pierce sank into a nearby chair. He had the whitest teeth in the entire world. In fact, I doubted that Pierce Scanlen would ever reach his twenty-fifth birthday before being kidnapped by ivory poachers. He was wearing a jumper with a large embroidered 'P' and 'S' on the pocket.

'Spoken by a bloke who has to have his initials on his sweater 'cause he's too thick to remember his own name.' It was difficult to think when I'd last met a man as downright pukesville as Pierce Reece-Scanlen Jnr (the Third).

Lounging in the chair like some Greek God, Pierce tilted back his head, exposing a slender neck, opened his lips and dropped in a round red grape. His Adam's apple rode up and down his throat like a tiny elevator. I suddenly realised that I hadn't eaten anything since the plane. I looked hungrily at the next succulent grape he broke off the bunch.

'I'd offer you one, but . . .' he gloated, glancing at my fingers which were splayed out on the formica counter in front of me, nails glistening wet with 'Malibu Sunset'. I leaned forward and, like a seal, gobbled a grape from between his fingers.

Pierce laughed. He had this warm, lovely laugh, like Golden

Syrup dripping off a spoon. Just as he was extending me another grape, a voice, swollen with insincerity, purred at my back.

'Dah-ling.' Rondah, now swathed in a silk kimono, kissed my cheek as though I was the most alluring person in the whole of America. She manoeuvred herself into the space between me and Pierce and shook free her popcorn-coloured hair. Up close I saw for the first time the hint of dark roots. Without a doubt, 'blondes' are the most significant contribution Science has made to the Californian way of life.

'No shit, Rond,' Pierce exclaimed, gobbling grapes. 'I didn't know your hair was highlighted.'

'It's *not*. This is my *real* colour!' Leaning into the mirror, she proceeded to take Pierce on a guided tour of each follicle. 'Cosmo dah-ling jest puts a little touch or two of streaks up here on top, and an incey, wincey, tincey liddle highlight here and there, but it doesn't detract from the *real* colour 'cause . . .'

'Sounds like a "yes" to me,' I said. It was a dumb thing to say, I know, but I just couldn't stand the way she was pretending to be so nice to me all of a sudden. I'd never met anyone so two-faced: this woman was positively *bi*-facial.

Pierce laughed and leant in front of Rondah to reward me with another grape.

Rondah's eyes, as she watched me nibble it from between his fingers, narrowed into two black holes of pure hate. She gave Cosmo the nod and my head was plunged back into the basin. I emerged, spluttering, in time to see Abe barging into the make-up room.

'Vondah!' Abe gushed, covering her in kisses. They were practically playing tonsil-hockey, for God's sake. 'And vot haff you got lined up for zee weekend? Somesing vunder-full no doubt?'

Rondah mused that she couldn't decide whether to opt for a raging time in New A'wlins or a quiet restful break in a luxury resort in the Rockies. 'And, well, for that I'd need to take someone recov-rin' from like *major* surgery, or someone deeply dull and borin'.' She flashed her insect-squashing eyes at me and smiled sweetly, 'Katrina, maybe y'all'd like to come?'

Honestly, Rondah Rivers made the 'bitches' on *Dallas* look like door-to-door collectors for the multiple sclerosis fund. Pierce miaowed and clawed the air.

Rondah looked at him all wide-eyed with innocence. 'What?' she purred.

My only other invitation was to Mimi's Colonics Party. I nearly accepted until Pierce explained the protocol of those parties. After dinner, group enemas are administered and guests help diagnose each other's dietary ailments.

People began packing up and making 'going home' noises. To tell you the truth, it made me feel just a little bit depressed. Forgetting about my nails, I grabbed at Abe, leaving a crimson splodge on the arm of his jacket. 'Abe, Abe, um, what are you up to at the . . .'

Abe peeled a pile of notes from the wad in his pocket and pressed them into my palm. 'Veal do lunch.'

'Great!' I enthused, relieved. This was the most interest anybody had shown in me all day. I flipped open my appointments diary. It looked like the Nevada desert in there, no kidding. A snicker ran through the room.

'I'll get my zecretary to get on to your zecretary, cupcake,' Abe said abruptly, and left. Ping and Phoebe Mercedez chortled derisively. I hadn't yet learnt that 'Let's do lunch' is a euphemism for 'Fuck off and die'. If Californians kept all the lunches they promised, they'd be booked out till the turn of the century. And that's if they had lunch for breakfast, dinner *and* lunch.

Abe was putting me up in a real posh place called The Beverly something or other, a giant, pink, 300-room marshmallow. I took a magazine from reception and followed the tuxedoed trail of waiters bearing trays of brightly coloured concoctions. They were rushing to and from a swish bar called the 'Polo Lounge'. It was full of glistening women and serious men in dark suits. The *maître d'* bloke slipped a surreptitious glance at my jaded jeans and perished T-shirt, trying to ascertain if I was just a common old dag, too poor to afford good clothes, or so rich and famous I didn't give a damn what I wore.

Exuding rich and famous feelings, I straddled one of the bar stools. Every seat was occupied by a woman. They leant sinuously on to the bar, all coloured talons, gi-normous cleavages and those white, bright teeth. It was the Barbie doll look again. I wondered if they could bend their legs up round their necks and rotate their arms 360 degrees in their sockets.

I ordered a drink, then flicked through the magazine. On page three, nestled between ads for super dooper pooper scoopers and designer space in Heaven (all you had to do was send $2,000 and a picture of yourself to a Reverend Hogg in Biloxi) my eye was snagged by an ad for a casino called 'Nirvana' in Las Vegas. I scoured the ad twice to make sure I wasn't misreading it. The casino was advertising a blackjack game in which they offered to show you the *second card*. Now, the only wisdom my father had imparted to his only offspring over the years was how to hot-wire a car, cheat in Monopoly, say 'fuck off' in sixteen different languages, palm cards, deal from the bottom of the pack, stack the deck, and play blackjack. Being able to see the second card was a mind-boggling advantage.

I imagined my father's face creasing into eager laughter. 'No bull? The second card? Hells Bells. A good punter never grumbles, a good horse never tumbles and a good mug never stumbles,' I could hear him saying in his strident voice, as he shucked on his shoes without untying the laces, squishing down the heel the way my mother hated, before disappearing into the depths of the casino with the rent money. (My father always told people that we lived in a nice little fibro bungalow overlooking the rent.)

With a start I realised that I'd been ambushed by thoughts of my father. Alarmed at this unexpected residue of affection, I slammed the magazine shut and swore out loud. The ladies at the bar glanced at me, disconcerted, and swivelled away. Their flaccid curves, corsetted into too-tight cocktail frocks, squeaked reproachfully on the bar stool leather. As I took a loud sip from my Jamaican Flirtation, it finally dawned on me that I was the only one who wasn't. Flirting, that is. I dismounted and moved to a small table by the bar.

A young woman was already sitting there. She was petite with large breasts that bulged over the top of her black cocktail dress. Plonked in front of her on the table was a huge handbag. I wondered what on earth was in there. Most probably all her vital organs, I decided, noting how thin she was. She wore a black cocktail hat, the veil of which shrouded her face. I remember thinking that it was the sort of hat you wear to a murder.

'Excuse me, do you mind if I sit here?'

She shrugged dramatically. We both stared straight ahead at

the row of sequined women. No kidding, if you could harness the glow from designer Hollywood dresses, you could illuminate all of Sydney for centuries. 'I think those ladies are on the game,' I whispered. 'What do you reckon?'

'Well, of course they are. Where do ya live?' my companion inquired sarcastically. 'In a *box*?' She lifted the veil, revealing a bright, eager, over made-up face that was examining me closely. 'You're Australian? No shit? Hey, what kinda cars do ya drive over there?'

'I don't drive,' I confessed.

She eyed me with a mixture of disbelief and alarm. 'What are ya?' she exclaimed. 'A weirdo, or what?' In the next breath she revealed that she'd just surfaced from a twenty-four-hour orgy with a rock group. 'I woke up' – she checked her watch – 'about an hour ago, upstairs in some suite, with a strange man's cock in my mouth. Shocked?' she asked hopefully.

Truth was, I'd needed a shock absorber for my brain ever since I'd arrived in this town. 'Huh? No, well, I mean . . .'

'What?'

'I just hope you don't grind your teeth in your sleep, that's all.'

She laughed then and sat back in her chair to appraise me. 'My name's Tash,' she said. 'Short for Natasha. My Mom wanted me to be a spy or a gypsy but all I could get was a job down the mall in McDonald's.'

A waiter briskly mopped the table and asked if we two gals would like another round of cocktails. Tash looked disapprovingly at the creamy residue in my glass. 'Sure, Mack. Get real. You're talkin' to *women* here. Two Lime Sodas.' She turned to confide in me: 'No calories. So,' she said, craning across the table to read the name on my drinks tab, 'Katrina Kennedy, what's ya favourite sexual position?'

'What?' I felt myself blush. Like I told you, the other reason I wanted to become an American was so I could stop blushing all over the place. It's positively illegal to blush in America. 'I dunno. At this stage in my life, anything involving a male. Why? What's yours?'

Tash didn't miss a beat. 'Standin' up, backwards, covered in custard.'

'Your boyfriend is a very lucky bloke,' I said. 'On the other hand, the man is going to *die*.'

'Got any drugs?'

My drug days began and ended on my thirteenth birthday when I'd sniffed some Airfix glue and stuck my right nostril to my upper lip. 'Sorry. In that department I'm about as useful as a screen door on a submarine.'

She looked at me strangely. 'You sure do talk funny,' she said in her thick gangster kind of drawl. *I* talked funny. Since arriving here, I had hardly understood one word spoken to me. People were always either trying to 'blue sky' me, or take me to 'the max' or 'run it past' someone or other. 'So, ya like it here or what?'

I shrugged. 'I'm azz-im-ilating,' I said grimly.

Tash suddenly stiffened, screwed up her eyes and stared intently over my shoulder. She clutched at her bag. I think she was actually trying to get *inside* it. 'Oh shit.'

This Arabian bloke was making a beeline for her across the carpet. 'Who's that?'

'An Arab.'

'Well, I can see that.'

'No. A *real* Arab,' she gushed. 'We're talking camels, harems, oil derricks.' She waved her arms in the air. 'The whole sheik shit.'

He pulled up short at our table and started blathering. I edged back. Well, you never knew in LA. The guy might have had a loaded pit bull in his pocket. He seemed to be saying something about a ring. Waiters and managers swooped. They locked Tash by the elbows and hoisted her up out of her seat. Her stilettoed legs pedalled the air like a cartoon character's.

'Yeah, yeah?' Tash's bluster returned in a flash. 'I've got ya ring, buster.' She grabbed a fistful of her stockinged thigh. 'Right here.' She kicked the waiter in the shin, slithered to the carpet and, pursued by the Arabian bloke's tirade, tottered towards the door. In her lopsided hat and high-rise heels that were too big for her, she looked like a little girl's drawing of what a grown-up lady should look like. I followed. A big bloke at the bar chuckled and, as we passed, asked if he could buy us a drink.

Tash's anger momentarily abated. She smiled demurely. 'Why thank you, sir.' Slapping our tabs into his hand, her voice shifted back into gravel rash gear. 'Two Lime Sodas and a – ' she glanced at me –

'Jamaican Flirtation,' I said, and raced after her out the door.

'Move ass,' Tash hissed at me, heading for the car park.

'Wait,' I darted back between the legs of the waiters, retrieved the magazine with the Nirvana casino ad, pocketed it and POQ-ed.

Tash didn't talk until she'd manoeuvred her battered black Chevrolet sports car (it had red upholstery, Mag wheels, a pair of fluffy dice dangling from the rear vision mirror and a dashboard carpeted in lime green shag. She called it her 'pimpmobile') into the 'Tow Away' zone on La Cienega. 'Camel fucker,' was all she said. I followed her into a café called Ed Debevic's. It was an old-fashioned Fifties sort of diner. The waiters rollerskated by, singing 'My Guy' and 'California Girls'. The waitresses whooshed by too, their hairy beehives toppling forward precariously. A sign by the door said, 'If you don't like the food, Mack, then go some place else.'

She perused the menu with delight. 'Ya must be starvin'.'

'No. Not really. I – '

'Ya must be. Rage burns up to about, oh, 200 calories per minute.'

'No, actually I'm not.'

'Yes. Ya'll have a wickedly creamy cocktail and a huge disgustin' cake and a Fudge Sunday Delicious Surprise Supremo,' she declared, relenting in her role as Calorie Kommandant. 'Oh and a cream donut.' Tash placed the order then inserted a quarter into the mouth of the miniature jukebox at our table.

'Where'd you meet *him*?' I asked finally. 'Through his parole officer?'

'Are ya sure you dunno where we can get some coke?' When I suggested the Golden Triangle she sighed and punched the jukebox buttons. 'I used to do some modellin' and shit, right? Well, on this shoot one day, I met this Arab guy. He kinda like, fell for me, ya know? Arab guys are kinda weird about women. They just, like, eat and play cards and ignore ya all night then, about midnight, grab ya for a few minutes of fast sex. They just kinda order ya up, like pizza. Anyways, then, in Paris, he, like, gives me this ring, see. I took it to Cartier's to get it like, appraised. They kept it for a day or two. And then, ya know what they finally told me?' 'What you have here, Madam,' she lapsed into a bad French accent, 'is a tiny piece of the moon.' This goddamned Arab guy had bought the rocks off of NASA. Can ya believe that?

Pretty poetic huh? A little piece of the moon.' Her wistfulness evaporated. 'So I sold it and high-tailed it home on the proceeds.' The little jukebox whined into life. The song she'd selected was 'Bikini Girls with Machine Guns', by the Cramps. 'That Arab guy was really startin' to give me the creeps, ya know?'

Tash looked just a few years older than me. About twenty-three. 'You just sleep with total strangers?'

'Only on a recreational basis.'

'For money?'

'No, but I get presents. Which I, ya know, sometimes sell.' She peered down the front of her dress with the professional detachment of an architect inspecting a building site. 'I'm savin' up for a breast reduction.'

'Why?' I said. 'Aren't two the normal number?' What was it about Californians? Why were they always melting, moulding or rearranging their body parts?

'It'll cost me four thou for both, with a medical rebate of $980 bucks, for each tit that is, and three to four days in hospital. And the only, like, side-effect, is a change in nipple sensitivity.' She took a slurp at her glass of water. 'I've gone, like, right into it.'

'Oh,' I said stupefied. 'Right. But, um, couldn't you, you know, save up on a straight job?'

'Had a straight job once, when I first came out here from Chicago an' all. As an office girl. But they only hired me for T and A.'

I gazed at her blankly. 'Travel and Adventure?'

She looked at me as though I was speaking a remote Bolivian mountain dialect. 'Are you yankin' my chain?' she snapped then, satisfied by my head shake, explained, 'Tits and Ass.'

'How do you know that? I mean . . .'

'They were always making me file things under "Z".'

'So?'

'Accounts and Beverages? Where do ya *live*?' she asked me again. 'In a *box*? They jest wanted me to keep bendin' over. Everybody's peddlin' their ass in this town.' Tash sounded like, not a B, but a C grade movie. 'We're all gettin' screwed,' – she trowelled the icing off my cake with her little finger – 'in one way or another.' And licked it clean. 'So why'dja come to America?'

I told her about the margarine competition and the show and about the actors and how everybody had ignored me and how

I had no mates here and how I desperately wanted to be an American.

'Well ya can't be an American without doin' drugs. It's our only culture, for Chrissake. Come to think of it, I do know where we could get some ecstasy.'

'Some what?'

'Oh, get real. *Ecstasy.*' She looked at me expectantly. 'MDMA?' She rolled her eyes. 'Methylenedioxymethamphetamine? It ain't everyone's drug. Some people experience like, nausea, sweatin', seizures, vomitin', blurred vision, coma, convulsions, delirium, ataxia, anxiety, anorexia, headaches, paranoia and jaw tension. Others report fallin' in love.' She ducked her head and with her tongue decapitated the froth from my Hot Fudge Sunday Delicious Surprise Supreme. 'Personally it gives me the most fantab-u-lous orgasms.'

'That's what *I* want.'

'Fantabulous orgasms?'

'No. To fall in love. That's the real reason I came to Americ . . .'

Tash suddenly catapulted forward, cross-eyed. She thrust her finger down her throat and started making choking noises. Before I had time to call an ambulance, she just as suddenly stopped. She leant back in her chair, legs akimbo.

'Don't make me sick,' she said. 'This is the butt end of the twentieth century. People don't fall "in *love*". I mean, get *real*. Believing in love is about as plausible as believin' in UFOs. You're gonna haveta toughen up, ya know that?'

She excavated the remnants of icing from beneath her long painted nail. About a week's worth of gunge came out with it. After examining the gunge thoughtfully, she scraped it on the tablecloth, screwed up her eyes and scrutinised me, as though deciding something important. She gave a dramatic sigh, then folded her arms across her ample bust. 'Didja know,' she asserted, 'that doctors at the LA County Hospital extract six to eight gerbils from the assholes of gay men every week.'

'Gerbils? Those little guineapigs? Those little furry . . . ?'

'First they de-claw 'em, chloroform 'em, and then insert 'em up each other's assholes.'

My mouth echoed the hole in the cream donut the waiter put down in front of me. 'Why?'

She shrugged. 'The sexual pleasure, apparently, comes from the little creature wakin' up and squirmin', ya know, as it suffocates to death.'

This was my first introduction to Tash's LA survival technique. She called it her TT – Tolerance Threshold. To toughen herself up for the abuse she regularly received from raving Arabs, megalomaniacal record producers, pushy landlords, and men in general, Tash was increasing her threshold of pain. Her theory was that by talking about disgusting things she could take herself to the limit, push out her pain envelope. It was sort of the Chuck Yeager Theory of Self Development. From Gerbils to German war atrocities, from real-life Rambos to rain forest destruction – every day she pushed a little further. One day there'd be this sonic boom and she would have broken through into the Shockless Zone. Then nothing could hurt her, ever again.

As I gagged, Tash touched my hand solicitously, before pouncing on my donut. 'It's the only way to toughen up,' she said, cream spurting between her fingers. 'Believe me, I was greener than you when I hit town.' She gave me a sidelong glance. 'Though maybe not. Anyway, I'll start ya on ya basic racist and sexist stuff, then, when you grow immune to those insults, we'll graduate to jokes about paraplegics, pederasts and fist fuckin'. Okay? Come on.' With that, she swallowed the rest of my donut, drained my cocktail and squeezed into her stilettos. 'Let's be culture-vultures.'

Tash was one of those people that you only have to meet for ten seconds to feel as though you've known her for ten years. That you went to kindy together. Got your first periods together. Smoked your first dope together. Got fitted for your first cervical caps together.

Assimilate, I said to myself, and followed Tash at a sprint, through the revolving door, without paying.

I felt like Scott leaving his Antarctic base camp.

Los Angeles has the shortest attention span of any city in the world. This town went through fads so fast that by the time you traded in your see-through suitcase for the latest swami and switched your dog from canine psychiatry to a Tibetan dietitian, you were already out of fashion. The latest trend this month, this minute, this millisecond, was clubs. Not *a* club. Just clubs. There were thousands of them. Some for tap dancing. Some for yodelling. Vampires Anonymous. There were even clubs for people who didn't want to belong to clubs.

Our first stop was a seedy saloon at the foot of the Hollywood Hills. It was a flimsy fibro construction. Snoring ceramic Mexican figurines lounged up against a neon sign which read 'Ugly Unlimited'.

The bilious lights of the lobby illuminated a strange assortment of dwarves, women whose facelifts had sagged unevenly, cripples, anorexics, transvestites and pincushioned punks with no part of their bodies unpierced. It was not such a beautiful sight. Tash slapped the back of a muscle-bound dwarf who was taking tickets at the door. 'Kat, meet Hercules, the bouncer. To keep the Bewdiful People out. Ain't that hil*a*rious! Got any blow?' she asked, lowering her voice. He led the way up the stairs, taking each step with panting ferocity.

The living-room was chock-a-block with prematurely balding men who looked as though they were all called Trevor, and large women with dandruffy shoulders. A lady in a lycra leotard, which accentuated the fact that one of her breasts was missing, ushered me into a photographic cubicle, 'No, um . . . see, I didn't come to join up or any . . .'

'Jest quit blabbin' and fill in the whatsamacallit.' She grilled me for details – name, date of birth, weight, star sign – then snapped a polaroid. I would be informed, she said, if I was considered ugly enough to be accepted as a member.

Well now, that was something to look forward to.

In the hallway, I flopped into an armchair. Hercules loomed out of the gloom. He waddled over and thrust me a menu. I smiled wanly and ordered an 'All-American Salad'. When he returned with my plate, he sat down, grabbed my hand and sent a fetid blast of breath into my face. 'Hey baby, how wouldja like to hear the pitter patter pat of little tiny feet in thuh mornin', huh?'

Just to top off my day, it was then I found a small brown cockroach lying on a lima bean. They only knocked a buck off the bill: 'Foreign Object in Salad' it read.

I decided to wait for Tash in the car.

'Got some downers,' she reported, climbing inside, as blasé as I was bamboozled. Who needed a chemical downer after that? I felt pretty depressed naturally all of a sudden.

Tash needed uppers to counteract the downers and downers to counteract the uppers and inbetweeners to make her feel like uppers again. The search for drugs is a hobby in Los Angeles. Everybody does it, day in, night out. Tash dragged me around to endless clubs with the same decibel-defying, seamless, acid rock music. She seemed to kiss and 'oh-dah-ling' everybody in the entire town, always concluding with 'and what's ya poison?'

'I need gluein' together,' she informed me at about midnight. We were sitting in the pimpmobile at the lights, surrounded by a maze of glass skyscrapers. 'What we need are some high class drugs.' Her black hat had slipped down over one eye. She looked like a pirate. 'Vertigo,' she said.

'What's that?'

'What's that?' she mimicked, 'Only THE hottest nightclub in town, that's what. Where do ya live — in a *box*?'

'You know, actually I've still got jet lag and . . .'

But Tash was already swerving out into the traffic and heading downtown. At the club car park, she strode around checking out numberplates. 'God! Spielberg's here.'

'Who?'

'Oh God! And so is Schwarzenegger's agent. Shit! And thuh heavies from Columbia. Oh Chrrrrist.' Her voice suddenly lowered. 'Check the line.'

Even though it was late, a queue of fashionably dressed hopefuls wound down the club steps and across the car park. The women wore Mao collars and flatties, topped with bleached crops of hair. The men all looked like paler versions of Pierce: regulation ponytailettes; loud, designeresque, baggy suits; topped off with studiously bored expressions. With any luck it would take about a fortnight to get inside, by which time 'Vertigo' would be out of fashion.

'Okay,' Tash grabbed my arm and took a deep breath. 'Think French.'

'What?'

Gesticulating and pointing, she ploughed to the front of the line with me in tow, and tried to push past the bouncer. His leg shot out across our path and a great hairy paw seized my upper arm. The bouncer's head looked too small for his enormous body. Pink rolls of neck fat bulged out of his suit: he was like a simmering sausage about to burst its skin. 'Whadd-thuh-fuck?' he inquired.

In fake, fractured French, Tash tried to persuade the Killer Sausage that we were in the Columbia party. It was about the dumbest thing I've ever seen anyone do. And I was no help. My French was limited to three words, 'lingerie', 'toupee', and 'secateurs'. Tash 'moiuserr-ed' and 'merci-ed' all over the place as the bouncer looked on – unmoved.

'S'pose your friend here, s'pose she's French too, huh?'

'Oui, oui.' Tash glared at me.

'Secateurs,' I said.

The bouncer folded his massive arms across his barrel chest.

Tash, defeated, lapsed back into her Chicago twang. 'Well, if I *were* French, honeybun, ya'd be right up my boulevard,' she told the bouncer and, leaning forward, playfully tweaked his penis.

'Yeah?' The fleshy portcullis of his leg lifted. 'Catch ya later, babe,' he winked as she sashayed through. This girl had more survival skills than a jungle commando, no kidding.

Tash pulled me in among the percussion of people on the dance floor. Everyone wore black and had perfect bone structure. They were like finely crafted shoes – sleek, soft, perfectly fitted. Next to them, I felt positively orthopaedic. The back of the head next to me looked a lot like Jack Nicholson. He turned around. The front of his head looked a lot like Jack Nicholson. He spoke. It was Jack Nicholson. I swirled around a lot, and stuck my leg out now and then so that he tripped over a bit and had to face me occasionally. Now I could write home and honestly say I'd danced with the most famous movie star in the Western world.

I was making a beeline for Warren Beatty, to try the same avant-garde dance technique, when Abe Epstein emerged from the dark groin of the disco. He was like a squat submarine surfacing. 'Vell, Good-day,' he boomed, his check-shirted belly bulging over straining denims. 'Hey babe. Don't I know ya from a past life?'

One of my major hates in life, is blokes who use 'pick-up' lines. They're always so stale. This one had definitely passed its amuse-by date.

'Yeah,' I screamed above the music, 'and you owe me a thousand dollars.'

As he threw his head back to guffaw, his huge hands grasped

a belt buckle the size of a satellite dish. I decided to get out of the range of his transmission. 'Veal do lunch,' I heard him call after me.

I found Tash in the toilets, hustling a miniskirted woman for drugs. I recognised her face from the covers of fashion magazines.

'Let's get out of here,' I bleated.

Tash maintained she was too 'out of it' to move an inch. It was impossible. A no-go idea . . . that is until I told her I'd seen her Arab bloke by the bar. Then she moved like a sprinter on steroids.

Things got blurry from then on, especially after ordering more and more drinks with bizarre names like 'Earth-Shattering Cosmic Orgasms on Ice' and 'Knee Trembler Screw Sideways with Milk'. I think it was me who wore Tash's black hat to stand on a table to sing the Talking Heads song, 'Stop Making Sense'. First in English. And then in Arabic.

At about dawn, Tash waved a triumphant fist in my face. 'Blow,' she announced.

We drove back to her place in Hollywood. The cool morning air must have sobered us up a bit 'cause we only hit the curb about ten times. Not that it made much difference when we did: the pimpmobile had no suspension. It was more like trampolining than driving.

'Shit, I'm burned out.' Tash threw her shoes through the door first, like a soldier checking for mines, before hurling herself after them. The weird thing was, her place was the opposite of what I'd expected it to be. Instead of an orgy of grot and grime she led me into a spotlessly clean room, done out in pastels and florals. As Tash made coffee, I examined the shelves of glass and ceramic knick-knacks. A United Nations of dolls dressed in national costumes jostled for space beside an entire zoo of miniature creatures, prancing across tiny, made-in-Korea, teak fields. Sprouting up from the corner of the room was a silver music stand supporting two slim volumes entitled *Vocal Exercises for Tone Placing and Enunciation* and *Twenty-four Italian Arias of the 17th and 18th Centuries*. The spice rack was arranged alphabetically, from Basil to Turmeric. As were the pills and vitamins in the bathroom cabinet. This girl even got healthy in alphabetical order.

'Do you live here alone?' I asked, retracing my steps to the kitchen.

I watched her inhale the cocaine she'd trowelled across a piece of silver foil on the table. She shook with pleasure as the raw voltage hit her blood stream. 'Ya wanna?'

I shook my head. 'Do you?'

'What?'

'Live here alone?'

'Sort of. Like I had this room mate, Karin Oppenheim. But the stoo-pid bitch has moved to New York.' Her exhaustion now evaporated, she moved at high speed towards the bedroom. 'She went an' like fell in yuppy-love with a tone-poemist-acupuncturist-crystal channeller.' I watched her strip off her cocktail dress. 'Another sucker for thuh romance shit.'

'Oh, come on. Haven't you ever been in love?'

'I'd rather be in a train smash,' she groaned, squirming into a pair of suspenders. 'I'd rather be in a supermarket line.' She threaded her pencil-thin legs into a pair of laddered black stockings. 'A high risk AIDS category. Mind you,' she paused to examine herself in the mirror, then slid me a sly slice of a grin, 'I'm probably already in that.' Her voice was momentarily muffled, as she tugged a school tunic over her head. 'Whyja wanna be "in love" for Chrissake?' she snapped, as her head emerged through the gingham neck hole.

I shrugged. 'There must be something in it. I mean, poets have been saying so for centuries. Don't you want to experience the whatsamacallit . . . intensity of passion. You know, the old emotional thrill.'

'I get more thrill changin' a tampon.'

As she finished getting dressed, I dozed in her double bed. After a few minutes I woke, panic-stricken. For a moment I thought I was at the bottom of Abe Epstein's Jacuzzi. Gasping for air, I struggled to the surface, the sheets entwined around me like seaweed. A sliver of sun streamed in under the pastel curtain. Through the gloom and the thumping beginnings of a hangover, I saw someone stir in the corner of the room. The figure turned to face the mirror. It was Tash, except she looked about thirteen. Her skin was extraordinarily pale, her face fragile. 'What time is it?'

'Time I got goin'.'

I watched her position a pigtailed wig on her head, snap a garter on to her thigh and hitch her school uniform up, until it puffed and pouted over her belt. She took another snort of her precious cocaine.

'I see this guy now and then, who likes schoolgirls,' she said in answer to my quizzical look. 'Chrrrist. A girl needs a lotta experience to fuck like a virgin, lemme tell ya.' She threw herself down on the edge of the bed. 'Hey listen. It just hit me. Now that Karin's like, become a walkin', talkin', two legged love-slave . . . why don'tcha move in? That is, as long as ya rinse ya plates before puttin' 'em in the dishwasher. I hate people who just like, put 'em in all gungy, don't you?' She paused to inhale the last blast of white powder. We'd spent the entire night scouring the city for what was gone in about two seconds. 'We ain't havin' ya goin' back down-under thinkin' we're all weirdos or somethin', right? I mean,' she sneezed, 'get real.'

I looked at her wig, sitting a little askew on her head, at her wild eyes, and at the strategic tears in her stockings. 'Hey thanks a lot Tash, but, you know, I'm sure the studio will keep putting me up at the hotel.'

She looked at me sceptically. 'Ah-huh.'

'See ya round,' she called, pulling the pimpmobile out of the Beverly Hills Hotel car park, hooting a percussion on the horn so loud that it drew both the doorman and the reception staff out under the entrance awning.

'And *who* are you?' interrogated the Doberman Pinscher behind the reception desk, before handing over my key.

I caught my reflection in the pink marbled walls of the foyer. A cockatoo-comb of hair framed a ruffled, red-eyed, drowned-corpse-countenance. Who was I? I thought. Kat Kennedy. A foreign object in a crazy American salad.

BONGA BONGA

There are only three things you need to know about Hollywood, I reckon. The first is that you have to learn a whole new language. No kidding. Like, if someone says to you, 'It's brilliant, I love it', what that really means is, 'It's kinda okay.' 'It's kinda okay' really means 'This is shit'. 'This is shit' means 'It's brilliant. I love it and want to buy the rights, *cheap*'.

Secondly, the writers and actors hate each others' guts. The only thing that draws them together is their hatred of the director's guts. The only thing that draws the actors, writers and directors together is their hatred of the audience's guts. The general public are referred to as 'knuckle-draggers', 'mouth-breathers' and 'tree dwellers'. And that's when they're being polite.

And the third thing you need to know is the 'Bonga Bonga' Joke. Everyone in Hollywood tells you this stupid joke about ten zillion times each day. The joke, in case you've been in a coma or living in Australia, is about these two blokes who are captured by cannibals. The chief tells them they have a choice: 'Death or Bonga Bonga'. The first bloke, not that keen on the old death option, opts for 'Bonga Bonga'. He is promptly sodomised by two hundred Watusi Indians. The second guy, seeing the bleeding, crumpled, whimpering wreck who opted for 'Bonga Bonga', chooses death. 'So be it,' the chieftain decrees , 'Death by Bonga Bonga.'

'That's it?' I asked Pierce, the morning he told me the joke. He was splitting his sides at its comic brilliance.

It was the first day of the readings and we were in the rehearsal room waiting for the other actors. The room was of ocean liner proportions, full of dust and dead ashtrays and dark corners. There was a kitchen at one end and a large oblong trestle table at the other, bathed in an egg-yolk yellow light. The exhausted writers, hunched over their coffees and Diet Cokes, looked like they'd rather be in Beirut. Like prisoners, they talked about their sixteen-hour days and 'life on the outside'.

As I tentatively nibbled at a bagel, Rondah, Ping and Phoebe Mercedez arrived together in a perfumed cluster and fell upon the food. Every day the production staff provided whole orchards of fruit, wheat-fields of buns and geysers of mineral water in every imaginable flavour. Now I knew why Americans had no wrinkles. Their food was so full of preservatives, they were positively *pickled*. And yet the weird thing was, their only topic of conversation was diets. Even though each woman had *the* perfect diet, they were all overweight and eating ravenously. Maybe they all had Bulimia Nervosa – but had just forgotten the purging part.

Well aware of the muffled stares and whispered asides of the other actors, I stayed sitting in my designated spot, pretending to flick through the script. Pierce was straddling the chair next to me, backwards. He looked tanned against his eucalypt-green shirt.

'Well?'

'It's a stupid joke,' I said dismissively. But it's kinda hard to dismiss a bloke whose presence is like an electric current running down through his chair, across the floor, into my big toe and up my jeans leg. It took Rondah to short-circuit it.

'Dah-ling.' Her big, wet, varnished mouth descended on my cheek. 'What a big day for such a little gal.' Her voice was as thick and moist as mayonnaise. 'Why, it's a downright testament to your talent, honey-child, your bein' here at all.' Pierce's left eyebrow pyramided up on to his forehead in amusement. 'I mean, alotta gals just get to Hollywood on the strength of their looks.' She flicked her hair off her face. I gawped at her, gob-smacked. Rondah Rivers was the Wimbledon Champion of the back-handed compliment. 'Why in no time at all, you're goin' to be *hot*, honey,' she said sweetly and sashayed away, her bottom cheeks jiggling through her stretch lycra.

Hot? Hot! I thought to myself. I would become inflammable. We were talking *thermo-nuclear*.

Pierce's mouth curled up into a cynical smile. 'Why not pay up now, kiddo?' he suggested magnanimously, patting me on the thigh.

'And why don't you just go find a cure for a major disease or something.' As my face reddened I buried myself in the script.

DINKS was the usual brain-bruising crap. Like every other situation comedy you've ever seen, there was a miraculously happy family, heaps of good-looking drongos called Brad, a lot of beautiful, wholesome women called Betty Jo, a lot of happy, puky, showy-off kids called Tiffany and Zachary, a lot of nosy neighbours who always dropped in without knocking, and a dog. Pierce played the de facto heart-throb. And Rondah played the bitchy career woman. She liked to remind you about 100 times a day how many Emmys she'd won for the role. Which wasn't surprising. When it came to being a first-class bitch, Rondah was pure pedigree.

Abe clapped his hands and called us to order. Ping, Phoebe, Rondah and the others, laden down with cakes and buns and hot coffees, dragged over to their seats. Abe had promised that the script introducing my character, Kylie, was 'some-sing new and original'. Remember what I told you about nobody speaking English? Well, 'new' and 'original' turned out to mean the kind of new and original stuff telly executives *always* fall back on at times like this.

Let me start by giving you a quick squizz at the old plot.
1) Rondah's character contracts deadly Southern Mongolian virus.
2) Needs blood transfusion.
3) Discovers she has rare blood type.
4) Only one other person in the whole world shares her rare blood type. It turns out to be a little Aussie, from the outback, called Kylie and, shock, horror (yes, the plot *sickens*);
5) Kylie turns out to be Rondah's long-lost little sister stolen by gypsies at birth.

Needless to say, when Abe explained this 'new' and 'original' idea to the cast, the prospect was greeted with funereal excitement. 'Zee premise,' Abe continued with the laboured ebullience of a Club Med Entertainments Officer, 'is that Kylie is flown back home to America from zee wilds of barbaric, outback Oz-strail-yar, vere ve vill civilise her.'

Civilise? Though dressed in denims and painted in lipsticks, the people surrounding me had suddenly taken on the murderous look of a tribe of Watusi Indians.

Blundering on into the stony silence (honestly, this guy could talk from under wet cement with a mouth full of marbles), Abe then lectured the surly assembly about the importance of cashing in on the 'Crocodile Dundee' phenomenon. 'Oz-strail-yars zoe popular now,' he continued with forced enthusiasm. 'And zoe vill be our own leetle Ozzie, yes?' Abe turned to look at me, as did all the others. I pleaded with myself not to blush. I made bargains. I promised to clean my teeth more regularly and not to squeeze blackheads. I promised to eat spinach and to do my pelvic floor muscle exercises. But my body betrayed me. Standing there feeling my face flush from rose to beetroot to acid-scarlet, I longed to be American like them. Why couldn't I have been born in California, where chutzpah and confidence are in the drinking water?

Abe finally put me out of my misery by starting the run-through. The script, though pretty contrived and all, was funny. But nobody laughed. Gags were greeted with a thrumming, numbing silence. Rondah, Ping and Phoebe read the lines flatly. They sabotaged punch lines by stopping mid-sentence to bite into cakes, munch loudly on apples, hitch clanking bracelets up tanned arms or dissolve into tubercular coughing attacks. Rondah had a rubber stamp in her hand. She slammed it down on every page. Craning across the trestle table, I saw that the stamp read 'NFF'. The writers winced each time she used it.

I leant over to Pierce. 'What does that stand for? NFF?'

Pierce's jeans rasped as he sprawled his long legs up across the desk top. He rocked back in his chair, pivoting dangerously: 'Not Fucking Funny.'

At the end of the script, when I was welcomed into the bosom of the American family and there were smiles all round, Rondah rose slowly to her feet. Every eye in the room was on her. Abe cracked his knuckles nervously, one by one. I nibbled a pattern around the rim of my styrofoam cup. The writers swapped weary glances, then squinted back up at Rondah. She flicked her hair from her face with conscious coquetry and smiled maliciously.

'Who wrote this she-eat?' she said, then frisbee-ed the script across the rehearsal room where it slapped up against the refrigerator.

Pierce lounged back in his chair and winked at me. 'Death,' he stage-whispered, 'by Bonga Bonga.'

So here, finally, was a punch line even I couldn't miss. In fact, if Rondah didn't pull her head in, 'punch line' was going to take on a more literal meaning.

As Pierce slouched from the room, Rondah and the other actors huddled around Abe, who was gesticulating wildly. 'Vell,' I heard him say in a clammy voice, 'maybe we haff overestimated zee popularity of Oz-trail-yar.'

Abe Epstein, I thought. Gerbil to the Stars. I wondered if the actors even bothered to get him drunk first.

Rondah turned to the writers and smiled condescendingly. 'Jest go back to your little booth and close your little eyes and switch on the little projectors in your hearts. I will pray for inspiration for y'all.'

When I closed my eyes and switched on my own personal projector all I saw was Rondah Rivers strung up by the nipples over a vat of sulphuric acid.

'We demand a rewrite,' she pronounced, then flounced from the room, the other actors hot on her haughty trail.

Abe lit a cigar and strode over to the weary writers. 'Ve need a new script,' he told them.

The writers all wore Identification badges complete with photos. The happy, healthy polaroid images – taken at the beginning of the season – bore no resemblance to their current wrinkled visages. You could trace, not just the day's, but the week's menu on their shirt fronts and they seemed to be growing plankton on their teeth. I kind of liked them, though.

'The script,' Max, the head 'hack', insisted furiously, 'is good as it is. It's a fucking embarrassment of riches!'

'Vell, you're half vight,' Abe snapped. 'Eats an embarrassment.'

'I thought you liked it? I thought you said it was original . . .'

'So? Jest change a verd or two. Eets not zee Rosetta Stone!'

The writers looked at Abe with undisguised disgust. As Amy crossed to the kitchen to console herself with a cake, I snagged hold of her sleeve. 'Why are the actors allowed to get away with that?'

She shrugged. 'Why do dogs lick their balls? 'Cause they can. Now you know why we call Abe "The Vet",' she added flatly. ''Cause he looks after the animals.'

'By tomorrow mornink.' Abe tugged on his cigar. 'Cancel all dinner dates,' he ordered, then disappeared, coughing in a cumulus formation.

The ten writers worked in a room called 'Das Booth' on the other side of the lot. They were locked in the 'gag gulag' all day, right through lunch, right through dinner, pitching jokes. They were like stand-up comedians, really – except sitting down. Even though 'Das Booth' was out of bounds to actors, I risked life and limb to cross the open battlefield of the car park. Jostling for space along the barbed wire fence surrounding the lot were the 'fans' armed with loaded, long-range cameras and the packs of young Hispanic men, bottle-swigging and chain-swinging. I didn't know which of the two was more lethal.

I came to a stunned halt at the door of 'Das Booth'. Max's head was sprouting a foam Statue of Liberty. Amy's cranium was crowned by a large tweed gumboot. A guy whose name tag read George was straining to keep aloft a pair of antlers. You see, to keep themselves sane, the writers adopted various themes for the week. One week, it was funny socks. The next, bizarre T-shirts. Silly underwear. Then silly underwear worn *over* your jeans. Then very silly underwear worn on your head. This week was silly hats.

Glancing around, I noticed that the room was windowless and the walls were padded.

'We've got no choice but to make the changes,' Max whined, his Statue of Liberty leaning backwards precariously.

There was a collective groan from the writers. Dave gagged, faking a vomit. Damien threw a jar of pencils at Max, who ducked. Lead shrapnel exploded as the jar hit the wall. As Max's hand appeared above the table, waving a Kleenex tissue in surrender, Amy noticed me standing in the doorway. 'Actor Alert,' she warned urgently, indicating my presence. The writers gawped at me in suspicious silence.

'Um, I just came to say . . .' God, what did you say to writers? Break a leg? Break an *arm*, more like it. I was beginning to wish I'd never come. 'Um . . . and I'm not brown-nosing or anything, but I thought your script, you know, the dialogue and stuff I mean, was tops.' They looked at me blankly. 'Ripper.' Still no reaction.

'Is that good or bad?' Max asked his incredulous companions.

'I think good,' Amy interpreted.

They thought *my* language was weird. These people spoke in tongues. All day I'd heard them yapping on about 'good buttons' and 'book-ending' scenes and 'chewing up scenery'. Things were 'on the nose' or needed 'handles' or 'headpieces' or 'lantern-hanging'. There were JLRs (Joke-Like Rhythms) and JTCs (Jokes-To-Come). There were 'two-fers' (a line with two jokes in it) and 'traffic jams' (too many actors on stage) and 'piping' (obvious exposition. *Our* scripts had enough steel pipe to bring oil out of Alaska). Not to mention 'refrigerator points'. This, it turned out, was a golden rule of sitcom writing. Never gloss over a point of logic 'cause it will invariably hit viewers at three a.m. when they're raiding the icebox.

Amy flung her scrawny arm around my neck. 'Listen babe, just keep thinking of the top left-hand corner of *Hollywood Squares*'.

Hollywood Squares, Pierce had already explained, was the place burnt-out actors went to die. To be placed in the centre row, or even mid-top or mid-bottom, indicated that you were still marketable, popular, 'hot', a 'go-project'. But to be seated in the top left-hand corner was the Hollywood equivalent of a death sentence.

The writers slumped around the table, like ten battered bean-bags. I contemplated the afternoon and night ahead of me. A cafeteria potato salad which was the equivalent of injecting cement straight into your veins, or watching *Hollywood Squares* in my hotel cell.

I decided to hang here for a while. I guess that's just the kind of girl I am – adventurous. I slunk into the booth and curled up in a corner of the couch. The room smelt hot and stuffy. It was a bit like climbing into a marathon runner's sock.

'A thousand stories in the naked city,' Max said finally, in a TV announcer's baritone, then lapsed back to his own Bronx whine, 'and we can't think of any of them.'

'Let's just kill all the characters in a car accident.' Amy's idea was taken up enthusiastically. For the next half hour, they discussed diabolical ways of disposing of all of the stars' bodies. A depressed hush fell over the room. Max took off his shoe and picked at his toes. Amy got the scissors and trimmed her split ends, collecting the hairy debris on her script.

They sat there in their silly hats for the next ten hours and came up with nothing. About midnight, Damien left the booth for a moment, returning with an armful of cookies, lollies, cake and chocolate. The writers unhinged their jaws like boa constrictors and devoured everything.

'Okay.' Max looked at his watch. 'Let's just give it a few minutes for the sugar to kick in.'

They all collapsed forward, heads resting on folded forearms, spotlit by the glare of the ceiling fluorescent.

'Quick!' Max ordered, seeing his comedy crew going down with the ship. 'Doesn't anyone know any *jokes*?'

Now, I'm not known for going straight for the jocular vein. But Garry, my ex-boyfriend, as well as lighting his farts and being able to sign his name in urine in the sand, was also a joke-teller. I cleared my throat.

'Where's the best place to have sex with a sheep?' It was out of my mouth before I realised how dumb it was. You know, I really should join Densa. 'On a cliff-top. They push back harder.'

The sound of my voice gave them whiplash. Rondah was right about my lack of personality. I was so charismatic that each and every one of them had completely forgotten I was there. They jolted back in their chairs and looked at me, goggle-eyed. There was a collective eruption into laughter.

Max came over and wrapped his arm around me. 'Hey kid, you're too intelligent to be an actor,' he said.

George announced that from now on, all sitcoms should be about sheep. 'My Three Sheep,' he said.

'Ewe and Me,' Amy added.

'Six Million Dollar Sheep.'

'We struck joke!' Max shrieked.

I guess the sugar had kicked in.

After a sleepless night, 100 cups of coffee and a vast mound of cakes and chocolate, we reconvened in the rehearsal room for another reading. The actors, fresh from their Malibu parties and prestigious film premieres, bantered and backslapped, then trashed the script once again. And back to Das Booth went the writers.

On Tuesday, Rondah, Ping and Phoebe scrapped the third draft because Rondah decided that my character's name, Kylie, was too ugly. The writers exchanged their silly jewellery for silly jockstraps and went back to Das Booth.

'Howzzit goin'?' Pierce asked me, fanning my face with the battered paperback he'd been reading.

'Fantastic! Excellent!'

He placed one foot on the rung of my chair, like a conquistador. 'That bad huh?'

On Wednesday, Rondah scrapped the script because there was a stage direction calling upon her to roll her eyes heavenward. 'It's blasphemous,' she said.

Pierce gave me a timetable of flights back to Sydney. I cut my fingernails on it, then shredded it over the bin.

On Thursday, the actors scrapped the script because the stage directions called upon Phoebe Mercedez to exit through the back door.

'That's racist,' Rondah announced mid-reading. 'Ain't that so Phoebe?'

Phoebe looked blankly back at Rondah. 'Is it?'

'Jest 'cause she's *black*, you have her exit out the *back door*.'

'Rondah,' Max explained in a snarl, 'she's exiting out the *back* door, because this scene is set in the *kitchen*.'

Pierce winked at me, then pulled his baseball cap down over his eyes. 'Television was so much goddamned easier when they just had horses that talked, doncha think?'

The writers retired to Das Booth wearing their underpants over their heads.

On Friday, the actors scrapped the script again. In the rewrite, Pierce's character had to enter wearing a chicken suit. Rondah stopped the reading. She refused to make jokes about a chicken while it was in the room. It was insulting to animals to play them as dumb.

Rondah was on her feet. 'Ping? Phoebe?' she called, and the two young women heeled, panting like trained pups, to follow their mistress out of the rehearsal room.

I spent most of the rest of the week in the toilets. Everyone must have thought I had Delhi-belly or something. But it was the only place where I could get any privacy. I was also fast becoming the world's cleanest human being. The shower was the only place where you could cry undetected. Well, nearly undetected. A golden head bobbed over the shower recess railing. 'Well, when do I collect?'

'Do you mind?' I struck a kind of fig-leaf pose. Who did this guy think he was? He was a total boof-head, a banana-bender. The guy was a regular ankle – three feet lower than an arsehole.

'Come on, kid. Pay up.'

'Rack off.'

'Well, stop blubberin' then. I'm sick of you hoggin' the goddamned shower.' He was a sympathetic bastard, he really was. Pierce opened the cubicle door and twisted the taps. The plumbing rasped with a bronchial shudder. 'There are no victims in this world.' He looked me up and down with a non-committal air. 'Only volunteers.'

I snatched my towel off the rack and cocooned myself in terry towelling. 'Yeah, spoken like a true oppressor. Why doncha give old Deng Xiaoping a call. You guys would really get on, you know that?'

'Hey, face facts kiddo. You're scum. Just like me. We sell lies for a living – a very competitive field in the good old US of A.'

I shoved past him. 'You're a real dickhead, do you know that?' My voice went thick as a milkshake, and I got that yucky wobbly feeling, when you're just on the brink of an ocean full of tears.

'Tell me,' he said witheringly, 'did these feelings of desperation and inadequacy appear suddenly, or did they just develop normally when you sold your soul to the Dream Machine?'

I bent my head and started vigorously drying between my toes. 'I don't know what it is exactly that I'm doing wrong. I mean, I'm trying to be an American. I've bought Raybans and Reeboks. I order "BLTs hold the mayo with legs" for lunch. I mean I'm practically a native for God's . . .'

'That's got fuck-all to do with it.'

'Well *what* then?'

Pierce looked me up and down. 'You're too goddamned thin,' he said. 'That's all.'

'What?'

'Haven't you noticed that there are never any food references in the scripts? Rondah has this thing about food. She's banned all fat, food, diet, stomach, mouth, meat, or kitchen jokes.'

'Can she do that? I mean, don't the writers . . .'

'Retaliate? Yeah. They give a weekly award to the person who comes up with the best Fat Joke in Das Booth. You know, she's so fat, people show movies on her. She's so fat, whales come to watch *her*. She's so fat that her butt has its own zip code.' He frowned in concentration for a moment. 'Oh yeah, she's so fat, Christo uses her raincoat to wrap islands in.'

'They can't hate me 'cause I'm thin. It's shapist.'

'Oh come on. Doncha get turned on by someone good-looking?' Pierce peeled off his T-shirt then bent to take off his shoes. His brown back was covered in soft down. His Nautilus muscles yawned into the stretch.

I looked away quickly, attacking my toes with the clippers. 'I used only to get the hots for blokes who attracted me physically, but that was when I was immature, before I *evolved*,' I said, my voice dripping with condescension. 'If I like someone, then they become sexy, that's all.'

'You're sexy,' he said suddenly. 'You've got a kind of Art Deco body, you know? Small breasts, strong legs, thin, muscly arms, tight tummy. You look like one of those Art Deco lamps, you know, where there's a chick in a real short skirt arching backwards, with a globe and everything, like this,' he demonstrated, 'topless.'

I became totally absorbed in a corn. Honestly, feet had never been so fascinating. 'So, what's *your* survival tip for LA?' I asked, changing subjects the way Tash changed lanes. 'Everybody seems to have one.'

'Don't stay.' He turned on the shower taps. 'Hollywood ain't the glamorous place it's cracked up to be. Basically, it's nothin' more than a hot and mangy town on the last S-bend in the plumbing of America.'

'Well, how come you stay then?'

He leaned close and blew in my ear. ''Cause I'm a shit, obviously.'

'At least, you pretend to be,' I said, flustered. 'I mean, I reckon you bung on the bad boy act a bit. You're the only one who's bothered to keep a hairy eyeball on me, for examp . . .'

'What?' Pierce turned away from me. 'Hey, don't flatter yourself. I didn't come in here to check up on *you*. I came into the john to *throw up*.'

I wanted to dissolve into the milky depths of the tiles. 'Why?' I said, instant sunburn suffusing my face.

Pierce shrugged. 'I'm an actor. Things are going too well. I get sick when I've got nothin' to get sick about. There's a guild guideline for actors. You have to be paranoid, neurotic, self-obsessed and drug-addicted. Doncha know that?' I heard the fly of his jeans descending and feigned fascination in the dead skin hanging off my big toenail. 'J'have to pick your goddamned toes all the time?' he said. 'It's disgusting.'

'Tell me, have you always been such a bullshit artist? Or do you take lessons?' I blurted, blushing some more.

To my surprise, Pierce's expression became hooded and dark. 'Listen, I used to be an okay kinda guy. No kidding. I believed in things. I had virtues.'

I almost believed him, I really did. Then I remembered the plucked nostrils. I looked at him, standing there, legs splayed, hands on slim hips, in his red Calvin Klein designer underpants. Did this guy go to Rent-a-Bulge or what?

'Oh, come off it. You wouldn't know virtue if it sat on your face,' I said. 'You're just scaring me off so you can get your hundred bucks.'

'Oh, save it for a rainy decade,' he yawned. 'You won't survive here.'

I wished he'd die and be reincarnated as a chair in Marlon Brando's house. 'Yer know what?' I raised my voice above the metallic throb of the water pipes. He was pukesville, he really was. 'You're the rudest sleaze-schmucko-ratbag I've ever met in my entire life!'

'Yeah, well, you have a nice day too,' Pierce said, slipped off his underpants and slammed the door of the shower cubicle. His buttocks, I noticed, were tanned.

Abe had suddenly cooled. Gone were the comments about 'High Concept Croc Dundettes' and lifetime contracts. Gone was the limo. With another empty arvo before me, I went back to the Beverly Hills Hotel. I lay by the pool and ordered a 'Jamaican Flirtation', then dived in and thrashed my way up and down. The other guests gawked at me as though I was a gatecrasher and should be thrown out of the hotel. When I gave the waiter my room number, I found out that I *was* a gatecrasher and *would* be thrown out of the hotel. My bill, he said, was no longer being paid by the studio. My bag had been packed and was waiting for me in the porter's room. As there weren't any cabs (LA, car-capital of the world only has *two* taxis and you have to wait a century to get either one of them), I walked all the way up Sunset, dragging my bag. It was one of those suitcases which is on a leash. I took to calling it Rover and stopped to let it lift its wheel on shrubs and bushes and stuff. It kind of took my mind off the fact that I was a homeless reject. A nobody . . . I mean, I used to pick my toes, but I didn't even do *that* anymore.

The Alice in Wonderland feelings came back. I had simply fallen down a hole in the world. A guy on rollerskates handed me a leaflet advertising a band called 'Sandy Duncan's Eyeball. Live'. Further along, a group of men were sitting on deckchairs on the footpath, having a picnic. A huge placard was propped up behind them. It read 'Gays Against Brunch'. I felt like the only normal person in the entire city – which was really saying something seeing as I'd just spent the whole afternoon talking to my suitcase.

When I tried to dash across the road on a red light, a hand pulled me back on to the curb. It was attached to an arm that belonged to a guy in floral boardshorts. As I waited for the lights to flicker to green, he informed me that he was a 'personal fulfilment manager'. 'Yeah, I was an airline steward, see, but I realised that I wasn't personally fulfilled. I left work and did a course on radical masturbation and a past life odyssey workshop, you know,' he yawned, 'the usual. And then I discovered that the thing that really fulfilled me personally, was fulfilling *other* people personally.' He flicked his card across to me. 'So now I consult, on a full-time basis. Well, what would make *you* personally fulfilled?'

I looked up at the flashing neon hotdog above the nearest café, and the camera shop shaped like an instamatic with the door in the lens, and the automated neon golf man who was putting a neon ball into a neon hole above the sports shop. Well, I wanted to 'assimilate' without turning into a dickhead. I wanted to become an American. I wanted to 'raise my tone'. (My dad's parole officer told me once that unless I raised my tone, I'd turn out just like my old man.) I wanted to meet a man who was romantic – you know, the type who talks to you after sex. I wanted to be famous enough to be able to tell Rondah Rivers to go suck a battered sav. I wanted to be rich enough to be able to hire someone to peel my pistachio nuts for me so that my thumb didn't get that little ridge in it. I wanted a cappuccino machine. To learn Russian. To take belly dancing lessons. But what would make me *personally fulfilled*? Standing there, waiting for the lights to change on the corner of Melrose and Fairfax, it hit me. The lights blinked to green. I looked him in the eye, appalled as the realisation reverberated through my body. 'Pierce Reece-Scanlan Jnr The Third,' I replied profoundly.

AUTO SUCK

Tash's place was dark when I got there, and the door was locked. She lived in a flimsy little bungalow just above Sunset Boulevard, on Dick Street. She chose it, she reckoned, so that she could tell people she 'lived on Dick.' I hoisted myself through the bathroom window, made a cuppa (the tea, of course, was filed under 'T' in the spice rack), then flicked through this book I'd bought on the way. Finding the section on Art Deco, I stripped off in front of Tash's bedroom mirror and compared my shape to a bronze and silver lady arching lithely backwards, one leg raised, holding aloft a golden globe. I couldn't see the resemblance myself. The only thing that made me look even vaguely like a lamp was the tampon string dangling down between my legs. I arched back a little further and tried a wry 1930s smile. This was how Tash found me.

'Lemme guess.' She slumped down on her bed behind me. 'Aliens have invaded ya body.'

'Oh, um . . . hi.' I scrambled for my clothes. 'I didn't hear you come . . . Hope you don't . . . The bathroom window was . . .'

'What a day.' She flicked off her high heels and massaged her toes. 'I'm like, ab-sol-utely zonked. First I go to do this recording thing, right, a jingle for a toilet tissue ad. I *know*, I *know*, but I'm broke. C. J. – that private D I told ya about, right? – is bleedin' me *dry*. The sonofabitch. Anyway, the sound recordist never shows up, asshole. So, not to feel I've wasted the *entire* morning, I like go to bed with the ad exec. I *know*, I *know*. Well, it turns out that, not only is this guy a lousy lay, but he's also this, like, total misogynist. First off, I only slept with this guy 'cause he told me he was single. So, what happens like, straight afterwards? I find a pacifier in his pocket. "Don't tell me," I go to him, "you're teething." Then he's, like, all shitty and he goes, "I only slept with ya 'cause ya needed it." He says that women get "in heat" which is why he reckons dogs are always followin' us down the goddamned street. I mean, can you believe this guy? And I'm, like, "hey, the only time dogs follow a woman down the street is when there's *sperm* dripping down her goddamned leg. 'Cause dogs, like men, are basically gay." How was your day?'

Even exhausted, this girl was manic. Tash was a walking, talking exclamation mark, with breasts. 'Have you . . .'

'What? Been followed by dogs when I've got sperm drippin' down me . . .'

'. . . rented out Karin's room yet?'

'Oh, nope. Let's eat.' Tash extracted a bottle from her bag, poured her evening meal of neat whiskey into a glass and then served me up my own liquid helping.

'Abe – the producer bloke I told you about – chucked me out of the hotel.'

'Oh well, surprise, surprise,' she said, a mocking twang in her voice. 'But hey, great. Move in. Look, I know I'm a bit kinda weird an' all, but hey, when ya need a shoulder-pad to cry on, I'll like, be there for ya, right? Have to charge ya rent though. *Banks*. I fuckin' hate banks. Banks only lend ya money if you can prove ya don't need any, have ya noticed that?' She frowned into her dressing-table mirror, fiercely intent on removing her make-up. Watching her daub her face, I began to feel calm for the first time since crash-landing in this crazy town. Tash *was* kind of weird an' all – the way she alphabeticised everything and the way she slept with dickheads and dyed her pubic hair different colours, but to me she was an oasis of warmth. '*Bon Appetit*,' she said, gulping at her glass. 'So, ya movin' in or what?'

I suddenly thought how good it would be to have my own fridge with my own jar of Vegemite in it. How good it would be to have someone to have secrets with and check that my undies elastic wasn't making a ridge in my jeans and to lend me emergency Modess and tell me I looked nice when I didn't. You know, the kind of things a good mate was for. '*Bon Appetit*.' The whiskey winced its way down my throat. 'Tash,' I hazarded, yanking my T-shirt up over my head, and arching back into lamp position. 'Do you think I've got an Art Deco body?'

She glanced at me in the mirror. 'Shit. I dunno. Wish I had ya tits though.'

'Rondah Rivers reckons they're too small.'

'Oh well, you can implant some of mine when I cut 'em off. So,' she added, with greedy curiosity, 'who said y'ave got a nice bod?'

'No one. Just this bloke.'

Tash gave me a knowing look and tore the current calendar page of August off the wall and turned it sunny side up on the dressing-table. 'Spell his name.'

'What for?' I watched her carefully letter the page in her own name, Natasha Marilyn Kerlowski. She bit her lip in concentration. Her little-girl look made a stark contrast to her punk paraphernalia of leather and lace.

'It's a game. We used to, like, play it as kids. It's called "Love, Marriage, Friendship, Hate".' She explained the rules. The idea was to write the name of a bloke over your own on a piece of paper, then cross out the letters common to both. Next, you count off the remaining ones, chanting, 'Love, Marriage, Friendship, Hate', to determine the 'attachment potential' of the relationship. Tash wrote down the name of her cocaine dealer. His name was Hank. It came out as "hate". I wrote down the name of Pierce Scanlen. It came out as 'love'.

Tash screwed up my romantic destiny and shot the paper ball into the waste paper basket. 'I s'pose y'are like, absolutely starvin'?'

'No, not real . . .'

'Come on.' She bounded off the bed. Before following her out of the room, I retrieved the paper from the bin. When I reached the kitchen, Tash was slicing of a piece of bright green dessert called Key Lime Pie, to go with my whiskey. She sent me a disapproving sidelong glance as I put the paper on the table and smoothed out the wrinkles with the palm of my hand. 'Oh shit. Y'are not, like, seriously still on this love kick, are ya? Kat, it was a joke.' She passed me a slice of pie. 'Kids' stuff.'

'Listen. The truth is, if dildos could kill spiders in the bathroom, we wouldn't need men at all. Got it?'

'Do you think I'm happy about it? This was not on the cards at all. Pierce Scanlen is the pits. He's vain, self-centred, up himself, arrogant, rude. And what's more, he makes me squirm with nausea every time I go anywhere near him – that's how I know it's the real thing.'

Tash reached across the table and used her orange, oval, glued-on nails to peel slabs of icing from my pie. They lay there in a pile, like gangrenous snow drifts. 'Forget it.' She nibbled at a piece of pie crust, *my* pie crust. 'Impossible.'

'What's impossible?'

'To fall in love with a man in California. Doncha know? Men in this town only fall in love with their cars. I mean they make television shows like – whatsamacallit – "My Mother The Car". A kinda womb on wheels. They call a one-night stand a "speed bump".' She now scooped up a wedge of pie filling, *my* pie filling, with her fingers and devoured it before flicking on the television. 'Look,' she instructed through a mouthful.

'Tash,' I said, exasperated, examining the few remaining crumbs on my plate, 'do you want me to cut you your own slice?'

The set flickered into life. Taking aim with the remote control, she machine-gunned around the channels. There were sports cars, cop cars, ads for cars, love scenes in cars, car chases, car smashes, plus a home-shoppers show that enabled to you buy your car without leaving your living-room, and buy your living-room without leaving your car. Not to mention the ads for 'automotive aftermarket car centres', complete with discos and sushi bars to keep customers happy while their cars were being serviced. There was even a news item on a hotel called 'Car Country International', a holiday resort entirely devoted to the pleasures of buying an automobile.

'Just as well I'm gonna be around to keep an eye on you, girl,' Tash concluded, silencing the television and spraying pie-crust crumbs. 'Ya wouldn't survive two seconds in this town without me. Still hungry?' she asked hopefully. 'I betcha are. I betcha ya'd like some chocolate cookies.'

We sat up all night, drinking whiskey and pretending that I was hungry so that Tash could eat, singing the theme songs to television shows we'd grown up with, making lists of all the rotten things in the world: the hole in the ozone layer (made entirely, we decided, by the hot air in Hollywood); the acid rain (according to Tash every cloud had a diochlorotetrafluoroethane lining); the methane emissions from farting animals; radioactive seas; the population explosion (mostly caused, Tash said, by people who used her brand of spermicide gel – she'd had two abortions this year already); the dolphins slashed into accidental sushi by Japanese fishing nets; the post-Chernobyl radioactive reindeers of Lapland; the fact that it takes fifty-five square feet of rainforest to raise enough beef to make one single American Hamburger, the threatened extinction of the elephant, the minke whale, the rhinoceros and of course, Tash added, the unmarried heterosexual male – until we were quite drunk on disaster. Then we both collapsed into laughter over the table-top, each wheeze sending us into another spasm. When our laughter finally subsided, I looked at Tash closely.

'But, at least,' I mumbled, 'there's still love.' I know it sounded kind of pukesville, but I believed it. I really did.

Tash shrugged and yawned mightily. 'I'd like wager ya some money on that, only I ain't got none. Speakin' of which, what's the time?' She retrieved my arm from the back of the chair where I'd flung it and peered at my wrist. 'Chrrrrist. Get your bikini.'

'What? Tash, it's seven in the bloody morning.'

'We're goin' swimmin'.'

Tash had five main expenses: hairspray, singing lessons, condoms, cocaine and C. J. The reason Tash had hired this private dick was to find her little brother. Her old lady had had more husbands than hot dinners and eventually all the kids were taken into state care. Some were adopted out. The youngest one, Elvis Raymond Kerlowski, had just got lost. 'Like a sock,' Tash said. That was eight years ago. Tash had been searching for him ever since. She'd told me how he looked just like her. For a second I thought she was going to cry, but then she'd steeled herself and grinned. 'Mom was, like, too crazy to go out an' get us a face each.'

C.J. had been on the case for two years now. His card read 'C.J. O'Connell. Private Detective. Leaves No Stone Unturned.' Judging by the size of his bills, he must have excavated a hole the size of the Grand Canyon by now. According to Tash, he'd seemed kinda reasonable in the beginning. There were to have been two payments: $500 to 'attempt to locate', and $1,000 for a 'successful location'. But C. J. had demanded more moolah every step of the way. Whenever he got a lead, some official had to be bribed to check a record or ring a contact. Tash's payments had escalated to $3,000 already. If you ask me, the only stone old

O'Connell had turned over went by the name of Blarney. So, it was mainly because of him that Tash was always trying to make money. Apart from her singing gigs, her advertising jingles and her 'presents' from the world's weirder male specimens, she regularly turned herself into a human guinea pig for the purposes of scientific research. For $100 bucks a shot, in the last month alone, she had drunk cough medicine for an entire day, smoked ten packets of cigarettes while standing on her head, and been wired up to track electric currents during orgasm. And now she was going to test whether or not you could survive swimming in the Santa Monica Bay.

'Whaddaya have to do exactly?' Yawning into a cup of coffee, I watched her hoik her breasts, one after the other, into her polka-dotted bikini top.

'Just take a quick dip, then report in later with side effects.'

I had started getting into my Speedos, but I now stopped, one leg lassooed in black lycra, and looked at her. 'Side effects? What sorta side – ?'

'Dunno yet, do I? The water's full of dioxin or somethin'. The fish they've been catchin' have like three heads, clubbed fins, little underwater wheelchairs. It's tragic.'

I shoved my cossie back in the drawer and trailed after her out to the car. A dip in dioxin or a day of dedicated naval-gazing. It was not as though I was exactly inundated with other offers. At that hour of the morning, the sky was awash with cool pastels, there was a warm aroma of jasmine, freshly bruised coffee beans and birds were singing. Even though we'd been up all night, I felt a surge of exhilaration.

'Whatcha grinnin' at?' Tash asked, as we clambered into the pimpmobile.

'I dunno, it's just that, well, the birds, and the flowers and all. It's kinda like that song. How does it go – "Love is in the air", ya know?'

Tash turned to me, screwing up her nose. 'Oh Chrrrist. It ain't love, you idiot,' she said, matter-of-factly, 'it's car exhaust.' Tash bent her head to fiddle with the loose wires beneath the dashboard.

'What *is* this dioxin stuff? You'd better not swallow.' I insisted, as the car hot-wired and fired into life.

'I never do, dah-ling.'

Tyres screeched and cars swerved as Tash caromed off the footpath a few times before launching her car out into the traffic on Sunset.

Tash often bragged that she had got her licence by bribing the supervisor. In exchange for a backseat blow-job, he'd agreed to overlook such trivial matters as two-wheeled lane-hopping, reversing into stationary vehicles and driving with one hand permanently pressed down on the horn. Gripping the dashboard in silent terror, I read the numberplates strobing past us. BIG BUKS, STAR LET, LUV CASH, MOGUL, BITCH 1 . . .

As we waited at the lights in Doheny Drive, six guys in the car next to us held up cardboard score-cards rating our sex appeal. Tash turned her face up to them and smiled broadly, before stabbing the air with a brutal finger. 'Sit on that and spin,' she advised them. The lights winked to green and Tash catapulted the pimpmobile forwards. As we raced, I risked another glance. Our rating had now dropped from an 8 to a 3. A sidelong peek at the next traffic lights revealed six pairs of pimpled buttocks plastered up against the windows. '*Now* ja believe me that guys here are only into *cars*?' Tash demanded as she ran another red light and rounded a corner into Wilshire on two wheels. 'And that ain't all. There are drive-in banks, churches . . . There's a twenty-four hour drive-in Taxidermist for God's sake . . .' She was positively exultant at proving her point. 'In fact, it's a wonder they don't have taxidermists for cars.'

'OK, I believe you that Californian men love their cars, but their cars can't love *them*, now can they?'

'Oh yeah?'

Tash hit the brakes. There was the usual swerving and screeching as the station wagon directly behind rammed into our bumper bar. (Tash didn't stop. She believed that's what bumper bars were for . . . bumping.) She hauled on the wheel, sending her pimpmobile into a full throttle spin that left us driving in the opposite direction. 'Fuck the beach, we're gonna go to the Pleasure Chest. If that don't cure ya, then nothin' will.'

The Pleasure Chest was a sex shop on Santa Monica Boulevard. Beside your usual range of pulsating, ribbed, rotating, or psychedelic dildos, leather whips and nipple clamps, this place had life-size, fully-warranted, electronic male dolls, called 'Dave' and 'Steve'. The salesman, a sleazebag in cowboy chaps, sidled up to me to explain 'Dave's' more alluring features. 'Meet Big Dave. The plastic, but totally realistic man of your dreams. Not only does Big Dave never say No, but, by pressing this lever, Dave can ejaculate with a liquid of your choice. He's macho, but a gentle lover,' the salesman assured me. 'He's insulated, for safety. And all for a mere $49.95. With tax.'

The Big Dave doll may have been shock-proof, but I was not. 'Ah, um, not today. I'm just here 'cause of my friend, and um . . . Tash?'

Beyond the plastic boys, was a row of gigantic, clenched fists, attached to plastic forearms. 'What do you s'pose people do with *those?*' I asked, incredulous, clinging to Tash's T-shirt sleeve.

Tash gave me a 'you've got to be kidding' kind of look. 'I suppose they use 'em for political rallies,' she said facetiously, clenching her fist and shooting her arm up into the air. 'Ya know, for when their arms get tired. Whaddaya you *think* they use 'em for! God, girl. It's time you had a little sex talk.'

'Oh come off it.' I lowered her arm and tried to look woman-of-the-worldly. 'Like what?'

'Oh, just your basics – like, who gets to hang upside down off the shower railings first – that kinda stuff.' Tash, exasperated, steered me by my elbow up to the back of the store. 'There,' she said, triumphantly pointing at what looked like a large single-teated udder tapering off into a rubber hose with a nozzle at one end.

I looked from it to her. 'Well?'

'*Auto suck,*' she gloated.

'So?'

'Guys plug it into their car cigarette-lighters and attach the nozzle bit to a, ya know, certain part of their *anatomy?*' she urged.

I shrugged.

'It performs fellatio,' she said impatiently. 'While they're *drivin'*.' She flicked the monster into action. It vibrated, making hideous slurping, sucking noises. The look she gave me was aloof, with a touch of the 'I-told-you-so's. '*Now* will ya believe me?'

I stood there, gawking at the serpent gyrating before me. All around me mysterious contraptions were whirling and gurgling. All the customers were speaking in the kind of hushed, reverential tones usually adopted by people queueing up for a Papal audience. I suddenly felt horribly oppressed. It was pukesville, it really was.

'Are ya okay?' Tash, balancing on one leg, was peeling a piece of gum from her other stiletto. With her dishevelled hair, smeared lipstick, nose-ring skewiff clothes, and one leg tucked up behind her, she looked like some exotic tribeswoman in a *National Geographic* magazine. She smiled wryly. 'A bit of *car sickness*, eh? Just out of interest, what size car does old Pierce baby drive?'

'What? I dunno. Big, I guess.'

'Oh well, he wasn't worth worryin' about anyway. That's one of the first things you learn about American men. *Big* car' – she wriggled her little finger in my face – '*small* cock.'

As if driving in LA wasn't complicated enough. The next morning in the taxi on my way to the studio I got whiplash from swivelling my head to see which men were driving *too happily*.

Once on the lot, I positioned myself on the silver fender of a red sports car across from Pierce's car space and studied my road rules. One thing I'd learnt about LA is that while you can drink blood, marry dogs and hold excretion parties – 'pedestrianism' is sacrilegious. As I was memorising how many feet you should park from a curb, Pierce roared up in his Ferrari Testarossa, got out, or 'de-carred', as the Californians say, and propped the bonnet up. Like a dentist, Pierce stuck his head into the motorised cavern. He didn't even notice me.

'That car's too big for you,' I called out to him crossly.

Pierce seemed preoccupied. 'Huh?'

'*Small* men always drive *big* cars,' I elaborated about ten decibels louder. 'It's one of the first things you learn about men – big car, small cock.'

Pierce extracted his head and shot a cursory glance in my direction, then strolled towards me. He snatched the pamphlet from my hands. An amused brow shot up across his flawless forehead.

'Road rules, huh.' As he flicked the pages, I drank in his presence. He was wearing his hair slicked back like a gangster. 'Okay, whaddaya do at a "Stop" sign?'

'According to Californian custom,' I replied defiantly, 'pull out my gun, and aim it at the person in the car next to me.'

Pierce's eyes glinted. 'Correct. Now, what is a Pedestrian Crossing?'

'Um, a trick to get pedestrians halfway across the road?' I suggested.

Pierce kissed his forefinger then pressed it up against my lips. I felt a tingling in the back of my knees. 'Very good. Go to the top of the class. Just remember to slow down for dogs and joggers and speed up for pedestrians. And try to avoid traffic jams. If you're stationary for too long in this city, someone will try to sign you up for a goddamned EST course.' I laughed. 'Now,' Pierce continued, peering over his Raybans, 'what gun is more effective on a freeway? A .38 Smith and Wesson, a sawn-off shotgun, or an automatic weapon?'

Before I could answer, Abe's sleek black limo oozed up next to us. An electronic, smoked-glass window lowered with a soft 'whoosh'. 'Vondah's looking for you,' Abe informed Pierce. The window re-sealed and the car crept away towards the security gates.

Pierce slammed his Raybans back up the bridge of his nose. His good humour evaporated. 'Shit.' He buried his head back under the bonnet and continued tuning.

To tell you the truth, we'd never been that big on ethics in my house. Dad said, basically, we couldn't afford them. But there were two things I lived by. One, never fake an orgasm, and two, never steal a bloke from another woman. Even though I thought Rondah was what we called back home, a total suck-back (her mother should have sucked her back at birth) it was against the Aussie Female Code to move in on her. 'How long have you and Rondah been on together?'

Pierce's head jerked up, cracking against the bonnet. 'What? Get real. That woman could make a vibrator go limp.'

'Well, I just thought. You were crying in her arms the first day I met –'

'That woman's vibrator has Harley Davidson written down the side of it.' Pierce circumnavigated his car, kicking each tyre in turn, the way men do. 'That woman has every marital-aid known to humankind.' Kick. 'She needs jump leads to start the things.' Kick. 'When *she* starts up, *LA* dims.' Kick.

'Then why do you suck up to her?'

He calmed down, leant back against the car and shrugged. 'I'm gutless. I told you. It's a helluva lot easier to string her along than to get on her bad side. Look what she's doing to you.'

Relief surged through my body. But, just because Pierce wasn't playing tonsil-hockey with Rondah didn't mean that there wasn't somebody else. How to extract the info without hinting at my own feelings for him? I would have to be suave, subtle, inventive. '*Are* you in love then,' I blurted, 'or what?'

Pierce suddenly slipped back into his cool self. 'It's the goddamned fanbelt.' He bent over the engine with the worried look of a parent bending over a cot, a mirror held up to the baby's nose to check that it was still breathing. 'Get in behind the wheel,' he ordered. I obeyed. 'Turn her over.' Inserting the key into the ignition, I felt a tinge of anxiety in the pit of my stomach. He called the car *her*. 'Now, hit the brakes. Accelerator. Brakes. Accelerator.'

'Well, are you?' I called out the window, pumping away at the pedals.

He stood back and laced his hands across his stomach. 'Shit.' His thumbs rotated around and around each other, like little fleshy turbines in an engine. 'I'm gonna have to take her into the shop. And I was gonna drive straight out to Malibu tonight.'

'Pantyhose.'

'What?'

'Well, see, when a fanbelt breaks, what happens is that the water pump stops pumping hot water into the radiator where it can be, you know, cooled. But you can make a kinda temporary fanbelt from a nylon stocking. You whack it round the pulley wheels, yank it tight, then tie a knot.'

Pierce switched off his thumbs and looked at me intently. 'You really know about all this car-fixing shit?'

I nodded. I know it must have seemed weird, seeing as I couldn't drive and all. But there was a reason I knew all about cars. My father hated them. He's the only gangster in the world to have a get-away pushbike. With Dad in the slammer so much I'd done all the repairs around mum's house, from lightbulb changing to lube checks, and all on the cheap. I may not know how to reverse park, but I do know how to seal cracked ignition coils in a car engine by using nail polish, fix a split heater hose with correction fluid and block up the cracks in a radiator by using egg whites.

Pierce looked at me dubiously for a moment, then tossed over the keys. 'Okay,' he said, and glided sinuously across the car park. 'She's all yours.'

The engine lay exposed before me. I peered down its gaping red throat, right into its shiny metal intestines. And then I did a really dickheaded thing. Pretending to myself that I wanted to play a tape, I slid back into the driver's seat. I glanced up and down the row of cars. The place was deserted. My legs sweated on the hot leather. I groped beneath the chair. Nothing. Hands clammy, I searched the back seat. Nothing. I rummaged through the glove box. And there it was – beneath the parking tickets, condom packets, swimming goggles, sweat-bands, lozenges covered in fluff, furry bits of hamburger, spray cans of hair-gel and mouldy jockstraps. An auto suck. I felt my heart contract. I was in love with a guy who was in love with his car. Great. I found it hard enough to compete with another female, let alone a sleek, red, mean machine which could go 0–60 in 2.9 seconds. I peeled off my pantyhose and entwined them tightly around the pulleys. I slammed the bonnet, sat on it beneath the searing sun, and sulked.

Well, I thought, it gave a whole new meaning to the term 'sex drive'.

THE COMEDY ASSASSIN

'Dunno why they call it a *live* audience,' Pierce scoffed, stealing up behind me and peering over my shoulder at the ten or twelve tiers of people in the studio. I examined the rows of impassive faces. The audience for *DINKS* seemed entirely made up of pensioners bussed in from sheltered workshops for the Terminally Boring, or teenyboppers who squealed at the mere glimpse of Pierce Scanlen.

When Pierce appeared in public, females fainted at a rate of one every twelve seconds. His autograph was currently selling for twenty bucks in school playgrounds and his fan club had recently run a competition for members to win a jar of his *breath*. Knowing Pierce, he wouldn't even have cleaned his teeth first.

Rondah had managed to stall my debut until just before Thanksgiving, when room was finally made in the taping schedule. The first and second scenes went as smoothly as thickshakes. It wasn't until my entrance that things started to curdle. No sooner did I get a laugh, than Rondah fluffed her next cue, waved away the cameras and clapped her hands.

'Sterling,' she commanded with casual arrogance, 'a toothpick.' Sterling was Rondah's full-time slave. He chauffeured her to and from the studio, fought off her fans and was made to grovel and brown-nose publicly. 'I simply *must* have a toothpick.' As he sprinted off the set, I wondered what he wrote under the 'Profession' entry on his tax return. Most probably 'Full-Time Toothpick Fetcher and Resident Bum-Wiper'.

I sat down on the edge of the couch in fidgety silence, surrounded by the monstrous cameras. They were like pterodactyls eyeing their prey. The other actors sprawled nonchalantly across the set gazing with open loathing at the gob-smacked audience.

Rondah beamed at her fans and wished them all a happy Thanksgiving; then, turning her back, she did an ape impression for the benefit of the other actors. 'Knuckle-draggers,' she hissed.

The cameramen idly jingled loose coins in their pockets. The writers frowned into space. Ping and Phoebe lazily grazed on leftover food on the set. Mimi selected an orange from the prop bowl, peeled it dexterously, discarded the flesh and nibbled keenly on the rind. 'That's where the vitamins are,' she urged, offering me a piece of pith. 'In the peel.' Yes, I thought, shaking my head in refusal, and that's exactly where they're going to stay.

Pierce positioned himself on the side of my armchair and unpocketed a fluorescent yo-yo which he cast off and reeled in expertly. 'J'know what I worked out?' he said to me. 'Just say you live till eighty – j'know how many years of your life you'll spend mating? Six. Plus, five years doing housework. Which is why I don't do any. Two years trying to ring people up, six years jerking off, and one year looking for junk you've lost. Have you ever thought about that?'

I looked at him blankly. All I could think about was how boring television really is. The poor audience would have more fun watching a spin-drier go round.

Pierce had executed ten 'walk-the-dogs' and twenty 'around-the-worlds' before Sterling reappeared, panting, and handed Rondah the toothpick.

She snapped the tailored twig in two and flicked it to the floor: 'Too late,' she announced. 'The moment has passed.'

Sterling's middle-aged face flushed. He nodded and walked rigidly back to his seat at the side of the stage. The cameras blinked into life again. The neon 'laugh' sign flashed and the rest of the scene rolled on.

But five minutes into scene four, Rondah derailed the comedy again. 'Whoa. Whoa!' She put her hand up, palm outwards, as though drawing a huge country and western wagon train to a halt at the sight of Injuns. 'Mental midgets?' she exclaimed about a line of my dialogue. 'You know, gosh, I jest feel that comment is totally offensive to persons of miniature stature,' she said, manoeuvering herself between me and the camera.

A notch of anger tightened in my stomach. 'Um,' I heard myself say, 'I can't see what all the kerfuffle's about.' A room full of eyes turned on me. 'I mean,' I faltered, 'if anyone mentally handicapped is watching, well, they won't understand the reference, right? And if they're midgets, they'll be too short to reach up to the phone to call in a complaint.' Rondah tapped her foot in irritation. This woman couldn't crack a smile at a joke-festival, no kidding. 'I think that . . .'

She whirled around to face me. '*I'm* the star of the show,' she hissed. 'When *you're* the star of the show, then you can think.'

Silence descended on the hall. Rondah signalled Ping and Phoebe to join her in a huddle over by the 'laugh' sign. Abe appeared on the set, his brow furrowed. Max slouched in after him with slow, heavy steps.

'I'm jest so sorry,' Rondah announced sweetly, 'but I just don't think we can go on with the tapin' until that line is removed from the script. Can we, gals?' Phoebe and Ping nodded, like the toy dogs with sprung heads you see in the back windows of cars. 'Sweet Lord, I just don't know how I let it slip past in rehearsals, I trooly don't.' She smiled so broadly and for so long that if she'd turned up in the city morgue, murdered, (now, *there* was wishful thinking) I could have identified her by her dentistry.

Abe turned to me, curling his lips. 'Don't take eat too zeriously. Eats not brain zurgery, cupcake. Veal get you a good line next week.'

Pierce peered up over his dog-eared book. Catching my eye he craned his neck and drew his forefinger across his pale throat as though it were being slashed. But he didn't have to tell me. I already knew that if I didn't crack it now, there would be no next week. There would only be the top left-hand corner of *Hollywood Squares*.

As Max and Abe withdrew into a conference of whispers, Rondah lowered herself on to the couch and patted me consolingly. Her fingers on my forearm were like padded claws. 'Don't take it personally, sweetiepie. It ain't your fault. No sirree. It's those damn writers. But at least it gives us time for a little chat, doesn't it, hmmm?' She twined a lock of her long hair around one painted finger. 'My spies tell me you've been seen hangin' round with Pierce. Don't waste your time, hon.' Although she smiled at me, her eyes had a diabolical glint. 'I know it's hard in a new town to get the hang of thangs. But, see, to be frank, honey-child, you're just not his type. Pierce goes for the more *sophisticated* woman. A class-act, y'all know what I mean? Someone with taste, elegance, breedin'. The sort of woman who can get into the best restaurants in town, with five minutes notice. No offence,' she let her hair untwirl, 'but you'd have trouble getting into McDonald's.' There was a rasp of pantyhosed thighs as she uncrossed her legs and stood up. 'I'm tellin' you this as a friend.' Turning on a spiked heel, she flicked a 'friendly' wad of hair over her shoulder and into my face, before crossing the stage to perch on the edge of Pierce's chair and brush proprietorially at non-existent dandruff on his shoulder.

I wished something really nice on her – you know, that she got abducted by a mad sex killer with halitosis.

Max shrugged a sign of defeat in my general direction and loped back to break the news to the writers. The taping staggered on, with yet more and more of my lines cut. Rondah succeeded in having all the humour removed from my part. At the end of the show, just when I was contemplating a date with a bottle of Seconal, Pierce sidled over.

'Hey kid, I forgot to teach you the fourth rule of Hollywood. Learn to bend over, stick yer ass in the air and grab yer ankles.'

'What?'

He hoiked up his jeans revealing a tanned and muscled calf. 'See? Permanent grip marks.'

'She just gave my part a total joke-ectomy.'

'Rondah Rivers,' he said, 'Comedy Assassin. Oh well, at least when you get fired, you've got a career to go to. You're a helluva mechanic, you know that?' He inserted his forefinger into the gap between his two front teeth and retrieved a flake of tobacco. 'The ol' Ferrari's still truckin'. Hey, I owe you one.'

I looked over at Rondah, wreathed in lipsticky smiles, signing autographs for the 'tree dwellers' she'd satirised earlier. 'Dinner.'

'What?'

'That's what you owe me.'

'Huh?'

'Out. Somewhere posh. I'll book.'

A CLASS ACT

Tash lay two pieces of cucumber across my eyes. 'What am I? A salad? I feel rid*icu*lous.'

'Sshhh.'

'It's going to be a disaster, I just know it. He's used to glamorous women. You know, who wear sequins and have tailored teeth.'

'Wouldja quit squirmin'.' Tash, open-mouthed with concentration, was smearing my face in an egg and mud pack. My hands were soaking in some napalm liquid and my hair, coated in henna, was sealed in a turban of Gladwrap. 'Yeah, well, you'll look just as fuckin' sophisticated as those chicks, once I've finished with ya.'

I removed one vegetable eyepatch and proceeded to eat it while staring at Tash like the Cyclops. 'Why are you so keen for me to go out with him all of a sudden?'

'Because once ya've been out with the guy you'll realise what a jerk he is and get over all this love bullshit.' She dried my hand and began sculpting acrylic tips on top of my own trimmed nails. 'An' then we can go down thuh Pleasure Chest an' buy ya yer first marital aid.'

'God,' I groaned wistfully, nibbling at my other eye-patch, 'I wish I was like you. You Americans . . . You're all so strong. So . . . I dunno . . . optimistic.'

'Of course we're optimistic.' Tash requisitioned the cucumber slice from between my fingers and repositioned it over my eye. 'This is a country where anything is possible. I mean, Chrrrist, Sylvester Stallone is like a *major star*!'

We'd gelled and sculpted and baked my left hand only, when one of Tash's human marital aids knocked on the bedroom door.

'Yo! Whadda youse chicks doin' in there? Lickin' each others *erroneous* zones?'

If Tash's boyfriends were any more moronic you'd have to water them once a week.

'Comin',' Tash called back. She cocked her head, timing his plodding retreat back to her bedroom, before whispering conspiratorially. 'Underpants-sniffer. Truly. He's got a whole collection, from old girlfriends and stuff.'

'Bull.'

'No kiddin'. It began when he was at college and got this job workin' part-time for a removalist company.' Tash picked up my hand by the wrist and proceeded to wave the wet nails back and forth through the air. 'He was always findin' ladies' panties under beds and stuff. He like, freshens 'em up by hangin' the crutch over a light bulb. Ya know, to – to – revive the smell. And then he just sniffs away. So watch it!'

'Ergh. Yuk. What a drongo. Why the hell are you going out with such a . . .'

'Drongo?'

'It means ratbag, weirdo. You know, total dickhead.'

She shrugged, 'I need a loan. He may be a deviant by night,' she said, turning the doorhandle, 'but he's a banker by day. Now,' she checked her Mickey Mouse Swatch, 'haul *ass*, girl.'

By the time she returned I'd tried on and rejected my entire wardrobe. A cascade of fabric spilt across the bed and on to the floor. Tash regarded my naked body slumped up against the mirror.

'Ya wanna borrow somethin' of mine?'

'Yes,' I addressed my puny reflection. 'Your head, legs and cleavage.'

'Look, it's not important what ya wear, okay, but how ya wear it. Just don't lose ya cool. Act kinda blasé.'

'*Blasé*? How can I act *blasé*? I'm having dinner with the sexiest man in the Western World and you want me to act *blasé*?'

'Look, if ya think you're gonna lose it and say somethin' totally stoo-pid well, I dunno. Just think of somethin' real borin'. That's the best way to look blasé.'

'Like what?'

'I dunno, do I? Recite the American Presidents in order. Count to ten in goddamned German. And order suave kinda food. That impresses the pants off a guy. Like, I dunno. Pâté.'

Tash unwrapped my hair, rinsed and dried it, cement-rendered my facial features in foundation, smeared on the lipstick, then levered me into one of her sequined dresses. It had the most ginormous shoulder-pads. I looked like an armadillo that had been taking steroids. The restaurant Tash booked for me was called 'Spago's'. This was the sort of place where you practically had to put your name down at birth to get a reservation. Tash had to pretend that it was my twenty-first birthday and say I was related to Paul Hogan and Princess Di and promise the *maitre d'* a fantasy phone-call before he'd even consider giving me a booking.

As I sat at my table waiting for Pierce, I finally realised why LA ladies favour sequins. Peering into the myriad of minuscule mirrors, you can pluck stray eyebrow hairs, squeeze the odd zit and check lippy leakage. I was busy doing all this, when Pierce made his late, head-turning entrance. He tacked across the room, berthing briefly at various tables to adlib rehearsed quips and kiss the cheeks of the BBBs (the Blond, the Bronzed and the Beautiful. Of both sexes. Believe me, living in LA you come to realise that the word 'bimbo' is not gender-specific). As he drew closer, I saw with horror that he was still in his sweat-stained training gear, gym bag casually tossed over one body-built shoulder. I sank down into my seat and longed for a dimmer switch on my sequins. Pierce slid into the chair opposite me. He reeked of hair gel and sweat. A pungent, intoxicating smell. Looking me up and down with mild amusement, he suddenly gagged and held his nose.

'What?'

'Your perfume.'

'Too strong?'

'Strong?! God, next time I'll bring a canary in a cage.'

I took a swig of my mineral water. It wasn't easy. For starters, Tash had only had time to sculpt those acrylic nails on to my left hand. I'm right-handed. Having to use my left hand was difficult enough but then there were the stiletto nails. No wonder glamorous women just sit around smiling lots. They can't *do* anything else. Frowning with concentration, I manoeuvered the glass back on to the table. 'I ordered us some pâté,' I said suavely, nudging the plate towards him with my elbow.

Pierce recoiled. 'I'm um, vegetarian.'

'Really?'

'Yeah. I can't eat anything that ever had a face.'

'Oh.' I edged the plate back out of view behind the menu. Tash's dress was so tight that at every movement I moulted about a thousand sequins. One fell into the centre of the pâté, and sat there, winking obscenely. 'It's ideologically unsound to eat French food anyway. I'm boycotting them. Well, *girl*-cotting them. I mean,' I rushed on, 'they're destroying the Pacific with all their nuclear testing and – '

'Yeah! I'm a Francophile. Total.' Pierce glanced idly around the room. 'Love everything French. Flaubert, Molière, Camembert.'

'Yeah, yeah,' I agreed suavely, not having a clue who or what he was talking about. 'Me too. All the bears.' I suddenly became aware that my left shoulder-pad was succumbing to the law of gravity. It had slipped slightly, descending in the direction of my shoulder-blade. It gave me a lopsided sensation. To compensate, I started to lean in the other direction.

Pierce ordered salads and two margheritas.

'What's that?'

He looked at me as though I'd just described my ovarian cyst operation plus post-operative infection. 'You're yankin' my chain. It's what *God* drinks in *Heaven*, is what,' he said. 'Jesus Christ, I'm on a date with a barbarian!'

Fishing into the pocket of his leather jacket, Pierce explained how after gym he'd 'swung by' the studio to pick up this week's script and been landed with a whole load of fan mail. Retrieving the perfumed wad, he peeled off the first few envelopes. 'Listen to this,' he chortled and proceeded to deliver a dossier of names and numbers. One fan confessed undying love and lust. Others promised fellatio and home-baked dinners. There was a declaration from a mystic that she and Pierce had been lovers in a past life. Included in one letter was a detailed sketch of a fan's labia majora. Another envelope contained a small lock of pubic hair tied in a pink bow.

I skulled my margherita.

The next fan letter revealed that during deep Freudian analysis, the author's psychiatrist had determined that only Pierce could satiate her physically, emotionally and mentally and that if she didn't meet him, their yin and yang balance would be diffused by the organic counter rhythm. 'Pretty horny stuff, huh?'

I shrugged coolly, tracing the rim of my glass with my tongue.

'Pathetic. How could anyone go to a psychiatrist.' Pierce eyed me from under half-closed lids. I rushed on nervously. 'I mean, talking about yourself day in, day out. It's so self-indulgent. It's just a hobby, you know. Like golf. That's it!' I asserted eagerly, my lips encrusted with salt. 'Analysis is just the American version of golf!'

Pierce folded the letters and dumped them in the ashtray. 'I go to a psychiatrist,' he said. 'Every week.'

I semaphored to the waiter for another margherita. 'Really? My hobby is whacking my foot in my mouth, just in case you hadn't noticed. I always do it. It's a feet accompli.' He continued to study me. I squirmed beneath his gaze. 'Get it? A feet ... oh well. At least tonight they're well shod. Look.' I levered my leg up on to the edge of the table. 'Tash, she's my friend, calls these her "follow-me-home-and-fuck-me" high heels.' Pierce, lazily scratching his ribcage, blinked with mild curiosity. 'I mean, not that I want you to ... I didn't mean that I ...' Thank God Los Angeles was in an earthquake zone. With any luck, one would come right now and get me out of this.

'Ya know what? Anyone living in LA who says they don't need a psychiatrist, needs a psychiatrist. Especially you.' Pierce leant back in his chair and crossed a sockless ankle over a tracksuited knee. I glanced at his tight pants and wondered whether or not he was wearing any underchunders. 'The trouble is, what with all our supersonic satellite dishes and tele-goddamned-communications systems and all, we suffer from a helluva shortage of *listeners*.' He lowered his leg on to the chair rung and rocked back dangerously. 'I mean, whadda you do? Who listens to you?'

No. Definitely no underchunders. 'Pardon?' I realised that Pierce had asked me a question. 'Sorry?'

He threw his hands up in the air. 'See what I mean? What-do-you-do-back-home-an'-all,' he boomed, 'when you're having a goddamned PLT.'

'—?'

'Personal Life Trauma,' he decoded.

'Oh well, we go fishing. Or dancing. Or down the pub with our mates and whinge for hours. That's what mates are for. I reckon you Californians go to psychiatrists instead of having good mates. You know. Someone you can have secrets with and stuff.'

'I have goddamned secrets with people.'

'Like what?'

'Like, well, didja know that I have a gym shoe collection? 147 different pairs.'

'No, I mean *real* secrets.'

'Before jerking off, I sit on my hand till it falls asleep – so that it feels like someone else's . . . What? I dunno. Ask me something. Go ahead. Ask me.'

I counted to ten in German, I recited the names of the American Presidents in order and then, blasé as buggery, I said 'Do you think believing in love is like believing in UFOs?'

I downed my margherita and signalled to the waiter for another. I could feel my shoulder-pad still slipping. It was moving glacially down my back and this wasn't the moment to retrieve it.

Pierce ran his hand through his gelled mane. It sprang back up off his face like a hairy halo. 'Love is bullshit. It's right up there on my Bullshit List, along with TV producers, politicians, parents and environmentalists.'

He reminded me, for one nauseating moment, of my old man. My father once painted a sign and hung it up outside the house, listing the people he hated. Besides cataloguing all of the neighbours, the list named politicians, car salesmen, screws, capitalist pigs, communist bastards, bullshit artists, blow-waved anchormen from breakfast television and, of course, Americans. *All* Americans. 'Environmentalists?' I quizzed him, snapping back to the present. 'Don't you worry about the state of the world and all?'

Pierce Scanlen pushed away his salad and shrugged. 'There's always the moon. Look, kid, this is the 1990s. We have to steel ourselves for all the shit and hard times ahead. Nuclear holocausts. Hispanic uprisings. America is going down the goddamned toilet. The eighteenth century was for the French. The nineteenth was the English century. The twentieth American. And the twenty-first is going to be the Sushi Century. Chrrrist. Pretty soon everything will be microchips and sashimi.' By now the shoulder-pad had descended below my bra strap. I felt like a hunchback. 'This is America. Consumer Capital of the World.' I could feel the eyes of nearby diners zeroing in on me. 'We get emotional about *things*, not people. We love our houses and I dunno, Jacuzzis and gym shoe collections and – '

'– and cars?' I asked quietly.

'Yeah and our *cars*. Not other humans for Chrissake.'

Anxiety began to spread through my body. *Eins, zwei, drei, vier, fünf, sechs, sieben, acht, neun, zehn.*

'So, how *is* the Ferrari?'

His face lit up like a traffic light. 'What can I tell you? Got her out of the shop today. She's bewdiful.'

She? She?

'Handles like a dream. Low revs, good mileage.'

'How interesting.' By now, my words were starting to slurr. My whirrdz were starting to slurrrrr.

He cocked one eyebrow cheekily. 'Hey, you're gettin' pretty tanked up, aren't cha?'

My margherita-ed mouth went dry. *Tanked*, he said *tanked*. I shivered, shedding another shroud of sequins. Kennedy, Johnson, who came after Johnson? 'Pierce. There's something I need to know about you?'

Just then my birthday cake arrived with twenty-one candles on it. The whole restaurant turned to applaud. I fished up my skirt and retrieved the renegade shoulder-pad and tried to hide it under my napkin. It looked a lot like a large white sanitary-pad. The other diners were now no doubt convinced that I was not just hunchbacked, but retarded. It seemed to me that they looked at Pierce with sympathetic eyes, the cockles of their hearts warmed to see a famous actor extending charity to a crippled moron.

'I didn't know it was your birthday,' Pierce said, scraping his index finger through a thick wedge of icing and licking it clean.

I felt a confession on the tip of my tongue. I could taste it. Blasé, I drilled myself. Stay cool. Hug the conversational corners professionally. Handle well on low revs. Nixon, yes, Nixon, Ford, Carter. 'Look, I know I'm not your type. In fact, I'm probably totally the wrong model. I mean, you're a kind of racing Porsche bloke, right. And, it has to be said, I'm more your basic, second-hand, Japanese, two-door, rust bucket, but . . .'

Pierce gave me an unblinking look. 'What the hell are you talkin' about?'

'But couldn't I get, you know, stripped down and resprayed?' Pierce's left eyebrow rose quizzically.

'Hey kid. You know that psychiatrist I was talking about, well . . .'

'What I'm trying to say is,' I gushed on incoherently, 'do you think you could ever like me. Just a little bit? Even though I don't have four wheels and I can't rear demist automatically?'

Through my tequila-sodden stupor, I suddenly noticed a flame shoot up from the table. There was a mild explosion. Then another. Five altogether. My hand was on fire. The birthday candles had ignited my new acrylic nails. Sozzled, I sat there and just stared at my barbecuing fingers. Pierce grabbed the flaming hand and dunked it into his cocktail. The benevolent smiles on the faces of the other diners evaporated. Their cute, deranged hunchback had just turned into a deranged, hunchbacked arsonist.

As the smoke cleared, the trendy woman at the table next to us leant over towards Pierce. 'Hey, aren't you from that comedy show *DINKS*?' Even though it hadn't rained in Los Angeles for about six months, she was wearing a transparent raincoat and high-heeled galoshes. You could see her designer underwear. You could see her appendix scar, for God's sake. Pierce smiled, revealing his faultlessly flossed fangs. She moved her chair over closer to him. 'Ya know what? You're much better lookin' in real life.' This was the worst birthday, when it wasn't really my birthday, I'd ever had. 'You're so funny on that show,' she crooned, positioning herself so that her back was completely turned towards me.

Kennedy, Carter, Ford, Reagan . . . no, Nixon . . . I could feel the crutch of my pantyhose slipping . . . '*Eins, zwei* . . . God. What comes after *zwei*?' I addressed the mole on her left shoulderblade. She shot me a 'drop dead you deranged groupie' look, then clasped Pierce's forearm and leant towards him to chat more intimately about the seductive subtleties of his on-camera presence. I mean, *please*.

There are three things I've always wanted to do.
1) Stand up at a wedding at the 'Does anyone here have any objections to this man marrying this woman?' part and say, 'Yes. I do. The guy's a total wanker and you'll be spending the rest of your life putting toilet rolls back on to spindles.'
2) Tell a man the truth when he asks me 'am I big, am I the biggest?' And
3 Throw a cake into someone's face. Especially in LA – the comedy capital of the world.

Well, everything from that moment on happened in slow motion. The entire restaurant swivelled to look at the cake-splattered socialite and the deranged human sequin. Ms Transparent Raincoat lunged at my neck, tipping me off my chair. I clung to the tablecloth as I descended to the floor, creating an avalanche of crockery. The *maitre d'* hoisted me up on to my feet. Sequins shot like shrapnel in all directions. I was carried through the restaurant and dumped unceremoniously into Pierce's car. He followed, close behind, dealing out greenbacks to all the people I'd kicked or scratched during my departure.

The dashboard glowed in the dark, as complex and mysterious as the control panel of a space shuttle. I twirled and yanked all the knobs. The hydraulic seats vibrated and rotated, then lurched forwards, backwards, left, right, up, down. The automatic soft-top cha-cha-ed above me. The hyperactive electronic windows wound themselves up and down. The frenzied wipers thrashed across the screen in time to the hazard lights. As Pierce attempted to steer while restraining my hands from the controls, I screeched and revved my voice into *broooom-broooom* noises, until I suddenly felt very, very sick. 'I'm gonna spew,' I announced romantically. Pierce swerved to the side of the road. But I didn't make it and projected a pâté and margherita vomit down the inside of his car and into the groove of the electronic window. Let me tell you, 'seductive subtleties' are kind of difficult to execute when you're puking all over a man's prized upholstery. The clogged window short-circuited and wouldn't close. 'Shit, Kat,' I vaguely heard Pierce sigh as he held back my hair, while I chundered yet again, 'It's a Class Act, kiddo.'

AT HOME IN THE HAUNTED GOLDFISH BOWL

I didn't hear from Pierce, post-puke. All I got day in, day out, was this daggy message on his answering machine. 'I can't come to the phone right now as I'm conducting a vampire orgy seance. Please leave your name, number and blood type when you hear the cosmic tone.' I got that for a whole week. I mean, how much blood and sex could one boy take?

My debut show had been 'sweetened' (that's what they call it when they overdub a track of canned laughter), edited down and put to air. At the end of the week, we would know the ratings and audience reaction and whether or not I'd be signed up for the season – or boomeranged back down-under. I moped around the house, eating frozen yoghurt and hot chocolate fudge and fantasising about inventing an auto suck equivalent for women. The days slid down like oysters. I just couldn't get my teeth into anything. Tash, meanwhile, kept trying to force-feed me her male leftovers.

'It's been so long since ya got laid,' she told me. 'If you get killed in a car accident, nobody will be able to identify your *body*.'

Friday and Saturday nights were like vaginal vaudeville at our place. It was the Ed Sullivan show of sexual acts, no kidding. Tash had a whole repertoire of boyfriends, who came (literally) at odd hours of the night. They were all blond, blue-eyed and blow-waved and were called Andy, Sandy, Chuck or Hank. I couldn't tell any of them apart. I also had to go shopping about every four hours to keep the fridge stocked. These blokes didn't just eat – they went through the cupboards *hoovering* food.

When I got home from the supermarket the Friday night of

my Mope Week, a blond, blue-eyed, two-legged blow-wave was leaning into the fridge, a towel knotted around his waist, spooning peanut butter straight from the jar. 'Hello, Andy, Sandy, Chuck or Hank,' I said coolly.

'It's Kat, right. Hey, doncha recognise me? Hey. I'm glad. How, like, refreshin'. I mean, I'd rather have you like me for *myself*, ya know?'

Andy/Sandy/Chuck/Hank rocked back on his heels waiting for me to say how impressed I was to have a semi-famous rock muso in my kitchen. Dumping the groceries on the counter, I slammed the fridge shut, then snatched the peanut butter jar out of his hands.

'Hey, ya want some? A peanut butter freak, eh. They say,' he added, 'that it's an aph-ro-dis-iac. Hey,' he grinned at me, 'have you got a bit of American in you?' He stood up close to me and had a sort of asthma attack in my earhole. 'Wouldja *like* to have a bit of American in you?' He was pukesville, he really was. 'J'know my secret technique for makin' love to a woman? I suck her toes.'

'Yeah?' I pushed him away. 'Well, I've got tinea.'

His smile fossilised, right in front of me. 'Yeah, ah. I'm kinda booked up right now anyway. Tash is waitin' for me in the bathroom.' He extended his thumb towards me and winked. 'Maybe later, huh?'

Ten minutes later, I heard the front door close and Mr Peanut-Butter-Gorger was gone.

'A premmie,' Tash explained, dripping soapy bubbles up the hallway carpet. 'The wimp came while we were kissin' in the goddamned bathroom.' So much for the aphrodisiacal powers of peanut butter, I thought. '*Men*,' she groaned, 'they either come too quick, or take too long. Premature ejaculators or Oh-my-God-the-ceiling-needs-painting-ejaculators, ya know? *Now* what am I gonna do all night?'

I watched her sip straight from the bottle in her hand, tilting her head back and gargling. Tash always used a mouthwash after she'd been with a bloke. She needed more than a mouthwash with most of them. She needed a whole body gargle, if you ask me. She swallowed loudly, then dialled the car-phone of one of her new lovers.

'Hello, Sandy?' But he was in the middle of a cocaine run.

Tash tried another couple of numbers. A married entertainment lawyer, who was into shiatsu massage and relaxation tanks, said he'd be over right away. They'd been ensconced into the bedroom for an hour or more when the doorbell rang and another Andy/Sandy/Chuck/Hank arrived. It was the cocaine dealer. He'd been able, he said, 'to swing on by' after all. Like in some clichéd French bedroom farce, the shiatsu lawyer was out the back door and Mr Cocaine was shown in.

I sat in my room putting my odd socks back in pairs. I pushed my cuticles back almost to the elbows. After an hour or two of that, I attempted a jigsaw puzzle of Pierce that I'd found in the local supermarket. I managed to reunite his nose with his mouth, but could only assemble one earlobe, half of one armpit and an Adam's apple that looked as though a bite had been taken out of it. Abandoning that, I read anything I could lay my hands on. When I'd learnt the personal histories of every American base-baller since the turn of the century, and found out from the Dear Doctor column of every magazine in the house what to do about failed liposuction, unwanted nipple hair and the joys of nude cooking, I lay down on the bed and pined for Pierce. A cloned voice on the radio was crooning that 'Love will find a way'. Yeah, I thought. Except if *you're* a kind, misunderstood, sensitive, lonely little Australian and *he's* a selfish, sexist, macho, sleaze-schmucko American ratbag. Sure, I'd wanted to fall in love. But not with *him*. I'd hoped to fall in love with someone daggy, someone who didn't mind if you bit your nails and spat them across the room occasionally. Someone normal. Not with the Most Wanted Man in America. And here I was, reaching for the stars. God. And here I was actually thinking such a pukesville sentence like 'reaching for the stars'. *What had happened to me?*

At about midnight, Tash poked her head around my bedroom door. 'Ya know what you've got?' she diagnosed, hurling herself down next to me on the bed with a long, contented groan. 'An affection-deficiency.' I watched her casually examine her inner left thigh for any renegade ingrown hairs. 'Dweezil's comin' over soon. Ya know, from the band. I was kinda thinkin' that he could bring over one of his pals. Like the drummer. Have you seen him?' She frowned in concentration as she squeezed a minuscule red blemish in the crease of her groin. 'We are talkin',' she paused to examine the results on her nail, 'Major Cute.'

'No.'

'Why not?'

'Just *no*. That's why. And don't start lecturing me. I'm in *love* goddamnit. I'm in love with Pierce Scanlen.' The words hung in the air between us.

'Well one thing's for sure,' Tash said coolly, 'the feelin's mutual. *He* loves himself too.'

'Seriously Tash, I know it's pathetic and stuff. But I can't think about anyone else.'

'Oh God,' she rolled her heavily made-up eyes. 'And people think that AIDS is deadly. Okay. Let's go over it again. What happened when you went out for dinner? It was a disaster. Now listen to me. And listen carefully. He's never gonna go for ya. Okay? Not unless you turn into one of those sophisticated, pseudo types. *They're* the sort he likes. Got it? The kinda chick who knows the pet names of at least three film directors. The kinda chick whose idea of a good night out is a tantric yoga dolphin meditation play group . . . ya know? And, who'd wanna be like them? So, *give it up*.'

'I can't.'

Tash shrugged. 'Okay fine. Have it your way. But while you've been sittin' in here veggin' out all night, I've had twelve sensational orgasms.' She lolled beside me in a voluptuous torpor. 'Got two tickets to the Eurythmics concert – and they're like *gold*. Wanna come? A discount at the dermatologists, two grams of coke, and,' she pulled a wad of money out from her bra, gangster-moll style, 'a hundred bucks.'

'Tash. You *didn't*.'

'Na. Course not. But I like didn't say no when he left me some. It'll help with C.J. I owe him squillions.'

'You're nuts.'

'And you're a prude.'

I drew my legs up to my chest. How could I explain to her what growing up in Australia was like? The trouble was I'd come from a country where the blokes called a vagina a 'muckhole' and the labia majora 'piss flaps'. Where the male version of foreplay was 'Feel like a fuck? . . . Well, do you mind lying down, while *I* have one?' I wanted something else. I wanted something more.

'I want something more,' I hazarded, 'I want, well, I know it's kinda corny-sounding . . .' I took a deep breath and said it.

'Romance.' I detected a yawn behind Tash's smile but pushed on regardless. 'I want passion. Intimacy.'

'Hey, I just whipped a guy with a bit of wet lettuce. Ya don't get more intimate than that.' Tash clicked open a compact and reapplied a layer of lipstick.

'Christ, Tash. You don't even know the meaning of the word. I mean, here you are sleeping with all these guys and doing everything imaginable and yet, well ...'

'What?' she pressed her lips together and ran her tongue back and forth across her front teeth.

'Nothing.'

'What?' Smiling, she peered once more into the compact.

'Well, I mean, you won't even go to the loo in front of them.'

Tash snapped the compact shut and looked at me sharply. 'Whaddaya mean?'

'Oh look. It doesn't matter. Forget it.'

'No. No. I won't. What were ya gonna say?'

'It's just, well, you wait until he's left the house before you go to the toilet. I've noticed.'

'Bullshit. Get real.'

'It's true.'

'Of course I go to the john when I've got a lover around. Jeez, whaddaya think I ...'

'Yeah, but not to *crap*.' I knew it was a disgusting thing to bring up, but it was true. 'And the blokes are the same. If they stay the night and stuff, they don't go to the loo until you've left the house.'

Tash shifted uncomfortably. 'Well, Jesus. Ya know, takin' the first cra ... doing number two's with a lover around. I mean. That's a big step.' Tash's eyes panned the room from left to right, right to left. She crossed and uncrossed her legs in agitation. 'It's hard to know how to do it. I mean, Chrrrist. This is a disgustin' conversation ya know that? Do ya not mention it and just do it and hope that he doesn't go to the john like straight afterwards. Do ya talk about it first? What? Let's face it. Takin' a ya know ... dump is not exactly sexy now is it?'

Tash, flustered, got up off the bed and balanced on one precariously high, red leather heel as she readjusted the strap of the other. She was wearing what she called her Regulation-Sex-

Slave-Shoes. 'No. No. It's too much of a – of a – I dunno, a commitment.'

'Well, that's what I want.'

'What?' Tash looked at me, squinting. 'To take a dump in front of a . . . ?'

'No, you dickhead. To fall in love. To have, well, total intimacy.'

'Which is why y'ave fallen in love with a guy who loves his car. Good one.'

As soon as Tash had disappeared into her bedroom with Dweezil, I went to the kitchen, hid all the groceries in the laundry hamper, then took a spoon and ate the remaining peanut butter, straight from the jar. Then to be really mean, I smeared the inside of the jar so that it looked deliciously full, before putting it back empty into the fridge.

On the morning the show ratings were due to be released, Tash gave me a triple dose of Survival Technique Yuckiness. Not only did she inform me that the ordinary plastic six-pack cover takes four hundred and fifty years to disintegrate, she also recited the names and crimes of ten Nazi war criminals still at large, and broke the news to me about 'apotemnophiliacs': blokes, she reckons, who can only get turned on by having sex with people with missing limbs. No kidding.

By the time the cab dropped me at the studio gates, I felt confident, ready for anything. The show would have rated well. I could feel it. I would be funny. I would be famous. I would become an American. I would make my home in the Haunted Goldfish Bowl.

A gaggle of teenage autograph hunters were clustered at the gate, pens poised. 'Who's that? Who's that?' they chorused, leering eagerly. I chucked a huge cheesy in their direction. They surged towards me, and then, just as suddenly, stopped. 'Oh, nobody,' their acned ringleader adjudicated.

All the actors, except Pierce, sat around the rehearsal room, nail-filing and name-dropping. Not having either – the only names I could drop would never get picked up again and my nails were still all melted – I slit open the cellophane on a pack of cards which I'd found in Tash's drawer that morning. Looking thoroughly absorbed, I sat up tall in my chair, aligned the cards carefully, then flamboyantly fanned them out between my fingers.

I have to tell you, there's not many things I'm good at, but I'm a whizz at cards. With an expert flick of my wrist, I snapped the fan shut. I shuffled and splayed them again before noticing that each card displayed a photo of a different naked man. I couldn't concentrate on the suits or numbers, only on clenched buttocks, long, hooded dicks and the wry smiles of moustachioed men with furry chests.

Rondah, who was handing out invitations to a Thanksgiving prayer meeting at her local church, stood in my light and peered over my shoulder. The tendons in my hand tightened and I snapped the pack shut. Not in time. Her fingers darted forward and snatched a card. Her nails looked like a shiny red set of Exocet missiles. I tucked my own charred specimens up into my palm.

'Hey, do ya mind? You're standing right in my . . .'

'My goodness, Katrina.' Rondah raised one perfectly plucked eyebrow, before slapping a brochure on the table in front of me. 'Drunken scenes in restaurants and now, pornography. We are seein' a rather tacky side of y'all lately, sugar. I heard on the grapevine about your little dinner at Spago's with Pierce.'

The *sour* grapevine. 'Yeah, well, whaddabout it? It was great,' I lied, trying to pretend that I wasn't blushing. 'I reckon he's a really nice bloke.'

'Oh yes sirree, that he is,' she agreed. flicking her hair back in that studied way she had. 'Still, it's a pity it's chemical.'

'What?' I strummed the edge of the card pack with my thumbnail.

'Anti-depressant pills.'

Tash reckons that everybody knows everybody else's business in LA, because they all share the same psychiatrists. 'Working with you,' I snapped back, 'he's got a lot to be depressed about.'

Her mouth contracted into a sour lemon moue. But even though her face had clenched up like a fist, she still spoke in her usual warm, curdled-custard tones. 'I know y'all must be feelin' a lot of hostility right now, honey. They have courses at UCLA ya know, on how to handle re-jec-shone.' The way my luck had been going lately, I thought, they probably wouldn't accept me.

'Don't beat yourself up, pet, ya'hear? As we come up to Thanksgivin', y'all should thank the Lord for all yer other blessin's. I mean y'all are really quite attractive, except for yer hair, an' of course, yer chest area. Y'all should have no trouble at all findin' some other line of work.'

'My *hair*? My *chest* area . . . ?' As I glanced down to check out my minuscule mammaries, I noticed that the church brochure she was distributing was dedicated to the evils of drinking and gambling. And then I did a really inspired thing. While cleaning out my jeans pocket that morning, I'd found, amongst the discarded dental floss, chewing gum blobs wrapped in foil and leaflets on driving schools, the magazine ad for the Nirvana Casino. Pushing up from the table, I stomped over to the telephone, ferreted out the number and dialled Las Vegas. The hypnotic purling noise of the long-distance call was shattered by the nasal whine of a croupier.

'Nirvana Casino?' I responded loudly, for Rondah's benefit. 'I'd like to inquire about your blackjack game.' The croupier put me through to the pit-boss. 'So . . .' I smirked at Rondah who was watching me, her face a knot of disapproval, 'Mack . . .' I was sounding more and more debauched by the second, I really was, 'you'll give the punter a squizz at the ole second card, huh?'

'Yes ma'am.'

'There must be some kinda catch buddy, huh . . . ?'

Rondah, *tch-tch-ing* self-righteously, continued doling out her church circulars, a totally insincere sort of saintly look on her chops.

'By the way, sugar,' Rondah informed me smugly, when I rang off (the casino, though refusing to volunteer any information, had agreed to answer any question I put to them about their unusual offer), '*nobody* goes to Spago's anymore. It's far too crowded.'

Before I could ask her how a place could be crowded if nobody was there, the telly executives slouched into the rehearsal room. They were a jittery, highly strung breed. Although only in their late twenties, they were all grey-looking and chewed constantly on smoking-substitute gum, or sipped from flasks of a stomach-soother called Mylanta.

'Well, I liked the show,' Jackie the only female executive volunteered nervously. 'I thought it was a very sound debut.'

'It was shit,' her boss, Nesbit, cried.

'Well, when I say I liked it,' Jackie backtracked, 'what I mean is it did need sort of like, more of the you know, same – but different. Don't you think?'

No one came to her rescue. She was left dangling over a Grand Canyon of silence, until Abe appeared. He paced the room, the ratings sheet clenched in his hand. The heads of the hushed gathering followed his progress back and forth, as though at a tennis tournament.

'Well, we gave it a shot, right?' Nesbit announced, pushing up on to his Reeboked feet. 'But I mean, what did we expect? The kid can't act, she can't sing, she's got no comic tim . . .'

Abe let out a whoop of delight. 'Zey luff her. She's tested positive wizz zee audiences.' Abe pinched my cheek between two fingers and squeezed it hard. 'Oh, cupcake. Does zee camera love zat puzz, or vot? Crocodile Dundette,' he slapped my other cheek. 'I am zigning you up for ever!'

This news prompted a collective cardiac arrest for the entire gathering of writers, actors, hair stylists, stage managers, couriers, cameramen, caterers, costume designers, make-up artists, wardrobe mistresses, warm-up comedians, publicists, production co-ordinators, network producers and the entire summit of Presidents. The astonished silence finally gave way to a long, low whisper which ran around the room.

Jackie took a gi-normous belt of her digestant. 'You were saying . . .' she sweetly inquired of Nesbit.

As the writers embarked on a blitz of back-slapping and the executives popped the corks on their bottles of vintage Mylanta, Rondah barged through the crowd to be the first to my side. The beaming face on her ID badge was in stark contrast to the hateful scowl she now turned on me. 'Well, shoot, how won-der-ful, sugar,' she lied, pressing her arctic cheek against mine. 'Con-grat-u-lay-shones pet.' She forced her lips into a strangled smile.

That afternoon, the limo magically reappeared, as did the flowers and 'High Concepts' and invitations to power breakfasts. Old, old friends, whom I'd never met before, kept gushing about how FAB-ulous and 'tastic I was. It hit the papers that I was to be signed up for the term of my un-natural life to a lucrative sitcom, and a strange brand of human being called the 'Agent' crawled out of the Holly-wood-work. People called Amyl, B.J. and Sky called, offering to do strange things like 'winging me a Gotham' for 'confabs' with 'highrolling honchos' – whatever they were.

But most persistent were members of the Gumleaf Mafia. Ever since *Crocodile Dundee*, California had been crawling with Professional Aussies. These blokes, going under the names of Bazza and Macka, wore a uniform of acubras, moleskins and R.M. Williams riding boots. They talked loudly about 'Olivia' and 'Paul' and peppered their conversation with lots of 'mates', 'G'days' and 'Don't come the raw prawns'. Their accents became more stridently nasal at the appearance of an American. An army of these two-legged cockroaches fronted up to my 'signing into the series' party. It was held at the Young Executives Singles Club – YES. Also in attendance were the TV executives, the press, and the brat-pack of teen actors currently moistening the underpants of adolescent females. The rest were the usual rent-a-crowd of ex-talk-show hosts, vaguely familiar weather-girls, former astronauts and urban cowboys. The only people in the whole of LA who weren't there were the actors from my show.

'Where's Rondah?' I screeched to Abe above the metallic throb of a song by the Decapitators, called 'We Rape Grandmothers'.

He looked embarrassed for a moment, well, as embarrassed as a megalomaniac amoral shark can look – then said in a clammy voice. 'Vondah? Oh, she ease here somewhere. Probably she ease plastered,' he winked. 'Or getting laid.' He threw his arms open. 'You vimmin,' he sighed. 'Two glasses of vine, and you haff vun leg in California, and zee uzzer in Connecticut.' He laughed immoderately, gloating over his wonderful wit. He then began a running commentary on every woman who passed by our table. 'Oohh,' he nudged me, 'I vish she'd come and zit on my face. Oh my God!' He pointed at a sad, overblown blonde by the bar. With a too-tight bubble dress, ponytail and lacquered face, she was one of the fifty-going-on-fifteen breed. 'Sheet,' he pronounced urbanely, 'I vouldn't fuck her with Cosmo's cock.'

I just hate it when blokes say stuff like that. Especially ugly blokes. I looked at Abe and his companions, at their flaccid faces and flabby jowels, their balding pates and piggy eyes. I mean, don't they shave? Haven't they seen their reflections? To put it bluntly, these guys were ugly as a bag full of bums.

'Vy are older vimmin like dog turdz? Because zee older zey are, ze easier zey are to pick up,' Abe informed us, shattering into laughter.

'Hey, ya know, you blokes are not exactly the Arnold Schwarzenegger types, right?'

Abe stopped laughing, placed a cigar the size of a sapling

between his thick fingers and lit it. 'You mizunderstand me cup-cake,' he said, waving the blazing baton. 'I am a Feminizt. I tink vimmin are zenzual and beautiful and horny and . . .'

'What about their brains?'

'Huh?' he glared at me, then waved his hand dismissively. 'Yes, yes, zat too. I like hiring vimmin. Zey are as competent as men, as dedicated as men – and there's always zee chance of a fuck at zee end of the day!'

A sudden urge to hit the dance floor overcame me. This simply meant wriggling into the whorl of dancers and just sort of squirm-ing a bit. It was buttock-to-buttock out there. Basically everybody was just standing there looking into each others armpits. But, eventually, through the dim light, I realised that it wasn't an armpit I was looking into, but the bulkiest groin in the entire world. It was Mt Rushmore, in denim. My eyes travelled upwards to a vast chest bulging with pectorals, which joined a thick, throbbing neck. On top of the neck, was a massive cranium, upon which sat a bionic smile beaming down in my direction. I was dancing with a Ken doll. You know, the sort of doll that comes with ski outfit, tuxedo, plastic scuba gear, racing car and obligatory Barbie. About six Barbies were smiling adoringly up at him now as he spoke.

'Hel-low there liddle lay-dee.' His capped teeth kinda gave him the look of a carnivore.

'G'day.'

He craned down to my level. 'Hey. No shit. You're the little Oss-sea?' He practically goochie-goochie-gooed at me. It was pukesville. 'Well, whaddaya know about that?' He lowered two massive arms around my waist and hoisted me into the air. He swung me to the side, tucked me under one bulging arm, put his head down, and, bellowing like a buffalo on heat, ploughed through the people towards the bar. From my horizontal position, all I could see was a mass of Reeboks and stilettos, as dancers in our path improvised spontaneous sidesteps into their choreogra-phy. With a cry of 'touch down', he desposited me on a bar stool, high-fived the bar tender and ordered drinks. A moment later he handed me a glass of some vicious green liquid flecked with coconut.

'What is it?'

'A Leg-Opener,' he said simply. 'Bottoms up,' and slurped his

Diet Coke. 'I'm in trainin', see,' he explained, pointing to his glass.

'What for?' I glanced up at him blankly.

'Ya dunno who I am? Chuck Larson!' He waited for my gasp of awe. 'Chicago Bears,' he elaborated, his voice swollen with self-importance. Chuck struck a studied pose. It looked as though he was preparing for a photo opportunity.

'Um, is that football or baseball?'

His dumbfounded expression gave way to a hearty laugh. He slapped me on the back. 'Fuckin' A,' he said succinctly. Chuck Larson was movie-star-handsome, with a curly mass of raven black hair cascading on to his massive shoulders. Judging by his conversation, he had more of the same between his ears. 'How long ya been Stateside, huh?' He delivered his jock-speak like punches, full of 'gotta' and 'wanna' and 'fuckin' this and that', punctuated with finger-snaps and high-fives.

'A few months,' I said, checking to see how many broken ribs had perforated my skin. 'Though it feels like a decade.'

'Oh . . .' His large face went all gooey, as though he was in a pet food commercial with a couple of cute kitties that had leukaemia or something. 'Homesick, huh?'

I waved my nose over the top of my glass and gagged. 'My mate Tash reckons I've got an affection deficiency.'

'Yeah?' Chuck swung eagerly towards me. 'Fuckin' A. I'm horny too.' I examined his large jaw and thick neck and vast expanse of sloping forehead. It was hard to imagine him as the end product of six billion years of evolution. 'Well, honey. This here's yer lucky day. Pucker up.' Even his lips looked muscle-bound. I ducked as they descended towards me. I mean, this guy was popular. You never knew where his mouth had been. 'Shoot, don't tell me yer shy?'

'No. No. It's just, well, I haven't had my shots yet.'

'Listen, babe. Have you any idea of how much I earn in a season?' He rested his gargantuan leg on the rung of my bar stool. Three and a half million bucks. I can have any piece of ass in America. But I wanna tell ya, ya know, with me, right, I neva just go for a babe's tits, or her legs or her ass or her . . . what turns me on is a lady's *face*.' He placed an arm either side of me so that I was pinnioned back against the bar. 'I s'pose a *facial* would be out of the question?' He pressed himself up against me. 'I like

THE LLAMA PARLOUR

the ladies see. I like to hold a woman down and feel her beneath me.'

As far as I could see, being beneath Chuck Larson was impossible. No one could be beneath him. He was about as low as you could get. Except, of course, for an amoeba or a piece of pond scum. I thought about revealing this information to him, but decided instead to tell him it was ideologically unsound for a woman to do it in the missionary position these days. 'Sorry Chuck, but we modern girls, we, um, only do it on top now.'

Old Chuck baby looked at me as though I'd stepped out of an alien spacecraft. 'Huh?'

I ducked beneath his arms and, parting the dancers with breast stroke motions, swam upstream. Another tidal wave of people surged on to the dance floor and I was caught up in the current. The social bends set in. I lost my breath. Just as my puny little life was flashing before my eyes, I felt a warm hand on my arm. It hoisted me to the side of the dance floor, and I was blinded by the flash of Pierce's smile.

After my eyes adjusted, I examined his face. He looked pale beneath his tan, if you know what I mean, and a little frayed around the edges. His hair was all tousled, as though a couple of wild animals had been grazing there. I felt a wave of longing so strong my throat dried. Then I noticed the three glamorous women he had in tow. You know, the suave, blasé breed. You could just tell by looking at them that they knew the pet names of at least three top film directors. These women would never have vomited in the car of a man they had the hots for. These women didn't vomit. In fact, these women didn't have any bodily functions at all.

Pierce placed a wad of money in my hand. 'One hundred bucks,' he said. 'Congrats, kid. You made it.'

'Nobody else turned up.'

'Are you kidding? Free food and Rondah's not here?'

There was a brittle, bright effort in his voice. A yawn unrolled down his famous face. 'Come on.' He gave me a conspiratorial wink and, shrugging off his lady friends, encircled my upper arm as we moved in tandem through the tables.

'Pierce, where are we going?' I asked, as we moved closer and closer to the ladies' loo. 'Pierce?' I said, as I realised he was going in. Like a gunslinger in a B-grade Western, he kicked open the door with one foot and slammed inside. Ignoring the women reapplying lipstick and rearranging cleavages, he marched straight into a cubicle, with me in tow, and locked the door. 'Pierce,' I whispered, 'are you having a gender crisis or what?'

He flipped down the lid of the loo and deposited himself on it. A wan island of light illuminated the tiny vial in the palm of his hand. He studied it devoutly, before laying out a few lines of cocaine on a small hand-mirror that magically appeared from his top pocket. My heart sank. It looked as though everyone in this town had a touch of the Tashes. As far as I was concerned, drugs in LA were totally superfluous. I mean, things were surreal enough already. And it wasn't that I was gutless either. I had promised myself to do most things − abseil, ride in a space shuttle, learn to play a Beethoven sonata. But there were some things I'd sworn not to do until I was eighty years old − parachuting, sleeping with two men at once, eating fugu fish (a Japanese delicacy which, even though a total what Tash would call 'palate-fuck', poisons to death about ten top gourmets every year) and cocaine. I mean, at that grand age, it wouldn't matter if I got squished, AIDS-infected, poisoned or addicted. But until then I had vowed to never, ever, ever do drugs.

From the pocket of his tight Jordache jeans, Pierce extracted a Biro, gutted it, stuck the plastic casing up his nose, hoovered up a white line and passed it to me. 'Wanna toot?'

The trouble was, Pierce could have asked me if I wanted to suck the brains of a freshly scalped monkey up through a straw, or even worse, vote Republican, and I would have said yes.

'Yes,' I said, inserted the pen up my nostril and mimicked his vacuum cleaner impression. I leant back on the dunny door − and exhaled a deep, dusty, spicy sigh as the warm rush of the drug exploded into my system. I had the distinct impression that I had just come from a tantric yoga dolphin meditation play group. I gave a cool smile, but then Pierce looked up at me, and I started defrosting.

'Pierce,' my voice was a stranger. 'Pierce.' Up until now I'd always thought the reason people gushed a lot in Los Angeles was because the whole place was built on top of oil fields. But suddenly I knew why Geyser Mode was the norm. Cocaine makes you talk fast. Reallyreallyreallyfastfastfasterandfasterandyoufelt-surewhatyouhadtosaywasfabulouslyscintillatingandinterestingandthateveryonewantedtohearitasmuchasyoudid. I took a deep breath. 'Pierce, I've been worried about you. Where were you? The point is, I may seem like a hick and all, but I've done heaps of stuff in my life. Heaps. You know, I can do tumble-turns, hot-wire cars, I can build a campfire, for God's sake, but this, this . . . feeling I have is something new to me. It makes me tongue-tied and tangle-toed. It makes me kinda – ' My lips felt numb, as though I'd come back from the dentist with a mouth full of Novacaine. 'Look, I know I'm not suave, and I can't dance and I don't know any film directors by their pet names. Even though I spewed in your car and all, I want you to know that I'm not always such a total one-hundred-per-cent-dag and well, won't you go out with me just once more, huh?'

This unexpected tirade startled a laugh out of him, which he promptly concealed behind his Raybans. 'Well, I'm pretty booked up for the next decade. I could wait-list you for the early part of next century.'

'No seriously.' I could barely talk, my mouth was so full of my feet. 'Any chance?'

Pierce shrugged. 'Well you are kinda growin' on me.'

'Great. You make me sound like a fungus.' His beautiful face remained expressionless. 'And you know what else?' I snatched off his Raybans. 'I don't believe all that tough crap you go on about, you know, not loving anyone and stuff. You just won't let yourself. Because it's unfashionable and beca . . .'

Pierce put his hand over my mouth. 'Don't sweet-talk me,' he said, inscrutable once more, behind his glasses. 'I'm emotionally diabetic. Sweet-talk could give me a goddamned seizure or some-thin'.'

'Do you always have to sound as though you're in a situation comedy?' I mumbled through his fingers. 'I-ve iss-d ooo.'

'What?'

I bit his index finger. He snatched his hand back off my face. 'I've missed you,' I admitted, then immediately regretted it. If there was a God, I now prayed to him to please, please, take some time off from the Middle East and get me out of this.

Pierce stiffened, looked warily about the cubicle, then unfolded to his feet. 'Don't weird me out. You're whacked. You dunno what you're sayin'.'

'I do. I do. What I want to say is . . .' But what did I want to say? I tried to remember, but couldn't concentrate. Strange things were happening in our cubicle. An army of ants was gnawing at my leg and there seemed to be octopuses swimming up over the edge of the toilet bowl.

'Oh, I forgot to tell you. This coke's cut with some pretty lethal shit. It's prob'ly too strong for a little marsupial like you.'

'It's not too . . . whaddaya think I am? A wimp?' I blustered, looking around for a spear gun.

'Yeah, well just don't worry if you start seeing God or anything.' Pierce slowly licked his finger, leant forward, ran it round the rim of my nostril, then rubbed the cocaine residue across his pink gums. 'If we see God, when we get high, whaddaya reckon God sees when *he* gets high? People?' Pierce peeled a few twenties from the wad he'd given me and nudged open the door with his foot. 'I owe you.'

'Where are you going?'

'I need to go for a drive.' There was a note of exaggerated ease in his voice. Though smiling confidently, he gripped his hands together so tightly that the tendons bulged.

My heart sank. 'In your *car*?'

'What else should I go for a drive in?' Taking hold of the door frame, he pivoted past me. 'My spacecraft. Warning! Danger! Alien Invasion.' Nobody paid any attention as he strode through the ladies' loo making Martian noises.

'You know what? I could go out with plenty of men. The *best*.' Trailing after him, I noticed that there were two pairs of feet under most of the cubicle doors. 'Chuck Larson is hot for me, did you know that?' I had a sudden flash of the seven-foot sleeping pill I'd left by the bar. 'He's *really* interesting. I really fancy him too actually. Pierce? Do you think I should go out with him? Pierce?'

Outside, the party was throbbing. I heard my name being called and saw Abe bolting towards me, arms semaphoring. 'Zee press vant to interview you.' As Pierce disappeared from view, Abe steered me towards the foyer with the grip of a policeman escorting a felon. 'Keep *laid back*,' he instructed gruffly.

Abe led me into a bubbling ooze of human lava. The lava spoke, blasting me with a barrage of stupid questions. For some reason, once you get your face in the newspapers, people want to know your favourite colour, your favourite food. They want to take pictures of you in your favourite pair of bathers, drinking your favourite cocktail, seated in your favourite chair. 'I don't have a favourite chair,' I replied to the lady from the *National Enquirer*. Abe rolled his eyes, making me dimly aware that I'd given the wrong answer.

'And how do ya feel now that yer've made it as a television starlet?' A camera light sizzled my corneas.

Sitting on the carpeted steps, I hugged my knees up to my chest and looked at my toes. If confusion, drugs and a broken heart were signs of movie starlet fame, then I would soon be down there with Marilyn Monroe and John Belushi. I shrugged. 'Dunno.'

Abe looked at me as though a family of tarantulas had taken up residency in my clothing.

'Whaddaya do for sex?' asked one sleazy slime-bag. I looked him in his tinted contact lenses and said that I'd bought a marital aid. 'And whaddaya think of the star of the show?' he persevered, 'Rondah Rivers. There have been rumours of artistic tension on the set. And she ain't here tonight, I notice.'

'I think she's a drongo.'

The reporters glanced at each other. 'Drongo?' one of them quizzed.

'Oh yeah,' I improvised, 'It's an old Australian word for a fascinating and truly nice person.'

'You weren't afraid to come to the party tonight?' a television entertainment reporter boomed, 'in spite of the death threats?'

I stared at him in complete stupefaction. 'I'm sorry?'

'The publicity department for *DINKS* received a death threat for you this evening. Didncha know?' he asked with greedy curiosity. The foyer, lined with mirrors, magnified the crowd. Conversation coagulated. They all looked at me ravenously – the way a woman looks at a chocolate biscuit on day two of a celery and water diet.

I turned to Abe, dry-mouthed.

'Yes, yes, she knew. But zey make zem tough down-under, yez?' He gave an indefatigable smile and yanked me to my feet. 'Sank you ladies and gentlemen.' I lost and regained my balance, gingerly grabbing for Abe's arm. He promptly steered me back into the party.

I felt numb from the brain down. Not just my foot, but my

whole body seemed to have fallen asleep. 'A death threat? Are you serious?'

'Didn't Vondah tell you? She volunteered to tell you just before zee function. I thought she told you.' I took this the same way I took Hitler saying that he would not invade Czechoslavakia.

'Why get Rondah to tell me when she's the one who probably made the bloody call in the first bloody place?'

'Look. Ve decided not to tell you, just in case you didn't show up for zee party. Besides, imagine zee publicity if you *did* actually get shot?' His treasonous eyes flickered wide for a moment. 'I'm joking,' he added, insincerely, before choking on a laugh.

The press reappeared around the corner. They were like ants, making for a dead lizard.

'Excuse me lady, would you like a photographic record of your special night?' Recognising the cheese-grater voice, I swung round. Tash, dressed as a French maid, snapped a polaroid of me. 'Sorry I'm late. I got a new job. Come on.' She dragged me into the throng of dancers, through the forest of tinsel that hung from the billions of balloons nudging the mirrored ceiling, then out the staff door into the car park. On the back of Tash's uniform, it read 'Pierre's Focus Pocus Photographic Services. Make your Evening Memorable'.

'I've always wondered who did that job. Going round to restaurants taking photos.'

'Well, now you know – desperates. It pays shit. But I get loads of tips. It's the maid's uniform. Men are like fish. Chuck 'em the right bait and you've got 'em by the gills, ya know?'

The fresh air calmed me down. I was no longer hallucinating. Only a couple of flimsy tentacles stretched towards my throat out of the cocktail glass Tash was clutching.

'Thanks for coming, Tash. Nobody turned up, can you believe it, except Pierce and he was so out of it that he wasn't really there anyway. Are you listening?' Tash had slumped down on the lid of a garbage can and was staring fixedly at her shoes. A cigarette was burning close to her fingertips, which, I noticed, were bitten down and bloody. With her other hand, she retrieved a flat band of red hair out of her face, tucked it absentmindedly behind one ear and said something I couldn't quite hear. 'What?'

'He's found him.' Unhurriedly, she let the cigarette drop between her fish-netted feet and lit another. 'Almost.'

'What?'

'Well, he *thinks* so anyway.'

'Who? Found who? Who's found who?' The ground dislocated itself and seemed to float up towards the sky. I wanted to sit down, but I was having terrible trouble trying to remember which way my knees bent.

'C. J.' Tash peered up at me as if through a mist. 'Hey, are you stoned?'

My brain came back into orbit. 'No! Well, a bit. Yeah.'

'He's tracked down the name of the agency who adopted him out,' she said flatly.

'That's fantastic.'

'But he ain't doin' anymore till I pay him what I owe him, the prick, plus more.'

'How much?'

'Six thousand bucks. He *says* it's to bribe the officials to get the info. The sonofabitch. I've bin thinkin'.' She addressed her champagne glass. 'Ya know, sleepin' with men for money? Well, it wouldn't be that gross.'

I thrust into her hand the sixty or so bucks left over from Pierce's wad. 'I'll get you some money. I'll get an advance on my, you know, salary.'

She counted it and shrugged dismally. 'Only men I *like*. It's either that, or topless modelling. Here.' She shoved her camera into my hands and hoiked up her top. 'Take a pic-sure will ya? They'll never believe my goddamned statistics otherwise.'

'Tash, be serious.'

'I am. They won't.'

'I can't.'

'Course you can. See the little red button? Ya just . . .'

'No. I mean I can't.'

'Okay, well, I'll just go hawk my fork down on Hollywood Boulevard. Would ja prefer me to do that?'

The flash illuminated her small frame against the stuccoed wall. A fleet of luxury limousines cruised the street outside the club car park, like a school of sleek black sharks. Tash pulled down her top. 'I'll send it off to a magazine, ya know, as a sample.'

'Tash,' I gasped, as the news finally got through to me. 'This might be it. You might have found him.'

'Yeah,' she shrugged.

I looked at my friend. She seemed about as excited as someone waiting for a Pap-smear appointment. 'Tash, are you okay?'

'Let's make a wish,' she said neutrally, raising her glass.

'What did you wish for?' I asked her as we toppled into the pimpmobile.

'Oh, nuthin' much. World peace, a patch over the hole in the ozone layer, the preservation of whales and elephants, a woman president, and democracy in . . .' she counted the countries off on her fingers, 'Saudi Arabia, South Africa, Kuwait, El Salvador, Iraq and China.'

'Oh.'

'Whadda 'bout you? What did *you* wish for?'

I took a gulp of champagne. 'That Pierce Scanlen gets a power surge on his auto suck.'

PART
TWO

THE RUDEST CHINESE
RESTAURANT

Being in love with Pierce Scanlen was like being in an out-of-control car – but for *three months*. Not only did he put LSD in the executive drinking fountain, but he was caught playing 'Spin the Quaaludes' with the fans at the entry gate. The game, apparently, involved each player spinning the Quaalude bottle and then devouring an amount of Quaaludes corresponding to the number rolled on the dice. Anyone who didn't overdose had to remove a garment. Two under-age Valley girls were down to their underwear – and up to their eyeballs – by the time Abe found them. Faced with having his pay docked, Pierce promised to go straight . . . while remaining as zonked as ever. I guess he thought he had us all bluffed, but you didn't exactly have to be Einstein to work out what was really going on. I mean, one night he made the entire cast and crew listen to a Jimi Hendrix guitar solo, *twenty-two times consecutively*, between takes. Christmas came and went, as did New Year. He stood me up both nights. Oh, he apologised each time, smiling his bionic smile, and asking me if I was angry. Well, let's face it, he might as well have asked me if he was lacking in sex appeal.

But it wasn't just Pierce who was headed on a collision course with calamity. There was Tash. She was running round like a headless chook, trying to raise the money for C. J. Not only was she writing songs in the hope of doing a demo tape, but she'd sold our record collection, stolen thirteen car stereos and started playing her saxophone on street corners. I had to pass around the hat – wearing a T-shirt that read 'Sax Appeal – Give Generously'. At nights she did seedy gigs downtown or in pukesville

111

grease-pits in the Valley. I was desperate to help her raise the dosh. Not just for the sake of her little brother, but because it was proving catastrophic for my complexion. You see, Tash's real addiction was sugar. While most rock singers are destroyed by drugs and alcohol, Natasha Kerlowski is the only rock 'n' roller who will be destroyed by cake. No kidding. She would come off stage every night and order six profiteroles. No, correction. She'd come off stage and make *me* order six profiteroles. See, by not ordering any, she could then pretend that she hadn't eaten any, which enabled her to pretend that she wasn't a certified cake-aholic.

Tash was so desperate for cash that she was even trying to write one of those blockbuster Hollywood 'shop 'n' fuck' novels. The only problem, she reckoned, was that she didn't know enough about the shopping.

Then there were the men. Basically, Tash's legs had been at a quarter to three for about the last four weeks. Besides the usual Andy/Sandy/Chuck/Hanks she was now also hitting the hay with an ad executive, another entire rock band and some married bloke called Brendon, from the Valley. She only saw him though, when he was coming downtown to take his car into the shop or to go to the dentist. Their entire relationship was based on tyres and teeth. Not that any of these blokes actually paid her in cold hard cash, but they did give her presents – which she cashed in coldly. She'd raised $2,263. Only $3,737 to go.

When I wasn't worrying about Tash, I was worrying about work. Since I'd been accepted and signed up on to the show, things had just gone right down the gurgler. Think of the three things you hate doing the most. For me, it's going for IUD fittings (the only time I ever want to see stirrups again is when I go horse-riding), cleaning out the toilet bowl, and attending rello reunions. Add them together and then multiply by about six million, and that would still look like a good time compared to daily life at *DINKS*.

To make matters worse, Cosmo had been crook, on and off, for weeks. At first he just laughed it off: 'Not a good idea dah-ling,' he said to me after he'd spent the morning spewing his guts up, 'to go on a vibrator bed after eating Häagen-Dazs ice-cream.' But I didn't believe him. Nobody could go on that many vibrator beds. Cosmo was sick, daily. So, not only was my only ally away more and more often with weird illnesses, but the actors were still sabotaging every script.

Rondah's technique for halting the show was to call for a stop-tape during my biggest scenes so that she could have her live sheep-cell injections. This was the latest in Swedish beauty treatment. When no one was around, Pierce and I put a bottle of mint sauce in her dressing-room. I paid for it though. That week's script called upon *her* character to slap *my* character across the face. Now, Rondah Rivers is what's known in the trade, as a 'one-take actor'. She gets it in the can first go. Well, *twenty-five* takes later, she just *still* couldn't get her lines right.

All the delays had the network heavies panicking. Because they were being paid to be script advisers, these dorks felt they just had to *advise* on the scripts regardless. As far as I could make out, points were scored by the number of points you raised, no matter how pedantic or just plain bloody stupid.

But, just when I was contemplating a more fulfilling career as a foot-odour-tester, or a fork-lift operator or a monitor of continuous-flow goods, I was summoned to Abe Epstein's mansion for a meeting.

Abe put his pudgy finger up to his thick lips, nodded towards the French windows and motioned for me to follow. He led me in silence down past the pool which nobody ever swam in, across the lush lawn to the dog kennels.

'Abe, where are we go . . .'

'Shhh.' He gestured me through the gate, then let out a long, low whistle. Thirty pedigree poodles hurtled towards us from all directions. They orbited around his legs like furry, malfunctioning sputniks. 'Now ve can tork,' Abe bellowed above the yelping. He bent down to enable the dogs to lick and nuzzle his hands. 'Vun can neva be too careful.' His eyes darted from side to side. 'Spies!' he hissed conspiratorially.

'What?'

'Spies! Ze house could be bugged. Zis ease ze only safe place to tork. Zee uzer netvorks vould do *any*-sing to get to my brilliant ideas. Of which' – he skewered me in his gaze – 'you, Crocodile Dundette, are vun.' A small, pink poodle chose this moment to start sniffing sociably at my crotch. 'You like being on zee show, yes?'

It was a little like asking a turkey if it liked Christmas. 'Oh yeah, yeah. It's great.'

The dog, having dispensed with foreplay, was now endeavouring to consumate our new friendship. It was attacking my leg with a dribbling ferocity. Nodding intently to Abe, I tried to shake free my new admirer. Abe broke off what he was saying, bent down, detached the dog's teeth from my inner thigh and scooped it up into his arms. 'Zis vun likes you, no?'

I cringed away from its pointy little face. Don't get me wrong. I like animals, but mainly in the past tense. Beef Stroganoff and Steak Diane in particular.

'Modern society,' Abe went on, 'no longer haz any concept of love or honour or religion. Today, zee only sing which sets vun person above zee rest is zair degree of Fame. My point ease,' he whistled again, sending the dogs into a louder and higher pitch of anxiety. 'Eef your popularity keeps up, ve vill spin you off into your own series.' He kissed the smelly pink blob on its snout. 'You like eat, no? My poodle?'

I patted the animated powder puff in his arms with feigned affection. 'Yeah,' I lied, gutless wonder that I was. 'Oh yeah. Lovely.'

Abe nodded approvingly as though I'd passed some secret test. 'Wiz zee right assembling and marketing, ve vill make a fortune out of you.' Abe Epstein called himself a Hit Factory, producing hit sitcoms like car parts. He prided himself on being able to pinpoint his audience, right down to the last pubescent pimple. He turned now to look at me. The glint in his eyes was like the blade of a knife. He ran a pink tongue around his salivating mouth, which seemed to have suddenly swollen with greed. 'It vill be like play-ink Monopoly, except ve vill just keep go-ink round and round ze board, passing Go.' His lips now looked like a couple of slugs copulating. 'Ven ve do zee deal,' said the slugs 'zis dog vill be yours.'

'Gee, um, thanks.'

Abe Epstein smiled, enraptured by his own magnanimity. The pink poodle suddenly strained forward in his arms and attempted to engaged me in a passionate tongue-kiss. Abe smacked it on the snout, before placing it in a separate pen. Next thing I knew, his arm was coiled around my bare shoulders. It seemed to suction on to my skin like a gold-braceleted tentacle. He whistled again,

114

so that we could talk beneath the sound of thirty yapping poodles. Abe went on to explain the sophisticated secret of his success – something about making simplistic, heat'n'serve shlock that sticks to the telly screen like chewing gum.

How sophisticated could you get, I thought to myself.

'I vill make you a star, Katrina, on vun condition.' The slugs curled up, as though someone had zapped them with pesticide. 'Stay avay from Pierce Scanlen. Zat boy ease a maniac.'

I almost laughed out loud. Staying away from Pierce would not be hard. The only time I ever copped an eyeful of him was when he needed to borrow money. When *DINKS* first started Pierce had signed the standard Hollywood contract with the standard Hollywood small print. So, even though the show was a smash hit, Pierce was still earning peanuts. His excuse for borrowing money was always for the monthly instalments on one or other of his cars. There seemed to be a monthly instalment due every day. Whenever I did fork out cash for him, he'd always promise lunch. But 'lunch' would invariably turn out to be a cup of cold coffee while he got his hair cut, or a warm ice-cream while we waited for one of his cars to come out of the shop. Still, I couldn't get too cheesed-off with him. The passenger window of his Ferrari still didn't close properly. Tash was right. As far as I could figure, the only way he would ever find me attractive was if I had a muffler and a steering wheel surgically attached.

So, to tell you the truth, I would probably have agreed to Abe's request, except just at that moment, the amorous pink poodle, thwarted in love, launched itself from the roof of its kennel. It sailed over the wire wall, straight at Abe, and sunk its fangs into his fleshy calf.

No sooner had word spread that Abe had been laid low for a day by a dog bite, than Pierce was organising get well cards – for the dog. By mid-afternoon of the next day, a substantial postbag had arrived at Abe's house. The tally, according to Pierce, was four sympathy cards for the patient, and 362 for the pooch.

Needless to say, when Abe limped into work on the following morning, his mood was far from jovial. It wasn't helped by Pierce's greeting. 'Hey Abe, what's that foam around your lips?'

Abe shot Pierce a lethal look – the sort of look that killer aliens give earthlings in comic books. Pierce had been arriving at rehearsals later and later, armed with wilder and wilder excuses, only to fluff more and more of his lines and then talk through everybody else's.

'Can you lend me the cab fare home?' Pierce addressed me, talking through Mimi's lines.

'Where's the Ferrari?' I whispered.

'Sold it.'

I snagged hold of his sleeve. 'You *sold* IT?'

Pierce flinched almost imperceptibly and shifted ever so slightly away from me. 'You see, my girlfriend prefers the less ostentatious kinda car. She's a minimalist.'

'Your *girlfriend*?' My stomach rode up and down my oesophagus like an elevator.

'Yeah.'

'You never mentioned that you had a . . .'

'That's 'cause there's not much to mention. Like I said, she's a minimalist. She's really got it together, see. She, like, owns one poetry book, one pair of silk sheets, one painting, one pair of jeans, one dress – designer, of course – sparse furnishings, white surfaces. She's a painter. Real artistic. A hell of an expressive face, you know?'

I hated this LA lady. She was obviously a minimalist because only a minimal amount of people liked her.

'So, how 'bout it? Cab fare?'

Abe zapped Pierce with another invisible death-ray. Pierce lifted one buttock up off the couch, frowned in concentration, then let rip with an explosive blast of flatulence. Every eye in the room bulged in Pierce's direction. 'The ability to fart at will is a virtuoso skill,' he explained. 'It's going to be included as a category in the Olympics.'

There was a reason Pierce had developed this Abe-proof force field. He'd been dropping hints about as subtle as Hiroshima that he was going to renege on his contract unless he got paid more moolah.

Pierce waited for the laughter to subside and the rehearsal to recommence, before taking me aside once more. 'Well?'

'God. Whadd'are you doing with all your money?' I whispered back, ferreting in my bag for my purse. 'Can't you balance a chequebook?'

'Money bores me,' he yawned. 'I'm bad at money.'

'Pierce *come on*. It's not as if I'm asking you to work out the circumference of the world.'

Abe clapped his hands to conclude the rehearsal and reminded the cast about the publicity photos the next day. 'Eats important zat you are all *on time*. Vight?' He fired off another killer look in Pierce's direction.

'Vong.' Pierce retorted.

Abe shut his script crisply. 'Vatch it Scanlen. Be zere, on time, or you vill be in zerious trouble.'

By the tone of his voice, he didn't just mean *trouble*, trouble. He meant testicles-cut-off-with-a-pair-of-nail-scissors type trouble. 'On time. Do you read me?'

'Sorry chief. I'm dyslexic.' Pierce pushed up from the couch and slouched from the room, torpedoing off another fart before departing.

All night, I practised being minimal. All night, I only moved when I had a purpose and only spoke when I felt profound.

'Wha-thuh hell's godinna *you*, for Chrissake?' Tash demanded, breaking off from her singing exercises. Her teacher had been on to her about her 'intercostals', whatever they were, and Tash had been practising like a mad woman for weeks now. At the same time as she trilled up and down the scales, she was busy concocting another of her weird culinary inventions: apple licorice turnover and cream because she just *knew* I was craving it. (I'd been trying to convince her lately that it wasn't a criminal offence to be seen eating in public. That food was, in fact, an important part of a healthy diet. But the message obviously hadn't gotten through.)

Lounging up against the counter, I told her the good and bad news. Pierce was not in love with something that had four wheels. He was in love with something that had two legs. 'Still, at least she's human,' I muttered, 'sort of.'

'Jeeezus. Okay.' Tash abandoned her arpeggios and thumped the spoon down on to the counter. 'Let's settle this once and for all.' She unwound the apple skin from the vegetable peeler. 'Turn around.' She swivelled me towards the wall. 'Now chuck this over ya shoulder.'

'What?'

She handed me the long green spiral of peel. 'Just *do it*. The shape of the letter it lands in is the first letter of the name of the man ya gonna fall in love with an' marry.' I gave her a 'you've finally cracked' look. 'It's true. Do it.'

Dutifully, I flung the apple peel over my shoulder. We both swung around and examined the shape on the linoleum floor. 'It's a J,' she announced. 'So ya can forget all about Pierce. It just ain't in ya destiny.'

'Tash, I can't forget him.'

'Look, if ya need somethin' large and thick in your life, why doncha just go to bed with, I dunno, a phone book, for God's sake. Now my turn.' She catapulted the peel over her shoulder, then squatted down to examine the results. 'It's a B.'

'B? How on earth do you figure . . .'

'It *is*. Gee,' she laughed, tracing the apple peel with her painted index finger. 'Maybe it's Bernard.' Bernard was the married bloke from the Valley I told you about. Mr Tyres and Teeth. 'I do like him an' all.' Her cooking apron was covered in pictures of cucumbers and jokes about their desirability ahead of men.

'Maybe it's a B for bullshit,' I scoffed and went to my room to practise artistic facial expressions.

The next day we assembled for the publicity shoot, faking camaraderie for the cameras. Pierce was missing. Abe strutted the set, cursing and gesticulating, the veins on his face standing out like they do in cabbages. Finally the door whooshed open and Pierce strolled in. For the first time in weeks, he looked well-dressed, wide-awake, clear-eyed and perfectly normal – except for the fact that his hair and eyebrows were completely missing. No kidding. A bald-egg-on-legs, he sauntered towards us and took his place in the front row.

The audible intake of breath sounded like a pneumatic drill.

The publicity shot was cancelled.

I found Pierce later, in the make-up room, mowing any remaining stubble from his scalp. Rondah, Phoebe and Ping were there too, fussing over Cosmo, who'd been sick again. Cosmo was the only person the three actresses were ever nice to. This was mainly because of the fact that *they* knew that *he* knew more about them than anyone alive. Cosmo had seen them all exposed, meek, naked, immobilised in the make-up chair. He alone had a full inventory of every wrinkle, crinkle, dimple. He alone had the power to make them look like a dog's breakfast.

'So kid,' Pierce said, as I approached him. 'What profession d'you think I'd be good at? Astronaut? Postman? Hey, what about President? Actually I've always fancied running a helluva good Chinese restaurant.'

I tried to make my face look artistic and articulate. Every time he glanced at me, I would pop an eye, flare a nostril, or cock an eyebrow.

'Yeah, it could be the rudest goddamned Chinese restaurant in the world,' he enthused, razor buzzing. 'All the meals could be called things like "Long Cock Soup". Or "Hot Fuck Duck" ... Hey, you couldn't lend me your pay cheque till the end of the week could you? I'm like, totally tapped out.' He switched off the motor on his razor. 'Well?'

'I . . . I can't. I owe rent.' Pierce shrugged and resumed shaving. 'Are you really going to quit?' I curled a lip provocatively, while looking up from beneath lowered lids.

'You betcha. I've had enough of this shit hole. Christ,' Pierce, glancing at my reflection in the mirror, asked nervously, 'you're not gonna barf again are ya? Your face has gone all kinda weird.'

'Won't you miss it?' I asked, relaxing my facial muscles. 'I mean the adoration, the fan mail.'

'Jesus Chrrrrist. You've read my fan mail? It's either from weirdo sex freaks or goddamned five-year-olds. The majority say, "I love you. I have two sisters and a cat and I live with my mom and dad." Although, look what I got today.' He extracted a condom from his pocket. Attached to it was a stamped, addressed envelope and a card reading 'Pierce, please fill and return'. 'Weird, huh?'

I felt my face warming up for its beetroot impersonation. 'But everyone in America wants what you've got. Fame, fortune, fast cars. I mean, it's the American religion. You're like a High Priest. You're like a – '

'God. The Gospel according to Abe Epstein. Has he offered you a poodle yet? We've all got one of those four-legged tea-cosies. I got mine four years ago when he promised me my own spin-off series. I keep the stupid mutt around to remind me never to believe anyone or anything in television.'

Cosmo, prising himself free of Rondah's clutches, affectionately rubbed his hand over Pierce's stubbly head. 'You've been summoned,' he said, his voice funereal.

'Come with me,' Pierce ordered.

'No,' I said – minimally.

Pierce seized my elbow and steered me towards Abe's office. He barged right in.

Abe's office was a shrine to quickly acquired wealth. Every square inch was crammed with ostentatious antiques. There were glass cabinets full of firearms (old Abe was forever going off to do courses entitled 'Learn to Shoot for Protection And Sport'), plus his collection of miniature model sports cars, which just happened to ape his lifesize assortment. But today the office looked completely different. I counted twelve, drop-dead-gorgeous male specimens, slouched in a nonchalant row. They wore denim shirts. Just like Pierce. They wore sockless topsiders. Just like Pierce. Their hair hung over one eye and a small pigtail bunched at the back of each neck. Just like Pierce – when he *had* hair that is.

Abe sucked on his Cuban truncheon, letting the ash cascade to the floor. 'Zere are plenty more vere you came from.' He pushed a piece of paper across the table. It was Pierce's contract. 'I've added a clauze saying you vill undergo zum "image maintenance".' Pierce's gaze passed slowly around the room, and finally came to rest on me.

'Pierce, what about the rudest Chinese restaurant?'

Abe picked up the pen and unscrewed the gold-tipped top. 'Besides, vot uzzer studio vill hire you vunce zey find out about your leetle problem, huh?'

Pierce looked from Abe to me and back again, snatched the pen, scrawled across the dotted line, turned on his heel and headed for the door.

'Crocodile Dundette,' Abe said sternly, as I made to follow. 'Stay right vere you are.' Recalling Abe's kennel of four-legged tea-cosies, I kept walking. 'Remember vot I said,' his voice trailed after me. 'Zere's plenty more vere *you* came from too.'

I caught up with Pierce in the car park. He was already behind the wheel of his freshly-sprayed car, engine gunned. 'What does he mean, your little problem?'

'Nothin'.'

'Pierce, let's talk.'

'Can't.'

'Well, what about tonight?'

'What? Oh, Jesus. Look, I gotta see a pal, okay? He's um, got this sick llama, see? It's overheating.' He turned and saw that I had my pay cheque extended towards him. 'Llamas are very sensitive to stress and strain.' He snatched the cheque, the engine flared and he left me there on the kerb choking on car exhaust. Personally I couldn't see why he needed help maintaining his image. The thing about Pierce was that he was so reliable – always there when he needed you.

VALENTINE'S DAY

When I got home that night the house was quiet. 'Tash?' I found her sitting all alone on her bed, laced into thigh-high boots and a black bra, a beautiful champagne flute in one hand, and nursing the biggest box of condoms in the entire world. 'Economy size,' it read.

She raised her glass to me. 'Happy Valentine's Day.'

'Is it?'

'Yeah. Two women all alone on Valentine's Day. How fuckin' symbolic.'

Another full glass of champagne sat fizzing by her side. 'Where's Andy/Sandy/Chuck/Hank?' I asked, kicking off my shoes.

'Bernard.'

I removed the huge box of condoms from her lap and placed it on the carpet. 'What? Didncha have his size?' I gibed as I plonked down on the bed.

She rolled her heavily made-up eyes. Honestly, she wore so much make-up, it must have been like weight-lifting her lids. 'Ya know wot? I thought he really liked me.' Her lipstick had smeared over the line of her lips and her too-red rouge was smudged. 'I told him I had herpes and he, like, freaked.'

I looked at her bleakly. 'You've got *herpes*?' I freaked.

'*Everyone* in LA's got herpes,' she said with casual calm, as though diagnosing a cold. 'The prick leapt off the bed like I had leprosy for Chrissake.'

'Really?' I said, leaping off the bed as though she had leprosy. I backed towards the door. I planned to disinfect the entire bedroom. The bathroom. The whole house. The entire neighbourhood.

'Ya can't catch it. God, girl, where do ya live?' she admonished. '*In a box*? It's only contagious about three goddamned times a year. Jee-zus, I can't believe how he sucked me in. I should've known. I mean, these days if a guy says he "wantsta getta know ya better" it just means he's trying to find out whether or not you've had an AIDS test.' She drained her champagne glass in one go, then ran her forefinger around the lip which emitted a high-pitched squeal.

'Nice glasses,' I ventured, 'Did Bernard . . . ?'

'It's stoo-pid gettin' presents from men. It's dishonest. I mean, why thuh hell not just sleep with 'em for money?'

'Oh Tash, don't flog them. They're too nice to – '

'Kat, I owe C.J. six thou. I've only raised two and a half. These oughta bring in a hundred bucks maybe.'

'Speaking of money. About the rent . . .'

'Chrrrist, Katrina. Where is all ya money goin', girl?' Tash drew up her formidable breasts. 'Ya didn't give in to that creep again, did ya?' Tash took a gulp from the full champagne flute this time. She now had a glass in each hand. 'God, we're too soft. That's our problem. Ya see what happens when ya show a guy any vulnerability at all? J'know,' Tash said, 'I have this over-powerin' urge to murder every man I've ever met – and my period's not due for *ages*.'

'Me too,' I confessed, flopping back on the bed.

'Here,' Tash passed me the bottle of champagne. 'Console yaself. Pierce would've been shitty in bed anyway. Good-lookin' men always are. 'Cause they don't have to try hard. Go for an ugly, scrawny lookin' poet or somethin' next time, will ya?'

Tash was right. My lack of imagination suddenly appalled me. I should have fallen for a Lithuanian librarian or a hunchbacked nuclear physicist. I was so clichéd. So predictable. I hadn't lost my heart to Pierce Scanlen; I had lost my mind.

Tash wet her finger again, and ran it round the rim of the glass faster and faster. 'Okay. It's time for a Survival Technique. Clit-ori-decto-mies,' she enunciated. 'J'know there are countries in this world where they still do female circumcision? Gross huh? Jordan, Indonesia, Southern Saudi Arabia.' All of a sudden, her arm shot forward, sending one of the glasses hurtling across the room where it shattered into the wall. 'Parts of Iraq, Iran and the fuckin' Sudan,' she shouted, sending the other champagne flute into flight. We both sat in stunned silence looking at the glass shrapnel. 'Shit,' she said finally. 'They were crystal too. Rejection brings out the worst in me.'

Just as well I hadn't eaten any lunch. I had a feeling it was going to be a *ten*-cake night.

'Oh well. Back where I began. $2,564 bucks.' Tash took the bottle from my hands and swigged at it. 'I've decided I'm gonna become a Feminist. Which means *no more men.*'

'Oh come on, you can be a Feminist and still like men.'

'Kat, get real! That'd be like bein' a vegetarian and still eatin' meat.'

I propped myself up on one elbow. 'It depends on the sort of man. Just like it depends on the sort of meat. I mean, you can be a vegetarian and still eat fish, right?'

'Well, I'm gonna be a *Vegan* Feminist then. From now on, I'm having a social diet completely free of *animal* products.' Tash took another swig from the bottle and passed it to me.

I thought of Pierce, of the ease with which he could lie, of the love-bites on his mirror. 'Me too. No more men on our menu, right?' I put my mouth over the bottle, tilted back my head and swallowed.

'Right!'

We slumped back against the lace pillows, silently passing the bottle back and forth between us.

'J'know,' Tash said sadly, after staring at the ceiling for a full five minutes, 'that more people attempt suicide on Valentine's Day than on any other day of the year?'

Make that a *twenty*-cake night.

Then, as though electrocuted, Tash leapt out of bed, tugged off her boots and started peeling down her tights, the nylon tendrils winding round her ankles.

'Okay, let's go out dancin' and get some uppers and get stoned off our faces and stay up till dawn. I need to *relax*.'

In another attempt to cure me of Pierce, Tash took me to a mystery club. I looked around. Loud music; pools of vomit in the loo; patrons slumped, legs splayed, heads lolling when their owners forgot to prop them up with their fists. It just looked like every other bar I'd ever been to. It seemed such an ordinary social cocktail: agenty-types on the take, actors on the make, mixed in with the usual male and female Barbie dolls, preened and creamed to perfection. I couldn't work it out. My only clue was my drink coaster. It was embossed with the name 'Simplex'. I frisbeed a coaster across to Tash, who was poised on the lip of a stool opposite me. 'I don't get it.'

'Simplex. Herpes Simplex. It takes the anxiety out of datin'.'

'You mean,' I said, anxiously, 'that everyone here has . . . that they've all got . . .'

'Put it this way, if some dude tells you about his personal growth, he ain't talkin' EST.'

Tash folded her lips around a pale green olive, sucked it into her mouth, then snapped the toothpick in two and flicked it into the ashtray. 'Ya see,' she said, warming to her theme, 'there's a new etiquette in LA. It goes like this – ' she paused to swallow her mouthful. 'Ya go on a date right? Things get, well, amorous. Ya tell the guy that you've got herpes. He freaks. You then give him your gyno's card. He then gets *his* doctor to ring *your* gyno. The doctors converse. After consultin' their calendars and comparin' the stress and biorhythms of their patients, doctors then advise their respective clients that it's safe to bonk on the third of June, at three p.m. 1995. And by that time,' she took a sip of her cocktail and was lost momentarily in the ornamental foliage, 'ya've prob'ly gone and gotta new disease and have to start all over again.'

'Gee. How romantic.' I suddenly became aware of the stool on which I was sitting. My dress was short and the seat was vinyl. It felt extremely hot and sticky. I was practically levitating, let me tell you. I decided then and there that from now on, I would only have relationships with Franciscan monks. And even then I would cover myself in neck-to-knee spermicide, wear six cervical caps and use a full-length condom. And that was just for phone-sex.

'But hey. It don't matter anymore, right? Now that we're Vegan Feminists. Drink up.' I took a sip of my cocktail. Tash nodded approvingly then suddenly sat up to attention. A young bloke was ricocheting across the room. He seemed to bounce from pillar to table to stool, collide with dancers, then rebound backwards or sideways into someone else. He was like one of those silver balls in a pinball machine. I knew from the languid limbs and the gleam of his shaven head that it was Pierce.

'Fuck off, ya schmuck,' a dynamic-looking girl with long, jet black hair advised him, as he sent a huge tumbler of icy cocktail into her lap.

'Well, you're helluva witty lady, aren'cha?' Pierce drawled, making an ineffectual mopping motion in her general direction. 'Did you think that up all by yourself?' Losing his balance, he made a grab for her, clutching at the long black ponytail. It came away in his hand. He looked at it as though it were a dead rat. Pierce lifted his eyes to hers with great effort. 'Don't fret Contessa. Your secret is safe with me, for I too am of noble birth.'

Tash was watching me closely. The DJ was playing 'My Funny Valentine'. 'Your looks are laughable,' the crowd crooned along, 'unphotographable. Yet you're my favourite work of art.'

Tash's fingers closed around my forearm. 'What happened to no more men on the menu?'

Shaking her free, I was on my feet and moving towards him, when it suddenly hit me where I was. If Pierce saw me here, in this club, he'd think I had herpes. God. I was having enough trouble getting him into bed while he didn't think I had herpes, let alone when he thought that I did. But, then again, what was he doing here? So that was why he hadn't made a move on me yet. He had herpes. In the time it took for all of this to seep through my muddled mind, Pierce, braying like a donkey, had attached the girl's switch to the back pocket of his jeans, hunkered down on all fours, kicked a famous film producer in the groin, and been tucked under the arm of a large bouncer with missing teeth. The only good thing was that, with his clean shaven head – an egg-shell blond we called it at home – nobody had recognised him. 'Each day is Valentine's Day,' the song purred on.

By the time I'd navigated my way outside, Pierce was lying in a pile of crumpled designer clothes in the car park.

'Have to take a piss,' he said, as I helped him to his feet. As he unzipped his fly, I retrieved his possessions. Along with the wallet and car keys, I found at least six plastic vials of multi-coloured pills. Nudging them down the drain I heard the soft hiss of his urine as it hit the wall behind me. It struck me that Pierce's piss would have a street value of about $6,000. So *this* was what all the money was for.

'So, how's the old llama?' I asked witheringly. The membership of the Southern Californian Skeptics Club had just gone up by one.

'Huh? Llama? Oh. Shit. The llama. Sick. Real sick. The llama is not looking good, kid. Shit.' He started groping round on the ground.

'Where's your girlfriend, then?'

'Huh?'

'Your girlfriend. You know, your "minimalist"?'

'Who? Oh yeah. Right. Um, yeah, well, we broke up.' Even stoned off his face, this guy was quick on his feet. 'Eons ago. See, the point is, kid, I'm too goddamned busy for a relationship. I go to bed stoned outta my brain and wake up so strung-out that I just have to get stoned again. And, well, there's just no time in between for anythin' else. Where are my goddamned pills?'

Snippets of music drifted into the cark park. I recognised a song by that Terence Trent d'Arby bloke. 'Sign your name across my heart,' it warbled, 'I want you to be my baby.' I luxuriated, just for a fleeting moment, in the idea that Pierce would sign my heart, would be my baby – then just as suddenly dismissed it. It sounded so, well, *Californian*. 'I want you to know ... that I'm not here 'cause ... I mean, see, actually, I came with a friend ... What I'm trying to say is that *I* don't have ... Do *you* have?'

'What?'

'It.'

'What it?'

'*It* it. *You* know.'

'No. I don't know. Where for Chrissake are my ... ? God. Is this my head? Or did my neck throw up?'

'Look, you don't have to lie. I mean, why else would you be here?'

'Where am I?'

'The Simplex Club.'

'Oh, is that where I am. Who did I come with?'

'If you *do* have, you know, I mean if you *do*, it's okay. *I* don't have it, that is, but if *you* do ... And, I mean, it's only contagious about three times a year, right?'

Pierce got back to his feet. He seemed suddenly sane again and stared at me steadily. 'What? Herpes? No. But that's a definite reason not ever to get involved with me, kiddo.' He touched my arm, absentmindedly, the same way people drum their fingers on a table-top. 'I'm sure I'm in a high-risk category. For herpes *and* AIDS and just about anythin' else that's goin'. And I'm not just *high*-risk, I'm ten-storeys-high-risk. I'm the World-Trade-Towers-high-risk. So, I'd stay right away from me if I were you. For Chrissake, where did I . . .' He rummaged once more through his clothing.

'Pierce,' I said, tucking his pills deeper into my pockets, 'why are you taking so many drugs? It's so bloody dangerous.'

'Well, it does limit my chances of being run over by a bus. Besides, this is LA, for Chrissake. A drug habit is a goddamned status symbol round here. Like a limo. Besides, I can handle it. Shit.' Pierce grabbed my arm to steady himself. 'Now I'm goin' back inside to find out who I came with. I just hope I had the good sense to come with someone who does drugs.'

Insects flitted around the fluorescent light high above the car park. I stood below them, in the dark, feeling the pressure of his fingers long after he'd taken his hand away.

So. That was it, I decided later that night, lying in my room. I was just going to have to learn to do drugs.

The debris of Tash's day lay abandoned on her bed. I sifted through the flotsam and jetsam of black boots, bondage ropes, a large pink dildo looking oddly exposed in the lamp light, school tunics, wigs, a box of false nails and a jar of opaque jelly jammed full of ball bearings. (I didn't even want to think about what she did with that lot.) But where, I wondered, was Tash's drug stash? I was sure she'd kept some for a rainy night. Ferreting through her possessions, I longed to be more like my best friend, brave, bold, tough as a toenail. I rooted through the usual hiding places: the toes of hardly worn shoes, the bottoms of tampax boxes, between the covers of a hardback bible. I found lots of things I didn't expect to find – a 2,000 piece jigsaw puzzle of the English Royal Family, half-finished; an Annette Funicello mouseketeer hat; a Girl Scouts 'Sewing Achievement' certificate and a school prefect's badge. But nothing as astounding as what I discovered on top of the cupboard.

Shoved back out of sight, against the wall, was a suitcase, blanketed in dust. It was locked. Feeling along the lip of the wardrobe door, my fingers fumbled on to the key. As I levered open the corroded lid, I was assailed by a chaos of scents. Standing on tiptoe, I plunged my hands into the box. It rattled with empty perfume bottles of all brands, shapes and sizes, hoarded away, just as I'd done as a kid with mum's cosmetic cast-offs, to scent my sock drawer.

Gob-smacked, I sifted through a botanic garden of dried and shrivelled floral bouquets. There were baby brag books – empty. Wedding invitations – empty. Photo albums embossed with wedding bells and love doves – all empty. As empty, in fact, as the eyes of the wrinkle-and-pimple-free young women on cover after cover of a magazine called *Bride to Be*. A matching battalion of blow-waved grooms beamed out at me from pamphlets advertising wedding reception centres, honeymoon destinations, marriage insurance contracts, dental plans for newly weds.

The breath went out of my body. Knowing Tash as I did, this box seemed as mysterious as Ming's tomb. I excavated further and found white stockings, unworn; white garters, unsnapped; a moulting teddy bear wearing an 'I Wuv You' T-shirt; heart-shaped cards of the sunset-teary-eyed-orphan-type, wishing non-existent couples happy engagements and blissful marriages. Finally, at the very bottom, lay a pair of white knickers embossed with a plastic cupid who played 'This Magic Moment' when touched.

I stood there, transfixed with embarrassment. It was as though I'd stumbled upon a spy-hole to Tash's personality. Even though the bed below me was strewn with the sexual detritus of Tash's day, it was this box, its secret contents, which made me squeamish with embarrassment. Losing my balance, I grabbed at the box with both hands. The underpants burst into song, serenading me with 'This magic moment, with your lips so close to mine' as I hurtled to the floor. I scrambled back up on to the dressing-table to slam the lid shut but nothing could silence those underpants. Though muffled, the tinny strains followed me across the room . . . 'will last forever, until the end of time'. They were still warbling ten minutes later when I dashed back into the room and blew along the wardrobe wood to remove all trace of my fingerprints.

CHOCOLATE CRAVINGS

'Pyjama,' Tash said, nudging her pimpmobile out into the traffic without even glancing into her rear-view mirror. 'Pyjama,' she repeated, as horns bleated and brakes squealed. 'Come on Kat, ya're not even tryin'.'

'Vasco da Gama,' I suggested half-heartedly.

'Who?' Having still only saved a total of $3,465, Tash's latest idea was to write a hit love-song for Madonna. An old boyfriend of Tash's worked for Madonna's recording company and had promised, in return for a grope or two, to get it to her. 'Pyjama, drama?' she glanced over at me. 'Whadda'bout drama, huh?' I sighed dismissively. 'Panorama?' she attempted, swerving to avoid a speed bump.

'Tash, will ya keep your eyes on the bloody . . .'

'I've gotta finish this song by tomorrow, Kat. Pyjama,' she repeated as she sped into the supermarket car park on two wheels. While we waited by the boom barrier, she looked at me pleadingly.

'Well, God, I don't know. I'm not feeling very inspired. Pyjama, karma?'

'What *you've* got lots of. Except it's all *bad*.' She slammed out of the car. It was true. Since Pierce had been banned from the set a month ago (we were still waiting for his hair to grow back), I'd been moping around, broke and miserable. Tash had done her best to cheer me up and not complain about my overdue rent, but you could see I was starting to get on her nerves. Not in a major way or anything. She just told me, in her usual understated fashion, that my presence was getting to be like a mild case of thrush. I loped after her through the turnstile into the labyrinth of laminex aisles. The row of trolleys, locked together, looked like a chrome centipede. Frustrated shoppers were playing tug-of-war with them. Some were even down on their knees, begging trolleys to please come quietly.

I caught up with Tash in the confectionery section, by the 'Easter Bargains' bin. A whole clutch of cardboard bunny rabbits, in tinsel and bowties and top hats, dangled from the ceiling above. Tash selected a packet of chocolate Easter eggs and ran her newly lacquered nail down the calorie contents table of its cellophane underbelly. 'God, if only guys came under the same packaging laws. Then you could find out what they're really made of.' She replaced the packet and selected another. 'Ten per cent malice, twenty-five per cent artificial sweeteners.'

'Yeah,' I laughed, lightening up for the first time in weeks. 'The number of preservatives added. Undetectable toupee. False teeth.'

'Youth Hair Restorer. Ugh. I hate that stuff. It always leaves this revoltin' orange ring on the pillow. Like rust.'

'Yeah, and by then it's too late. You've got Bedroom Botulism.'

'Oooh look. Caramel-filled.' Tash bent to extract her favourite Easter cookies from the back of the shelf. 'Gee, Kat, I think ya might be gettin' a cravin' for those later.' Tash was about to deposit the biscuits in the trolley, but paused to hold the packet up to my face. I looked at the moreish photograph. 'Looks good, huh?' Her eyes glinted. 'Well, listen to this.' She rattled off a list of the chemical contents, a diabolical cocktail of sugars and sweeteners. 'They're lethal. These cookies could kill. That's what happens when ya get hooked on somethin' that looks good. It's the same with guys. "Ooh, yum," ya think – "great pectorals." It ain't till ya read the packaging contents that ya find out the dude's a dud product.'

I groaned loudly. I'd been waiting for her to have another crack at Pierce. She hadn't mentioned him for at least one whole hour. Snatching the packet of killer cookies from her hand, I defiantly slit open the cellophane and gobbled one whole.

'Look Kat. Love is like a chocolate cravin' . . .' Tash steered the trolley with one hand while she ran the lacquered talons of her other hand along a shelf of 'Hot Fudge Upside Down Easter Sunday Decadence Cake'. 'Love is a chemical addiction,' she lectured, her fingers lingering near the Turkish Delights before she wrapped them firmly around the handle bar of our trolley. 'And ya gotta resist. I mean,' she exclaimed, moving rapidly on to Nibbles and Nuts, 'the guy's a *jerk*,' Tash called back to me. 'What can ya possibly see in an asshole like him?'

I picked up a packet of dull, dry crackers and examined it with elaborate interest, while I thought about Pierce. What *did* I like about him? . . . I liked the fact that he'd worked out how many years of your life you spend trying to ring up people. He was the only person I knew who had wondered if *God* saw *people* when He took acid. I liked the way he touched me all the time. Unlike Aussie blokes, Pierce Scanlen was fluent in body language. I liked the way he wondered why he couldn't tickle himself. And how could I *not* like a bloke who'd faked an orgasm with a prostitute because he didn't want to hurt her feelings? I liked him for the battered paperbacks he always had on him. My father reckoned that Californians only ever read menus, Tarot cards and bank balances. I felt like a water-diviner in some desert. My stick just wobbled when I was near him. Maybe when I found his hidden well it would be stagnant or silted up or toxic or something. I didn't know. But I would find it.

Tash was glowering at me. 'Well?' she said impatiently, tapping out a tune with the toe and heel of her shoe.

I shrugged. 'He's funny. He makes me laugh.'

'Funny? Chrrrrist. Even inanimate objects have more personality than Pierce. A toilet seat. A toenail clipper!' Turning on a spiky heel, Tash gripped the handlebar of our trolley and abruptly manoeuvred it out into the stream of trolley traffic. There were shouts and curses as three or four shopping vehicles collided behind us. Oblivious, Tash accelerated down the aisle. The trolleys' club-wheel meant that we kept lurching sideways, mowing down customers. At the crossroad, she swerved into Frozen Foods. 'Just forget him,' she snapped at me, frisbeeing packets of Fish Fingers and pizzas and Chicken Bits into the trolley. 'The guy's a selfish asshole livin' out the Hollywood Brat Pack cliché, takin' too many designer drugs, lookin' all wan and wasted an' havin' people say, "Oh he has so much potential . . ." He's just locked like *forever* in adolescence. It's pathetic. Par-thetic.'

The trolley skidded precariously close to a stand of Instant Dairy Whip. 'Look,' she said when I caught up with her. 'Ya can getta lotta things in America.' She gestured up and down the aisles to the products of every imaginable type in every imaginable flavour. There were pagodas of imported fruit, pyramids of hand-made, brightly wrapped chocolates, Taj Mahals of exotic teas. 'Ya can getta mink jumpsuit worth $20,000 bucks. Ya can get an expresso machine for your goddamned car. Ya can getta stereo system for ya pet rodents. But not *love*. That's one commodity Hollywood don't stock. We're too cynical. Am I gettin' through to ya, girl?' Tash marched on ahead of me, her neck drawn up, her back stiff, her shoulder-blades sticking out sharply through her cotton T-shirt.

'Tash,' I trotted after her, appeasing with tiny, nervous smiles the irate shoppers she'd run over, 'I didn't want to fall in love with Pierce. But love just, sort of, I dunno, seeks you out,' I shrugged hopelessly.

'Seeks ya out?' she scoffed. 'Ya make it sound like a Cruise Missile.'

'Well . . .' I squirmed under her gaze. 'It is a bit like that.'

'Romance was invented by advertisers to sell breath-fresheners and panty-liners. I'm immune to all that crap, thank Chrrrrist. If I can't eat it or fuck it, I'm not interested.'

'Stop actin' so tough. That's bullshit. You care about other stuff.'

'Yeah, True. You're right.' Her face softened for a second and I looked at her hopefully. 'Drugs. I care about drugs. And orgasms.'

'Well, then, what about the stuff on the top of your wardrobe?' The words had marched out of my mouth before I realised they'd left base-camp.

Our trolley collided into the one in front of us. They locked together as though copulating. Tash's knuckles on the handlebar were clenched white, the veins in her tiny hands bulging. 'Whaddaya mean?'

'Nothing.' My heart felt like it was doing a Jane Fonda work-out all by itself in my chest. Picking up a frozen chook I examined the cooking instructions in minute detail.

Wrenching the trolley free, Tash butted it towards me. 'WHADDAYA MEAN?'

'Tash.' The chook fell to the floor, skidding across the aisle. 'Watch it! Jesus.' I slammed the trolley back at her. She charged me again. I dodged it, matador-style.

It seemed as though we were marooned in the middle of the longest supermarket lane in the world. It was as wide as a highway and just as congested with people and prams and renegade shopping carts. The customers who'd been bustling and shoving to get by, their arms festooned with brightly coloured plastic bags advertising everything from baked beans to peek-a-boo bras, now stood and stared. The sign above us read 'We Take the Worry Out of Shopping'.

I tentatively grabbed her arm. Don't say it, I said to myself, don't say it, and then, of course, I said it. 'The box. On top of your wardrobe. It's full of baby books and bridal bouquets and booties and – ' Tash jerked away from me as though I were a live socket – 'and singing underpants,' I added in a small voice.

Tash shrank before my eyes. The colour left her body. Then a sudden surge of rage consumed my friend. 'How dare ya snoop round in my room!' she yelled.

'I wasn't snooping, I was just – '

'That box don't mean nuthin'. I'll dump it. I'd just forgotten about the fuckin' thing that's all.'

'Look, I wouldn't have mentioned it, only that it does seem off – the way you put me down for believing in love. It's a bit hypocritical that's all.'

'Hypocritical?' she detonated. 'You're the goddamned hypocrite. Here ya are constantly whinin' about your father bein' this bludgin', selfish schmuck. And then ya go and fall in love with a bludgin', selfish schmuck. Don't talk to me about hypocritical!' With a mighty thrust, she hurled the trolley towards me. I dodged to one side, and it thudded into the mountain of Dairy Whip cans, sending them crashing in all directions – just like a special effect in one of Abe's sitcoms. I watched the domino effect down the aisle with horror; ricocheting cans collided with other tin pyramids, which in turn collapsed, haemorrhaging their contents across the floor.

I glanced around. Tash was strutting down the aisle. 'Tash. Tash! I'm sorry!' I ran after her, ankle-deep in the debris we'd created. 'What about the song? Iguana,' I called out after her. 'Botswana. Armour, um, embalmer? Wait, I've got it, Llama?'

The hem of her skirt twitched crossly as it rounded the corner of the aisle. By the time I got there, she was nowhere to be seen. A battalion of staff stood staring at me. I smiled feebly.

Not only was I made to reconstruct the tin monuments but I had to put everything in our trolley back where I'd found it. Tash hadn't left me any money and Pierce had pocketed all mine.

Walking home up San Vicente, I thought over what Tash had said. Maybe love was nothing more than the romantic equivalent of a chocolate craving? I had definitely been gorging daily on a family-size block of self-pity. Why had I ever wanted to fall in love in the first frigging place, I asked myself? I had always prided myself on my will-power. When my gang at school, Cara, Fang, Chook and Co, went through the obligatory hippy stage, I was the only one in Year Ten not to fall for one of the swarm of pseudo-swamis who were doing the rounds. When they got into heavy metal head-banging, I was the only one not to take up smoking and sleeping with the band. Even when we all went punk, I was the only one not to pass the time nipple-piercing and arm-tattooing. I had a finely-tuned crap-antenna. I could give a man a hairy eyeball as soon as look at him. The truth was, I was just not the type to fall in love. It wasn't in my blood. I mean, look at my parents. My Oldies had a His and Her Honeymoon. *His* was in the remand section of Long Bay jail, and *Hers* was working two jobs to get his bail. You see, it wasn't until they were married that she discovered dad had a record as long as a Wagnerian opera, three ex-wives, a drinking problem, a debt to the Marrickville Mafia of $8,000 and that he'd recently taken out a similar amount of life insurance on her. When she confronted him with all this, do you know what he said? That *the first few weeks of marriage were always a settling-in period.*

And now Tash was telling me I'd fallen for a man just like *him*? My stomach tightened. The very idea was totally pukesville. She was right. 'Love' *was* just a matter of having an emotional sweet tooth. It was time to go on a romance diet. Starve myself of his company. Book myself into the Betty Ford Clinic for Incurable Romantics. Love sucked.

When I got home, the house was in darkness except for the message light on the answering machine, blinking insistently in the gloom. I pressed 'play'. It was Pierce asking me if I wanted to drive down to his parents' place for the Easter break.

I started packing. Like I said, I'd always prided myself on my will-power.

SMOTHER-LOVE

Pierce's parents lived in Palm Springs, a shimmering city smack-bang in the middle of the desert a few hours out of LA. We drove down Frank Sinatra Way and Dinah Shore Drive. Pierce pointed to a gi-normous pink house on the rocky ridge above us. It loomed over the entire town like a mutated butterfly.

'What's that? Some kinda temple?'

Pierce snorted. 'Yep. Sure is, kid. That's where we joke-nig-gers' – his name for people who worked on sitcoms – 'come to pay homage to the great Joke Master in the sky.' We flashed past the street sign. It read 'Bob Hope Drive'.

The wind was hot, as though someone had turned a hair dryer on us. The whole place gave me the same feeling in my guts I'd had at Abe's party. The same sensation that something was missing. But *here*, I couldn't figure it. I asked Pierce if he could put his finger on the problem.

'No blacks. No Hispanics,' he said automatically. Pierce drove casually, one lean forearm lying along the hot metal rim of the open window. The wind whipped his little pigtail up behind his head like an antenna. Perhaps now he'd receive the messages I'd been sending for the past eight months. 'Earth to Pierce,' I secretly transmitted. 'Come to bed with me.'

Pierce swung into the driveway of a place called the Palm Springs Paradise Country Club. Fences topped with discreet twists of designer barbed wire, surrounded the entire compound.

Pierce wound down the window and inserted a plastic security card into the slot. The huge iron gates groaned open. We drove along perfectly paved and empty streets, with regulation-sized trees and short-back-and-sides lawns. Sealed off from the outside world, it was all safe and sterile. As though it were a side arm,

Pierce aimed a remote-control gadget at the garage door of a large condominium. 'My parents' place,' he said. The garage yawned open as Pierce eased the car inside. The door sucked shut behind us.

'Why do they live *here*?' We climbed out of the car and the air-conditioned cold slammed into us. It was like running smack-bang up against an iceberg.

'For the air,' he sneered. 'They came here for the hot, dry air and then, 'cause it's so hot and dry, they spend all their time inside in the goddamned air-conditioning. And that,' he said grandly, 'is America for you. My mother,' he warned, hauling my bag out of the backseat, 'is unbearable. What do you eat by the way?'

'Oh everything,' I bellowed above the tape still thudding out of the car speakers, 'except chilli. And anything with tentacles.'

'Tentacles?'

'You know seafoody stuff. It makes me kinda squeamish.'

He snapped off the music. 'Well, whatever we're havin' it will be Ideologically Sound, that's for sure. See, my mom's a Born-Again-Greenie. That means no food from Alaska, Iran . . .'

'Alaska? Why on earth . . .'

'The clubbing of seal cubs. Iran – mad mullahs. South Africa – sanctions . . . Basically, all we're left with are a few Nicaraguan coffee beans and New Zealand zucchini.'

'Oh yum,' I said despondently.

'She also hates people who wear leather.' He yanked the tongue of my belt. 'Or make-up,' and ran his finger around the line of my lips. 'She's a bitch basically. And my father is pussy-whipped. I only see them when I need money.'

As I struggled to unthread my belt through the denim loops, Pierce opened the side door and we stepped into a mirrored hall, offering me about twenty different images of Pierce's taut, tanned and totally aerobic mother who stood waiting to greet us.

'Dah-ling!' She launched herself at her son, locked her arms around his neck and dangled there. Pierce winced. 'Running short of cash again? I only see him,' she vaguely addressed me, 'when he needs money. Isn't that right dah-ling?' She smiled up into her son's face. 'Well the answer is No. What? No kissy-wissy for Mumsey-wumsey?' Pierce, looking as though he was at the dentist's for a filling, dutifully lowered his expressionless face. His mother's lips lingered on his cheek. 'Oh, I'd forgotten. You really do have the most beautiful skin. Always has,' she said in my general direction. 'Especially on that cute little butt of his.' With that, she yanked down on his tracksuit pants, revealing two perfectly rounded buttocks.

'Mom. For Chrissake.' He pushed her roughly away and retrieved his trousers from half-mast. Mrs Scanlen was examining me with an expression of mild hunger. When I turned towards her, she regally extended a cheek, making a vague 'kissy' noise somewhere in the vicinity of my earhole. 'And *who* are *you*?'

'Kat. Katrina Kennedy.' Her expression was now carnivorous. I patted my wild wads of hair. Her blue eyes travelled the length of my body. Twice. I tucked my nail-polished fingers up into my palms and waited for her to volunteer her name. She didn't. 'And, um, who are you?' I asked finally, dimly registering that perhaps this was not the right thing to do.

Her left brow executed a gymnastic trick halfway up her forehead. 'Lydia. Lydia Reece-Scanlen.' She was an ironclad, firmly coiled woman with a well-preserved shape shown off in a tailored jogging suit, the top of which was studded with badges reading, 'Solar Not Nuclear'; 'Feed The Poor, No More War'; 'Think Globally, Act Locally'.

'And what do you *do*?'

There was a loud rumbling from my abdominal area. It sounded like an orchestra was tuning up in there. I realised that I hadn't eaten for about a day. 'I um, work on the show, with Pierce.'

'Oh. Mar-vellous,' she said neutrally, scooping bags and packages from Pierce's arms and leading the way inside. The orchestra in my stomach was now launching into the gastronomic version of Beethoven's Fifth. Mrs Scanlen glanced at me with faint disdain. 'I do hope you're hungry. I've concocted a rather *wonderful* bouillabaisse. I've been cooking the stock for about *two years*.'

The air-conditioning was working its way through to my marrow. I shivered. 'Bouill-a-what?' I asked nervously.

The mother of the man I loved looked at me as though I was a spastic retard. 'Delicacies from the Garden of the Sea,' she pronounced superciliously.

Pierce winked conspiratorially, as we followed his mother into the condominium.

His mother sent Pierce away to get the mulberry (no colourings or preservatives added) organic champagne. 'You may not realise this,' Mrs Scanlen confided, firmly guiding me into a chair, 'but Pierce is a mistake. I call him "The Incredible Jumping Sperm".' Pierce Snr and I were using the Rhythm Method because I was worried about the side-effects of the pill, and IUDs, well, I was right about *them* wasn't I, what with Delcon Shield law suits. And so Mr Scanlen was withdrawing.' Pierce's mother was one of the 'tell-all' types common on the West coast of America. 'So be careful. Diaphragms are best I think. Or cervical caps. Pierce is only a baby himself. We don't want any accidents now, do we dear?'

Before I could explain that we hadn't so much as touched tongues, let alone done the horizontal tango, she took hold of my chin and sort of wrenched me forward to face her. 'You're terribly pale, dear. Are your bowels all right? I get *terribly* constipated when I travel. Oz-trail-yan. Well. We've never had an Oz-trail-yan before. You *are* a novelty.' She crossed to the big bookcase – the first bookcase I'd seen in America actually – and retrieved a leather-bound photo album. She positioned herself at my side and flicked through the brightly coloured collection of photographs. Pierce beamed out at me from every page. It was like looking at a brochure for the different doll models in the Ken range. And the Barbie dolls were there too. A new one in every shot, draped decorously on Pierce's arm, smiling seductively. 'Amanda, oh yes, *she* was nice. Beautiful figure. Oh and Susan. Oh yes. Just look at that mane of lovely hair.' She traced the face of each beautiful Barbie with a nail. 'Mary-Ellen, lovely, delicate hands, perfect skin, I remember, and soft, lovely eyes. Oh and Blair! Now *there* was a beauty. So poised, so graceful, with the most gentle, supple hands and soft, soft face and, oh, Carrie. Sensational. Look at that. Beautifully proportioned figure. Firm, gorgeous breasts.' She turned to look me over once more. 'You've got nice *teeth*,' she said eventually.

I felt like a horse at an auction. No kidding. I was worried that next she might ask me to count to five with my feet.

'Dah-ling,' her voice vibrated as Pierce approached, bearing the wholemeal champagne. 'We're just looking at you in your various *stages*. The Bikie thing, remember? I got leathers and rode around with him too. Didn't I dear?' Pierce got out a roll-your-own and lit it. He blew a luxurious cloud of smoke in the direction of his mother's 'Stop smoking. I ask you from the bottom of my lungs' badge. Resolutely, Mrs Scanlen continued talking. 'You see, I've always believed that the way to communicate with our children is to experience life with them.' Pierce took a sip of his wholemeal wine then poured it into the nearest pot-plant. Mrs Scanlen's flinch was almost imperceptible. 'Oh look. The hippy stage, remember? I smoked dope with you then too. Didn't I dah-ling? Well, let's face it. It's not nearly as damaging as alcohol.' Pierce threaded the belt I'd discarded through his own jeans loops. He toyed with the leather tongue lying across his left thigh. 'And the punk stage. *That* was fun, wasn't it dah-ling? I've still got my outfits somewhere. I really liked that, not having to wash. And the hours I'd spend making my hair stand up on end till it looked like I hadn't brushed it for a month . . .' She turned to smile at me. 'It must be handy having hair that is like that *naturally.*'

By the time we sat down to dinner, I was feeling as light-headed as a mountain climber. It wasn't the freezing cold, but the social altitudes. Mrs Scanlen left me dangling off conversational precipices, or staring down the vertiginous slopes of icy silences. She wanted to know how much I earned, what my father did, how much he earned, was my mother a Feminist, what were my politics and was I aware of what caused the hole in the ozone layer?

Pierce started acting like a maniac. First he got out a bottle of nail polish from his kit bag and proceeded to paint the little fingernail of his left hand. Then he lit up a joint. He offered it first to me and then to his mother.

To make matters even worse, the first course was sushi. Seafood was pukesville enough, but *raw* seafood. If you ask me, there's a very fine line between sushi and fishing bait.

When his mother continued to ignore him, Pierce removed his shoes and socks. He inserted the chopsticks between his toes and attempted to eat his sushi with his feet. I looked at his mother, dry-mouthed. Mrs Reece-Scanlen didn't blink an eye.

'So,' she delivered her counter-attack, 'what's my son like in bed? Innovative?'

'Um, sorry. What?'

Pierce's mother looked up at me, while I dangled. '*Our* sex life,' she indicated her husband, who had just walked in, with a disdainful toss of her head, 'is practically non-existent.'

I stared at Pierce's father. From the waist up, he seemed very serious in shirt and tie, but from the waist down, he wore striped, synthetic trousers and fluorescent plastic sandals.

'Oh my God,' Mrs Scanlen snorted dismissively, glancing grimly at her husband's attire. 'He's gone native again.'

Pierce Snr was protectively clutching a bottle of wine (preservatives and artificial colouring added) which he placed next to him, out of the reach of his wife. She eyed him glacially. He seemed a gentle man, withdrawn and preoccupied, with the permanently puzzled expression of someone trying to remember where he's put the car keys. 'Hello, son.' He also seemed totally unperturbed by Pierce's virtuoso feeding-with-feet performance. He nodded at me, then quietly added, 'Could you possibly pass the salt, please, dear?'

I handed him the small silver bowl. We all watched as he ladled the salt over his meal.

'Go ahead,' Mrs Scanlen said, 'harden your arteries. See if I care.' Mr Reece-Scanlen, without pausing, immediately ladled on another two loads.

Mrs Scanlen sighed, then passed me the seafood bouillabaisse. I trawled along the bottom of the pan with the serving spoon. But the only sea life I could recognise in this exotic aquarium were the oysters floating like clots of grey phlegm on the murky surface.

'Oysters,' Mrs Scanlen informed me with resolute indifference, 'are an aphrodisiac.' She pushed the pot towards her husband. 'So, eat up, won't you dear.'

Pierce's father rubbed his hands together compulsively, like a sad little insect. As he reached for the butter, Mrs Scanlen slapped his wrist. 'I thought you were sticking to the polyunsaturated?' His Adam's apple was the size of a grapefruit. I watched, intrigued, as it bobbed up and down in his throat.

Pierce, tiring of the lack of response to his performance, lowered his feet to the floor and passed the butter dish to his father, who proceeded to paint his roll in thick yellow slathers.

'Believe me,' Mrs Scanlen said to no one in particular, 'relationships are finite. That's why I've always advised my own offspring never to get married.' Her fork shot across her plate, harpooning a piece of squid with a sharp, short-tempered jab. The forkful of tentacles disappeared into her delicate mouth. Her lips first pouted and then enfolded the entire fork, so as not to smudge her whole-earth-animal-testing-free-wind-chafe-protection lip-gloss. 'He's never even attempted cunnilingus. As they say in bathroom-graffiti, he thinks it's an Irish airline.' She erupted into a volley of firecracker laughter.

My mouth resembled the garage door we'd driven through earlier. It gaped, then slammed shut. Then gaped and slammed shut again.

'I just *know* you want seconds,' Mrs Scanlen insisted to me, retreating with the casserole dish for hot reinforcements from the kitchen.

'Well, Mr Scanlen?' I asked desperately. Pierce Snr was in a sort of trance, from which he only briefly emerged to wrap himself around his precious glass of wine. 'Tell me about your business?'

His lachrymose eyes lit up. 'Oh,' he enthused, 'are you interested?'

'Yeah. Yeah, I am.' Anything to get away from Pierce and his mother and the weird game they were playing.

'Well, you see, dear,' he said, 'I don't know if you've noticed this, but we Americans love to consume. It's our religion, you might say. And so I invented a firm that creates products that can be used only *once*.' He then launched off on to a colourful inventory of his products: condoms, candles, Christmas crackers, cattle castrators, designer tampons, exploding whoopie cushions, dissolving swizzle sticks . . .

At the reappearance of his wife, Pierce's dad deflated, just like one of his own party balloons. Mrs Scanlen placed the casserole dish in the centre of the table. The tide in the bouillabaisse had come back in, a king tide of treacherous oysters and people-eating octopuses. 'Oh God, he's telling you all about his brilliant business schemes, is he? Manufacturing papier mâché heads that look like pop stars and presidents. Now, *there's* something really useful to do. Don't you think?' she asked contemptuously, ladling a shoal of fish on to my plate. 'You see, my husband's business attention span is on a par with his sexual span. Short-lived, one might say. I mean, it's disgusting. Here is the world on the brink of an environmental holocaust, and what does he do? Make things that can only be used once and then thrown away. I do wish he'd do a line in *husbands*. What about some mayonnaise?' she asked

Pierce, who was now blowing bubblegum balloons so huge they obscured his face.

'Na,' he grunted through a bright pink mouthful.

'Of course you do.' Mrs Scanlen bobbed up and down like a piece of bread in a toaster, fetching things Pierce said he didn't need – soy sauce, a fresh table napkin, mineral water, more wholemeal wine, yoghurt dip.

'The boy's fine, Mother,' Mr Reece-Scanlen kept saying. 'Leave him be.'

I glanced at the bowl of yoghurt dip suspiciously. 'What is it?' I whispered to Pierce. 'A facial?' Mrs Scanlen glared at me. Chastened, I made a dutiful stab at a piece of squid. It was tough as a radial tyre. Honestly, all it needed was a chassis and a tape deck and it could have driven itself back to the sea. I tried again, but it squealed out from under my fork prong and shot across the table with the speed of a Formula One racing car.

'Oh dear. Pierce seemed to be doing better with his feet,' jeered Mrs Scanlen, mopping up. Her quick, efficient movements made me feel even more clumsy.

Pierce Snr slurped more wine into his glass and gulped at it nervously. 'Don't worry husband-dear, I don't mind if you drink alcohol. You're a business man – you're already brain-dead. Don't you think I'm right, Katrina?' she said, turning to me.

What I thought was that this woman should just make like a turtle – shut her gob and pull her head in. Pierce's dad went to the kitchen, reappearing with a packet of chocolate Easter eggs, which he tore open defiantly.

Even though we were only halfway through our main course, Mrs Scanlen got up from the table and returned with a huge dessert. 'A mucus-free, carob soufflé made from soya milk, defatted soya flour, emulsifier-soya lecithin and eggs, free-range.' It sat quivering in the centre of the table. 'My own recipe.' Mrs Scanlen cut off a slice and passed it to Pierce.

Mr Scanlen immediately extended the packet of chocolate eggs towards his son.

Pierce just sat looking from one to the other of his predatory parents. It was so quiet you could hear the sprinklers outside, whirling neurotically.

'Go ahead, dah-ling,' Mrs Scanlen said to Pierce, 'eat the chocolate. As long as you don't care if you ruin your teeth. Not to mention your talent. Bad food fuels bad brains. I mean, look at your father.'

Pierce's father gave a helpless little flap of his arms. He was like a wounded bird.

Pierce's face, hands and body, even his hair, kind of clenched. And then he snapped. 'I'm just glad you're sitting downwind,' Pierce rounded on his mother. These were the first words he'd uttered all meal. ''Cause your politics are *on the nose*, Mom, j'know that? They stink. You want it all, doncha? A compact disc *and* whales in the ocean. Bucks *and* buckwheat. The truth is, you can only afford to go Green 'cause of all the goddamned greenbacks Dad has earned over the – '

'Is that right, Mr Know-all? I only wish I'd discovered an environmental consciousness earlier. Then I could have recycled *you*. And maybe got a son with integrity. Some Moral Fibre. A son interested in more things than money, and fast cars. I've given you every opportunity; that course in palaeontology, the painting trip to Morocco, Russian lessons . . . And how do you repay me?'

Pierce's eyes lit up slyly. Mrs Scanlen, catching his triumphant expression, and realising she'd been ambushed, suddenly took a deep breath, raised her herbal tea to her lips, took a long, slow sip and then returned the cup soundlessly to its Wedgewood saucer. 'But, what am I saying? Celebrity status, even in television, is now a source of power in its own right. It's Pierce's way,' she confided to me, 'of changing the system from within. He pretends otherwise, of course, but we know,' she winked, 'don't we? This little acting phase is all part of a grander plan – after all, look what happened to Ronnie Reagan.'

Pierce slumped in his chair, his face collapsed like the mucus-free soufflé in front of him. He then thumped up from the table and disappeared from the room.

Mrs Scanlen folded her arms victoriously. 'Well, well, well,' she said, spooning yet more bouillabaisse on to my plate, 'I'm just so glad that Pierce has gone and got himself another nice little friend. We must get a photo of you – for the album.' She moved over to the mantelpiece and retrieved a square of gilt-edged cardboard from amongst the forest of Easter cards. She thrust it towards me. 'There's a charity do I'd like Pierce to be seen at. It'd be good for his image. You could accompany him.' Mrs Scanlen touched my arm, the way you touch the pet of an acquaintance, even though you're allergic to it. 'Absolutely *everybody* will be there. Of course, you'll have to put up with the usual phonies and photographers, which will be *terribly* tedious.'

'Oh, yes, terribly,' I said. She was right. It would be full of fakes dropping their own designer names and pretending they didn't want to be photographed by the paparazzi – and I wanted *desperately* to go. My eyes glinted at the thought of Rondah's face when I arrived with Pierce as my Human Handbag.

Pierce took his place again at the table. He selected an Easter egg from the packet and started nibbling on it. He was completely naked. Starkers. In the bollocky. All bronzed six fabulous feet of him.

If his mother was shocked, she didn't show it. She simply turned once more to me. 'And so Katrina, you didn't tell me, *is* my son good in bed?'

It was then that I bit into the chilli. My palate hit the stuccoed ceiling and my eyes began whirring. The world tilted. There was a blur of white light. I heard a loud crack, which I dimly thought might have been my head hitting the table.

How to Impress the Parents of the Man you Love.

Rule 1. Do not ask his mother who she is and what she does.

Rule 2. Do not ask if the food she serves can be worn as a facial.

Rule 3. Try not to let them see you, on the first meeting, with your head in your dinner plate.

When I came to, my tonsils still up around my eyebrows, my eyes stopped swimming long enough for me to recognise Pierce's parents, who were peering over the edge of the table to where I lay stretched out on the carpet.

'Oh,' Mrs Reece-Scanlen said, with what sounded like the tiniest hint of disappointment. 'For a moment there I thought we could add you to my husband's collection of disposables. Australian girlfriend. Hardly used.'

I sat up in time to see Pierce's tanned buttocks retreating from the dining-room.

Once I'd recovered, I tracked Pierce down to the gurgling Jacuzzi. I squatted down in the shadows. 'Your mother is interesting,' I volunteered.

'She's a fucking cunt.'

'Oh. Well, that's one way to put it, I suppose.' Pierce was

gulping furiously at a margherita. 'She wants us to go to this charity thingo.'

'What is it this time? The Charity Ball for Reformed Bondage Sex Slaves and their Pet Ferrets? Jesus. The fund for Sons Who Want to Kill Their Fucking Mothers.'

I had never seen him so riled. 'I'll go with you, if you like. You know, to keep you company. I'd kinda like to go.'

'I *hate* charity do's. They're addicted to charity balls in this city. They have charity balls to raise money for other charity balls.'

'Your dad's nice,' I said, sidestepping.

'He's pathetic. That's the worst thing about family get-togethers. It drives home to you just how mutated and horrendous your gene stock really is.'

'She's not all that bad. I mean, at least she tried to understand stuff that was going on in your life, when you were growing up an' all.'

'She lived my goddamned life for me! She put me into a crash-crèche-class when I was two! You know, where they give you intensive learning with flash cards and stuff . . . She attended pre-natal university, for God's sake. That's where they read you Shakespeare and shit while you're in the womb. She's been disappointed ever since that I didn't turn out to be a genius.' Pierce disappeared from view beneath the frothing duvet of foam. Re-emerging, he drained his drink and sighed loudly.

'My dad encouraged me to play truant,' I prompted, breaking the silence. 'He reckons that a "school" is just something fish swim round in.'

'Yeah?' he said calmer now. 'What does he do? Your dad? You gettin' in, or what?'

'What? Oh.' Gingerly, I stepped out of my clothes, all except my undies and lowered myself in. It was like getting into what we'd just had for dinner. I sank down into an awful bouillabaisse of discarded bikini bottoms and Bandaids, spiced, no doubt, with a decade of sweat and hair-balls. 'Failed bank-robber and part-time gambler. He used to borrow my pocket-money. "I'm good for it, kid," he'd say. "You know that." But he never was. Bastard. I read in the papers about some bloke in Boston who sued his parents for bringing him up badly. That's what I'd like to do.'

'God. I'd like to sue my parents for bringing me up too well.'

'Whaddaya mean?'

'At thirteen,' he blurted, 'my mother told me that it was about time I started to rebel. At fourteen she offered me my first hashish. At fifteen she suggested it was time I had my first sexual experience. Whatever I did, she just accepted.' He sliced the cellophane off his cigarette packet with the one long nail he cultivated on the little finger of his left hand. 'And get this. When I got picked up for drunk-driving, j'know what she said? That the only justice in this world was poetic. She said that in today's corrupt system, "criminal" is merely a euphemism for someone who gets caught.'

I laughed. Pierce shot me a withering look. He leant back against the pebble-crete rim of the Jacuzzi and exhaled a sibilant stream of cigarette smoke. 'Most kids get dragged off to church, right? Well, I got dragged off to demonstrations. One year I got involved with the goddamned IRA. I thought that would be too extreme for her soft-centred, Chardonnay-socialism.'

'And?'

'My mother started wearing green a lot. So I abandoned that for the PLO. And she starts making hummus. I finally told her that I wanted to be a priest. They're both atheist, right, my parents? And j'know what she said? That "the Catholic Church had a fascinating and intellectually rewarding theology". I mean *puh-leaze* . . .'

'And acting?'

'Ah. Now there I thought I really had her. She hates television. Even more than she hates "toxic food stuffs". She doesn't even have one in the whole goddamned house. I honestly thought I'd finally found something that would make her crazy. But she told her friends that acting was a noble and artistic calling . . . I mean, Chrrrist. Tell *that* to Abe Lincoln!' He stood up to go and refill his margherita. In the dark, the tan marks on his arms were like the stripes of an exotic animal.

'What *was* your first?'

'What?'

'You know,' I swallowed. My throat constricted. 'Sexual experience.'

'Animal, vegetable or mineral?' he asked, not missing a beat. 'Nice, huh?' he said, sinking back into the frothing water.

'Lovely,' I replied, entranced by his soft brown forearms on the lip of the pool. 'I wonder what Rondah's was?'

'That's easy. She mated with a man and then ate him.'

I laughed again. Watching him, I felt a totally delicious ache in the pit of my stomach and the tips of my fingers. Bits of his naked limbs jutted like rocks out of the frothing water. I wanted to be shipwrecked on them. Like a deep-sea mariner, I began to negotiate my way across the Jacuzzi. My ardour was, however, momentarily dampened by a geyser of boiling water surging into me at groin level. 'Christ,' I squealed.

'Chrrrist!' Pierce echoed as I overbalanced and trod heavily on his submerged foot. 'Wouldja sit thuhfuck down?' he said, in his usual romantic fashion.

Feeling my way with my feet, like an octopus on the bottom of the sea, I located the seat next to him and anchored there. He threw his head back and gazed up, eyes glistening, at the stars. He stretched for his drink. As he moved, his skin gleamed wetly in the dark. Wishing it could be in my hands, I ran my eyes over his body. It was now, I thought, or never. Pursing my lips, I lunged towards his dark profile. But he turned his head at the wrong time. My kiss ended up somewhere on the back of his neck. I touched him. But his skin was unresponsive. It had all the sensual appeal of one of those blow-up male dolls I'd encountered at the Pleasure Chest. 'Don't, don't you want to?' I didn't recognise my own voice. It was so quiet, small enough to fit in someone's pocket.

'Listen,' he said urgently, 'you've seen my parents for Chrissake. I'm totally emotionally fucked up. It's in my goddamned blood.' He fumbled for a towel, dried his hand and hurriedly lit up the half-smoked joint lying in the ashtray. 'I need some breathing space.'

My crap-antenna started wobbling. What was he, I wondered, asthmatic? 'Don't you . . . find me attractive?' I sank down in the bubbles so that they blanketed my bite-size breasts.

He drew back hard on his joint. 'I'm celibate,' he exhaled.

'You're what?'

'Celibate. Amoebas have got it pretty well sussed, I reckon. I mean an amoeba just kinda lies round in the primeval sludge having sex with itself. Didja know that? Single-cell reproduction. That's the answer. No chocolates, no fussing, no condoms no "Hey, have you had an AIDS test?" Not to mention the worry of goddamned kids. I am *never* having kids. It's not that I'm worried they'll grow nostrils in the middle of their goddamned foreheads or sprout eyes in their chins, an' all that shit. I'm just worried they'll grow into my mother. Sorry.' Pierce kissed me on the nose, and stepped out into the shadows. ''Night,' he said. I just sat there in stunned silence. Sweat was pouring down from my forehead, mingling with the tears. I sniffled loudly. I was par-boiling.

'Oh, Chrrrrist. You're not crying all over the goddamned place are you?' I could feel his presence in the gloom. 'Jeeeze. Whaddaya want from me?'

To go to the ball, of course, I thought to myself, like all Cinderellas. *God. What was happening to me!'*

'Well?' he insisted.

What did he think I wanted? I wanted to be his, six-kids-and-a-dishwasher-his, till death do us part his, forever and ever. Instead I settled for a slurp of his abandoned margherita.

'Look, you're attractive, okay?'

'Well then, why won't you go to the charity thingo with me?'

'Look, if it's that goddamned important I'll go. Okay? OKAY?'

'Okay.' After I heard the screen door slam, I swirled a towel around my body and went and got my pack of cards. I'd been doing so many practice hands lately – just to get Rondah's sanctimonious knickers in a knot – that I'd accidentally worked out a system that could beat the bank at the Nirvana Casino. I dealt out yet another hand of blackjack, and just sat, staring at the pack. Great. Things were going so well. I'd left Australia because the men there treated women like sperm-spittoons, and now, here I was in America, throwing myself at a bloke and whingeing 'cause he wouldn't make love to me. If the Aussie definition of foreplay was 'are you awake, love?', the American version of foreplay was turning out to be marriage. Since AIDS, the only thing dirty about LA was the air. I suddenly got an irresistible urge to do something totally tacky.

Poking through the ashtray, I resurrected and lit up the stub of Pierce's joint. I poured myself the remains of the margheritas. I straddled the bar stool, as brazen as Madonna. I flicked my hair out of my face like a film star, and rang the Nirvana Casino in Las Vegas with another question.

THE MEAT MARKET

When Pierce dropped me home with 'do or die' promises to take me to the charity ball (I was going to make him swear on his mother's grave but then I realised that there wasn't much point really), we drove right past my house. That's because there was a stretch, chauffeur-driven, customised, chocolate-and-red-leather-upholstered-limo with smoked windows pulled up in the driveway. It looked a lot like the sort of car you'd go to a funeral in.

'Tash?' I called out urgently, pushing past the screen door. Tash, who was in her bedroom shovelling layers of black eyeliner on to her lids, bobbed her head around the door. Even though she was beaming, her eyes were faintly troubled and didn't hold mine with their usual impertinent gaze. 'Waddabout this?' She thrust her latest culinary creation in my direction – an asparagus and strawberry cake. It looked like something regurgitated by a Rottweiler. 'Well, whaddaya think? I invented it for you,' she insisted, ignoring the tell-tale strawberry stains around her mouth.

All I could think was that she'd dyed her hair blonde. 'I dunno,' I ventured. 'To tell you the truth, I kinda liked apple and licorice crumble better.'

'Yeah,' she laughed nervously. I laughed nervously. 'Asparagus and strawberries. I wonder what colour piss we'll have?' And then we fell on to each other in a big bear hug. We disguised the tension of our last words in the supermarket, by laughing excessively at things that were only vaguely funny and squeezing each other's hands and arms a little too vigorously.

'Where've ya bin?' she said, squeezing my shoulder a little too vigorously. 'I've bin worried sick . . .'

I told her about Pierce taking me to meet his parents and how

150

that must really mean something (I wouldn't let *anyone* meet my old man. As far as I'm concerned, coagulation is the only proof that blood is thicker than water). And I told her that I was going with Pierce to a charity do.

'Oh. Great,' Tash said flatly. Her eyes said, 'I'll believe it when I see it.'

'What's with the limo?' I asked her.

''Member that polaroid ya took of me? Well, they phoned. I'm booked for a photo call. Today.'

'Oh. Great,' I said neutrally. My eyes said, 'Don't do it.'

'Look,' Tash elaborated, 'the way I see it, Christ died for our sins, right? So we might as well make it, like, worth the poor schmuck's while. Come with me!' she urged, wielding her make-up spatula. I practically went blue with nausea at the very idea. 'As my, ya know, bodyguard.' But just as I was going to say that I'd rather be stuck in a holding pattern for ten hours, jettisoning fuel, seated next to a talkative insul-batt-salesman with body odour, I glanced up on top of Tash's cupboard. Her Hope Chest had gone. Disappeared. Tash caught my glance in the mirror. But neither of us mentioned it. We kept it separate: those hard words we'd had wouldn't flavour the rest of our friendship.

'Okay,' I said hurriedly. Tash was my best mate. At that moment I would have done anything to make things right between us. Except, perhaps, eat strawberries with asparagus.

To tell you the truth, I should have got out of the stretch limo and run like the billyo, the minute we got to the mansion and I heard a rock speak. No kidding. As we sat in the back seat, fiddling with all the gadgets and gizmos, a voice emerged from the large boulder at window level. 'Have a nice day,' the rock said. 'Please state your name and business.'

Tash – after a few false starts – zapped down the electronic window. 'Natasha Marilyn Kerlowski. I believe ya wanna see mah tits,' she said shamelessly.

The gates abracadabra-ed open and the limo purred past the security cameras, through the groomed gardens, around the circular drive, before crunching to a halt outside the magazine's headquarters. Tash and I looked up dumbfounded. We had pulled up outside a castle, complete with galleries and gilded turrets, truncated columns, towers and pleasure domes. It reminded me of that Fantasyland castle at Disneyland. And there were lots of Tinkerbells. A row of them, with luscious breasts, and lubricious thighs, formed a welcoming party.

'Well, hi there, Miss Kerlowski,' said a glamorously dressed woman with a voice to match. Miss Kerlowski. That about cracked me up.

'Holy shit,' Tash whispered to me, as we got out of the car. Women thrust bouquets into her hands. A porter whisked her bag out of the back seat and a butler proceeded to lead her off on a tour of the mansion, with me in tow.

Inside, the walls were chockers with paintings I'd only ever seen in school art books. Outside, peacocks strutted around palm-fringed ponds and stone nymphs cavorted in glistening fountains. Tethered across the lawns, Spider Monkeys cocked their quizzical little heads to one side and examined Tash and me – the latest acquisitions. The silent butler led us through aviaries of rare birds – toucans, parrots, pelicans, all displaying their exotic plumage.

'Hello,' a neon-bright parrot greeted us. 'My name is Cindy and my hobbies are travelling and meeting people. Hello, my name is Cindy and my hobbies are travelling and meeting people. Hello, my name is . . .' Tash jabbed me in the ribs as we choked back our chortles. Next, we were pressing our faces up against the glass of an indoor aquarium full of electric eels and irridescent fish that flashed past, small as fingernails.

As we re-emerged into the dazzling daylight, Tash whistled, 'Jesus Chrrrist. This place is amazing.'

And it was, except I couldn't help thinking that this entire magazine empire was built on *sperm*. I mean, the very foundations of the mansion were probably mortared with semen. It kind of killed the old glamour to tell you the truth.

We were then taken to meet the boss. The hard, modern furniture looked alien in the old, wood-panelled room. The bloke behind the desk introduced himself as Stefan, a wiry, muscular man, just starting to run to fat, his hair cropped to disguise an advancing bald spot. The wooden plaque on his desk read 'Artistic Director' which, in a magazine like this, was a euphemism for a guy who spent his days examining photographs of the female crotch.

'Well, Natasha Marilyn Kerlowski.' Despite the smile, Stefan said her name as though it were a disease. A South Efrican, his accent was like a vocal karate chop. I eyed him with chronic mistrust. 'Hmmm,' he said, staring intently at Tash's eyes. 'Yes.'

Tash, uncomfortable under his scrutiny, shoved one hip out to the side and placed her hand on it. 'I thought ya wanted to see my tits?' she said stridently.

The photographer, a he-man whose T-shirt bore the face of a cartoon character I couldn't quite remember, snickered. Stefan shot him a scathing look and he fell silent immediately.

'No. You see, it's all in the eyes. Cut the head off a girl, and there's nothing. Just a lump of meat. The eyes have to look sexy, intelligent. The polaroid you sent us was only from the neck down. You used a hellava photographer.' Tash winked at me surreptitiously. 'Now,' Stefan slid up out of his chair and circled Tash in a predatory fashion. 'The first photographic session will pinpoint what the problems are with the entire body.'

'Problems?' Tash said challengingly, turning her head over her shoulder to follow him.

'Oh yes. The pubes may be too hairy, bottom too big, knees knocked, feet gnarled, tits not the same size . . .'

'Whaddaya mean?' Tash snapped defensively.

'Quite often they don't hang in the same position – one nipple may point forward and one may point to the side.' He paused, too close to her, and stroked her arm. 'I'm an expert on the female form. Does she have a hairy top lip? Can we bleach it? Does she have thick ankles, thick arms, thick thighs?' Or a thick head, I thought, like you. 'I can fix anything,' he added, in a voice both aloof and malicious. 'Age?' he snapped, moving efficiently back to his desk.

'Counting past lives?' Tash said provocatively.

Stefan shot her a supercilious look. 'Of course, I'm not forcing you to co-operate. Obviously, the money for this gig is not so important to you.'

'Twenty-three,' she acquiesced.

'Well, then, we're just in the nick of time. Over twenty-five and girls start to show signs of wear and tear. Drooping, cellulite.' He threw his hands in the air. 'The whole catastrophe.' Tash's bravado momentarily evaporated. 'Height?'

'Five foot two,' she responded meekly.

'Eyes of blue, good. Five foot two, long-waisted, well-endowed girls are our favourite – aren't they Carl?' So much for 'the eyes have it all'. We all turned to catch the photographer bloke ogling the contours of Tash's figure. And he wasn't just looking, he was consuming her. 'They photograph the best,' Stefan hurried on, drawing the attention back to himself. 'Does your boyfriend know you're doing this?'

'I don't believe in boyfriends.'

'Does your mother know?'

'My mother sucks shit.'

Stefan looked up suddenly, his eyes hard. 'Have you done any hooking?'

'No,' she lied.

'When are your monthlies? We must work around Uncle George's visits.'

Tash executed her famous rolling of the eyes, just as I knew she would. 'What am I? An idiot? A bimbo? Ya think the peroxide leaked through my skull and bleached my brains? Would I be here, bum-breath, if I had my periods?'

The score, I reckoned, was Tash – two, Stefan – one.

'You are a natural blonde, aren't you?' Stefan interrogated. He was looking at her with a weird expression, both wistful and contemptuous.

'Yeah, of course,' Tash fibbed effortlessly, studying the nail varnish on the little finger of her left hand.

I watched as Stefan's cold eyes slid, ever so slowly, down Tash's neck, focusing, finally on her chest. He smirked with admiration. 'With most girls we put them on the pill and tell them to come back in a month or so. It makes their titties bigger. Natasha, you ain't most girls. They are a serious set of jugs.'

'Major League Hooters,' the photographer chorused.

'We'll do you tomorrow. This, you may have gathered,' Stefan gestured towards the man in the immaculate, white T-shirt, 'is Carl. If you don't like him, you tell me and we'll find you another photographer. But,' he smirked as Carl readjusted his belt buckle, in a mock-self-conscious gesture that emphasised the Olympic-sized bulge in his left trouser leg, 'most girls like our Carl.'

I don't know about major hooters, but these two blokes were Major Bozos. As if reading my mind, Stefan suddenly slewed around to face me. 'Who's the side-kick?' I copped a fetid blast of his breath, the stale, oniony smell barely masked by the peppermint he was sluicing obscenely round his chops. 'We don't allow our girlies to be accompanied.'

'My lover,' Tash lied with cheerful aggression. I gawped. The two men chuckled with only thinly disguised revulsion. I made a mental note to give her heaps later. HEAPS. Stefan flipped open a copy of his magazine, stopping at the centrefold. 'These are the sort of shots we want.' A woman lay spread-eagled across the page, displaying what the boys back home would so eloquently call her 'meat curtains'. 'Got any problems with that?'

Tash craned over the desk, then shook her head. Stefan smiled a fraudulent kind of smile and handed her a 'Model Release' form to sign. As Tash scrawled her name across the bottom of the page, old Onion-breath delivered his final spiel. 'From here on, during your stay with us, you'll be treated like a princess. But, bear in mind, we entertain lots of Businessmen. And we like to make them feel happy. In other words,' his voice became low and scornful, 'if you get your ass grabbed, don't complain, okay babe?'

'But,' I piped up, scandalised.

'Feminism is bad for business,' he silenced me. 'As are dykes.'

Being in that holding pattern, jettisoning fuel for ten hours, seated next to the talkative insul-batt-salesman with B.O., was starting to look more and more attractive, let me tell you.

Tash was taken to the beauty salon for her make-over. She was scheduled to have her nails painted, hair tinted, face packed in imported mud with 'special anti-inflammatory' property, her pubes waxed and shaped . . . and that was just for starters. I decided to leave her and do some exploring.

In the middle of the lawn was a swimming pool. Lying around the edges, on deckchairs, was a host of beautiful, if slightly shop-soiled models. All topless. I looked at the ponderous symmetry of their silicone, regulation-sized breasts. Tash had told me that a centrefold spread can take up to two months to shoot. Practically one whole wing of the mansion was taken up with potential centre-folds recovering from plastic surgery to nose, toes, eyes, thighs, hips, lips, tits and bits. (I was so sick of meeting people who were having their faces *lifted*. Couldn't they have their bodies *lowered*, you know. Just for a change?) Others were staying here with orders to exercise, or starve down to the required pretzel-thin proportions. They spent their nights as table decorations for visit-ing company directors at executive dinners, their days as garden ornaments, being ogled by sexually famished Midwest businessmen.

I sat on the edge of the pool, dangled my legs into the chlorinated cool, and watched the women. They lazed in the sun like bored pedigree cats. Men buzzed around the pool like insects, laughing lecherously and volunteering all too eagerly to rub on suntan oils and fetch sodas.

I sat there in the searing sun for hour after hour and not one man approached me. Not that I wanted them too, mind you – but I wanted to *know* that they wanted to, if you know what I mean. Rondah was right. I had the sex appeal of a toenail. Ingrown. It seemed as though everyone in the whole of America was busy bonking, *except me*.

When I finally squelched my way up to Tash's room in the guest wing, I could hear her guffaw before I opened the door. I nearly didn't recognise her. Her new blonde hair was curled and swept up off her face, which was painted in about six coats of high-gloss lacquer. She was trampolining, not on the bed, but on the floor. 'Try it!' She yanked me over the threshold. The spongy carpet yielded beneath my feet, then bounced back, propelling me into the air. It was like moon-walking. 'It's for floor-fuckin', she squealed, airborne. 'This place is the carpet-burn-capital-of-the-Western-world. And look,' she shrieked, 'there's twenty-four-hour room service. And light dimmers at floor level! And,' she bounced over to the bathroom and opened the cabinet, 'everythin' ya could ever need. Razors, vitamins, uppers, downers, dildos, condoms, whipped cream. Even Pepto Bismol, for the upset Bimbo tummy.' We bounded about, doing Space Odyssey impressions, before splashing down in a mass of limbs on the ginormous bed. The ceiling was mirrored.

'Hey, ya wanna watch the porn channel?' Tash giggled, groping for the remote control.

'Erggh. No. Why?'

'I dunno. Don't you ever just wanna check that you're doin' it right?'

Doing *what* right, I thought to myself, in despair. Addressing our reflection on the ceiling made us feel we'd lost all gravity. But actually, I was feeling very grave. About everything. 'Tash, let's go home. Let me get you some money. Pierce owes me squillions.'

'What am I? A charity-case? I'm doin' a centrefold! We're talkin' serious coin.'

'But Tash, the bottom line is . . .'

'The bottom line,' she interrupted, 'is *money*. And it's not just the bottom line. It's the top, middle, bottom, in between, and every other goddamned line. Money doesn't just talk in this town it SCREAMS. So don't go into Prude Mode, okay?'

'It's not that! I'm trying to get down and get dirty, I really am. But there's something wrong with me.' A sob constricted my throat. 'I mean, not even the one man I love in the whole world will go to bed with me.'

'Huh?'

'He's gone celibate,' I groaned.

'But whaddabout Palm Springs?'

'It wasn't exactly a one-night *stand* – more your one-night *sit*. We just sat and talked about his parents for hours.' Tash laughed loudly, quickly smothering her hilarity in the pillow. 'It's not funny,' I said sharply.

Tash raised her head from the bedclothes and looked at my dejected reflection in the ceiling mirror. 'Well, maybe he didn't know you were like, comin' on to him?'

Tash reckoned I was too reserved in the old sex department. She reckoned I needed to be more 'up front'. That I should 'wear my cunt on my sleeve', as she put it.

'Tash, I practically raped the guy, for God's sake . . .'

'Well what's wrong then? Is the old sperm count down or what?'

'I dunno. He just says he's celibate.'

'Kelp, milk, oysters, honey, raw nuts and wheat germ oil.'

'What?'

'Wheat germ oil is like, high in vitamin E, which increases the dude's sperm count and the volume of seminal fluid. Kelp is like, packed with iodine which stimulates the endocrine glands which make men horny. As does the gonadotropic hormone in honey, and the glycogen in raw nuts. And oysters are like, major high in protein, not to mention calcium, iron and vitamin A – which can't hurt, right?'

I looked at my friend in astonishment. Tash may have left school at fifteen, but she had a PhD in heterosexuality.

'Why ya lookin' so skeptical?' Tash demanded.

'It's not that I don't believe you, Tash, but it's just so hard to think of a recipe that combines milk and oysters.'

'Well, don't worry about it now. If ya wanna get laid, wait till tonight,' she laughed. 'We're gonna be treated like princesses.'

And we were. We were wined and dined and spoilt rotten. Drop-dead-gorgeous men asked us to dance and flirted compulsively. But all the time, our sleazy minders, Stefan and Carl, were watching us. While I could gorge myself to death, Tash wasn't allowed to eat anything more substantial than a bit of wilted lettuce. At 10.30 were were marched back up to our rooms and tucked in.

'Hey, ya wan us to say our fuckin' prayers?' Tash scoffed, as Stefan, with strict instructions for an early night, sealed the door shut.

At 10.45 Tash was dragging me down the corridor of the mansion. We stole into the private kitchen where she proceeded to raid the fridge. Renavigating our way back through the maze of stairs and walls and halls, we drank toasts straight from a bottle of champagne and scrawled graffiti.

'F*** Censorship,' Tash tattooed with nail polish on the first-floor landing.

'Porn is the theory, rape is the practice,' I authored in lipstick on old Onion-breath's oak-panelled office door.

'I think we're a bad influence on ourselves,' Tash decided, as we cracked open our second bottle of Bollinger. Which is quite possibly the reason we slept through the early morning wake-up call, and why, when Tash finally did appear in the photographic studio, an hour late, wearing, as ordered, only a tracksuit and no undies – so there'd be no elastic marks on her body – she looked like a chook's breakfast.

'No, of course I'm not angry,' Carl said. He was carrying his camera like a weapon.

The gay make-up artist started fussing with Tash's face. 'Oh, my God. What lurvely skin. Bewdiful. Oh, and lervely hair. Whaddaya do for skin care? Great titties, too. Nicest lookin' girl I've had in the hot seat for such a long time.'

Tash cocked her hip one way and tilted her head the other. 'What's this?' she said, in a clear and challenging voice. 'The old "massage the girl's ego" bit?' Carl and the make-up guy exchanged a wary glance. 'I guess ya're tryin' to relax me, is that it?' She then began to speak as though the men weren't there.

'Hey Kat, notice how they only use a gay make-up guy. That's so I won't feel threatened. I bet he'll start talkin' dirty soon, ya know, to put me in the mood.' She flashed a knocking, mocking look at the make-up guy, who shrivelled into a guilty silence.

'Cute,' Carl said, a lethal glint in his eye, 'real cute.'

About a year later, Tash was released from the make-up chair. After she'd changed into lacy underwear, Carl strapped her into highheeled, cream, cowgirl boots, out of which her legs rose like matchsticks. He arranged her limbs on the sofa, patted her scrawny shank, and started shooting.

'I betcha there's no film in the camera at this stage, am I right?' Tash, indefatigable, sang out. 'I betcha just shoot a few fake rolls first, ya know, till I get warmed up. Like toast, right?'

Carl wielded his camera with scarcely restrained violence.

'Ya see, they hope you'll get the hots for the photographer,' she informed me, for his benefit, 'and, hopefully, fuck him durin' lunchbreak, so then you'll be more relaxed. Ain't that right, Carlie-Warlie?'

Carl stopped clicking for a moment and glanced at the make-up guy, who shrugged dismally.

'Okay, babe,' Carl said with contrived warmth. 'I want to see one nipple.' He switched into his pre-rehearsed preamble. 'Imagine the camera is someone you're trying to make very horny.'

Tash shot them a skeptical look. 'Listen, fuck-face, the only thing makin' me horny is the amount of cashola I'm gonna be paid for the centrefold.'

Carl's face turned into a rigid mask of fury.

Painstakingly, they progressed from one nipple to two, and, finally, to full nudity. As Tash kicked off her teddy ensemble we all looked in amazement at the red splodge of pubic hair between her little legs.

'A natural blonde, eh?' Carl said, his voice slovenly.

'Oh yeah,' Tash said casually. 'Forgot about that bit.'

Carl considered this for a moment, then kept shooting. 'Oh well, it kind of goes with the nose-ring.'

Overwhelmed with hungover weariness, I curled up on a prop sofa behind a screen at the back of the studio, and sank, totally knackered, into a dreamless sleep.

I awoke to the sound of men's voices.

'Centrefold, my ass.' Recognising Stefan's South Efrican

inflexions, I peeked around the side of the screen. He and Carl were pouring over the polaroids of Tash. 'No way. I mean, fuck, she's got tits like roadmaps.' Tash was so pale that the flash had made the veins show through her translucent skin. According to the men, they looked like two bulbous blue-vein cheeses. The same breasts they'd both salivated over earlier, they now dissected coldly. 'Christ, and whaddam I s'posed to do with the inverted nipple.'

'I can tease that out with ice. She could still make the centrefold in my op – '

'Hey. What the hell do ya think I'm talkin' for? My health? Even if you do get it out, they're dark nipples, too. She must've had a kid.' Stefan went on, his voice subtly contemptuous. 'Check for stretch marks.'

'And dye that muff. We'll give her a few days to tan up, then do a pictorial piece. I mean, okay, she's lousy for the centrefold, but she has got such *Guinness Book of Records* hooters, I'll use her for a secondary pictorial. Yeah, a fantasy pictorial. I dunno, with another babe maybe.'

'Whaddabout that little chick she's with?'

I tucked my head back behind the screen and stopped breathing.

'Don't make me laugh,' Stefan said. 'She's what we call in the trade, a 'two bagger'. Put a paper bag over her head – and then another one, in case the first one breaks.'

I decided to go. I left Tash a note saying I'd be back, said goodbye to the talking rock, and went home to put my head in a paper bag.

THE BALL

The Easter break had done nothing much to improve things at work. The writers had graduated from gorilla costumes to cross-dressing. Mimi was now pushing me to attend a nude aromatherapy class. The 'touch of flu' keeping Cosmo bed-bound had now progressed into a 'mysterious illness'. Pierce spent most of the time in his dressing-room being measured for his life-size model at the wax museum. (They took casts of his nostrils and minute details of his inside leg measurements. They even brought in a tray of eyeballs for him to select from.) Abe was still promising that we'd 'do lunch'. And Rondah, as well as having her usual sheep-cell treatments, was booked in for a series of silicone injections in the lips. According to Ping, BRL (the Big Red Lip look) was the latest fashion. Rondah kindly suggested I got my lips and breasts done simultaneously.

What worried me was how the silicone would be able to tell what was what and which was which? I didn't want to end up with lactating lips and mammary glands which gave monologues.

Because Rondah's lips would be out of action for a day or two after surgery, she was busy devouring everything in sight. 'Well, chickadee,' she confided, 'my spies tell me you're goin' to the May Day Charity Ball tonight. With Pierce.' I watched a large hamburger disappear into her gob.

Rondah should have been born a snail. Snails are perfectly designed for gluttony. See, their mouths are built into their feet, allowing for maximum consumption while on the move. For a fast food junkie like her it was the perfect solution.

'Yeah, yeah I am. So what?' I said, doing fishmouth exercises with my lips to make them pout out as far as possible.

'Well, I must say, you have excellent taste in partners. Pierce

161

is so witty and wonderful and clever and elegant and sensual.'
She paused to devour the last of her Big Mac. 'It's jest amazin'
isn't it, how *opposites attract*.'

I left Ms Snail Features to go and buy some kelp, milk, wheat
germ and oysters.

On the way to Pierce's place, I was so excited my bones were
burning. I really knew I was in a bad way when, sitting in the
back of the cab, clutching my box of oysters and bottle of Kahlua
(it goes well with milk), I sang every lyric to every love song that
came on the car radio. And, what was worse, *they made sense*. We
drove up a wide street in Beverly Hills, upholstered with palm
trees. Mexican gardeners rode what looked like huge mechanical
vacuum cleaners, suctioning up leaves and grass clippings. Only
in LA, I thought, would people get their lawns blow-waved.
Pierce's house looked like something from a kid's drawing. Set up
off the road, it was the typical blond brick, disinfected Californian
mansion, all sharp lines and hard surfaces. It was the architectural
version of a migraine.

I got the cabbie to drop me off in the street behind Pierce's
house and climbed, as he'd instructed me, through the hole in
the back fence. The pavement in front of his house was continually
crowded with a herd of pubescent girls. Tonight they periodically
broke out of their giggling huddles to chant, 'Pierce. Pierce.
Pierce.'

I moved past the slimy swimming pool – his was the only pool
I'd ever seen that had plaque – and into the house. The first
thing I laid eyes on was Pierce's poodle chasing his tail in the
middle of the room, barking and snapping at invisible invaders.
Next I took in the squalid debris of a week's worth of fast food.
The carpet was buried beneath grease-stained pizza cardboard,
compact disc boxes, Pepsi cans, overflowing ashtrays, half-gnawed
dog biscuits, chewed up Doonesbury cartoon books and discarded
clothes. 'Pierce?'

Pierce's head popped up from his prone position on the floor.
His eyes were alert and shiny, like those of a small marsupial
disturbed in the dark. 'Wow. Hey, speak quietly will you? My
mortal remains have only just come back to the land of the livin'.'

I waited for him to notice Tash's slinky black dress I'd poured
myself into, and the crowd-stopping-gob-smacking jewellery

welded to both ears (gigantic photos of James Dean studded in diamantés). He didn't. 'Well,' I said, executing a kind of Doris Day whirl. (Honestly, for a minute I thought I was going to start singing. *What had happened to me?*) 'Do I look hot to trot or what?'

'Huh?' Pierce attempted to fix me with a stare, but ended up addressing the space six inches to the left of my head.

'Oh Pierce.' I put down the Kahlua and oysters in dismay. 'You're not stoned are you? What've you had?'

'Oh not much,' he said, scratching his balls absent-mindedly. 'Some Quaaludes, some Valium, a face-full of amyl and a snort or two, or three.'

'Oh, is that all.' I flopped on to the lounge chair. The room was full of brand-new white furniture, all of it covered in shiny, clear plastic, which screeched horribly every time you shifted your weight. Old Abe had appointed someone to take care of Pierce's image maintenance. House, haircut, the works. Pierce reckoned that Abe had tossed up whether or not to have Pierce's nose broken to add character to his face.

'Hey, there are only two laws about drugs, kiddo.' Pierce lurched into a sitting position, cupped his hands to his face and lit up a joint. 'Always mix 'em and always do more.' He drew back on his joint like a starving man. 'I mean, you never just have one course of a meal, for Chrissake, now do you?' The flickering light briefly illuminated his face, which looked as though it hadn't been shaved for the entire week. It wasn't just mere stubble. This was more your basic Harris Tweed. He offered the joint to me.

I shook my head. 'I don't wanna be stoned at the ball. Otherwise it'll be like last time. I'll start thinking about God and Art and Death and –'

'The what? Huh?' He got up slowly and weaved his way across to the kitchen.

'– and the Universe and all that kinda stuff.' I found myself fighting a terrible feeling of despondency.

'Duck,' he said, before hunkering down on all fours and crawling over to the fridge. 'The what? Huh?'

'The charity ball. Ouch.' I collided with a dark shape in the gloom.

'Get down. No kidding. If I put on the fucking light, they start screaming. One of them threw a goddamned bottle through my window last night, with this note in it from someone called Petra.

You know what it said? That she'd had this really vivid dream she was having my baby, for Chrissake.'

I felt my heart contract. He wasn't coming.

'It's tonight. You forgot. Pierce, you promised.'

'Did I?' He was momentarily spotlit by the murky light from the fridge. 'You should know better than to pay attention to me, kiddo. You know more shit comes out of my mouth than out of the Malibu sewage plant.' I watched his hand disappear into the mouldy interior and retrieve two beers, before I heard the door suck shut. 'Besides, it's a full moon. If I go out tonight I will undergo some hideous chemical change.'

'You promised.'

'And turn into a warlock. Or worse.' He crawled back across the kitchen tiles, the beers tucked into the waistband of his jeans. 'A television producer.' Back in the relative safety of the living-room, he extracted a can, peeled back the aluminium ring, then extended it towards me.

'I brought Kahlua,' I said dismally. I felt clogged, like when you go swimming on a full stomach. 'It's my lack of lips isn't it?'

'What.' He ashed the joint lazily, his fingers lingering over the butt-congested pizza box.

'Do you want me to get them, you know, surgically enlarged? I mean, would that help?' My voice sounded all wobbly. 'Pierce?'

He responded with a loud belch. He then bared his teeth and inserted a finger into his mouth. 'Hey, are my gums bleeding?' Without waiting for my reply, he curled up in a semi-foetal position at the foot of the television screen.

'Why did you have to get so stoned, *tonight?*' A wave of helplessness went through me.

'Hey, it's like this – the coke was offered to me. I couldn't turn the guy down. You see, I'm not all bad. This is my little contribution to the betterment of humankind, for Chrissake.' He sprawled his legs out across the carpet and rested his head back on his folded arms, like a sunbather. 'If I took the drugs, then he couldn't take them, which lessened his chances of overdosing, dying, getting addicted, having a seizure or burning out his mucous membranes. It's just proof of how self-sacrificing I really am.'

My head felt shrunken. Pierce Scanlen – urban witchdoctor. 'My mate Tash and I had a talk about you the other day.'

'Oh yeah. Whaddabout? Lemme guess, the size of my cock. But no, no, I suppose you're not into small talk.'

I blushed, thinking of the oysters congealing in their cardboard box. 'Tash reckons that you're a selfish, self-indulgent asshole.'

Pierce considered this for a moment. 'Uh-huh,' he agreed.

'She said you were a spoilt little rich boy.'

'Yep.' He eyed me vacantly. 'Is that all? She left out "bitter, cynical and twisted".'

'You just want to live out the entire Hollywood Brat Pack cliché. You want to keep blaming your parents for everything. You want to take too many designer drugs and get big bags under your eyes and look all wan and wasted and have people saying, "Oh, he's a symbol of his lost generation". You want sympathy. Well, I don't feel sorry for you.' Indifferent, Pierce, reached for his beer can. I kicked it out of his reach. 'Christ! Doncha know that aluminium cans take about 500 bloody years to disintegrate?' I recited. 'Doncha know that there are still countries in the world that perform clitoridectomies – Saudi Arabia, Iraq . . .' Pierce looked up, as though he was going to speak, but instead, peeled off a little piece of pastrami from an old pizza and threw it in the general direction of the garbage can. '. . . Iran, Jordan. Doncha know, are you listening to me? That there are Nazi war criminals still at large. And what about the bloody ozone layer? Huh? What about that? When the icecaps melt, Bangladesh is going to just bloody well sink!' As I ranted at him, Pierce launched more and more meat frisbees across the room. 'Doncha know that there are hundreds of endangered species like the, the Woolly Spider Monkey and the . . .'

Pierce now extracted a balloon from his hip pocket and started blowing it up. His own face began to take shape. As I talked, it got bigger and bigger and more swollen until his rubber visage loomed before me, grotesquely misshapen. 'The Northern Square-lipped Rhinoceros . . . the spotted prairie dog.' Pierce didn't seem to be listening. 'Pierce?' Holding the warped, inflated version of himself aloft, he was gazing at a distant spot on the wall, rocking back and forth from the balls of his feet to his heels.

'Dogs have one major advantage over people,' he suddenly said. 'J'know that? Yep. If they're geriatric or sick or just plain depressed, they're allowed to have a merciful death. By law.' He pressed the tip of his joint up against the balloon, which burst deafeningly. 'Wouldn't it be good, eh? And then I could become an eggtimer.' He picked up the remains of the balloon, a shrivelled piece of red rubber, and went on, his voice rasping. 'I got this letter today, from some asshole fan club or other in some asshole shitheap of middle America, asking if they could have my ashes to put in an eggtimer.' He started to laugh. He doubled up with laughter. 'Not only that, but some other dude rang up offering to collect my sweat and sell it in bottles for twenty bucks each. He wants to call it, "The Sweat Smell of Success".' He clutched his belly and roared.

'Personally, I don't see the funny side of it.' I flicked the gold-embossed invitation across my knuckles crossly. 'Look, it's getting late. Are you coming with me,' I took aim at his guilt-gland, '*like you promised*, or are you just gonna do the complete Dingo Act?'

'An eggtimer,' he whimpered, trying to control his voice. 'A fucking eggtimer.'

'It's perfect, if you ask me. You're always running out on people.'

My angry words hovered in the air – ugly, loud, out of place. As we contemplated different corners of the room, a slime of self-pity seemed to engulf us both. I stood there, trying to tell myself that humiliation was character-building. I considered my options. I could

a) Turn on the lights and set the fans outside screaming like cop sirens

b) Sock him in the cake-hole

c) Walk out and hope the hell that he'd follow me. I strode towards the door, well, more like minced, considering the designer straight-jacket I was wearing. To my relief, I heard Pierce padding after me.

'Hey . . .'

I turned, grinning, thinking of the grand entrance we would make, press photographers snapping, fans clapping, Rondah agog.

Pierce thrust a piece of paper at me. 'Cash this for me, will ya?' I peered at the paper. It was a cheque for $3,000. Made out to me. Signed by Pierce's father. 'I told dad you were broke and needed a loan.'

My mouth went dry. 'Is that why . . . is that why you took me to meet your parents?'

'Well mum won't lend me any money. Bitch. And well, I knew

they'd like you, especially dad.' I just stared at him in mute dejection. 'Look, I told ya I was a prick. I've never pretended to be anything else.' I pressed my fingers into my eyelids which felt dry and scratchy. 'I'm sorry about tonight, okay? But it's gonna be an awful goddamned night anyway. Wall-to-wall dinner-suited schmucks and dinner-suited-schmucks-in-training and their designer-dressed female schmuckettes. These people are like rodents – they'd eat each other to stay alive.' I felt a clot of anger rising in my throat. 'Besides, the whole point of being an American is to become so goddamned famous that you can never leave your house, doncha know that?'

My love for him was suddenly cauterised by a blind, white fury. I picked up the box I'd brought and hurled it at his head. He ducked and it detonated against the wall. I seemed to have taken over from Tash in the field of gastronomic invention – this was Oysters Nagasaki. As the screen door slammed, I glimpsed Pierce's poodle, a blur of fur, chasing his tail round and round the room.

'And here we have...' The compere peered down her cosmetically-reconstructed nose at the notepad clutched between her painted talons. '... Bob Hope's sock. Yes. What am I bid for Bob Hope's sock.' Around the reception room, tuxedo-ed guests briefly consulted their sequined partners, before raising manicured hands. All the women looked anorexic. You could whack on a stamp and post most of them, no kidding. I noted, reluctantly, that the place was chockers with wall-to-wall dinner-suited schmucks and dinner-suited-schmucks-in-training and their designer-dressed female schmuckettes.

'One hundred dollars,' the man across from me bellowed, his female postcard giggling shrilly by his side.

Since my late arrival, the other guests had so far bid for a jar of jelly beans donated by Ronald Reagan, Zsa Zsa Gabor's garter, Rin Tin Tin's collar and a rib bone that had once, supposedly, belonged to Cher.

At a charity function like this you can gauge how important you are by where they seat you. Once I'd explained to the lamé-clad hostess that there was no Pierce, I was quickly reassigned a seat up the back, near the dunnies, with a totally interrupted view of the stage and three monosyllabic dinner companions who turned out to be an ex-barrel girl from a cancelled game show, the obligatory astronaut from an abandoned mission and an aged child-star from a fifties sitcom who now did ads for orthopaedic girdles and lint-removers. It was the sort of company you could spend about an hour talking to for a few minutes, if you know what I mean. Just to top off my night, it was then that I noticed Rondah. She swept into the room in a cloud of billowing silk, on the arm of some glamorous toy-boy. She began to circulate, greeted celebrities and dignitaries with indiscriminate affection. She was like a cat, pissing territorially in every corner of the room. She orchestrated her silken gown around her as she was seated at the foot of the stage, right in the line of fire of the cameras and spotlights. The whole room strained to listen to the murmur of idle chatter and smug laughter coming from her table.

I felt like a licorice jelly bean, you know, the one that's always left at the bottom of the pack. Toying with my bread roll, I tried to look as though I was devising a new fuel formula for the Exocet missile, and to look as if I didn't mind – in fact *preferred* – to be here on my own. When Rondah spotted me I immediately started up a riveting conversation with the peppermill. I nodded and smiled, I feigned laughter, I had my attention diverted, momentarily, by the water jug. I gave little flutters of my eyebrows to display my great enjoyment of its amusing conversation.

The ex-barrel girl and the aged child-star looked at me with vague alarm. The grounded astronaut would have too, but his eyes were orbiting his tenth martini and he'd lost all communication with ground control. Just as I started up a sparkling conversation with the butter dish, I saw Rondah moving across the room towards me.

'Well hell-low.' She quickly assessed my three dead-beat companions. 'What? All alone, sugar?' she asked hopefully. '*Men*,' she went on before I could utter a word. 'The trouble with Pierce is that he jest walks all over nice gals. Didja threaten him? Didja cry? Didja walk on out? Listen honey, I don't mean to cramp your style – mind you,' she said, looking me up and down, 'between you an' me, there ain't all that much to cramp – but threats jest don't work with Pierce. It's best to jest come right out and degrade yourself and *beg*.'

I despised Rondah then. For a moment, I saw right into her. Rondah was the sort of person who would have relished telling all the other kids on her block that there was no such thing as Santa Claus or the Tooth Fairy.

'He'll be along later,' I lied. 'He just had some, some business to attend to.'

Rondah raised a skeptical eyebrow. 'My Lordee, what a sweet dress,' she said, rustling her silken gown. She was so flamboyantly dressed, that I felt dishevelled just looking at her. 'It really encapsulates your personality – simple.'

Rondah drew a deep breath, but before she could humiliate me any further, the background percussion of polite applause was suddenly shattered by a rowdy cheer. A vaguely familiar voice rose above it, booming over the amplifier. 'Well, howdy, y'all.' Craning around the column in front of our table and then peering through the pools of light and shrieking people, I could see Chuck, the Chicago Bear. He was standing on the stage, his muscly contours still visible through the thick weave of his dinner suit.

'And what am I bid for a night – one whole night – with the horniest man in America?' The compere yelled. The room throbbed with applause and excitement as the women whooped wildly. Chuck nonchalantly pumped his massive arms. He stood erect, his mighty thighs akimbo. This wasn't a man. This was just one gigantic muscle, in cowboy boots. He flexed a mischievous smile. The squeals reached a crescendo. 'Let's start at $1,000,' the compere brayed.

'Oh God,' Rondah groaned, 'who let *him* out of his cage for the night... DAH-LING!' Her attention and her arm were seized by a gossip columnist from a notorious showbiz magazine, and Rondah, back into Territorial Cat Mode, was off, once more, on her celebrity circuit.

The bidding was now up to $2,500. Sequined arms thrashed. Press photographers machine-gunned volleys of shots. Women wearing little more than predatory expressions tried to thrust their way up on to the stage. Restrained, politely, by dinner-suited bouncers, they resorted to throwing their house-keys and phone numbers. The whole room was suddenly charged with raw sexual voltage. The amount escalated, as did the squeals, until Chuck, beaming, finally went under the hammer for $10,000 dollars. 'A dollar per inch,' he crooned into the microphone as the lady who'd bought him swooned.

It was interval. Music shuddered into life and people started dancing, lip-synching the same saccharin lyrics that had sounded so poignant to me earlier in the evening. Suffering from terminal tedium – well, it doesn't take long to exhaust the conversation possibilities with a peppermill – I wove through the tables toward the exit. I passed Chuck. The paparazzi were moiling around him, squabbling for position. As I waited in the phone queue to call a cab, Rondah swept by, now on the arm of a famous producer.

'What?' she said, with mock-sympathy, pausing beside me. 'Still not here? I always thought Pierce had a God Complex – *He's* s'posed to be comin' back one day too, ain't he? Frankly, sugar, I think you've got more hope with the Second Comin'.'

I decided to walk. As I made a beeline for the door, I glimpsed an enormous shape in my peripheral vision. It loomed larger and larger until I felt a great hairy hand on my shoulder. 'Hey, babe! With me, see, I never just go for a lady's tits or her legs or her ass. What turns me on is her face. I suppose a –'

'– facial would be out of the question.' I chorused. The horniest man in America threw back is head and roared with laughter. 'Fuckin' A. Hey, you wanna know some-think? You're funny. You know that? You're one hellava funny little lady.' He broke away to welcome two autograph hunters while simultaneously indulging in a boisterous exchange of hosannahs and high-fives with a passing host of soap opera stars. 'Assholes,' he whispered, turning back to me, the fake smile still warm on his lips. He returned his pen to his pocket, checked his watch, cocked his head to one side and appraised me. 'Okay, I'm outta here. Let's hit the hay?'

'What?'

'Let's ride the one-eyed express. Let's mix body fluids. Let's . . .'

'Dah-ling.' Rondah disentangled herself from her producer and lunged at Chuck's lips. She lingered there long enough for the cameras to click. 'I just so ad-mire what y'all have done for charity, Charles. You don't mind if I call you Charles do you?' The accent was hurtling South by the second, no kidding. 'Most men in your poz-i-shun, just don't care enough about the de-fence-less of this world.' She widened her eyes defencelessly. She practically purred, for God's sake. I suddenly decided that, with her over-made-up face, exaggerated cleavage and coquettish ways, Rondah was the world's first *female* female impersonator.

'I thought you reckoned he belonged in a cage?' I reminded her.

Rondah turned her back on me and focused Chuck with her old wide-eyed and innocent look. I can't believe men find that kind of expression attractive. If you ask me, she looked like a dog that had just been spayed. 'Won't you join me, for a little cock – ' She rolled the first word round in her freshly lipsticked mouth, before tagging on the second syllable ' – tail?'

'Gee, I would sugar,' Chuck said, shaking himself free, and taking hold of my arm, 'but fuckin' A, I got my hands real full, right here.'

At that moment, illuminated by the coloured foyer lights, Chuck Larson seemed to me to be the most incredibly handsome and wonderfully mysterious man in the entire world. Kind of.

'J'know how many chicks I've been to bed with?' he asked, after fobbing off Rondah, who flounced back to the bar, having warned me as she left that God was watching my every move. '9,999.' He placed his calloused paw around my shoulders. I thought of Pierce. Of his soft hands. Of his curly lips. Of the way he rocked forward on the balls of his feet when he was excited. 'An' I was a late starter. No shit. Neva scored a touchdown wiv a chick till I was sixteen. Not bad for ten years eh?' I thought of the little pigtail coiled at the nape of Pierce's neck. 'And I've never, ever been shot-down.' I thought of how he smirked, in that certain sidelong way he had. 'You wouldn't break my record, little Oss-sea, would ja? So, are we gonna play with the pork sword or what?'

He was a smooth-talking bastard, he really was. I glanced at my profile in the mirrored door. What was so bad about small breasts anyway? At least you could always read the entire message on my T-shirts. Not only that, I'd never had to wonder *why* I got a job.

'Hey,' I said, suave as hell, 'when you put it that way . . .'

Chuck's apartment smelt like the inside of a very old and scungy jockstrap. I picked my way around the dumbbells and weights – Chuck had told me that he had a personal trainer, who came every morning to give him a work-out, you know, a bit like being a dog and getting put on a lead and taken out for a run. The bathroom was steamy with damp towels and carpeted with discarded tracksuits. Jock straps dripped from the railing in the shower recess. It was a tropical jungle in there.

My heart was beating on triple time. My face, in the mirror, was kinda pre-coronary pink. I splashed it with cold water, smeared a space in the mirror and looked at my stunned expression. 'Okay,' I said calmly, 'your name is Katrina Kennedy. You're twenty years old and you're living in Los Angeles – even though your old man would say that was a contradiction in terms. The man you love thinks that your breasts are too small, your best friend is baring all for one of the tackiest meat market magazines in the whole of the Western world, and you're about to have sex with a man who was just sold for one night, for $10,000.' I took a deep breath and strode back into the living-room. The lights were now so low that it took me a while to spot him. A six foot two inch naked tower of male flesh rose up from the dark groin of the room.

'I wancha to know, right,' Chuck said, unbuttoning my dress at the back, 'that I ain't no butt-head, got it? You see, most people, right, reckon that footballers are just meat-heads. That shits me, right. That burns my ass.' He slid the dress off my shoulders, and down over my hips. 'I'm gonna tell you somefink I don't normally tell like nobody – but I know a loddabout art, see. Yeah, I do. I have the Pieta, by, oh, by lott-sen *lots* of different painters and I have, oh, Dalis and Rodins and Magrittes and Hockneys and – it's all over the fuckin' place. I'll show ya later, eh?' He threaded my legs out of my underpants. 'An' it's all good, too. Ya know, if I tell ya I have a Merv Moon-Unit sculpture, j'know his work? He's this real hot Californian-type artist. This one's kinda of two women bein' kinda chainsawed by these two rats in tutus, hangin' right smack-bang next to a Giacometti. You'll go, "no way, never, ugh". But when you see it, it works. 'Cause, art, see, is like people. Great art and great art will kinda meld, right? Just like great people and great people.' As if going for a try, he scooped me up in his burly arms and deposited me on the enormous bed. And not just an ordinary bed. It was a transparent waterbed, stocked with goldfish.

He stood over me, a triangular mass of bronzed muscle, hands on hips. I smiled lamely up at him.

'These,' he said, puffing out his chest, 'are my pecs – pectorialis major,' he elaborated. 'Feel.' He placed my palm on a muscly mound of breast flesh. I prodded it, as you would a wounded

animal in the road, to see if it was alive or dead. It rippled. I drew
back my finger in vague alarm. 'And these . . .' he revolved so that
I was staring at a brown wall of sinew, '. . . are what I'm really
workin' on now – my lats.' Two little wings of flesh appeared on
the sides of his torso. 'Latisimas Dorsi,' he explained, continuing
the guided tour of musculature. 'And then, of course, there's the
old delts.' Chuck squared his shoulders and loomed over me. He
was panting like a dog. 'Check the gluts. Ripped huh?' As he
placed my hands on his boulder-solid buttocks, I thought about
what he'd told me, 9,999 lovers. I shifted a little so that he could
now rub his undulating abs against mine. That meant, let's see,
I worked it out in my head as his quads gripped my thighs and
rubbed back and forth. Ten years of sex, 9,999 lovers, that meant
about 1,000 a year. His bulging triceps and biceps lowered across
my body, as he placed his hands under my gluteus maximus. He
raised me up a little, and, flexing his anterior posterior medials,
rolled over on top of me. That meant, I analysed, three and one
tenths of a woman a day. Christ! Didn't this guy ever have to go
visit the rellos? I mean, he might be a stud and all, but didn't he
ever have to spend a day buying groceries? Didn't he ever come
down with the flu? Or maybe just not feel like it? 'Ooh, baby!' I
looked at his undulating slabs of flesh poised above me, at his
pulsating pecs, his throbbing ads, his oribis muscles – which were
descending towards me in a state of puckered contraction and
thought, Kat Kennedy, you're about to have sex with the biggest
liar in America. I dodged his kiss, rolled sideways and climbed
out of bed.

'Hey,' Chuck grunted as his lips collided with the pillow.
'Baby . . . ? Kat . . . Nice puddy-tat.'

'Listen, I'm sorry,' I stammered, fumbling into my clothes. 'But,
ya know, I'm not your type, really I'm not.'

'Huh?'

'I don't know anything about football. In fact, I hate sport. You
know, I once played tennis with the racket still in its cover. No
kidding. The most exercise I get is cleaning my teeth. I mean my
body is just a mess. Look,' I extended my arm and wobbled the
flesh on the upper part of it. 'Kimono sleeves,' I said. 'I'm just
not good enough for you. You'd be slumming it with me. It's an
insult to your deltoid-latisimas-whatsa-ma-call-its. Okay?'

'Whaddabout my art collection, huh? I ain't even shown yer

Mervyn Moon-Unit's sculp . . .' I made for the door. 'Hey, happy May Day to you too,' he called out after me. 'You've gotta problem, lady. J'know that? A real big problem.'

I knew it. I knew I had a big problem. And I was going to see him and sort it out, right now.

MAGGOTS IN THE MEAT MARKET

I hitch-hiked uptown to Pierce's place. The back gate groaned open. I pushed the back door. The television cast a tubercular blue pall over the room. 'Pierce?' The dog tilted its head and appraised me, then cocked its leg and pissed on the floor. I negotiated my way through the maze of overturned chairs, and dog turds towards the kitchen. I could make out a dark shape hunched over the kitchen table. I switched on the light, triggering a scream from the fans outside. I glimpsed them through the window, in giggling tête-à-têtes. They launched into their ritual ear-splitting chant: '*two, four, six, eight* . . .' A pool of cold coffee was congealing with a trickle of blood from where his head had cracked down on the table. I moved like a deep-sea diver, weighted down with tanks and flippers and leaded belts. I lifted his delicate head and cradled it in my lap. '*Who do we appreciate?*' His hair was plastered to his face with perspiration. I smelt the sour reek of vomit from the corner of his mouth. I saw the pills scattered on the floor where they'd fallen. '*P-I-E-R-C-E.*' I thought he was dead. And then, he twitched, like a fish on the deck of a boat. '*PIERCE!*'

It was morning by the time I left the hospital. I nosed Pierce's black Porsche out into the torrent of traffic. Just as well the car was automatic, because last night had been the first time I had ever actually driven a car. As I could barely see over the dashboard, manoeuvring it was like trying to steer a house down a highway.

I spoke to the rock and was let inside the walled mansion. The harsh morning light now revealed the long, grimacing cracks in

175

the castle walls, the algae choking the fountains, the noses chipped off the ornamental stone goddesses. The atmosphere was soiled and seedy. You could almost smell it.

Tash was in the middle of her morning's shoot when I burst into the studio, panting, ashen-faced.

'You'll have to wait, Missy,' the make-up guy told me snidely as I pushed past him.

Tash, wearing black panties and fish-net stockings, was standing with her hands on her hips, as Carl lifted her breasts, one at a time, to stretch a piece of what looked like masking tape across the crease beneath. He then camouflaged the transparent tape with a flesh-coloured paint. Carefully lowering each breast, he stood back to examine his artistry.

'Kat. Hey there,' Tash shouted, turning her gravity-defying bosom in my direction. The sticky tape had created a cantilever, a kind of flying bust-rest. 'Can ya believe this?' she laughed. 'Here's every woman in the goddamned world lookin' at the women in porn magazines, thinkin' desperately, "why don't I look like those women," when *no* woman in the world looks like those women. It's all a scam,' she chortled, before blowing a big, pink balloon of bubble gum. 'Hey. Whatsamatta?' she demanded, finally focusing on my face.

'Pierce . . . he overdosed. Last night. I found him. It was my fault. He was freaked 'cause someone wants to make him into an eggtimer and . . .'

'A what?' Carl was now strapping her into an iron-laced corset. Her new, aerodynamic breasts pouted over the top.

'And I told him about the sea otters and the rain forests.'

'Is he dead?' Her lipstick was arterial-red.

I shook my head. 'I've been at the hospital all night. I had to drive him there. I can't drive.' A terrible sob came out of me. Brushing Carl away, Tash was by my side, wrapping her arms around me.

'Natasha,' Carl admonished, wearily tapping his wrist watch.

Tash got to her feet and led me defiantly towards the door. 'Take a break, fellas, okay?'

Carl slammed down his masking tape. 'This behaviour is just not acceptable!'

Tash replied with a one-fingered salute and led me, sobbing, across the lawn and into the indoor bird sanctuary. The birds squawked uproariously at our arrival. 'J'like the get-up?' she laughed, gesturing at her lacy corset. 'I was born to be cheap. What can I tell ya? Here, this'll cheer ya up,' she winked, guiding me over to the parrot cage. 'Hello, pretty girl.' The parrot ruffled its feathers, took a bad-tempered peck at Tash's fingers, then retorted, 'Hello, Polly wants a cracker. I am a mindless bimbo. Hello, Polly wants a cracker. I am a mindless bimbo.'

'Like it?' Tash laughed, rotating towards me. 'That's what I've been doin' for the last few days.' I gave a crooked little smile. Tash took hold of me by the shoulders and pushed me firmly down on to the cold stone seat. 'Now,' she said sternly, 'I think it's time for a Survival Technique.' Her navel, I noticed, was glistening with baby oil. She sat next to me, snagging her stocking on a stone. 'Oh shit. Now,' she gazed into my eyes intensely, 'I know at times we all think that our life is the pits and that nothin', ab-sol-ute-ly nothing in the whole wide world, could possibly be worse than what we're goin' through. But, like, there is one thing worse than anythin' imaginable. In Calcutta, an' this is true, where labour is, like, dirt-cheap and there are squillions of people, when the sewerage pipes under the city get all clogged up, ja'know how they unclog 'em? They, like, tie a rope around a guy, a human being, and they pull him through the pipes of shit – to clean them!'

'Really? Like a two-legged Rotor-rooter?' I asked, appalled, remembering the grisly dunny-cleaning gadget I'd seen advertised on TV.

'Yep! So, neither of us should ever, ever complain again. Okay?' Exhausted, drained, I nodded.

'Now,' she said. 'I'd better get back before old Carl-baby kills me. Ya see, it's nearly lunchtime, and we're still only up to tits and pubes. Still no "beaver shots". I know what'll happen – after my lunch of, like, one stick of celery, Carl will come back and tell me that the shots so far are lookin' fab-u-lous, but that Stefan went nuclear 'cause the photos are too soft. Carlie-Warlie will then pretend to be really pissed. Ya see, most models would be desperately in love with the photographer by now. Most would have been screwin' his brains out durin' the last few days. And he's told them he loves them and, oh, the whole catastrophe. So, now that he's pissed at 'em, they'll, like, do anythin' to make him love 'em again. Like spreading 'em. Here.' Generously, she extracted the piece of gum from her mouth and inserted it into mine. 'Their psychology sucks. I mean, get this. Yesterday, in the polaroid session, Carl kept tellin' me to wet my finger and moisten myself. "You're dryin' out again dah-ling." But, ya see, they've got fake pussy-juice, made from some kinda silicone, for that. They just want me to get turned on by touchin' myself. How could anyone get turned on under a room full of lights, with gaffer-taped tits and those two sleaze-schmuckos lookin' at ya? . . . I mean, *please*. The only thing which is turnin' me on is the thought of the money I'm gonna get for the goddamned centre-fold.'

'What?' I sniffled.

'Have I filled ya in on how much cashola I'm gonna make?'

'Tash, haven't they told you yet?'

'Told me what?' she asked distractedly, examining the hole in her stocking.

'They're not using you for the centrefold.'

'Huh?' she said, poking an inquisitive finger into the tear.

'I overheard them.' Still sniffling, I groped for a tissue up the sleeves of Pierce's jacket that I'd thrown over my shoulders at the hospital the night before.

'What?' Her head jerked upwards like a periscope.

'When I fell asleep. In the studio. Behind the . . .'

'What did they say?' She accidentally tore the hole even wider with her fingernail. 'What did – '

'They said that your tits were too pale, or something.' I sifted through the debris of dead matches, parking stubs, snapped swizzle sticks, martini olives and various vials of coloured pills in the pockets of Pierce's coat.

'But I've *tanned*. Whaddaya think I've been doin' up here the last . . .'

'And that your nipple, I dunno which one, was partly inverted.'

'But we got that out with ice. These guys are talkin' outta their assholes.'

'Not just that. They also reckoned that your nipples were too dark, from having a kid, or something. Morons. I mean, shows how much *they* know, right?'

Tash froze. 'They said that?' she asked quietly.

'Yeah.' Giving up, I wiped my nose on Pierce's sleeve. 'They kept going on and on about a secondary pictorial.'

'No. No. About the baby.' Her voice reminded me of car tyres crunching on gravel.

'Yeah. Typical. And there was Stefan bragging about how well he knows the female anatomy an' – '

Tash stood up. The abruptness of her movements set the birds squawking and squealing in a raucous cacophony. She stalked out of the sanctuary and across the lawn to the studio with me hot on her heels, her very high heels that skewered the grass.

When she burst into the studio, the make-up guy rose to his feet, clicking his tongue in mock-anger. 'Would you just look at the state of that face. Oh, and the hair!'

Tash's dishevelled hair was sticking out like a head-dress. Which was apt, 'cause she was on the warpath. 'Fuck off,' she said to him calmly, before ripping off her layers of sticky tape. It fell on to the floor like skin.

'Whaddaya think you're – Oh my God! And your tights are laddered! Carl! *Carl*! Come quick!'

Carl swaggered over, all smooth and suave and full of tenderness. 'Baby, love, hey, honey-child. Okay, get a grip. You're boodiful babe, you really are. Get Stefan!' he hissed to the make-up guy.

'Why the fuck didncha tell me you'd changed your mind about the centrefold?'

'Oh, is it about the *centrefold*? Heck, I was gonna tell ya. Of course we were.' This guy had the moral integrity of a cockroach. 'But a secondary pictorial, I mean, just saying we don't use you for the centrefold, an' all.' He backtracked, his eyes fidgeting. 'A secondary pictorial is still real big, babe.'

'A secondary pictorial is $1,500,' Tash said, her voice icy. 'A centrefold is *six*.'

Carl's face suddenly congealed into hateful scorn. His pretence of politeness evaporated. 'Ya know, I've met chicks like you before. You dykes are all the same. Basically you just wish you were a man.'

'*I* don't,' Tash said calmly. 'But I bet *you* do.' For a second I thought Carl was going to wallop her. Gone were the Gucci manners. He was now beginning to look like the Photographer From Hell. 'J'know why women have cunts?' he spat. 'Well, do ya? – So men'll talk to them.'

'Women, I'll have you know,' Tash hissed back, 'are far superior to men. A penis is jut an oversized clitoris. And a clitoris is the only part of the human body that exists purely for pleasure. So chew on that fuck-face!' She strode out of the studio. I scrambled after her. Other guests, baking themselves poolside, glanced up in amazement, as she stalked past in her peek-a-boo corset. A big-bellied businessman stretched out his hand to pat her posterior. She wheeled around and thwacked him across the head, before strutting over to the Spider Monkey cage. She opened the door. 'Go on, you suckers.' But they just sat staring at her, moon-eyed. When she untethered the peacocks an army of gardeners came galloping across the grass.

She stomped towards the drive and got into the passenger side of Pierce's car. Once inside, she drew her legs up to her chest, folded her arms around them, buried her head and started to cry.

'Tash, hey, it's only a centrefold,' I soothed, climbing in beside her. 'It's no big deal, you know.'

'It's not that,' she said funereally. And then she started to rock back and forth, her arms locked around her legs, back and forth, sobbing silently. *Then* it finally made sense. The private detective, the money, the secrecy, the hope chest, the wedding paraphernalia, the brag book.

'Your little brother,' I addressed her elbows, 'he's really your own kid.'

'They took the baby away as soon as he was born.' She kept rocking. 'They didn't even let me see him. The only way I knew I'd had a boy, was 'cause one of the fuckin' nurses said, "Give him to me".' She rocked forward. 'I never got to see him.' She rocked back. 'They wouldn't let me see him.'

PART
THREE

WHO DO I HAVE TO FUCK TO GET OFF THIS SHOW?

Tash took to her bed and didn't get up. She abandoned her daily singing exercises and favourite TV soaps. She wouldn't even acknowledge my knocks on the door. She just ordered in take-away sushi and bottles of whiskey. Once, I pressed my lips up to the keyhole to sing the television commercial for Rotor-rooter . . . 'Call Rotor Rooter, that's the name, and away goes troubles down the drain . . .' But there was no response. Occasionally I'd catch a glimpse of her on her way to or from the loo, her kimono stained and wilted, the silk tie trailing behind her on the carpet like a frayed little tail.

What she'd confessed in the car was that at fifteen, Tash, who was in state care at the time, had got in 'the pudding club' as she called it, and had been coerced into signing adoption papers. No one had told her she had a choice. She called her kid Elvis Raymond, but he had a different name now. She'd been searching for him ever since.

It was a bad time all round. Cosmo still had some terrible bug which he couldn't shake off. The writers had graduated to wearing full period costume. Abe was still busy power-lunching his way to indigestion. Mimi was hounding me to join her Rainbow Reflection Centre, which taught channelling classes at $25. To keep young, Rondah was now undergoing a course of Hydergine, a prescription drug for Alzheimer's Disease. There were a few side-effects, ranging from mild nasal congestion to extreme coma. No need to tell you what I was rooting for. The days were getting hotter and hotter. The sky was so blue it made my eyes ache.

But, worst of all, nothing was said about Pierce's absence.

In the first week's script, his character was just conveniently sent on an unexpected business trip. The next week had him injured in a car accident – which meant Abe could hire a stand-in and just swathe his mug in bandages. By the third week, the studio was running out of ideas, which explained why Pierce's character was suddenly abducted by mad mullahs. By the end of June, just as the writers were contemplating turning him into a Martian spy who had been recalled to the Star Ship, Pierce appeared back on the set. He was his usual wise-cracking self, a little pale, but still the black-belt master of the art of tongue-fu.

In Los Angeles, there's a special law relating to information. It's called Freedom of the Suppress. Abe paid off everyone imaginable to keep Pierce's 'wobbly' out of the papers. Nobody would talk about what happened – least of all Pierce.

'Why didja take all those pills?' I cornered him in the make-up room. 'Did you mean to take so many?' We were alone, except for Cosmo, who sat, slumped and asleep, in one of the make-up chairs. On the rare days Cosmo did turn up to work, he would just doze off all the time, even right in the middle of a conversation with you. But nobody was mentioning that either. I couldn't understand this town. Everyone was so eager to talk about their impotence, penile implants and herpes pustulences, but when it came to talking about real problems – there seemed to be a conspiracy of silence.

'The trouble is, Pierce, you're living your life as though it's a movie.'

He was sitting cross-legged, arms folded across his chest like an Indian chief.

'Huh. If that were true,' he scoffed, 'doncha think I just might've picked something a little more goddamn interesting? A Marx Brothers film perhaps, or *Sex-Crazed Amazon Women in Love*.'

I glowered at him. 'You know what I mean.'

'Okay, look, I'll tell you the truth. I took the drugs for one reason.'

I leaned forward eagerly, 'Yeah?'

'To make myself more intelligent, charming and goddamn sexy.'

The truth was, he was looking the opposite of all of the above. He looked worn-out. His green eyes were bloodshot, as if he'd been underwater for too long. His hair was matted together and his face, when I stroked it, was slick with sweat. 'It was accidental, though, right?' I persisted hopefully.

'I just needed a few drugs to help me forget,' he said seriously.

'Forget what?' My voice was a Rescue Squad cop coaxing someone back from the edge of a cliff.

'To forget that I take drugs, of course.' He swung around and around in his swivel chair, grinning maniacally.

Rondah glided into the room like a large ocean liner looking for a berth. She steamed in our direction. Pierce bolted. I made to do likewise, but Rondah cruised across my path. 'Oh, ain't you havin' make-up today, sugar?'

'I've *had* it.' Where were the good retorts when you needed them? Why could you never, ever think of them until you were at home, cleaning your teeth and putting out the cat.

'Oh.' She smiled her Academy Award-winning smile. 'Still in-er-ested in Pierce, huh?' I tried to manoeuvre past her, but she blocked my escape. 'I know I do tend to run him down, a liddle, tinsy, insy bit now and then, but one of the good thangs about him is that he's not in-er-ested in superficial thangs – like *appearance*. Still, I suppose Pierce has enough good looks for two people, hasn't he, hun?'

She anchored herself in the make-up chair. She wouldn't need any make-up for the role I'd cast her in – the butter in *Last Tango in Paris*.

'But the truth is,' she purred, 'I just hate to see y'all makin' such a damn fool of ya-self, sugar.' The seam of her stretch jeans parted her labia perfectly – what we called in Australia a 'front bum'. 'Can't you see that Pierce is just not pickin' up the option on your friendship? Your relationship is in Turnaround. Face facts. Pierce needs a strong woman. Not some little chickadee he can jest walk all over. Why, he jest up and left the detoxification programme at Cedars Sinai. And sweet Lord, Abe paid twenty thousand bucks for that. Oh, gee,' she said smugly, clocking the look of shock on my face. 'You did know he's a certified addict, didncha honey?'

By the time I got outside, Pierce was pulled up alongside the security gates. I opened the passenger door and slid into the seat beside him. He glanced at me, a look of exhaustion in his eyes. 'Well, howdy pard'ner,' he said, gunslinger style.

'Have you been in a detox unit?' I persisted.

'God, eat one person and they call you a cannibal. Sodomise one guy and they call you a queer. I don't need no detox unit, okay?'

'Is that where you've been?'

Pierce flicked on the radio as he waited for the boom gate to rise. As soon as it was in salute position, we revved out of the lot. The leather seat was hot and sticky on the backs of my legs. I rested my forearm along the window frame, but it too scorched me. The crackly voice of the radio announcer was giving details of the predicted heatwave. Pierce, inscrutable behind his smoky Raybans, remained silent until we ·swung into a car park. The sign over the gates read, 'Forest Lawn. The Final Retirement Home. A poignant way for people on both sides of Life to say Goodbye'.

'A cemetery? You brought me to a cemetery?'

'I kinda like it. It's real quiet.'

'Pierce, normally I don't approve of this sort of thing but – are you still seeing your psychiatrist?'

'Why bother?' He flung his legs out of the car and stood up. 'They never cure you of anything. It's not a helluva lot in their interest. I mean, a cure means the loss of a client, right?'

If Tash's magazine mansion was the Disneyland of Sex, then this place was the Disneyland of Death. The lawns rolled on luxuriously, acre after acre with musical fountains, signposts advertising the graves of the famous, and elaborate obelisks that looked, in the dazzling sun, like marzipan confections. To the left was a drive-in funeral parlour with picture-window rooms, where relatives could view the remains of loved ones without the inconvenience of leaving the car. You haven't lived until you've died in LA. No kidding. I followed Pierce across the grass to where he'd deposited himself in a clover patch. A circle of silence stretched around him. I just sat and waited for him to let down the forcefield.

'I love this place,' he said finally. 'It just cheers me right up.'

In the garden below us, an extended family of Italian mafiosi in sinister suits and wide ties, with lacy-dressed little girls and bow-tied little boys, were trailing behind an ominous black coffin. It was pretty cheery, I have to tell you.

'Pierce,' I turned to him, grim and determined, 'All those pills. Why?'

'Why? Well, pills are a helluva lot less messy than most other forms of self-destruction, doncha think?'

'So, you really meant to . . .' My blood temperature dropped to glacial levels.

'Commit suicide? Na.' He lay back on the grassy bank. 'Look, if I really was gonna commit suicide, I would've, you know, laid some kind of groundwork early on, right? I would've been giving interviews, you know, about what a helluva sensitive and soul-searching guy I really am. I would've been seen crying in public a lot. I would've taken up, you know, writing poetry and playing Leonard Cohen records.'

My crap-antenna was wobbling so violently I could hardly sit still. I had motion sickness. 'Couldn't you quit being so *glib*. Just for once.'

'I'm serious. Look kid. Quit worryin'. If I really had meant to top myself, wouldn't I have left a goddamned note? Something really profound and heart-warming for Chrissake. That made absolutely everybody feel really guilty?' Although he was smiling, his body was tense, his neck muscles fanning out like a frilled-neck lizard. 'I would've dressed for the occasion too. Something that goes with the colour of puke. A little beige number, I think, with flecks of orange.'

The whole time he spoke, I studied the shifting planes of his face. Even though his voice was light and flippant, his jaw was clenched. It moved jerkily from left to right. Right to left. His moods seemed to be going up and down faster than a TV evangelist's underpants. 'Pierce,' I insisted, 'how did it happen? I have to know.'

'Wouldja give it a rest? Jeesus. What are ya? My mother?'

Pierce sprung up and made for the car at a sprint. By the time I'd caught up to him, the car was idling impatiently. I climbed inside. As he injected himself into the traffic, the horizon was spectacularly stained with streaks of neon orange and vulgar yellow. 'Ironic, isn't it,' Pierce said, 'that air pollution produces the most fantastic goddamn sunsets in the world.'

'So, what happened?' I made a car salesman look timid, I really did.

'It's the same with sex and stuff too,' Pierce continued, ignoring my question. 'Too much sex increases a chick's chances of contracting cancer of the cervix, right? And too little sex increases a guy's chances of getting cancer of the prostate. Bizarre, huh?'

'Pierce?

Pierce answered my question by slotting a tape into the machine. Some mindless rap music thudded out of the speakers. 'PIERCE,' I yelled above the din. 'You can't just go round pretending this didn't happen.' He thwacked his palms against the dashboard leather in time with the beat. 'Do you want to end up emotionally anaesthetised? Like your old man? Is that what you . . .' He bellowed along to some bass-thumping monosyllables, completely drowning me out.

Back in the studio lot, Pierce silenced the tape deck and turned to me. 'Look, kiddo,' he said kindly, 'you've just gotta stop being so considerate and all. This is *LA*. We don't behave like that here. People are gonna start labelling you some kinda social weirdo or something. You'll get locked up.'

I stretched my hand towards him, tentatively, as though he were a bewildered nocturnal creature, caught unexpectedly in daylight. 'I'm worried about you.'

'Why bother?' Pierce said, scratching his arse.

I took a deep breath. I could feel every pore, every cell, every follicle, prickling with embarrassment. 'Because . . . because . . . I love you, I guess.'

Pierce frowned into space. His brow furrowed. He then turned and leant towards me. For one cardiac-arresting moment, I thought he was going to kiss me. But instead, he held his hands up the air, thumbs and index fingers extended, as if holding a piece of string. Threading the imaginary string into one of my ears and out the other, he then began sawing rhythmically back and forth.

'What are you doing?'

'I'm dental-flossing your brain.'

It was then that I felt my chin start to tremble. I tried to speak, but my voice was all wobbly and weird. Please don't cry, I begged myself. Please don't cry. I made a plea-bargain with my body, promising not to eat the leftover Eater eggs I'd hoarded, to exercise daily and go to bed early, if only it would not betray me now. 'What's going on with you?' I blubbered, my chin crumbling, my face caving in. Swabbing at my eyes with a hanky, I vowed to stuff myself to the gills with chocolate and stay up late as often as possible. 'I mean, there's always some excuse. When I first met you, you led me to believe that you only loved your car.'

'I suppose buying you a car would be out of the question? It's my best pick-up line,' he joked.

'Then there was the mysterious girlfriend. Then you tell me you're in a High Risk AIDS Category. *Then* you decide you're celibate. Meanwhile, you're stringing me along and pretending you like me so you can get all my money and use me to get cash out of your parents.'

'Hey, I keep trying to make ends meet, no kidding. But the goddamned ends keep moving.'

'I've finally got you sussed: the only person you love is yourself. Deep down, you're skin-deep, Scanlen, do you know that? So quit with the bullshit and just tell me straight out *what the bloody hell is going on with you?*'

We sat for a long time saying nothing in the hot, bleak car park. The asphalt bubbled in the sun. The fans at the gate screamed. The crack dealers dealt. The whole city was stupid with heat. A fly zigzagged its way across the windscreen. I lashed out at it with my hand. It stalled, midair, then plummeted to the dashboard where it jerked and gyrated. We contemplated it in dismal silence. It took longer to die than an Opera singer, no kidding.

'Okay,' he said at last.

'What?'

'Okay, kiddo. I'll tell you everything.' He eased himself up out of the car. 'My dealer's at the gate.' He fiddled casually in my handbag. 'Ya know where he keeps his coke? In his shoe. He's the only man in the world who enjoys puttin' his foot in his mouth.' Calmly extracting some notes from my purse, he slid out of the car. 'Just lemme score some toot an' I'll siddown an' tell you everythin'. Okay?'

It was the last I saw of him for three days.

And they were three terrible days.

I spent most of the time searching for Pierce. I looked for him everywhere – up at his garage, down at the gym, over at the cemetery, in his favourite civilian (meaning they were off the lot) snack bars – 'Nature Strip' and 'The Munch Hour'. But nobody had seen him. Nobody. I dialled his number all day, every day, letting the phone ring and ring and ring, till my ear felt all squashed and numb. Nothing. I rang his doctor. I rang his dealer. I went around to his house and pounded on the doors. But the windows were shuttered. The doors bolted. The gates barred. I joined the straggling crocodile of pubescent females on the pavement, and kept watch. The whole house, locked up like that, looked as though it were scowling directly at me. Finally, in desperation, I rang his parents.

'Did you get the cheque, dear?' Pierce Snr asked.

'The what? Oh, yes. Yes. Thanks a lot. I'll pay you back just as soon as I can.'

God, I thought, now he's got me lying for him. What's more, I did it with such ease. It was my father, I thought with dread, coming out in me.

Pierce had to be written out of the show again. The mad mullahs came back and this time, *they* were discovered to be Martian spies, sent, we were told, on a top-secret mission – to steal Rondah's treasured donut recipe. 'Oh Lordee – who wrote this sheat?' Rondah screeched from the stage and led the actors in their usual walkout.

The predicted heatwave was beginning to crackle its way through the windows from outdoors. Rings of sweat stained each armpit, as the cast and crew collapsed on to the set, waiting to see what would happen next.

While Abe tried to negotiate between the actors (all except Mimi, who had decided to take a vow of silence to cleanse her inner aura) and the writers (who had resorted to fire-eating acts until George accidentally flambéd his head), we received a message that Cosmo was dead. All the flu viruses and 'tummy upsets' and cold sores and sleeping sickness had been symptoms of something far more serious. In the trade papers his obituary read 'Cosmo Vinyl. Bachelor. Age 42. Cause of death – liver cancer.' His coffin, according to Californian law, would be marked with a large and unmistakable 'A'. These days the words 'bachelor' and 'cancer' were a euphemism for AIDS.

While all of the crew and catering staff went into quiet mourning, Rondah reappeared wearing a surgical mask.

'Well,' she said defensively, 'nobody knows jest exactly *how* it's spread. Those germs could be all over this very make-up room.' She also announced that she wanted the entire place sterilised and that no make-up artist was allowed to touch her ever again, unless wearing surgical gloves. Rondah Rivers made Charles Manson look compassionate, she really did.

The next day, the writers, who had been up all night substituting Martians for mad mullahs and mad mullahs for Martians, appeared at the camera run-through wearing T-shirts which read 'Awful Punishment Awaits Really Bad People', and then proceeded to laugh hysterically at every line of their own dialogue. The more they laughed, the more deadpan became the actors' delivery. It was going to be a long day. I pressed my fingers into my eyeballs. They felt sunburnt, on the inside.

The third day was taping day. It was also my twenty-first birthday. Most of us were late to the studio because we attended Cosmo's funeral at the Disneyland of Death. Needless to say, Rondah and the other actors hadn't bothered to turn up. The producers and television executives who did bother, talked business – Cosmo's death had turned into a 'power funeral'.

By the time we got back to the lot, the audience for the four o'clock taping was already streaming through the gates, armed with autograph books and Instamatics. The feeling backstage was one of terminal panic. None of us knew our lines or our moves; the script was being changed by the minute; and Pierce was still missing. Jackie, the television executive, kept rifling through the pharmacy she called a handbag, popping different coloured pills and wheezing on her Ventalin pump. She was, by now, drinking Mylanta straight from the bottle. Pretty soon she'd be pushing round an intravenous drip of the stuff.

To make matters worse, the air-conditioning had broken down. Being inside the studio was not unlike being in a microwave oven.

Mimi was refusing to wear underpants on stage because, thanks to acupuncture, her vaginal juices had just come back. Rondah was refusing to remove her AIDS-barrier gloves.

There was half an hour to go before taping.

Abe ricocheted between the control room and backstage, and the actors and crew were all ringing their agents to see who they had to fuck to get off this show. News came that the writers had locked themselves in Das Booth, in the nude, and had gone, officially, on strike. Rondah announced that they might as well stay that way. She refused to put into her mouth words written by such dee-praved pee-pull.

While the panic continued backstage, I watched the audience file into the studio. They craned and strained for glimpses of their pin-up stars. Jeff, the comedian (and I use that term loosely) who 'warmed-up' the audience with recycled jokes, was positively haemorrhaging charisma into the microphone. 'Welcome. Welcome. Well hel-lo sir,' he gushed, bounding up the stairs and addressing a member of the audience in the third tier. 'And where are you from?' Jeff thrust the microphone into the old guy's bewildered face.

'I'm retired.'

'Oh, you're retired?' Jeff repeated encouragingly.

The old guy uttered something inaudible. A spotlight had now searched him out. 'Sir,' Jeff oozed smarmily, 'Wouldja mind speaking up?'

'I'm *retarded*,' the old bloke shouted.

In the midst of this, Abe arrived back from his summit meeting in Das Booth. He was tethered to a swivel chair by a pair of handcuffs. His only way of moving was to paddle with his feet, as though on a skateboard. 'Zey chained me up, zose bastards.'

A key was found in the lock, but the writers had filed down the edges. One of the crew got out a flick-knife. 'There'll be a bit of blood, man, but not much,' he said to Abe. 'Okay?'

As he hacked away at the chain and Abe's face twisted with terror, word came that the writers, still barricaded in their booth, were ordering in champagne and caviar. And charging it to Abe's expense account.

It was five minutes till taping time.

Fuming, the cast of *DINKS* made its way on to the set. The audience sounded like an orchestra tuning up – screams and squeals and squawks erupted at a hundred different pitches. As we sat at our designated positions and waited for the cue from the floor manager, Rondah leant towards me. 'Have you heard from Pierce?' I caught a strange look in her eye – a flash of haughty desperation which made me think that perhaps she felt as desolate and abandoned as I did.

There'd been hints in the gossip columns lately of Rondah's 'maturity', an LA euphemism for 'over the hill'. Which was why she was spending every spare moment trekking to Swedish alpine and Mexican desert and Rumanian mud spring retreats to be massaged with crushed goat foetuses and animal placental protein. I shook my head and gave her a gentle look, full of camaraderie.

But Rondah made a sudden adjustment to her mouth and reassembled her facial features. The glimmer of vulnerability vanished. 'Oh well, he's prob'ly off with his lover some place. Oh, he has told y'all about that, hasn't he, honey?' She was speaking once more in her air hostess voice. Rondah should have carried a Boeing 747 around with her at all times, no kidding.

'He broke up with her, eons ago, for your information.'

'Her?' Rondah stage-whispered, all the time smiling insincerely at the audience. 'You mean *him*. Pierce' – she articulated each word with delicious relish – 'is buy-sex-shall.' She snuck a glance in my direction, feigning surprise at my shocked expression. 'You mean, you didn't know that? Oh, well, shoot, I'm sure he meant to tell you.'

The floor manager snapped the clapper-board and the familiar theme music thundered out of the speakers. I looked down the muzzle of the camera. Suddenly I had an image of my mother, the last time I'd seen her, in hospital, dwarfed, like I was now, by grey, indifferent machines. The studio was hot with other people's breath. The neon 'laugh' sign was flashing neurotically above the stage. Looking around the set, I began to feel detached, invisible, as though I were the camera. But minus any soft filter lens. Finally, after nearly a year in Hollywood, I'd got the picture: the bewildered audience, the shell-shocked crew, and Abe and his cast – the SS of sitcom.

For the first time, I saw myself from outside – marooned in the Dream Machine as it relentlessly pumped entertainment to the four corners of the earth. Just like terrorists tamper with a city's water supply, Abe Epstein, if he'd had half a brain, could have changed the flavour of the whole world's fantasies. But it'd never happen. It was all poisoned. If we were fish, we'd be floating, bloated, belly-up.

The truth was, I'd been so busy seeing through everybody else, I hadn't bothered to take a look at myself. I was miserable. I was miserable right through to my marrow.

The theme music ended, the applause died down, the lights went up and the floor manager gave me my cue. I got to my feet, crossed the stage and left the studio.

I hauled open the Emergency Exit and ran out on to the street. The heat slammed into me like a punch in the stomach. I ran across the car park and out on to Hollywood Boulevard. I paused panting at the street corner to strip off a layer of clothing. The air was leaden with twice, *thrice*-breathed air.

Looking up and down the dusty, unshaded street, the Alice in Wonderland feelings flooded back. I felt disoriented. Everybody looked so busy, so purposeful. I listened to the medley of accents and car horns and tape decks and sirens and station jingles and I realised I had never been so lonely. I felt like a single sock. I was overcome with a sense of homesickness, but the awful thing was, I didn't know for *who* or for *what*.

'Yo. Whip some skull on me, bitch.' The voice belonged to a member of a heavy metal gang, in regulation spiked bracelet and Def Leppard T-shirt. 'Put a lip-lock on ma hoagie,' he invited, pointing at his crotch. Scurrying past him, I found myself amongst a group of bemused tourists cowering on the corner of Hollywood and Vine. Cameras and autograph books in hand, they'd come to catch a glimpse of someone famous. But all they could see were male prostitutes, listlessly plying their trade in front of the greasy diners; drug dealers in spandex, zebra-striped pants; and street kids, begging for food and money, sleeping rough on the construction sites in Franklin Avenue – not runaways but throwaways. This was, as Pierce's father had taught me, the Ultimate Throwaway Society. Through it all, an amplified voice announced that the 'bus tour of the stars' homes – fifty of the most famous homes in the world' – was about to commence. Price just twenty-five bucks.

Trudging downtown, I passed a billboard advertising 'Merge Therapy', a course which promised to teach motorists how to merge into freeway traffic streams. That, I realised, was exactly what I needed. Not for lane-hopping, but for everyday life.

I started buying myself birthday presents – things I never even knew I wanted. I bought a 'blaster bra' with speakers instead of cups and an electronic, self-stirring saucepan. I spent all the big notes in my wallet then started purging myself of all my small change. I staggered along with all my packages and parcels, but the relief I'd felt at having got rid of all my *DINKS* money suddenly evaporated. There was one fatal flaw in the American consumerism myth.

You can't have everything. I mean, *where would you put it?*

I dragged my birthday packages into a café on Melrose. The walls were lined with brightly coloured photos of hepatitis-yellow chips, and pock-marked sausages. 'Whaddle it be?' The gum-chewing waitress took my order for iced tea with a surly curl of the lip. But no sooner had she pushed past me than she suddenly retraced her stilettoed steps. 'Hey,' she gushed, 'ain't you that little Or-strail-yan from that show on TV?' Before I could deny all existence of any such person, any such place even, she was off on an account of her life, starting with her boyfriend's penis size, and then moving right along to her suspected lesbian tendencies. 'Me name's Marie, I pump iron two hours a day, I'm heavily into suchi and I like to be the dominant partner.'

I stared at her. Californians have this habit of talking at you, out of the blue. They just launch off into the most intimate conversations – well, you couldn't really call them conversations. They're more like monologues really. Which is okay, I guess, if your ambition in life is to be a full-length mirror. But mine wasn't. Not any more. Before I could reply that I wasn't into eating anything raw – including her – she was off again, this time explaining how her neurotic psychosis stemmed from being the third child, which was why she continually 'underachieved' in life.

I picked up a *National Geographic* magazine from the counter top and pretended to be riveted by an article on sow insemination. But Marie pressed on, undeterred.

'I knew you'd understan', bein' so famous an' all.'

Marie's other customers were now catcalling and complaining. Leaving my last remaining dollar, I dragged my birthday packages out into the blistering sun, crossed the street and just stood on the nearest corner. In the heat, my studio make-up was running. The mascara left two black trails like skid-marks down my face. I realised then that I was still wearing my woolly winter costume for today's taping.

But I nearly jumped out of it when a strong hand suddenly clamped down on my shoulder. 'Excuse me ma'am. Can I see your driver's licence?'

I turned toward the voice, dazed. 'Sorry?'

'Your D-r-i-v-e-r-s L-i-c-e-n-c-e. Wot? Ain't I talkin' English here?'

It was a policeman, in those silly jodhpurs they wear, complete with hard hat and compulsory intimidate-your-suspect dark sunglasses. 'What for?'

'You were jay walkin' ma'am.'

'What?'

'Walkin' against the lights. Licence?'

'Why do you want to see my *driving* licence? I was *walking*.'

'Ma'am, you were progressing at two miles per hour in a Non-Walking Zone for which the City of Los Angeles must inflict a fine.'

'Happy Birthday. It's my birthday. Did you know that?' I told him, for no particular reason. 'This is a preposterous city. I mean, the place is chockers with nude car washes and auto sucks and Jacuzzi orgies and – I dunno – people overdosing on every kind of drug, and you're fining me for using my *feet*? *I don't have a licence*,' I snapped at him. '*That's the whole problem*. I can't *merge*. People don't have friends in this city, they have *contacts*. No one has a lover, they have "enlightened, non-hierarchical, non-sexist co-partners". Address books – have you noticed this? – are only written in *pencil*. But then there's all the "indiscriminate intimacy" – that's what Pierce, my boyfr . . . this guy I know calls it. Like just now. I met this waitress who told me all about her lover's penile implant, her lesbian tendencies and her untapped star potential. No kidding. Everyone I've met in this town, from bank clerks to hairdressers, has an acting degree or a film idea. I'm desperate to meet someone who'll just say, "Hi, I'm a plumber." I mean, you're probably only a cop by day, and a mime artist by night, right? Do you see what I'm saying? This town isn't "laid back" at all. Everybody is from some place else. It's the "go west" mentality of America. "Go west and make your fortune." But, you see, if you fail here, *there is nowhere further west to go*. This is *it. Finito*. It is *now* or never. Which explains why people are always shooting each other on the freeway. Every day there are new inventions and gadgets and mobiles to save time, so that people can have more time to dream up new time-saving inventions and gadgets and mobiles. People, like my boyfr . . . this guy I know, then have to take drugs to alleviate the boredom they feel with all this time on their hands. He just buys bigger and better cars, so that he can see less and less of more and more, faster and faster. He's suffering from a terminal case of Hollywood – all because nobody will ever say "No" to him. *Including me*. And then there's my *girl*friend. She pretends to be tough and brash, but beneath all that bravado, what is she? One long ache of insecurity. Now she's locked herself in her room and won't come out 'cause her nipples are dark. And *worst* of all, my *father* might have been right about something for the first time in his life. I hate that. I hate him. I hate this city. Mimi Zarbo. Do you know her? Well, she should stop worrying about her *own* colonics. I mean, if they were going to give an enema to the earth, they'd stick it in right here. Los Angeles is the arsehole of the world. The point is, *I don't want to be an American anymore.* Okay?'

The policeman was staring at me. He shoved his hands up in the air in surrender. 'Hey lay-dee. Calm down, okay. Why doncha just go home and have a nice rest. Sounds good, huh?' I shook my head, sobbing. 'Okay, okay, whaddaya want, huh?'

'What I want,' I wailed 'what I want, is to be the way I was before I wanted to be the way I am now.'

I walked the rest of the way home in a daze, whether from heat-exhaustion, inhaling too many car fumes, or the fact that I'd just had a complete nervous breakdown in front of a policeman, I'm not sure.

Things could not get worse, I told myself. Things were as low, as we said at home, as a snake's prostate. That is until I opened the letterbox. Inside was a letter addressed to me. Hoping against all hope that it might be from Pierce telling me where the hell he was, I slid the remains of a gnawed-off nail into the seal and snapped it open. It was from Ugly Unlimited. I'd been accepted as a member.

I would have gone straight to the bathroom and got out our best wrist-slashing razor, except for the fact that Tash had surfaced at last. Seeing her again shocked me out of my self-indulgent stupor. Cocooned in her cigarette-scorched kimono, soiled with soup and wine stains, her hair dangling over her gaunt face, she sat dejectedly at the kitchen table. A tumbler of whiskey was in one hand, a slab of cake in the other. She was so thin, I thought, if I touched her I might puncture her skin.

'Happy birthday,' she said, toasting me.

'You remembered?'

'Here.' Wielding an eggslice, she sawed off a slab of chocolate cake and thrust it across the table in a shower of crumbs. I took it in my hand, plonked down in the chair next to her and just gazed at it. She poured me a glass of whiskey and sent it skimming across the table top. Her kimono fell open and I saw that she was wearing nothing but the pair of singing underpants I'd seen in her hope chest. 'So where's lover-boy?'

I shrugged dismally.

Tash chewed her lip pensively then let out a long weary sigh. 'Can ya believe it?' Chocolate was smeared around her pale mouth like lipstick. 'Two hot-to-trot, horny, absolutely beautiful, witty, wonderful women all alone on your twenty-first birthday, eating cake and getting shit-faced. It's a crime. It should be banned. It's a' – she burped loudly – '*tragedy.*'

We sat there in a gloomy, half-tipsy torpor, fiercely intent on the cake in front of us.

'J'know. I've been thinkin' the last two weeks – they hate us, really,' Tash said suddenly, through a gigantic mouthful.

'Who?'

'*Men.* Why'ja think they tell those terrible jokes. Like Carl's witty one, remember?, "Why do women have cunts?" '

'Oh that's off. I hate that one.'

'On and on they go about how bad we smell and how bad we taste. I mean, sperm does not exactly taste like zabaglione, but do *we* make jokes about it? *No.* Because we're nice. Too nice. Which is why I've decided to sleep with men for money.'

I choked as a bit of cake went down the wrong way. I remembered what Tash had told me about her tolerance threshold, how one day there'd be a sonic boom and she would have broken through into the shockless zone. Well this was it. She was through her threshold. Nothing could hurt or shock her any more. As Tash leant forward to thwack me on the back, her underpants spluttered into song. 'For she's a jolly good fellow, for she's a . . .' they warbled tinnily. 'Correction. Not *men.* Man. I'm gonna find one rich honkey an' screw him for everythin' he's got.' The battery in the heart-shaped knickers was going flat.

'It's the only way I'm gonna make that money. You should toughen up too, kiddo,' she said, regarding me with an expression of fierce affection. 'Hey, what's to eat? My stress level is up. I could eat this entire table.' Things must be bad. The only thing Tash usually admitted to eating were men. 'Get the Supremo,' she demanded, passing the pizza menu.

'How big?'

'Orphanage size.'

'What is it about the American male?' I asked, hanging up the phone. 'I thought this generation would be different. But they're worse in a way.'

Tash placed her unshaven legs up on the chair opposite and

wrapped her face around the now empty cake plate, nodding encouragingly. Her pink tongue darted in and out.

'I mean, sure, they can sit around analysing every nuance of feeling, but at the same time, they seem, well, sort of emotionally dyslexic. J'know what I mean? Like, they can all talk about G spots, but can't get it up.'

'Tell me about it,' Tash interrupted. 'Some of my men make the Giant Panda look virile.'

'They're in a kind of limbo-land. Not the macho meatheads they were brought up to be, *or* the Male Feminists they claim to be on telly chat shows . . . They're sorta . . . I dunno, fractured.'

'I take it,' Tash said calmly, her face elongating with the effort not to break into a triumphant smirk, 'that Pierce-baby bit the dust.'

Refusing to give her any satisfaction, I crossed to the fridge to fetch the peanut butter jar which, due to Tash's curtailment of carnal activity, was full.

'Don't worry,' she added sagely, 'time heals all things – except herpes, period cramps, and radioactivity.'

'J'know,' I told her, as proof that I was toughening up, 'that a pig's penis is in the shape of a corkscrew? I read about it in *National Geographic*. It'd be great, wouldn't it? You could have sex and then open the bottle of wine afterwards.'

'Followed up,' Tash snorted, 'with a bacon sandwich.'

'I wonder if pigs have trouble in the "keeping it up" department?' I said, greedily gobbling a golden brown spoonful.

'Dunno,' Tash yawned. 'Never been to bed with a – oh, wait! Come to think of it. Yes, I have!'

'Me too.'

'Is there any other kind?'

Our laughter soon evaporated. We sank once more into a slime of self-pity.

'Maybe we should just go gay,' Tash sighed despondently. 'I mean if you can't beat 'em, lick 'em, right?'

'I'd rather go Jewish. All the funniest people in the world are Jewish. In fact, I feel *guilty* about not being Jewish.'

'Me too.'

As Tash's underpants wheezed into song, we both flung ourselves down into our chairs again, watching the tide go out in the whiskey bottle.

'*Now* what?'

'Chocolates,' Tash announced. 'I've got some *some*-where.' She was on her feet, rifling through cupboards. 'Experts say women eat chocolate in lieu of sex. The truth is women have sex in lieu of chocolate!' It was then we found the note from Tash's Mexican cleaning lady. Neither of us had washed up since last time she was here, and we hadn't seen it buried beneath the greasy pots and pans. Tash read it first then passed it solemnly over to me.

'Dear Misses,' it read, 'Tank you for pay rize. Tank you. Maria. P.S. The washing machine is licking.' Tash's eyes lit up. Clutching the biscuits she'd excavated from the bottom of the washing hamper, she manacled my arm and hauled me through the house to the laundry. 'Kat,' she enthused, 'This is every girl's dream.'

'What?'

'Didn'tcha ever sit on the washin' machine when you were a kid? Ya know, for the vibrations?' I shook my head. 'God, girl,' she said, back to her usual self, 'whereja live? In a *box*?' Tash twirled the knobs and then hoisted herself up on top of the lid. 'Well, come on. Don't just stand there. A washing machine that *licks*. We'll never need men again.' She reached out a scrawny arm and dragged me up on to the machine. 'I mean, ya don't have to talk to it, or massage its ego. Ya don't haveta hold in your stomach for hours and hours neither.'

I sat there by her side as the vibrations shivered through the cold steel. A look of pure joy passed over Tash's face. 'Happy Birthday, Kat,' she said, biting blissfully into a chocolate biscuit.

'Thanks, mate,' I clinked my glass up against hers, just before the machine thundered into spin dry. We looked at each other and started to laugh, a loud, uncontrollable cascade of laughter, spraying chocolate chip shrapnel in all directions. It took me a while to realise that not just the washing machine, but the entire laundry, the entire house in fact, was shaking. A framed poster of Bette Midler slithered to the floor, spitting glass shards. The cupboard doors hurtled open and swung back and forth on their rusty hinges. Drawers catapulted out of their sockets. The bottles on the shelves cha-cha-ed closer and closer to the edge, then smashed to smithereens on the tiles below. Tash and I were flung off the machine. The whole house had gone into Triple Speed Spin.

'Oh Chrrrist. It's a fuckin' earthquake,' Tash shouted eloquently, gripping the lip of the sink.

I gave her an 'Oh, no kidding' look. 'Let's run,' I shrieked, staggering to my feet. I lurched on legs that no longer seemed to be mine.

'Where?'

I remembered the tales of airborne cars and fallen power lines sizzling like snakes. Stop, I thought to myself. Think. What would a grown-up do? I clung on to the legs of the gyrating ironing board.

'Phone book,' Tash said. Thank God the underpants had stopped singing.

'You want to *call* someone?' I wailed, incredulous. '*Now?*'

She crawled on hands and knees down the hallway, dodging the debris. By the time I caught up to her, she was flicking through the front pages of the phone book, running her index finger down the page marked 'Earthquakes'. I peered over her shoulder. It was full of really useful stuff. 'Have handy a can of baked beans, a flashlight, powdered milk, and a monkey wrench,' it read. 'Portable stove, fire-escape ladder, non-electric can-opener and make sure your smoke-detector is properly installed.'

'Great,' I howled. 'Now they tell us.'

'It says to stand under a doorframe.' We staggered, phone book in hand, to the doorway and stood there, clutching each other as the building shuddered with the after-shocks.

'What else does it say, for God's sake?'

She ran her finger further down the page. 'It says, let's see, "Arrange beforehand a rendezvous point with friends".'

'Oh, this is so helpful I can't believe it.'

'Or loved ones.'

'I don't have any loved ones!' I was, by now, bordering on hysteria. 'That's the whole problem.'

'Well,' Tash interrupted, putting on her most matter-of-fact voice, 'where'ja wanna meet?'

I looked at her woefully. 'Sydney,' I whimpered and started to cry. This was just topping off the entire day really nicely. I felt totally betrayed. I mean, there are certain things you expect from life. You expect to put on weight when you're dieting. You expect men to be lying when they say, 'No, I'm not married'. And you expect the earth to be there when you put your foot down. The fact that it wasn't, well, left you feeling downright cheated.

We stood in the doorway waiting for the next shock. I was too frightened to look out the window. I thought I might see San Francisco. Finally Tash ventured across the shattered living-room, retrieved the remote control and activated the television. California, it seemed, was still all here. Well, as 'all here' as California could ever get, that is.

'Sorry, folks,' the newsreader advised, 'but we're getting under our desks.' Abandoning his Autocue, the pinstriped anchorman ducked out of view. A voice rose up beneath the table-top. 'And now, the world news.' But the station cut away instead to a helicopter report of the damage. Freeways were blocked. Overpasses were now underpasses. Roads had bubbled. Buildings had buckled. Plate glass windows downtown had come loose, turning into lethal frisbees. Pavements had concertinaed. Houses had been swallowed whole. The earthquake was 5.9 on the Richter scale, we were told. Tash whistled through her chocolate-coated teeth. From under his desk, the news-reader predicted another big quake might take place that night. He advised all viewers to 'stay somewhere safe'.

And so that is just where we stayed, huddled beneath the door frame, clutching our monkey wrench and phone book, the whiskey bottle and the remains of the chocolate biscuits. And that is exactly how Pierce found us, when at half past ten, he walked through the door. Just like the stunt my old man pulled – coming back to mum after two years.

'Oh hello,' I said, 'didn't he have your brand?'

THE LLAMA PARLOUR

Too drunk by now to care whether the earth went into spin rinse again or not, Tash told Pierce he was a piece of shit, kissed me sloppily on the ear, and picked her way through the wreckage to her bed.

'Are you okay?' Pierce studied my face.

'Fine,' I said, startled at the tremor in my voice.

'Well, how 'bout that?' he said. 'The earth moved. I had to rush over straight away.'

'Why?'

'To see if you'd finally got laid,' he grinned at me sheepishly.

I surveyed him with a composure which surprised me. 'What have you come over for? To tell me that you're *gay?*'

This unexpected accusation startled a laugh out of him. 'What?'

'Well. Are you?' This time Pierce reeled back from the whiplash in my voice. 'Is that why you wouldn't let me get close to you? I mean, didn't you have the guts to say it?' Pierce's halo of hair feathered across his face. He blew it out of his eyes and stared forlornly at his old training shoes. He was sporting his favourite ones, with the scuffed heels and curled-up toes. They looked like something an astronaut would wear. 'Oh, what's the point!' I made to move away, but his hand shot out, like the mechanical probe of a spacecraft, and seized me.

'Kat,' he said hopefully.

'What?'

He let my arm drop and began to jingle the loose change in his pockets. After staring some more at his footwear, he turned and picked his way through to the kitchen. I heard the blender whirl and stood, paralysed, as he returned with two frothing margheritas. He took a big gulp, and looked at me pleadingly. I felt drained. Pierce, after all, was made of kryptonite. Women just lost all power within a two foot radius. Fiercely intent on distracting myself, I leapt to my feet and started straightening furniture accordioned by the earthquake.

'You still haven't answered me. What are you doing here?' I snapped, straining to prise apart two armchairs. 'Did your parents send me another cheque?'

'They've even named a fucking board game after me. Don't you see?' blurted Pierce finally.

All I could see was mess. Armed with a broom, I propelled the shattered glass and crockery into a pyramid in the middle of the room. Pierce followed me, gabbling non-stop.

'The players have to build up this heart-shaped jigsaw of my fucking face by answering questions about me. Kat, are you listening? Who's my favourite historical figure? What's my favourite telephone prefix? How many pairs of underpants do I own? Well, shit, the only thing they got right was my goddamned foot size!'

I snapped open a sheet of newspaper and placed my feet on the edges. With violent jerks, I swept the debris aboard, completely obscuring the photo of a man eating live gold fish to raise money for the 'Gay Unmarried Mothers Association' . . . 'My favourite figure in history,' I said, 'is this guy who stowed away on the First Fleet that took all the convicts to Australia. The *ultimate optimist*. He's probably bloody well related to me come to think of it.'

Pierce seized the broom and spun me around to look at him. 'Kat! With all the bullshit written about me, I *forget who I am*!'

'I thought you were a survivor!' I said sarcastically, jerking free of his hand. 'I thought after the nuclear holocaust, there was just gonna be you and a couple of cockroaches?'

Pierce's face was a mask of despair. 'Chrrist. Can't you see that I'm just like those Aussie men you're always whining about. Whaddaya call 'em? Emotional Vacuums.' To disguise his anguish, he concentrated on biting off a bit of dead skin on his thumb.

'Is that the reason you took the overdose?' My voice was tighter than Rondah's panty-girdles.

'I just had to get out of the goddamned Llama Parlour.'

'What? The llama – whaddaya call it?'

'That's what we're in. You and me. We're locked up in the Llama Parlour. It's like this,' he said, moving on to another finger and gnawing at it neurotically. 'The rich in America like to have fashionable pets. Miniature crocs, house-trained boa constrictors. Then it was pedigree pink rats. Llamas were the latest. Everybody had llamas. Every pop star, socialite, up-tight, out-of-sight groover on the block wanted a fuckin' llama. So, this jerk, this smartass entrepreneur thought he'd cash in. He flew all these llamas to an island in the Caribbean. Well, they waited and waited, and, you see, *nobody came*.' Cause the llamas that everybody had craved and raved about, were suddenly passé. Ya know, as passé as *DINKS* was before it was even thought up.'

'Okay, okay,' I interrupted coldly, moving once more out of his kryptonite range. 'Cut to the chase.'

'Well, it was hot. The llamas got sick. They got thirsty. And now they've just been left to starve to death on this island called Antigua, miles and miles from home. Fashionable one minute, fucked the next.' Pierce gestured out the window. The lights of LA shimmered below us. 'Welcome,' he said savagely, 'to the Llama Parlour.'

'And that's why you wouldn't let me close to you? In case I found out you lived in a LLAMA-BLOODY-PARLOUR?!' He nodded.

It was then I walloped him fair and square in his cakehole.

He looked at me, stupefied.

'You bastard! You great, hairy bollock. You sleaze-bag. You bloody great drongo. Why didn't you say so? I was just about to have *breast implants*.'

'What?' A welt was erupting on his face where I'd whacked him. He rubbed it absentmindedly.

'Everyone kept telling me, Rondah and Phoebe and Mimi and Ping and Abe an' all, that I'd never get anywhere with Hollywood, or with you, unless I dyed my hair blonde and got breast implants.'

This startled another laugh out of him. 'But Kat. Breast implants. Look, they're gross. *And* non-biodegradable.' I looked at him dubiously, but for once he wasn't joking. 'The silicone takes about 500 million years to biodegrade. Rondah and Mimi and all the other babes ya see walkin' around with body bits which defy gravity, well in fifty years time, when they're dead and buried and worms are eatin' their bones, all that will be left are those squidgy pieces of silica gel. Those women are walkin' environmental hazards. You can't even cremate 'em. They won't burn. Crematoriums will soon be clogged with gooey, sticky, tit implants.

They'll have to take them out *before* the body's burned or buried. There'll be an implant mountain. Women will prob'ly bequeath the goddamn things to each other. The Breast Bequest. But Chrrrist, who in their right mind would ever want anything that'd belonged to *Rondah*?'

We looked at each other and burst out laughing. We laughed till we cried. Then we flopped on to the couch and sipped at our margheritas in silence, listening to the dogs and sirens yelping faintly in the distance.

'The good thing about you,' Pierce whispered, 'is that you're the only person who doesn't want to souvenir bits of me . . .'

I looked at his chaos of unkempt curls. At his red mouth. At the scungy Bandaid looped forlornly around his forefinger. 'I just want a cuddle,' I said in a tiny voice.

And, then, ever so slowly, Pierce lifted my bare foot up off the floorboards and kissed the arch. He leant towards me. He smelled like freshly baked bread. He lay his head on my shoulder, then turned his face towards me. His arms encircled my body and his tongue slid down my throat.

To tell you the truth, I'd never, ever played a game of tonsil-hockey like it.

I don't know how long we kissed. We lost track of time – unheard of in LA where time is money and money is everything. When we finally surfaced, we were both a little dazed and goose pimpled, as though we'd been scuba diving for too long.

'Okay,' Pierce said, drawing breath, 'let's lay our cards on the table. I'm twenty-five, two years runnin', which really makes me twenty-seven. I owe you a couple of thousand bucks. I can't cook, I take too much cocaine and um, oh yeah, I don't speak any languages.' He raised an eyebrow, which said 'your turn'.

'Well, um, I'm confused, and um, unemployed. I just survived an earthquake and a nervous breakdown in the same day and I'm hopelessly besotted with the biggest sleaze-schmucko in America.'

Pierce dipped his finger in the glass and ran it down the line of my throat. I couldn't move. I was taut as a wire. He kissed my eyelids, my nose, my chin, then slowly nudged his way down my throat, nuzzling into the nape of my neck. He opened my shirt and looked at my breasts. 'Art Deco,' he whispered tenderly. He ran his index finger around the rim of the cocktail glass. Then kneaded the salt into my nipples. I felt my body arch towards him.

I was twitching – like a jazz solo. Retrieving the lemon slice from the lip of his glass, he squeezed icy droplets on to my skin and licked them up slowly, lingering. The lemon and salt stung and tingled. 'Salt,' he licked one breast. 'And lemon,' he licked my bellybutton. 'And creamy froth,' he placed his hand between my thighs. 'Kat the Margherita.' The doorbell rang. It was the orphanage-sized pizza. It buzzed again. It rang and rang and rang.

BEAUTIFUL BEGINNINGS

One of the best things about America is that you can sing your entire way around it from 'New York, New York' to 'San Francisco'. From 'Highway 51' to 'Route 66'. From 'Galveston oh Galveston' to 'Meet me in St Louis'. From 'I'm Going' to Kansas City, Kansas City, Here I come', to 'Kentucky Woman'. There is a song about every place imaginable. The road Pierce had chosen was measled with potholes, so we had to drive slowly, which suited me fine, 'cause I didn't want this trip to end. Ever. As Pierce and I dodged ditches and warbled our way through a vast repertoire, it struck me that I didn't know any songs about my own country. Dapto, Toowoomba, Wollongong and Wagga just didn't have the same rock 'n' roll ring about them somehow.

The road to las Vegas was what we called at home a 'crystal highway', which meant it was a long stretch of lethal bitumen where windscreen breakages were common. Every time a car hurtled past us from the opposite direction, I would lean forward and press my fingers on to the glass in case of a ricocheting stone. The rest of the time, I kept my hands firmly, possessively, on a part of Pierce. I snuck up next to him, like a teenager in a bad B-grade road movie and nibbled his neck and stroked his hair. To have Pierce caressing my cheek, kissing my fingers, cupping my chin, well, it was unbelievable. 'Feel good?' he asked me.

What I felt like was one of those army-survival ration biscuits – the dried ones that don't expand until placed in water. I thought I might burst for joy, that's how I felt. I nodded. 'How 'bout you?'

Seeing him beam at me the way he did made me feel as though I'd won some kind of Emmy.

'Where are we?' I asked Pierce dreamily, about two hours and two thousand songs into our journey. Pierce, one hand on the wheel, the other draped around my shoulders, glanced down at the map in his lap.

'Well, let's see, we're about between the "F" and the "O" of "California",' he told me.

'Gee, well aren't you the navigational whizz,' I whispered into his warm neck. 'Must be in your blood. America is an accident, didja know that? You were only discovered 'cause old Columbus went off course. No kidding. At least, that's what my dad reckons.'

'What did your mum think of your old man, you know, teaching you all his gamblin' tricks an' all?' It was the first time Pierce had ever shown any interest in my past. I felt vaguely exposed and suddenly shy.

'Not much, but then they didn't think much of anything the other did. Take my mum. She was kinda keen on gardening, yoga, vegetarian food, that sorta stuff. My father likes drinking, gambling and red meat.'

Pierce laughed. 'They must've had somethin' in common for Chrissake.'

'Well, they both liked going to the beach – but not together.'

'Yeah. It's totally beyond me why the world wants to live together as one big, happy, family. Families are fucked.'

But it was a different sort of family Pierce was currently pre-occupied with. It was a horses-head-in-your-bed-no-knee-caps-type family. Pierce owed the local LA drug mafia a lot of money. He'd told me last night, after we'd made love, that they had generously offered to pump him so full of holes you'd be able to make a colander out of him.

I'd seen Latin mobsters on Hollywood Boulevard, brazen as all get-out, in their giant Rolex watches and waistband beepers. They drove Mercedes and white stretch Cadillacs with photos of Jesus dangling from rear-view mirrors. These were the guys Pierce owed money to. He admitted he'd 'put the odd drug of theirs into his body'. (The odd drug? I'd say the Iraqis could open him up as a petro-chemical plant.) Which was why he'd got behind in his house payments, forfeited his three cars, hocked his prized $400 airpump Reeboks and been in hiding. It was why we were headed for the Nirvana Casino, Las Vegas.

Over the last year I'd rung the casino maybe four times. As promised, they'd answered all my questions. Yes, they would tell me the rules on doubling and splitting. Yes, you could insure against the blackjack. No, the blackjack didn't pay three to two. It paid even money. That was a statistic I'd worked into my calculations and experimented with, over and over, in practice hands. I'd been working on a system all year, sort of.

A squadron of insects suddenly hurtled themselves up against the windscreen. I leapt back, startled, then looked at their splattered technicolour innards. 'Pierce,' I said, suddenly serious, interrupting his vibrato rendition of 'Long distance information, give me Memphis, Tennessee'. 'Listen, I'm going to win this money for three reasons: One, to pay off your debts. Two, to buy out your *DINKS* contract. And three, to give some to Tash. Not for drugs, okay?'

'Relax,' he said, with equal solemnity, 'I've gotta quit coke. I know it. Yesterday I blew my nose and half my brains came out.'

'But what about the other stuff? The pills and, I mean, Jesus Christ, if you need chemicals – *breathe*. This is California. Smog Capital of the Western World.'

'I *said*, I'll quit, okay?'

'Rondah reckons you're an addict. She said you ran out on the detox programme 'cause you couldn't handle it.'

Pierce flicked on the windscreen wipers and the mangled insect bodies disappeared. 'I'm *not* addicted, okay? And I'm *not* doing any more drugs. One of the reasons is that I want to know when I'm having a good time.' He placed his warm hand on my inner thigh. 'Like last night. No shit, Kat. I'm bored with dope. I've done every drug known to civilisation for Chrissake. From Aspro to Airfix glue. From marijuana to car defrosting fluid. There're no more highs left now.'

'*Love* is a drug,' I hazarded, sneaking a glance up at his face. I should know, I wanted to say. In that department, I was speaking as a true-blue junkie.

'Yeah?' Pierce gave me a sidelong glance, then smiled his widest smile. The air around him seemed suddenly luminous. I looked at his hair, bleached golden on top by the sun. Even his eyelash tips were tinted blond. I devoured every detail of his face and form and I had never, ever felt so, well . . . Schmaltzy as it was, the only word was – *happy*. God. I almost gagged. I couldn't believe such a word could come out of my mouth. It sounded so well . . . Californian.

And you know what? *I didn't care.*

'Let's have happy childhoods,' Pierce said suddenly, 'except as grown-ups.'

Staring ahead at the white line stretching over the horizon, spumes of dust spiralling up behind us from our wheels, I was seized by an icy premonition. 'I feel as though I've made you up,' I admitted softly. 'I think I'll look over and you'll be gone.'

Pierce, without warning, swerved his Bronco down a track on the side of the road. He turned off the ignition. 'I wanna kiss you between your legs,' he said matter-of-factly. 'When we made love again this morning, it was too fast. As though we had a great meal, but missed a course, ya know?'

We'd pulled up in a massive forest of cacti. As he stretched me out on the back seat, I saw them flanking the car, vegetable soldiers, their prickly green arms up in surrender.

Nevada was made up of the sort of landscape spaceships land in. After we arived in Las Vegas, parked the car, took to the pavement and met some of the local people, I realised that not only had the spacecraft landed but the aliens had taken over. Dinner-suited spruikers, sweltering in the midday sun, hustled passers-by to come inside their casinos. Scantily clad, middle-aged women, their swollen legs squeezed into support-hose, tried to lure us in to see shows. 'Debbie Does Alice' or 'Naughty Natalie Needs a Nightie' starring Bambi Jnr and the Bimbos. Walking the main street gave me the sensation of being inside a pinball machine – lights, buzzers, bells, flashing neon signs, large, luminous shapes and rotating figures, hub-caps rolling past like silver spheres. I grabbed hold of Pierce's T-shirt sleeve, to anchor myself closer to him. Up above, psychedelic pinwheels of neon light transformed themselves into one cartoon character after another, each suggesting that you 'try our hot slot spots'. That you 'come on in and win'.

The one good thing about landing in such alien territory, was that no one recognised Pierce Reece-Scanlen Jnr (the Third).

'Well, whaddaya think?' Pierce asked me, when we reached the end of the main drag and turned to observe the chaos of lights under the harsh desert sun.

'What I think is that this place must have the biggest electricity bill in the whole of America.' Pierce laughed and kissed the palm of my right hand. I curled my fingers over the place where his lips had been and vowed not to wash off his lucky touch.

Every hotel in town was grafted on to a casino. Some floated, others revolved; one could only be reached by gondolier across a sea of pink bubbles. My favourite had elevators shaped like rocket ships. There was a countdown, before the zero of 'take off'.

We hocked Pierce's watches and rings, withdrew my meagre savings from the bank, and then counted up our kitty. $6,465 dollars. There was a flicker of guilt as I thought of Tash. But after I'd won at blackjack, I could give her all the money she needed to find her kid. Pierce squeezed my arm reassuringly and we headed off to find our hotel.

The Nirvana Casino was off the main drag. A ten foot billboard above the foyer advertised the day's fun activities. It was blank.

We rode the lift up to the floor marked 'Cloud Nine' and found our room, 'the Royal Flush Suite'. It wasn't exactly what you'd call four-star accommodation – it was more like four exclamation marks. The bed sagged. The bedspread was mysteriously stained. There were cigarette scorch marks on the laminex counters and a dead cockroach floated forlornly in the toilet bowl.

'What a goddamned honeymoon suite,' Pierce laughed, drawing across the shabby curtain. The billboard opposite was flashing incessantly its promise of an 'all-you-can-eat-for-$1.00 breakfast'. Next to that was a quickie wedding chapel called 'Beautiful Beginnings'. We read the neon-lit list of the chapel's twenty-four-hour-a-day services from the tux and gown rental prices ($50 an hour) to the ring bearer's pillow ($10.00). There was a courtesy limo, to and from your hotel, a complimentary video, a penny for the lady's shoe and a frameable copy of wedding vows. 'What would our vows be?' Pierce asked, resting his chin on top of my head and hugging my waist.

'To have an orgasm every day,' I said, 'and to laugh at each other's jokes.'

'And to get a jukebox that plays all our favourite road songs. Done. I mean, we'll need to celebrate, after our win and all.'

'Yeah, of course we will.'

'So.' He looked at me provocatively.

'So?'

'So, let's get married. Now *there's* something I've never done before.'

Gob-smacked is too tame a phrase to describe my reflection in the warped glass of the Royal Flush Suite on the Cloud Nine floor of the Nirvana Casino, Las Vegas, Nevada.

Lemme tell you, the Nirvana Casino, with its plush carpet, and polished chrome and throbbing galaxy of fluorescent lights, was just a tad different from the illegal gambling joints in Redfern and Rozelle where I'd been with my old man. These were derelict rooms above greasy hamburger joints, with steep, dimly lit stairs and a cockatoo, usually a teenager, stationed on the corner, to look out for cops.

We crossed to the nearest blackjack table. There were seven players. A surly croupier shuffled four or five packs together. They rattled like automatic gunfire. For the first hour, I just stood and watched, gauging whether the bank was on a winning or losing streak. I'd roughly calculated how often the bank should win; usually about two or three per cent more than the punters. When I thought the bank was about due for a bad run, I would make my move, cool as a cucumber. At least, that was the plan.

But watching the game unfold, a spasm of dread went through my entire body. After all my zillions of practice hands, my meticulous calculations and phone calls to the pit boss, I realised, sickeningly, that there was one question I'd forgotten to ask him. Well, hadn't even thought to ask, actually. See, usually in blackjack, when the player and the bank tie, the bet is void. Anyway, to compensate for the privilege of letting us punters take a quick squiz at the second card, the Nirvana Casino – the dirty, rotten, mongrel bastards – had ruled that when it was a tie, *they* won. I had a loaded feeling in my throat. This information was not incorporated into my calculations. I don't wanna bore you with a whole lot of technical cardsharp crap, but I just want you to know why I was on the point of complete cardiac arrest. All my instincts told me to get the hell out of there. I had a sudden urge to go trekking in the Gobi desert, or, failing that, to sit and watch my bath water running out for about a year. Anything. Anywhere, but here. Just then, however, I felt Pierce's hands softly cupping the small of my back, encircling my waist, squeezing firmly. I remembered his upcoming appointment for a Mafia shoe-fitting. 'I wonder what size cement shoe I take?' he'd mused in the car. 'But, then again, I suppose one size fits all, really, huh?' And, as though lowering myself into a cold pool, I eased my way slowly into the game.

The stool wobbled uncertainly as it took my weight. The other players, all middle-aged and all male, glanced at me with undisguised disdain.

'These stools are reserved for players, liddle lay-dee,' the croupier chided snidely. He had rancid breath, with a suit to match.

'Draw,' I said crisply, placing a pile of plastic tokens on the table.

Old Rancid-breath looked at me as though I was a laboratory specimen, glanced in bemusement at the other players and shrugged. He lazily dealt us all two cards from the metal, self-sealing shoe. He dealt himself two cards, and then, as advertised, flipped them both sunny side up. A drink materialised. I drained it.

I started low, tailoring my bets while testing my calculations. In the first game, I scored a picture card and an ace. Blackjack. In the second hand, I was dealt two eights. 'Split,' I told the croupier and started playing two hands against the bank. I drew another eight. 'Split,' I ordered. I was now playing three hands against the bank.

The croupier suddenly quit smirking and concentrated on the cards. All three eights drew aces. I stood on nineteen. The dealer, stuck on fourteen, had to draw again. Another eight. 'Bank busts,' he muttered and paid us all out.

Pierce stood behind me the entire time, a silent sentinel, his breath soft and regular on the nape of my neck. We remained like that for three hours. Begging off, on a pee-break, I sat on the lid of the loo and re-examined my calculations. I was still up four per cent. Okay, I'd calculated on six, but four was still good. It seemed to me that the number of tied bets was statistically very low in blackjack. It would take a little longer before Pierce and I could go into MM (Millionaire Mode) and put a deposit on that jukebox. But my system was still intact. Back at the table another drink surfaced at my side. I raised the glass and my bets. And my winning streak continued.

After five hours, Pierce nibbled my ear lobe. 'How's the blushin' bride? You're a genius,' he laughed, collecting some chips. 'I'm going over the road to book us in. Remember,' he winked, 'an orgasm every day and to laugh at each other's jokes.'

Beaming, I watched him saunter across the shagpile, his hands sliding into his hip pockets before he was swallowed up by the scene – the middle-aged drink waitresses, their black lycra hot pants bucketing swollen buttocks, the gaggle of gawking tourists and the anti-gambling protesters, who'd suddenly appeared, bearing neon signs, saying 'Jesus Saves'.

The guy straddling the next stool, an amateur player, but with a friendly, crooked kind of smile, swayed towards me. 'Zat your boyfriend, honey? There's over one thousand weddin' chapels in this here town, ya know,' he winked broadly. 'Maybe you'll get lucky, huh?'

But there were no 'maybes' about it. The luck I'd somehow lost since coming to America was back. It was all over me like a rash. Black cats, pointed bones, voodoo dolls, nothing could harm me. If there'd been a ladder around I would have walked right under it, no kidding. It seemed I could only draw picture cards, aces, doubles and splits. I skulled another drink and, for the next few hours, luxuriated in my success. I would cancel Pierce's Mafia shoe-fitting. I would pay off Tash's detective and get her a recording contract. I would fly all my old mates Stateside: Chook, Fang, Deb. I would finally be rich enough to 'raise my tone'. I wouldn't just buy a jukebox, but an entire orchestra to play road songs, day in, day out. I wouldn't just hire someone to peel my pistachios, I would buy the whole goddamned plantation. I would purchase zillions of live cells and re-inject all the sheep Rondah had fleeced. And best, best of all, I could finally lop my family tree – my father's branch of it anyway.

'Ain't you gettin' a little tipsy there, hun?' my neighbour asked, as I siphoned up the dregs of yet another celebratory margherita. 'See up there,' he said, little pinky extended to the ceiling. 'That there is a transparent ceiling. Yep. There are catwalks up there. And they see every move we make.' He leant back on his stool and gave a cheerful wave. I craned upwards too. The stool teetered precariously. 'They ply us with drinks, see,' my neighbour warned, restoring my balance, 'while they're pumpin' the room full of oxygen. We're totally shit-faced, yet wide awake enough to keep playing'. It really chaps ma hide! Clever turkeys, in't they?'

It was true. Hypnotised by the croupier's movements, dulled by the free drinks, intoxicated by my initial success, it took me another half hour or so to realise that things were slowly going wrong. Something seemed to have happened to my system. I had calculated a few losses into my scheme, but not a losing streak like this. Every second hand seemed to be a tie. That question I'd forgotten to ask the pit boss gnawed at my drink-sodden brain. To compensate, I started betting too high. Time skidded past, as did my life-savings.

'Las Vegas,' my inebriated companion droned, as much to his drink as to me, 'has to put out two goddamned phone books every year. Didja know that? Most transient place in the world. See, they come to make their fortunes, get shafted and then they're stuck here till someone bails 'em out.'

Seized by panic, I then did what my old man had drilled me, over and over, never to do. I abandoned my system. I could hear him now. 'Rule number one – ignore your winning and losing streaks. Resist. *Stick to your system.*' But I doubled, I tripled, I quadrupled bets. Like a classic losing gambler, I hadn't quit when I was ahead and now I was trying to recoup by pulling stunts both dangerous and dazzling.

The truth dawned on me about four a.m: I was skint. Broke. Busted. The air seemed to shrivel. The croupier drummed his tobacco-stained nails on the tabletop. The other players were waiting for me.

'Can I play a credit?' I pleaded.

But old Rancid-breath just yawned as he examined something his forefinger had excavated out of his ear-hole. He flicked the foreign object at the floor.

I got up from the table and wandered unsteadily through the hotel. I could imagine the mysterious men above me on the invisible catwalks, laughing convulsively. My reflection loomed out of countless light-studded, gilt-edged mirrors: someone dispossessed, lost, awkward. To escape the maze, I blundered into the ballroom. On stage, a tuxedoed MC was wise-cracking into the microphone. I stood and listened to his spiel, as he introduced a 'cunt-tree and west-stern' singer called Crystal Gayle. To drunken, tumultuous applause, all six foot two inches of Crystal swept on stage. Her hair came down to her knees. Even though I had just lost my entire savings and Pierce's most treasured possessions, all I could wonder was whether she had pubic hair to match. 'Howdy you all,' she said, before launching into 'Don't it make your brown eyes blue', a ballad, I supposed distractedly, about contact lenses. Why had I told the croupier that, yes, I wanted to keep playing? That wasn't just a slip of the tongue . . . that was a slip of the whole mind.

Overcome with weariness, I squeezed into the elevator. I watched the floor numbers blinking by as though it were a nuclear countdown. But, by the fourth floor, I was already formulating an escape plan. Ideas bubbled into my brain. I grasped at the thought of running away. We would just keep on driving. We would get odd jobs here and there. We would live on sex and margheritas. We would have endless adventures and tell each other all our secrets. We would laugh at each other's jokes and make love every day. We would just keep on driving until we'd been to every nook and cranny of America. I mean, we had zillons of songs to sing yet.

The door to our room was open. I nudged it with my foot. The room was crawling with cops, all of whom wore guns. They were shredding pillows, pulling apart clothes, decapitating bottles and pouring the contents down the sink. Most of them were under-cover officers – tanned, tightly jeaned, sneakered. They watched me narrowly. A policewoman patted me down. As she did so, the head Detective explained to me that they were a SCAT squad – Street Corner Apprehension Team, and that Pierce had been picked up by an undercover officer buying two grams of speed and a vial of cocaine. Pierce sat in the corner of the room, huddled up like a drab, abandoned parcel. He wouldn't look at me.

'I don't believe it,' I told the D, my strangled voice two octaves higher than usual. 'He's *straight*!' I spun towards Pierce. 'You're straight. Aren't you?'

'Answer the lady, punk,' ordered one of the tough, leather jacketed young cops.

Pierce shrugged and closed his eyes like an angel.

'You've made a mistake officer.'

The Detective tapped the breast pocket of one of his subordinates. 'Ma'am, O'Conner here was wired for sound.'

'You *didn't*!' I pleaded with Pierce, 'Did you?'

I watched him calmly unseal his packet of Drum, fold the paper, fill it with tobacco, roll it adroitly, lick the seal, place the cigarette on his bottom lip and light it. 'Are the Kennedys gun-shy?' was all he said.

The breath left my body. Blood beat in my temples. I felt cool, wet sweat in the small of my back. It was true. He was just like my father. He set himself the lowest standards possible – and then failed to live up to them. It was useless betting on either of them. They were both wild cards.

I glanced at him. He looked demolished. The urge to hold him in my arms was overpowering, like a desperate thirst. I concentrated hard on not throwing up (what Pierce called 'enjoying yourself backwards'). I focused on the warped glass of the window-pane. I concentrated on the illuminated, revolving donut on the breakfast sign opposite. And next to it, the marriage chapel. I re-read the neon list of what was on offer. 'Economy – $125. Regular – $175. Deluxe – $225. Joan Collins Special – $300. No blood tests required.'

'Kat.'

'What?' Although I wouldn't look at him, the thirst came back, searingly.

'I, ah, I guess this means the wedding's off, huh?'

'You've got the integrity of, of – *Abe Epstein*,' I detonated. 'Do you know that?'

'Kat, hey, I was joking.' There was a throb in his voice which I'd never heard before.

'Go bite your bum,' I said profoundly, and went into the bathroom to throw up. After scrubbing the palm which he'd earlier kissed, almost scalding myself in the process, I left without looking back.

As I crossed the hotel room Pierce made a move towards me. 'Kat, wait!' The darkly dressed men closed in around him like beads in a kaleidoscope. 'Fuck off, pigs,' he howled, flailing, trying to push past them.

'These Hollywood types,' the Detective drawled, strongarming Pierce. 'Think they're too good to crap. Ya ain't above the law *here*, punk.'

I saw him then in the mirror, haunted, hollow-eyed. 'Face it,' I said to his reflection, addressing myself as much as him. 'You're an *addict*. You need *help*.'

When I got back to the Bronco, it had been almost totally stripped. The radio and tape deck were gone, the leather seats slashed, the chrome trimmings and personalised numberplates wrenched loose. The tail-lights were smashed and a scratch like a hairline fracture ran the entire length of the duco on the driver's side. Hoisting myself through the shattered windscreen, I revved the engine, gritted my teeth and lurched uncertainly out into the road. The improvised ventilation made my eyes water. There was a muffled *clackity clack* as the axle came loose. Sparks flew. It trailed behind, like the tail of an injured animal.

On the way home to LA I noticed all the dead things on the side of the road, which I'd somehow not observed on the drive up. Large dogs, small dogs, decomposing cats, huge furry piles that could be beavers or skunk or small bears. It hit me then that I'd been so busy, so desperate not to turn into my father, that I'd become my *mother* instead — faded, jaded, bitten down, in love with a lying bastard. I glanced into the rear-vision mirror. The fabric of my face was pinched, my lips pursed as though I was sewing and had a mouthful of pins. I didn't need a doctor for diagnosis. I knew what I'd contracted. A terminal case of the Pierce Scanlens.

'A mess of dead animals bleachin' in the sun . . .

All squashed out on Highway 61,' I sang sadly.

They *looked* how I *felt*.

OBSCURITY KNOCKS

By the time I got home the next day, the details of my stay in Las Vegas were already becoming hazy. The only clues I had about what had gone on was a drink coaster with the words 'Joan Collins Special' scratched on it, two olive pips, a couple of paper napkins with Keno numbers scrawled on them, the word 'Help' and the name of the jail in LA to which Pierce was being extradited.

I deposited all this in the garbage bin, made myself a coffee and sat in the dark of the living-room. I surveyed the note pad by the answer phone. There were no messages for me. The heatwave still hadn't broken. The air was so hot, you could practically hear it shimmering off the street and crackling through the crevices of every building. The house smelt of alcohol, stale cigarettes and take-away pizza. In between searching for a cooler spot on the couch, moving fretfully from cushion to cushion, I peeled at my split ends, tuned into re-runs of old gangster movies or watched bow-tied weather men pointing sticks at satellite photos predicting more heat. I even watched the test-pattern. I then scratched the labels off the take-away all-in-one-ready-mix margheritas I had been drinking on the road. After that, I looked up 'romance' in my dictionary. It said 'remote from everyday life'. 'To exaggerate, to fabricate, to lie.'

I finally slid on to the floor, in the dark, and shuffled back through my tattered deck of days. I felt exposed. Finessed. Caved in, like a house of cards. The night noises of my neighbourhood drifted into the house. I could hear sprinklers whirring lazily, Jacuzzis throbbing, canned laughter from other people's television sets. I felt an ache of loneliness through to my bones. It seemed that everybody belonged somewhere, to someone, except for me. For the first time, I missed my mother. I wanted to be tucked up in her bed, eating Vegemite on toast and sharing the cryptic crossword. The mug of coffee in my hand was cold. The surface was a skin of grease. I drank it anyway.

I probably would have sat there for the rest of my life if Tash hadn't come home and found me. She galloped into the room, all breathless and dishevelled, loaded with packages. She switched on the light, saw me huddled on the floor in the dark, and stopped still. 'Good day, huh?' she taunted, arching a pencilled brow.

When I confessed to her what had happened, she silently crossed to the kitchen and returned with a huge whiskey. I drained it in one gulp. I felt the liquid fire burn the back of my throat and make a hard landing in my empty stomach. It made my eyes tingle. Tash fetched me another, then stood, hands on hips, like a ward nurse administering medicine.

'I need a job,' I told her. 'Got any ideas?'

Tash gave me a sly glance. 'How desperate are ya?'

'Desperate.'

She ripped open one of the packages she'd dumped on the carpet and unravelled a satiny bodice and suspender ensemble. It was like something you see on the dust jacket of a Harold Robbins novel. 'Come on. We're late. Two hundred bucks each, for an hour's work. All ya have to do is stand there and look pissed off.' She glanced at my face. 'Believe me, tonight, you're a natural.'

'Tash,' I said wearily, realising that I hadn't slept for about forty-eight hours, 'what are you talking about?'

Tash was now scooting around the room, slashing plastic carry-bags and tearing open packages. 'I joined an agency. Yesterday. I should've done it eons ago. Don't look like *that*. It's all very kosher. Candida – she's the Madam – she's like a grade school teacher, no kiddin'! Pleated skirt, starched white blouse, the *works*. I nearly started doin' my multiplication table! Anyway, she gets about seventy bucks for introducin' ya to ya client, right, an' then ya jest like, make ya own arrangements.' Peeling off her clothes, Tash beetled into the bedroom where she proceeded to dust her naked body with baby powder. Trailing behind, I watched her lie on the carpet and wriggle her legs into a tiny rubber skirt, talking ten to the dozen the whole time. 'And it ain't really like bein' a prostitute or anythin'. I mean, you get a *choice*,' she emphasised. 'Candida offered me about, oh, ten guys from her books. The first dude she dredged up likes his "escort" – they call ya "escorts", funny huh? – to be doin' the ironin', see, while he, like, breaks into the house. Another schmuck wants ya to hit him with a feather duster while he licks the goddamned floor boards. Nice guy, Candida reckons, real successful an' all.' She paused, panting, the skirt marooned halfway up her thighs. 'This other guy on her books has this, like, heirloom fantasy. The "escort" see, has to hide his ring in her – you know – while he searches the goddamned room. When he can't find it, he, like goes *bananas*. Finally, ya have to give him the ring and say "Sorry, lord and master" and then be kinda "mock-raped" ya know, as punishment.' With one final, forceful tug, she gasped and the tight rubber skirt snapped against her waist. 'That was just like, too weird for me. Chrrrist, I'm never gonna get this off again. I've cut off all circulation. Tell me if I'm goin' blue, okay?' she gasped, jackknifing to her feet. 'So, that left it down to two guys. The first one she told me about likes ta dress up in the chick's underwear an' do her housework. Well, that didn't appeal to me – ya, know, havin' the guy in ya own house an' all. Besides, like I told Candida our house is such a mess, after the earthquake an' all, it would take him, like, about a week and cost him a fortune at two hundred bucks an hour. So –' she levered herself on to the chair in front of her dressing-table and uncased a lipstick. She spoke into it as if it were a miniature microphone while she applied her lippy. '. . . At 'eft 'is 'uy, 'oel 'ulman.' She smacked her lips together and ran her tongue hard across her front teeth. 'So, that left this guy called Joel Schulman,' she repeated. 'All he wants is a bit of light bondage.'

'What a low-life.'

'No way, José!' Tash swung around to face me, her eyes fierce. 'With Joel Schulman I'm scraping the *top* of the barrel. No kiddin'. 'Cause, guess what?' She craned back into the mirror, massaging foundation on to her face and dusting her complexion vampire-white. 'The guy is like, the head of one of Hollywood's major studios. Went for my first session last night, believe it or not.'

'But Tash,' I whispered, aghast. '*Bondage?*'

Tash shrugged, appraising her reflection. 'Some people like country. Some people like classical. Others rap, or rock 'n' roll. What's the diff?' She was now darting and diving into drawers and cupboards, fetching shoes and garter belts. 'It's justa matter of keepin' an open mind about it all, okay?'

'Okay,' I replied stoically.

'Look, the truth is, he's got stale breath, body odour and a picture of his wife by the bed. But he pays well, it doesn't hurt and afterwards, when I told him about my singing an' all, he offered me a recordin' contract, for a demo. Not only that, but he's teachin' me about classical music – ya know, Andrew Lloyd Webber an' those guys.'

I could suddenly feel a draft blowing through my open mind. So I closed it. 'But Tash, these men are, well, they're sick.'

'Men are like babies. That's all. They need fantasy. I figure somethin' must of just happened to 'em, when they were young an' all. And they, like, can't get it outta their systems. Candida says we're analysts. Practical analysts. She says that if they didn't have us girls an' stuff, they'd probably go out and, like, attack someone.'

'But last night, didn't it, you know, well . . . revolt you?'

Tash shrugged. 'The only thing which revolts me is his *ego*. I mean, how dare a sixty year-old guy think he's turnin' me on. Ugh.'

'Sixty. Jesus, Tash. Are you sure he's up to it?'

'God yeah. Look, he's real fit. In A–1 condition. A ten K-a-day guy. So . . .' She turned to face me, transformed into a cold and icy Sex Siren. 'Are ya comin' or what? He told me to bring along a friend whenever I wanted. He likes two girls. One to watch. An' he'll pay double. We're talkin' serious coin here.'

I looked at Tash's tiny, shiny body, her wiry little legs and fierce eyes. My past flashed through my mind, as if I was in a car smash – Chuck and his gluteus maximus muscles, Rondah and her liposuctioned hips and silicone lips, Mimi's colonics, pet psychiatrists, Pierce Scanlen's plucked nostrils – I could feel the whiskey in my bloodstream now, thick and treacherous. I took another swig, gulping it down, one, two, three. It was time to toughen up. 'Okay,' I hiccoughed, and put down the empty glass. 'Why not?'

Things couldn't get worse.

DEATH — A FATE WORSE THAN LIFE

Couldn't they just!

Tash prodded the dead body of Joel Schulman with her big toe. 'Isn't he supposed to be stiff?' His complexion, by now, was the colour of curdled milk.

'Give the man time, for God's sake. He's only been dead,' I checked my watch – it was nearly midnight, 'two hours.'

Tash fiddled pensively with her varnished toenails. 'Didja know that hair and nails keep right on growin' after ya die?'

'No Tash. I didn't know,' I said, averting my eyes from her feet. 'Thanks for enlightening me.'

'Try Epstein again.'

Reluctantly, for about the twentieth time, I dialled my ex-producer's number. With a sinking heart, I listened as the purling phone clicked once more into his answering machine. I hung up. '*Now* what will we do?'

Tash shrugged. 'To tell ya the truth – I have no fuckin' idea. Wonder what's on the old boob-tube?'

I looked at her as though an alien life form was taking over her body. '*How can you think about television at a time like this?*'

'Okay, okay.' She put her hands in the air, imitating the victim of a stick-up. 'Just try him once more, okay?'

Dialling the number, which I now knew by heart, I was so surprised at the sound of a human voice that I nearly hung up.

'Oh hi, um, may I speak to Abe Epstein? It's Katrina Kennedy calling.'

'What? What!' Tash, demanded, now having a go at her finger-nails with her teeth.

I covered the mouthpiece with one hand. 'She's put me on hold.' The music playing down the phone was 'Got so Many Troubles I Wanna Die'. If we had been in a Woody Allen film it would have been funny. But we weren't, and it wasn't.

'Mr Epstein can't be disturbed. He's in the Jacuzzi.'

'Well, it's kind of an emergency. It's kind of a matter of . . .'

'Life and death!' Tash urged, sitting alertly up on her haunches.

'. . . life and death.'

'Literally,' Tash added, gnawing at the nails on both hands at once.

'Look,' said the female voice at the other end of the phone — I could *hear* the blonde hair and siliconed breasts, no kidding — 'Mr Epstein can't jest take calls from strangers in the middle of the night. For your information, Mr Epstein is *the* most famous television executive in the whole of Holly — '

'Yeah, yeah, I know all that. Could you just get him to call?'

Reluctantly, Ms Hospitality of the Decade wrote down the number I read from the plastic aureole on the phone in front of me. I rang off. We were stonkered. '*Now* what?'

'Okay, it's time to stop fartin' around. What we need,' said Tash, caroming off the floor and vaulting over the furniture to her handbag, 'is a lawyer.' She grabbed her address book and flicked the pages over. 'Remember Hank the Hunk?' Tash, predictably, kept all her men alphabetically indexed under 'L' for 'Lawyer', 'D' for 'coke dealer', 'T' for guys who could get her tickets to concerts and so on. Personally, I felt they needed refiling — 'A' for 'asshole', 'S' for 'sleazebag schmucko', 'D' for 'Major-Drongo-Dickhead-Ratbag-Fart-Face-the-Third'. If so, Hank the Hunk would have come under the latter category. A native New Yorker in his mid-thirties with a hair transplant that nobody mentioned, Hank made his fortune from 'ambulance chasing' medical negligence cases. Having tired of hanging around hospitals, he now specialised in palimony suits for the discarded, live-in male lovers of rich widows. He had also been known to take his fees in sexual favours. From both genders.

Tash called him up. Within ten panting minutes, he was sidling into the apartment. 'Well, little ladies,' he oozed, casting a condescending eye over both of us, 'bitten off a little more than we can chew, huh?'

'Hi, Hank,' I said. 'How's the hair transplant?'

His rosy-cheeked baby face darkened and his beady eyes narrowed. Tash kicked me hard in the shin, before placating Hank with a tasty tongue-sandwich.

'Well,' Hank said, when he surfaced. 'I did some research on your case on the way over. Male death during carnal activity is not so rare as one might imagine,' he said slimily. Hank produced a large encyclopedia from his briefcase, snapped it open at the dog-eared page and proceeded to read aloud. 'Felix Faure died of a heart attack while . . .'

'Who?' I said

Tash shushed me.

'. . . in a special sex-chair with his mistress. Attila the Hun, stroke during sexual intercourse. Leo VIII died the same way . . .'

'Shit,' Tash said, craning over his shoulder, 'and he was a Pope for God's sake. See?' she beamed at me, 'Things could be worse.'

I couldn't quite see any grounds for optimism. Hank dumped the huge tome in my lap. 'Here, you might learn something,' he snarled and, even though it was night, put on his regulation Raybans. I looked at him with loathing. This guy needed a pair of sunglasses for his bum. I mean, that was obviously where he thought the sun shone out of.

By the time I'd skimmed the encyclopedia's pastel illustrations of sputniks and brontosauruses, New Guinean head-hunters and hammer-headed sharks, the Human Hair Transplant had convinced Tash to give up all idea of her recording contract and get on the phone to Joel Schulman's studio Vice President, Arnie Grossman.

I'd seen pictures of Joel and Arnie all round the apartment. The majority of photos showed them beaming, arms slung round each other, receiving industry awards. There were lots of chummy fishing and hunting trip shots and many more of the two buddies on the sets of their various blockbuster movies, arm in arm with the Stars. A knot of anguish gripped my stomach. There are nicer things to have to do than break the news of the death of a dearest pal. But, as it turned out, I needn't have fretted. The first thing Arnie Grossman did when he arrived was to kick the body of his best friend with the toe of his Italian tennis shoe. 'Are you sure he's dead?' he said sensitively.

'No,' Tash said, rolling her eyes at me. 'He's just pretendin'. The guy,' she added, barely containing her hysteria, 'is as *dead* as a mutton *chop*. He's *dead* as a weekend in *Dubuque*. Are ya gettin' the picture buddy?'

I looked at her perplexed. 'Where?'

'Oh well,' Grossman sighed, as he unravelled the cellophane from his Cuban cigar and inserted the aromatic truncheon between his rubbery lips, 'at least he's not worried about box office takings.' It struck me then that Grossman, of course, would be next in line for the studio throne. Even though he was attempting to manufacture a degree of sorrow, he couldn't keep a self-satisfied smirk from sneaking into his eyes. Though obviously slimmed down by aerobics, Grossman was still heavily jowled and his excess paunch was corseted by a Gucci tracksuit. He wore a portable phone strapped to his waist, like a gun in a holster.

The Human Hair Transplant — who'd never been in the presence of such a Big Shot — got all flustered and grinned with pukesville insincerity, as he filled Grossman in on the details of the situation.

'It's impossible,' Grossman interrupted.

'What?' asked the Human Hair Transplant. 'That he had a stroke?'

'No. That he had a *heart*,' Grossman chortled. Tash and I exchanged a look of nauseated disbelief. He choked back his laughter, suddenly sober. 'This news can't get out. It would be a disaster. We must keep it quiet. At least until the close of Wall Street tomorrow. Otherwise, Jesus Fucking Christ!' Pacing the apartment, cigar in one hand, portable phone in the other, Grossman was like a caricature of a studio executive. 'Company shares will plummet. There's been takeover speculations circulating for weeks. Of course, we've denied it all, but things are kinda rocky, already, ya know?'

'I see,' the Human Hair Transplant agreed sycophantically. 'And this will tip the boat?'

'Tip the boat?' Grossman snarled. 'Tip the fucking boat? This will turn us into the fucking Titanic.'

Tash was standing slightly behind the tracksuited bulk of Arnie Grossman. She caught my eye, and, her face working overtime, mouthed, 'Can ya believe this guy?'

'Look, *Gross*person –' she said, spinning him around to look at her. She came up to about his navel – 'or whatever your goddamned name is, I don't care a shit about ya studio shares,

WHAT ARE WE GONNA DO WITH HIS BODY?'

Grossman looked at her the way you look at something smelly on the sole of your shoe. 'You want my help? Huh?' he snapped at her. 'Huh? Then *shut thuh fuck up*. That's taken care of. I've got a pal, Homicide Squad.'

'The cops?' The words caught in Tash's throat. 'You're gonna call the cops? Oh great. We could have done that our . . .'

'Listen, this guy's a lieutenant.' He talked to her as though she was taking speech therapy. 'We used him when we did the TV series on the drug-squad. The guy's totally cool. Trust me, babe.'

Grossman drew his portable phone, and loaded the number.

The next hour I can only describe as surreal. The tame Lieutenant, his yellow face damp with sweat from the climb up the stairs, panted into the room with two detectives in tow. He stood there, mopped his brow, and simply said, 'Where's the stiff?' All seven of us then filed into the living-room and dismally contemplated the body of Joel Schulman. His face had taken on a bewildered look – like someone stuck on a crossword puzzle. Being in the presence of a stiff seemed to make the younger men hungry. As the Lieutenant inspected the corpse, the detectives inspected the crisper. 'Whad thuh fuck's this?' the younger one asked, withdrawing his head from the second shelf. His hand followed shortly afterwards, clutching a bowl of seaweed kelp. 'Check it out will ya?' He began to strip-search the refrigerator, lining up the various edibles, like suspects, along the kitchen counter. 'Pritikin bread, miso soup, lecithin, lettuce,' he pronounced in an incredulous rollcall, 'bees' jelly, ginseng. The guy's a fuckin' health food freak.'

'Yeah, well it did him a lotta fuckin' good, didn't it?' the other D added. He picked up a bowl of miso and sniffed it tentatively. 'Shit. What's this? Bats' urine?'

The dilemma over what to do with the body then gave way to an even more pressing problem – what food to order in. The Lieutenant wanted Chinese. Grossman was against it because of 'that monosodium glutamate shit'. Hank put in a bid for sushi. The younger detective didn't bother to hide his disgust. 'Christ,' he only half-whispered, 'doncha hate fuckin' lawyers.'

As Tash and I crouched in a corner of the living-room, the men took off their jackets and loosened their ties. They argued about the pros and cons of pizza and spare ribs, Cajun and Kentucky Fried, before radioing through a food order to the nearest squad car. Grossman, Hank and the Lieutenant adjourned to the master bedroom to plot in private. Tash made a run for the door, but they shut it resolutely in her face. The detectives then started up a conversation between themselves about baseball teams. Mid-sentence, the elder D snapped his fingers and pointed at Tash. 'You,' he said, 'suck my cock, and you – ' singling me out, he jerked his thumb in the direction of his partner – 'suck his.' Nonchalantly unzipping his fly, he then resumed his conversation about managers and homers and steals.

I scuttled across the carpet and seized Tash's thin little arm. 'They think we're prostitutes!' I gasped. 'This is awful!'

'Well, of course they think we're prostitutes. We are.'

I looked at her, totally flummoxed. 'Tash, the only thing I do in bed is sleep. I've only had sex like once in the whole past year. That hardly classifies me as a – '

But Tash was up on her feet and moving obediently across the room. I watched her, sick to my stomach. She stood right next to the cop. 'Tell me,' she asked sweetly, pouring her glass of Diet Pepsi right over his head, 'with a penile implant operation, is there pain afterwards?'

He gawked at her, his pure amazement giving way to undisguised disgust. 'Fuckin' bitch!' he spat.

'Hey,' Tash retaliated. 'If God had meant us to give blow-jobs, She wouldn't have given us teeth.'

Half an hour later, two boys in blue arrived with the take-away. Of course, it being LA, they all knew each other. 'How's the little woman, Johnno?' one of the cops asked as they rooted through the grease-stained cardboard boxes and dived in with flimsy plastic forks.

The aroma of food lured the Human Hair Transplant out of the meeting room. He whispered to us that Grossman was now in contact with the DA's office, trying to do a deal. But the DA was insisting on a post-mortem, which would mean an investigation. That was when Grossman got his brainstorm. Joel Schulman had been making lots of contributions to the Republican Party. Maybe it was time to call in a few favours.

As the heavies plotted and schemed behind closed doors, the younger detectives and their cop mates broke out the cards for a game of pontoon. Feeling grottier and grimier than I ever had in my entire life, I slithered off to run a bath.

As the water filled, I cleaned my teeth till the gums started to bleed. Submerging myself in the hot, soapy water, I had the distinct sensation that I was dissolving. Tash tiptoed in and locked the door after her. 'Hi,' she said gently. I ignored her. 'Mind if I get in?' I kept my eyes closed. 'Don't worry,' she said sarcastically, 'I'll take the tap end. It's the least I can do, right?' I felt her step into the bath and settle herself, with a long sigh. 'In a bad mood?' she asked tentatively.

Bad mood? The mood I was in made Sylvia Plath look high-spirited.

'I brought ya some biscuits,' Tash said brightly, when I didn't answer. Craning over the side of the tub, she retrieved the plate from the floor. 'Thought ya might be hungry. I mean, killin' someone really works up an appetite in a girl.' She proceeded to munch and crunch her way loudly through the lot. What had begun as a mosquito bite of annoyance suddenly flared up into a major rash of anger.

'You know what I hate about you?' I suddenly snapped, sitting up and splashing a tidal wave of water over the sides. 'I just hate the way you never, ever say you're hungry and never, ever order any food, and then eat all of mine. It drives me *bonkers*.'

Tash's face momentarily crumpled. She looked at me, shocked, then a hint of defiance flared in her eyes. 'Hey, I didn't make ya come!' she bawled back. 'You said ya needed the money.'

Grunting, I furiously lathered my left armpit with soap. 'Doncha think I know that? Doncha think I know that my whole life is totally rooted?' Lifting my arm, and craning to see into the mirrored wall, I negotiated the fleshy contours with the razor. 'Pierce is right. Parents ruin you. I've inherited my father's criminal genes – I'm downwardly-mobile.'

Tash stiffened. Her lips twitched crossly. She traced her finger through the steam on the glass. 'J'know what *I* hate?' she said abruptly. 'I hate the way ya're always puttin' down ya old man. That's what I – '

I squinted up at her in surprise. 'The bloke's a bloody no-hoper. He's on the bludge. He's a gambler, for God's sake!'

'So what? The guy's got an addictive personality. I s'pose you're *above* all that. I s'pose love's not addictive, is that right?'

'It's *not*. I told you. I never wanna see Pierce Scanlen again. I neva wanna . . .' I stared at her, inarticulate with rage.

'You can't change people,' she rushed on. 'Okay, he ain't the father you'd hand-pick in Heaven, but he's *yours*. So, why not just accept him the way he is?' She erased her steam etchings with one swipe of the hand. 'Parents ain't perfect. They make mistakes sometimes, just like everybody else.'

I felt betrayed by her unexpected defence of the old ratbag. And then, just as her erased drawings were re-emerging on the glass, the real meaning of her words became clear. I took a deep breath and looked at my friend calmly. 'He'll accept you,' I said softly. 'Of course he'll want to know who his real mother is.'

'I dunno his name, even.' Tash gnawed at what was left of her nails. 'What if they've given him a terrible name like – I dunno – *Dwayne*? Or God, I dunno. *Percival* or somethin'.'

'The name doesn't matter.'

'Maybe it'd be best if I jest neva meet 'im.' Stretching her left leg over the edge of the bath, she ferociously sandpapered her thigh with a loofah. 'I mean, he's prob'ly gonna grow up to be a goddamned ad executive or a, I dunno, a blow-dried game show host. No kidding,' she said bleakly, 'the more I mull it over, the more I think it might be best to just leave it alone.'

'Look, it'll all be okay.' I took the loofah from her hands. Her leg was red where she'd attacked it. 'I promise you it will. Right now, the most important thing is to get C.J. the final payment and just *find* him.'

Tash tilted her chin up, the way she does when she's fighting back tears. Her fingers were latticed around her knees which she'd drawn up tightly against her chest. 'I've found him,' she said simply.

'What?' The soap shot out of my hand and torpedoed into the water. I groped for it around our tangle of legs and feet.

'Address, name of adoptive parents, phone number. The works. I borrowed the final two grand from a goddamned loan shark. But, the thing is, now that it's finally happened, I'm too scared to go see him.' Her small, goose-pimpled frame was shaking. 'Hey, I'm sorry I got ya into all this. I was just gettin'' – big fat tears were rolling down her face, mingling with lilac swirls of eyeshadow – 'ya know, desperate. I had to get money. I didn't know what else to do.'

I felt a rush of affection for her pencilled brows, her little silver nose-ring, her two-tone hair, growing out red at the roots. Sloshing water over the sides, I leant forward and hugged her close. 'It's okay,' I said, rocking her back and forth, cascading suds on to the carpet. We sat there, holding hands like two people at a seance. Maybe, I thought, we could just stay in this bath for ever. Tash shifted her weight and leant back against me, exhausted.

Outside, I could hear one of the men snoring. I remembered how my father snored. He called it 'sleeping out loud'. With Tash asleep in my arms and the warm water lapping my chin, thoughts of my father started sneaking up on me. I frogmarched them out of my mind, but back they would come, indefatigable. I suddenly saw him singing 'God Save the Queen' in the aisles of our local supermarket. He wasn't a walloper, my dad. If I threw a tantrum or something, he'd just start singing the anthem – in football stadiums, churches, trains, at family reunions, he would just launch off, loud as anything. It was so embarrassing I would stop crying instantly. I remembered him too, reciting poetry when I was sick. 'The Man From Snowy River' and Byron, in his loud and luscious voice, a faint Irish twang in his vowels. Then I saw him, the year he came home on Christmas Day, his arms buckling beneath the weight of presents. He'd been inside for two years – picked up by the gaming squad for running an illegal casino. The 'cockatoo' had scarpered, and the whole kit and kaboodle had got snitched. All that time I hadn't seen him. Mum marched to the screendoor. There were words. And then he was gone. Peering through the venetian blinds, I watched him slowly retreating down the street towards the railway station, shimmering like a mirage, stooped in the scorching summer heat. It was the only time I had ever seen him in a suit.

The thing about my dad was that he just hadn't found his place in the world.

Like Pierce.

We were woken by a pounding on the door. I realised, with a dull thud, where I was and why. My fingers were all shrivelled up – a condition we used to call as kids, 'deadman's fingers'. Pretty ironic, huh? We'd fallen asleep with the taps still trickling and bathwater was now lapping over the enamel sides.

'For Chrissake,' a rough voice said, 'Whad thuh fuck are you

232

two doin' in there?' I recognised it as belonging to the older of
the two detectives. We felt his shoulder ram against the door. I
checked my watch. It was six a.m.

'Okay, okay,' Tash said, groping at the taps and scrambling for
a towel. 'Christ almighty, What's the hurry? Somebody die?'

I stepped out of the bath and into a shagpile squelch.

'Ha-de-ha-ha, Miss Smartass.' This time I recognised
Grossman's imperious drawl. 'We gotta get this body into the
bath. It's decomposing.'

For a minute I thought I was going to throw up. As we opened
the door, still tugging on pieces of clothing, the cops barged past
us, and levered the naked body into the bath. It was the opposite
of pushing a whale out to sea. Grossman and Hank followed with
ice-cube trays and cast the frozen blocks into the water. Like
miniature icebergs, they bumped up against the outcrops of Joel
Schulman's flesh. Old Joel, pale and gloomy, was looking a bit
like an iceberg himself. As I watched him, one lid suddenly opened
and surveyed me accusingly with a pale and jellied eye.

Tash made us both coffee. Cradling the cup, I buried my face
in the steam. The livid morning light seeped in under the doors.
Tash was drumming her bitten-down fingers on the breakfast bar.
'The way I see it, we're gonna get done,' she announced flatly. I
looked at her bleary-eyed. My brain was benumbed, totally lacer-
ated by the events of the last three days. So, what was new?

And, sure enough, during the next hour an argument erupted
over what to do with the body. Grossman wanted it 'disappeared'.
The best solution for that was to get it down to 'Chicken Wire
Charlie'. His technique, according to Lieutenant Scrutin, was to
wrap the body in chicken wire, weight it down, then dump it out
to sea. That way, the evidence would just be nibbled away by
various sealife, and end up in somebody's fish and chips. Just
chucking it into the sea meant that arms and legs, which were
traceable, might turn up in a shark's tummy.

Personally, I was praying that Joel Schulman would just magically combust. Though, being a Harvard graduate, a Hollywood
studio executive and a member of the Palm Springs Country
Club, it would definitely be the first spontaneous thing he'd done
in his life.

'Or a simpler way,' suggested the older detective, the one Tash
had saturated in Diet Pepsi, 'would be to wait till thuh end of

Wall Street tradin' and then come clean. Just let the chicks take the rap.'

All eyes in the room slewed around on to us. I honestly don't know what would have happened, if what happened, hadn't happened, if you know what I mean. There was a noise not unlike a long, loud burp and the building shuddered. I was about to go into Earthquake Mode and bury myself in the phone book beneath the doorframe, when I realised that the disturbance was coming from the bathroom. Grossman, Scrutin, the two Ds and Mister Hair Transplant broke all known records in a sprint down the hall. By the time Tash and I reached the bathroom, the door was swinging casually on its hinges. The air was charged with floating dust. What we saw, squinting through the pall, astounded us.

The bathtub had fallen through the floor.

Joel Schulman's apartment was on the very top of a glass tower that rose thirty storeys above the street. Most of the penthouse cantilevered out into space, beyond the rest of the building. Tash reckons it was our fault because we left the taps running all night and the extra weight sent the tub tumbling. But I reckon the whole structure had been weakened by that bloody earthquake. Freeways had been buckling and buildings cracking ever since last week's wobbly. The white walls were criss-crossed with hairline fractures and huge hunks of tile had come away. We peered over the edge of the carpeted hole. All we could see were the bristling heads of palm trees and the chrome snake of cars crawling down the freeway.

But there was no sign of Joel Schulman. From this height, he'd have been pulverised. Basically, he would look a lot like the orphanage-sized pizza.

'Well, gentlemen,' Tash gloated, 'it looks as though the stiletto is on the other foot.'

'Whaddaya mean?' Grossman snapped.

'Well,' Tash added sweetly. 'Does the word SPLAT mean anything to you?'

As used as he was to movie special effects (it was rumoured that Grossman was solely responsible for the C-grade 3-D thriller, 'Revenge of the Mutant Vegetable Man') he was completely discombobulated. As were the coppers. Mister Hair Transplant promptly threw up all over Arnie Grossman. Tash was the only one who kept cool in all the heat.

'The Perfect Crime. A murder without a body . . . Accidental death. Natural disaster. Let's talk business, gentlemen, shall we?'

Nauseated, I burst out on to the balcony, where I stood inhaling the smog. LA must be the only place in the world where you have to go *inside* to get a breath of fresh air. Even this early, the sun was like treacle dripping off a sluggish spoon. The city seemed a grey smudge made by a giant thumb.

It must have been eight-thirty when Tash emerged, clutching two slips of paper. She handed me one. It was a cheque. I looked at the amount. $50,000. She was standing, legs splayed, her little hands on her slim hips, her nostril ring sparkling in the sun. I looked at her, perplexed.

'I sold the film rights,' she said, matter-of-factly.

'To what?'

'To *this*. To *us*. All I hadda do was convince that Grossman goon of the publicity potential. This is, like, how I pitched it: two naïve, young girls, out on their first hookin' assignment. They're broke, inexperienced. And the guy, like, goes and dies on 'em. Now, what are they gonna do with the body?' Her eyes glinted wickedly. 'It's a comedy, a black comedy. With the perfect ending. Grossman's already talkin' about castin'.'

My first reaction was that she had either gone stark-raving bonkers, or that she was, as she would say, 'yankin' my chain'. But then I looked around me. This was Hollywood after all. A city where they said 'have a nice day' and then shot you.

'So,' Tash said, hoisting herself up on to the balcony wall. Her legs dangled dangerously over the road below, where a crowd surrounded half a dozen emergency vehicles. 'Whatcha gonna do with ya money?'

I looked down at the slip of paper in my hand. 'I dunno.' I listened to the sirens below, the staccato car horns, the pulsing radios, the screeching tyres. 'Go home, I guess.'

'Kat,' Tash said kindly, backlit by the sun, 'I dunno much about life an' all, but I do know one thing. You can't go backwards. Y'know where Pierce is?'

I shrugged.

'Look, just 'cause he sounded so sincere about givin' up drugs and stuff, doesn't mean he wasn't, ya know?'

I peered up into her face. 'I thought you hated the guy's guts? I thought a toilet seat had more personality? I thought you said . . .'

'Yeah, yeah, I think that. But *you* don't. You love the prick.'

'I do not,' I snapped. 'Not any more.'

'Listen,' she placed her hand on my hair. 'There's only one thing worse than bein' in love.'

'Yeah? What's that?'

'Not bein' in love. I should know,' she said despondently.

We slouched there in dejected silence for a while.

'What are you gonna do?'

Tash flung back her head defiantly and squared her shoulders. 'Go say hi to my kid, I guess.'

I looked at my friend, at her tight and wiry frame, at her fierce and sad face. And I knew it was the bravest thing she would ever have to do.

One of the detectives poked his horrible head out the sliding door. 'Phone,' he said curtly. Tash made a move for the door. 'For *her*.' He jerked his thumb in my direction.

'Hello?' I took the call in the master bedroom. The silk ropes were still trailing like limp strands of spaghetti from the four wooden posts. With the blankets scraped back and the sheets twisted, the bed gaped like a wound. I couldn't look at it.

'Vot!' a voice shouted, 'you sink you can just vork off my set, zen come crawling back. You are vashed up.' In the background, I could hear empty bottles being stacked and women being put back in drawers. 'You vill never verk in zis town again!'

When I told Abe what had happened, his whole manner altered. 'Film Vights?' he stammered, 'Film Vights? Hold on a zecond.' Abe put his hand over the receiver and cancelled all calls for about the next year. I got the feeling that he'd suddenly be free for lunch. His voice shifted gear. It was full of long-lost-daughter kinda kindness. The old crap-antenna started to wobble.

'Don't do eat,' Abe panted into the phone, 'for a small zlice of zee action, I can get you a much better deal at zee rival studio. Sink about it.'

'Na, Abe, I don't think so.'

'But I haff given you every-sing.'

Yeah, I thought, a couple of lifelong hang-ups, an inferiority complex, an identity crisis and a complete nervous breakdown. With slow deliberation, so as to savour every second of it, I hung up in his ear.

'Well, at least we've learnt one thing,' Tash philosophised as she entered the room. 'No matter how bad it gets, death is definitely a fate worse than life.' She shoved my bag into my arms. 'Get goin' girl. I'll woman the fort.'

'Will you be okay?'

Tash gave me one of her 'who are kiddin'' looks. 'Where'ja think I live — in a *box*?' She winked at me and then snapped open the venetian blinds. The sun lit up her eyes and hair. That's how I would always think of Tash. In technicolour.

Making my way down the stairs, I had the distinct feeling that my luck was going to look up — any decade now.

ROOSTER ONE DAY – FEATHER DUSTER THE NEXT

On the way to the prison, I did two things. First, I posted the Nirvana Casino ad to my old man – including details of their rotten mongrel rule on tied bets. (The only gambling dad had access to was two-up and Chinese dominoes. They were still illegal, but easier to hide from the cops. It'd been about two years, he reckoned, since he'd seen a roulette wheel in Sydney, and three since he'd found a blackjack table. This would just about rot his socks off.) The next thing I did was to buy a ticket back to Australia. The plane was leaving that night.

As I left the airline office, I noticed that the sky had turned a metallic grey. The streets were full. Overcrowded bars belched people out on to the pavements. Fireworks erupted. It was like a mini-Vietnam. It dawned on me that this was the Fourth of July. I'd been here one year exactly.

'You wearin' panties, honey?' inquired a biker outside International Burger. The streets seethed with the usual human minestrone: intimidated tourists; style-shamans; short-back-and-sides soldiers; Rastafarians in hairy, rainbow jumpers and Afghan slipper-socks; leather-clad bikers wearing their dreamy, post-hit smiles; scrupulously scrubbed Jesus-Freaks; fans of heavy metal, black metal, speed metal, satanic metal, of bands called 'Electric Vomit', 'Satan's Penis' and 'I Spit on Your Gravy'.

The leaden clouds rumbled and for the first time since I'd been in LA it started to rain – big, juicy, indecently plump droplets. A warm, earthy smell filled the air. Even the buildings seemed to soften. I lifted my face up to the sky and inhaled.

At the remand section of the prison, I left an envelope for Pierce containing a cheque big enough get him out *and* to permanently postpone his Mafia shoe-fitting. Then I went to wait for him in the visiting-room. It was so familiar to me – the nostril-numbing smell of disinfectant, the hushed desolation, the ever-watchful security camera, the denuded walls, bare except for a few bits of unimaginative graffiti. Then there were the inmates, twitchy, as though covered in swarms of invisible ants, their women visitors, worn down, and the infinitely sad sound of a baby crying. I picked Pierce out of the crowd straight away. He spotted me and moved towards my table. He had a black eye and a cut above the nose. I felt a spasm of fierce, protective love and nearly ran towards him. But then I steeled myself. I controlled it. This time I would play my cards close to my chest. Stick to my system.

'Didn't think you'd come,' Pierce said, sinking into a chair opposite me. His unkempt hair looked like the polygraph of a chronic liar, all up and down jaggedy.

'Neither did I.'

'Sour grapes?'

'A-huh. A whole bunch.'

We sat in silence for a few moments.

'I'm glad you did,' he said finally, his voice small. 'Come, I mean.'

The test, I thought coldly, would be whether or not he asked me for money. 'So, how are you?' I inquired, resolutely indifferent to the livid semicircles beneath each eye.

'Oh well, the odd guy has felt inclined to use my face as a goddamned ashtray. But apart from that, fine, great,' he replied with subdued irony. 'Never better.'

'I wasn't sure if you'd still be here. I thought they'd let you out on bail.'

Pierce shrugged. 'They're going to. But who can I call? Epstein? My mother? *Please*! I've got some kinda goddamned social worker on my case. Her name is, wait for it, *Moira Dykes*. Can you believe it? I think that's a name you make up for an Arts Grant Application, isn't it? She's probably the author of a book called *Aren't Men Assholes*.'

'Sounds like a good book,' I said coldly. I kept waiting for Pierce to ask me for that bail money. He didn't.

'She wants me to go on a detox programme. I kinda walked out last time.' Pierce volunteered uncomfortably.

239

'And? Are you gonna do it?' I asked, expecting a fight on my hands.

'Yeah, yeah I am,' he said solemnly. Although the rain on the tin roof was deafening, the silence between us seemed louder.

'So,' he finally shouted above the din, 'how'd ja find me?'

I shrugged. 'Tracked you down. They told me you were bein' brought back to LA for writing dud cheques.'

Pierce shifted uneasily. Another silence hung heavily between us. 'So,' he said, a note of exaggerated carelessness in his voice, 'how did they write us out of the show? Bizarre hide-a-bed-accident? Attacked by a giant waffle-iron. What?'

'Well, from what I've gleaned, I found God and went off to Botswana to fight the Tsetse fly, or something like that. And you went down to the basement to get the skis and just never came back up again.'

'Woa! Woa!' Pierce put his hand up in the air, like a traffic cop halting cars. 'This is a series in which I've been kidnapped eight times, shot three times, pushed off a cliff, gone deaf twice, had cancer, been brainwashed by Russian spies, cloned by Martians, and come back from the dead. And they just *sent me down to the basement?*'

'Apparently the same thing happened to some French girl Abe tried to introduce into the series eons ago. When Rondah got her sacked, the script just called for her to go up to the attic to get the Scrabble board and she never came down again. She's been up there for twelve years as far as Amy could figure it.'

'Well kid, it looks like it's the top left-hand corner of *Hollywood Squares*.'

'As we say at home – "Rooster one day, feather duster the next".'

We smiled then, in tandem. Pierce placed his hand over mine. The two fingers closest to his thumb, I noticed, were stained from tobacco. 'God, I could handle a margherita,' he said, flashing me a conspiratorial smile.

For a moment, I too, felt overcome by thirst. But then, remembering where we were and why, I retrieved my hand. For a while, there was no sound but the rain thudding on to the roof. Fans stirred the stagnant air. I watched Pierce roll a cigarette.

'You're pretty quiet today,' he said uneasily.

'Yeah. Silent, like the "P" in swimming.'

'What?'

'Oh, nothing. Just something my dad used to say. I visited him in jail a lot as a kid, you know. He called it the "B and B" – Bed and Breakfast.'

Pierce glanced quickly away, and shredded the cigarette he'd just rolled.

'So,' I shifted gear, 'what are you gonna do when you get out?'

'Moira Dykes wants me to apply for a "Youth Unemployment Scheme". Which kinda sounds okay. I mean, I'd like to be unemployed and I'd like to be youthful. Hey,' he said, mock-cheerfully, 'maybe we could just keep on driving? You know, all over America.' He lit up with a glimmer of optimism. 'We haven't touched on the Country and Western repertoire yet, or the Blues – Memphis Blues, Tennessee Blues. "I've got Dakota on my Mind".'

'Pierce . . .'

'No. Listen. I wanna say something. I've behaved like a total asshole with you, right from the start. If they gave out Oscars for Assholes, I would win, hands down. No kidding. I would probably win Greatest Supporting Asshole too. I lied to you, I took your money, I let you down. And all the time, you hung in there. But I'm gonna change . . .'

'Oh yeah. What?' I said doubtfully. 'A Born-Again-Human-Being, huh?'

'I know you don't believe me. So, I'm just gonna have to prove it to ya. Which is why I'm going on the detox programme. Jesus Chrrrist. I hate those goddamned places. Believe me, that's the biggest sacrifice I can make – well, that doesn't involve a virgin and a volcano.'

'Pierce . . .' I placed my plane ticket on the table between us. His face registered a quiver of alarm. 'Where you headed?'

'Home.'

'When?' As he bent to examine my ticket, I noticed the glimmer of a grey hair on his famous forehead. The thing about Californian kids is that they get old so young.

'*Tonight?*' Pierce looked at me as though seeing me for the first time. Suddenly he leant forward and coiled his fingers around my upper arm. I pulled away. It felt hot where he'd touched me. I looked down, half-expecting to see a bruise in the shape of his hand. 'You *can't* leave. You're the only sane person in Los Angeles. The whole of California for that matter. . . . You're the only sane person in my life!' Sane? I thought, recalling the shattering absurdity of the last twenty-four hours. 'You can't go. Not *now*.' He looked down at his scuffed sneakers.

'You can always come and find me – when you get bail an' all.' Now, I thought. Now he'll ask me for money. 'That is, if you really mean it.'

'I'll get bail. Today. I'm coming after you. Kat!' My name caught in his croaky throat. 'YOU CAN'T GO,' he shouted into the sweat-dampened air.

The inmate sitting at the table next to us grinned. He had no teeth. I glared at him until he looked away. 'You don't believe in relationships, remember? It's right up there on your Bullshit List.'

Pierce was looking intently into my face. He was now so close it was as though he had three eyes.

'Kat,' he said, cupping my face in his hands. I waited for my usual attack of embarrassment, but for the first time since coming to America, I didn't go into Blush Mode. My cheeks didn't turn vermilion, nor did a geyser of sweat saturate each armpit. 'The thing is, I've ... I've ... well, I've fallen love with you, I guess,' he said.

Bloody hell, I thought.

I squinted at him mistrustfully. But there was not a trace of the usual mocking laughter, not a hint of the customary casual arrogance in his eyes.

'I have to go,' I said hurriedly, getting to my feet and moving across the room towards the security gate.

Pierce burst into song, a mad medley full of ballads about love and no-good men and stay with me baby and it's gonna be alright and get me through the night and sign your name across my heart.

As he warbled on, indifferent to the hostile stares of the other prisoners and the fish-mouths of contempt on the faces of the wardens, I felt another great wave of longing for this Oscar-Winning American Asshole. But I steeled myself. I controlled it. I was like a reformed gambler, still in love with the game, but no longer willing to be enslaved. This time I would play my cards right.

Maybe he would come after me, and maybe he wouldn't. All I know is that by the time he'd stopped singing and reached me and turned me around to face him, two gi-normous tears had welled up in his eyes and spilled down his stubbled cheeks. Not only had he stopped calling me 'kid' and not asked me for money, not even once, but when I kissed him goodbye, there by the wire-mesh, under the evil eye of the security camera, I stole a surreptitious peek up his nostrils. They were hairy. Both of them. Not only that, but for the first time since coming to this crazy town, the old crap-antenna . . . well, it wasn't wobbling.